Crucible

By

Miguel Torres

Dedication

I dedicate this book to
My youngest son.
He, who has pushed me harder than any other,
to open my heart with love and patience.
For a world I would have never known
without him.
I thank God everyday for such a wonderful
and blessed experience.
Manny you are the stardust in my eyes each day I
rise.
You are the reason I was brought to Romans 15.1
and each time I look at you
I am given the fortitude to stand for it.
With all my heart and soul
son,
I love you.

Crucible Foreword

Many people go through life facing difficult challenges in jobs, school, family, and relationships. Rarely, however, do people take the opportunity to step back and take a look at the big picture, evaluating what common threads exist between all those challenges. While we are growing up, we create a pattern of behavior that helps us cope with whatever difficulties and challenges we may be facing. As children, we have very little resources to pull from that will teach us good, healthy habits. At the time of our struggles, we pull on whatever will get us through at the time. Although this skill serves to benefit the child during that immediate situation, quite often the skill is never revisited and evaluated as to its effectiveness once the child becomes an adult.

Author, Miguel Torres, grew up in an extremely challenging environment among the streets of Bedford Stuyvesant, Brooklyn, where he suffered various challenges no child should ever have to endure. As a very intelligent and creative child, he created his own patterns of behavior that taught him to cope with his struggles in order to be a guiding light for his three younger sisters who he was responsible to care for at a very young age. His skills serve to get them all out of childhood alive and well. However, what was still required was the necessary evaluation of those skills as to their effectiveness in the life he currently leads.

Over the past several years, Miguel Torres, has walked on a spiritual journey where he has learned how to convert those skills that are still applicable while discarding those that have hindered his life as an adult. His journey was one of love. This story he depicts, in Crucible, details that love story. This walk he tells so eloquently in this tale of lovers is both passionate and full of desire. But unlike many of today's tales, it is based strongly in a reality that rings true to the reader.

Although he says a few times in the novel that it is HIS STORY, this story isn't to be taken literally. True enough it is HIS TALE, but it is not a complete work of non-fiction, meaning all the details cannot be taken at face value. The story is real and true enough to get across this powerful message of love in its truest form. This is not about hurting anyone, or airing dirty laundry, but about triumph and overcoming past hurts to heal all in a place of love. So many of us today who don't know the way, this should serve as a great tool towards that path. There are so many questions about love; here lies some much needed answers. This journey, which has brought him to a place of peace, promising to provide him the life he wants and a legacy for his children was not easily gotten. But, in sharing, the hope is that it will make that road but a bit easier for those that follow.

Introduction

Ephesians 6:11 Put on the whole armor of God, that ye may be able to stand against the wiles of the devil. . . . having on the breast plate of righteousness, taking the shield of faith, wherewith ye shall be able to quench all the fiery darts of the wicked and take the helmet of salvation, and the SWORD of the spirit, WHICH IS THE WORD OF GOD.

With this in mind, I set out to become a tool to be used by the Almighty to help others to find their way to the place that they cannot only pick up their swords but prepare by sharpening it each day as they enter the world, ready for battle; wielding it against the darkness that invades our lives, families, love and all our relationships. We

6

*can defeat the enemy
with truth as our light,
and still have
preparation of peace
at our feet; ready to
be laid. We just have
to know how. There is
an ancient art to
bringing this into your
life that is 100%
effective, if followed
correctly.*

*2 Corinthians
3:2 Ye are our epistle
written in our hearts,
known and read of all
men: 3 forasmuch as
ye are manifestly
declared to be the
epistle of CHRIST
ministered BY US,
written not with ink,
but with the SPIRIT of
the living God; not in
tables of stone, but in
FLESHLY tables of
[our] HEART.*

*The process
sounds so simple;
picking up and then
sharpening my sword
will make me a more
effective weapon
against the evil that
men do. Taking this
into my heart, I
become the weapon so*

*each time I sharpen
IT, I sharpen ME.*

*But for
anyone who has even
thought about it, let
alone tried, you know
the world is filled with
all sorts of challenges
and temptations. This
is ESPECIALLY true
within our love lives
and our pursuit of
romantic love.*

*Throughout
time Crucibles have
been used in the
process of **creating** a
sword.*

*Although our
modern knowledge of
historical techniques
is limited, we do
know, historically,
sword fabrication has
been, effectively, a
high military
technology.*

*Therefore, just
as the techniques of
producing modern
weapons are often
closely guarded, the
techniques developed
for creating superior
swords were also*

guarded and rarely, if ever, published.

As in many endeavors, war and strife have fostered this art.

The necessity for a Crucible, however, is cemented, life long, to the process. Its fundamental purpose is to heat metal, so hot, that it actually MELDS two different types of metal into one; thus providing the raw materials to make the absolute best swords.

For no sword can be made purely from one metal. This sword will always be brittle; it will always break. Just as man was not meant to be alone, the metal that makes up a sword, too, is at its best with another.

Once those TWO metals are completely broken down and formed again as ONE fluid

9

liquid, it is ready to be formed.

The metal is then poured into a mold in the shape of a sword. Once cool and back in its solid state, heat is again applied in order to forge the metal.

This process is called tempering, whereby the heat from the Crucible is used to again soften the metal so that it may be hammered and thereby hardened.

This process is done over and over until the sword is strengthened to its potential. No sword leaving this process can be called superior if it does not contain ridges because ridges generally increase the swords overall structural strength relative to its mass.

This process is called FULLering and it must be done down the LENGTH of the blade. This means no blade should ever look completely smooth. Just as no one is perfect or does this perfectly, these unique "imperfections" actually ADD to its overall structural strength.

The final step of the process is called **'NORMALIZING.'** *Here the blade is carefully and evenly heated and then cooled; this time slowly without hammering.*

The purpose of normalizing is to **remove the stresses** *which may have built up within the body of the blade while it was being forged.*

During the forging process, the blade may have been heated and cooled differentially creating undue stress, whereby some parts may have been hammered more than others. This is called WORK HARDENED.

If these stresses are left in the blade they could affect the finished product. Unchecked, the hardening and tempering might not be as even. Potentially, enough stress could have been added that the blade would be weak in spots; weak enough that it could fail under enough strain. So normalizing is essential.

Finally hardened, the sword must be sharpened if it is to be used as a weapon at all. It may be shaped into a finely balanced, perfect edge.

*However, gripping the device constitutes the cutting component of the weapon. Even a superior sword with a **weak grip** is useless.*

One must remember that the SHARPNESSS of the sword, and ability TO KEEP ITS EDGE, is a

*BALANCE between
VOLUME AND
SUPPORT.*

*At this point,
the <u>sword smith</u>
should then be most
concerned with
maintaining the state
of the blade itself. He
would likely,
IMMEDIATELY, be
involved in the work
of fashioning the
guard and sheath.*

*This book will
walk through one
man's journey to take
this ancient art in
creating a weapon
through the trials of
fire and realize it in
human form.*

*Psalms119:9
Wherewithal shall a
young man cleanse his
way? By taking heed
thereto according to
thy word. With my
whole heart have I
sought thee: O let me
not wander from thy
commandments. THY
WORD HAVE I HID
IN MY HEART . .
teach me thy statutes .
. . I will meditate in
thy precepts.*

13

*This is not a
religious book and I
am not a preacher,
minister or pastor.*

*This is a real
story about real
people who had been
seeking love their
entire lives,
unsuccessfully.*

*This is an
incredible, inspiring
story about those two
people and how they
found the greatest love
they have ever known.*
***This story is also
about keeping it.*** *But
make no mistake, this
is not a love story.
This is a story ABOUT
love. This is my story.*

*Proverbs 4:23
Above all else, guard
your heart, for
everything you do
flows from it.*

Chapter 1
Wrought Iron
(A Hard Head . . .)

It was another late Friday night as Tony turned over, once again alone, in the massive, king-sized bed he had bought specifically to have more room. He never imagined he would have it all to himself once he had moved to Florida. He had moved to the sunshine state with his fiancé and newborn son with hope that he would have been married by now. After all, they had been there two years already and spent far more time fighting than they ever did building the family they had moved there to build. As he thought about it, one would discern that his being alone in that bed, at this point, considering the state of his current relationship, would make perfect sense. Each time his fiancé failed to come home at a decent hour, failed to call, and left him alone with their son, his blood boiled. All he could think about was, "How the hell did I end up here?"

He tossed and turned in a pool of his own sweat and he remembered what it was like to be in that old bed with the woman he loved sweating out the sheets in passion instead of the stress and loneliness that now forced his perspiration. All he had left to look at were those bright red numbers that told every minute she was gone. It was 2:45a.m. and she hadn't even called to tell him she was safe, or on her way home. Tony got up, no longer able to take the silence, and decided he was going to check on his son Angel, whose room was at the other end of his apartment. Realistically, this act gave him a reason, or permission, to go over to the window for what must have been the twentieth time, to search out her headlights which he hoped would be coming into the parking lot. He did not.

As he let the blinds fall and headed out of his bedroom door toward Angel's room, he listened out for the door downstairs just in case she had pulled in before he had looked. Again, nothing. He peeked in and saw that his son was indeed still fast asleep, as he had been for several hours. Although he knew this from the baby monitor in his room, he had gone to check anyway.

There was a tall, fifty-five gallon fish tank in Angel's bedroom with tropical fish that Angel and his daddy loved to watch. Tony sat down in the rocking chair and watched the fish's repetitive pattern of right to left, over and over again. He pressed the button to the small CD player he kept at Angel's bed side. He kept Sade in the player as this was Angel's favorite thing to be rocked to sleep to. On the nights that Sade wouldn't suffice, his daddy would sing to him until he fell asleep holding his face or ear. He was such an affectionate child, with the most tender heart.

Although his agitated mood faded and he began to calm down to the mellow tune and tranquility of the fish swimming to its rhythm, his loneliness never subsided. Tony reached down into the crib and gently took Angel out of the bed and pressed him up against his chest, listening for every breath, and feeling every beat of his tiny heart. As his son's chest rose and fell, their breathing became one and Tony could feel the emotion building up within him as the tears began to roll down his face.

"What has happened to my life?" He could never have imagined that he would be so utterly happy with the child portion of his family while the mom/dad equation was completely lacking. After all, Tony was the father of four children now and Angel was the only child he planned, asked and prayed for. He was certain this was it for him and his wait for a family he had dreamed of was finally over. From the moment he had laid eyes on his fiancé, he was certain he loved her in a way that said marriage and forever. CERTAIN.

Yet here he was again, alone? The squirming body of his tiny son alerted him to the fact that he needed to calm his emotion and wipe away his tear streaked face. With a mere look at the precious love in his arms, he began to smile and the tears easily subsided. He shut his eyes, put his hand on the tiny back of his baby boy and squeezed him slightly. Without much effort, he tried to get into whatever dreamland his son had found. And soon enough he could feel himself falling asleep. As he caught himself falling limp with his son still in his arms, he was startled and stood up at once to place Angel back into the bed safely. He was now tired enough to not care about where she was at this point. He stumbled back into the bedroom without having to convince himself not to go back to that window, and sleep fell as soon as his head hit the pillow.

He was awakened by the chimes from the door alarm, which told him that she was finally arriving home. He rolled over and looked at the clock to see it was almost 4 a.m. and rolled away from the clock. He could hear her kick off her shoes and began making her way up the stairs. She turned the hall light on which shined directly onto Tony's face. This forced him to throw the covers over his head to block out the 75 watt bulb that rested in the hallway's socket. His movement revealed signs of life, alerting Sharon that she had woken him up and she turned the light off at the top of stairs. She entered the room as quietly as she could but it took Tony ignoring her to keep his eyes closed and his temper down.

From the outside of this thing it would appear that she was doing everything she could not to wake him up but the truth was that she was full of drama and was looking to share some of it at that very moment. She knew he was upset and would easily get a rise out of him. She could clearly tell he was doing his able best not to go in that direction. She walked to the opposite side of the room, slid her pants off and began to unbutton her shirt. Undoing the last button, she entered into the bathroom and closed the door. Tony was fuming as he could clearly smell the cigarette smoke and alcohol on her breath, but again went within himself not to let the peace he had managed to find escape through the temptation to give her a piece of his mind and hurt feelings. He could hear the shower running and he knew he had a little while to get his thoughts and feelings under control before she would be out of the shower. If he was lucky, he would be back asleep before she even came to bed.

As the water ran, and the minutes passed, he could feel his temper come down. His slumber began to overcome him when his last thoughts seemed to scream that this is not what it was supposed to be - love. This is not the love he brought his child into the world to. This is not the love he intended on spending his life with. This could not be the love he dreamed about his entire young life. There had to be a mistake. There must be something else. He closed his eyes and began to fall off to sleep while his anger slowly began to shift to sadness, haunting him like the rain on opening day at Yankee stadium. You can ignore it, but you know its coming. You know when you know, but you fought the urge to bring that umbrella because you knew that meant defeat. Or is it just common sense?

Chapter 2
Tells from the Crypt

It was another lonely Friday night as Tony stared at his computer screen feeling accomplished after just acing another law school exam. He was on his way as far as his career was concerned and felt on top of the world. It had been less than twelve forlorn months since he had left the mean streets of New York City for a life here in the lonely southern call of Florida. Heartbroken, he had decided on a life that would be filled with love, life and children - plenty of children. There had to be plenty of children. He loved them and the measure of the success of his life would be measured in the amount of love and support he would give those beautiful children and grandchildren he desired to be around him during his final hours here on earth. He had always dreamed and imagined a large family far removed from the life and love he was brought up in, on the mean streets of Brooklyn, New York. He wanted to get as far away from those streets, and the type of love he was raised in, as he could. After spending nearly thirty years in pursuit of that dream in every way imaginable, he decided to take the woman he thought knew him best, strike out into the world, and find a path that would lead to what seemed to be their dream now. Without the impediment of the sick love that came from both of their families, they decided not to wait for approval. They knew it may never come. Considering how far they had come, and from which they escaped, they chose to step out of their comfort zone, away from what everyone else thought they should do, and seek their dream - their union. Once they got here, they had not married, although they intended to. But life had a funny way of making those types of decisions for folks before they ever knew what hit them.

So here he was a year and some change into this country-living with the son that he and his former fiancé had bore together - once again alone. As great as he felt about his career and its future, he felt equally as crumby about his love life and the dream that he had harbored since he was old enough to dream of such dreams. His intended was off running, ducking and hiding from any possibility of a life, let alone the one they had once dreamed of. It was all fine and well to dream and speak of such fantasies when they lived in the realm of the harsh realities of New York City streets, so far removed from such tenderness and love. But once they got halfway to their desired destination and she could see things start to take shape, she knew she was not the woman in that dream.

She only hoped to be one day and was actually quite shocked that Tony had brought them to such a place as quickly as he had. She was not nearly as ready to pursue their future as she thought she was, and realized it almost immediately once they arrived in the south. So she ran by keeping herself busy with working about seventy hours a week. Her commute to work was an hour at best each way which meant there was no time left to build the life they set out to have and she knew it. This was something she did purposely; this way the excuse could be made to blame it on the job rather than her unwillingness to do what was necessary for the couple to move forward. As each week passed, their love and their life faded like an old worn out quilt, leaving only dirty patches of what their life used to be and had once hoped to have. They just simply grew apart, spending no time together. Their lives included things and people that neither one, knew, or partook in. Soon they were both lonely, just not for one another. It was a really sad thing to cover their lives with.

The worst part about it was the impact on the son that they had made in trepidation of this grand life that they had moved here to have. He was an infant so he was completely unaware of the flawed life he was born into as his father did the best he could to make everything look like the family he had promised him upon his birth. Tony had waited for what felt like an eternity to get over the fear of having a child and pursue the life he dreamed of; the one he knew he was meant to have.

He had been married before when he was younger; in his teens, in fact. He had always done things early. It did not work out for the young couple who seemed to love each other so much. Nor did the son they had. He had died of crib death and the emotional damage killed their marriage. Now here he was over a decade later standing a bit wiser and a hell of a lot more afraid than he was the first go round. The sting from that failure felt less real when he rationalized that they were just too young and dumb to have ever figured out all the things one needs to figure out in order to make something like that work, coming from where he was from. He didn't know it at the time but his history was damning him before he had ever left the gate and he had so much more to overcome than he was ever willing to admit to. He had beat himself up for about five or so years then found the strength in God to move on through the divorce, and through the loss of the precious gift that was their son. He never thought he would have the strength to hold another child again much less one of his own. But he found strength and healing that he knew only God could provide and there he stood albeit alone.

He wanted the world, and this time he was more determined than ever to have it. This time not only did he know what he wanted but he knew how he would have it. But more than that, he was fully prepared to go out and do the work to make that desire a reality. Sadly, since their arrival, he wasn't motivated to continue down that path with his intended. It wasn't until he got sick and tired of being sick and tired that he decided to go out into the world and find his life and love again. It was one the hardest things he ever had to do but he sat down and had the adult, heart-to-heart with the woman he had asked to marry him. After several conversations about the same subject and a failed attempt at couples' counseling, the decision was finally made to end their twelve plus year relationship in pursuit of a life.

Sharon lived in denial her entire life, so for her this decision was not as tough as it should have been. She just went to her safe place and walked on as if this thing never happened. Contented in the idea that Tony had always loved her and could not possibly have stopped now, she chose to believe that they still had a chance even if it was remote. She believed that after some time to cool off he would be back just like every other time he had left after she had failed him. She had not been the ideal woman even then, and she knew it. But one thing she always was, she was always there. Even at her worst, she was able to provide the one thing Tony needed; to feel like he was with someone who would never abandon him. She had, long ago, been abandoned and was certainly aware of the feeling and leaned in on him for the same support. They lived a life full of fear, using each other as codependent crutches. It had been a sad existence that they had hoped to parlay into a life. Like a spring board on a swimming pool, she had hoped all their years of history would take them to new heights as they jumped into the pool of life. Surely it would at least count for that? She never even considered that when Tony said it was over that it was for real. Even as she moved her things out and left their son behind with him she was still steeped in denial that this thing was only temporary.

Tonight, Tony was online after having successfully completed yet another hurdle of his first year in law school and was feeling awesome about himself. He had been getting the spam emails about dating services and meeting people for as long as he had email but never thought of even trying to meet anyone that way. He just thought it was too weird and impersonal trying to sort through pictures of people and deciding which one would be most compatible based on how someone looked. For him, things were far more complicated and he knew a pretty face would not be enough. Sharon was pretty and it meant nothing in the final hour when it was time to put in the work for their relationship and life. He needed someone with whom he had more in common with than just good looks. After all he was no slouch, but she had to be more than that. He was feeling good with himself and full of the confidence from that exam when he decided to join the website and began his search for love and, hopefully, a wife. He had to laugh to himself about that thought. Finding a wife had been reduced to your mouse and a click on your computer.

"KRS one did say the art of navigation had been reduced to a Lincoln," he said out loud to himself, as he laughed.

He was now a member and began clicking on photo after photo, reading profile after profile. He found some that were interesting but most didn't appeal to him and his nature but it didn't stop him from looking. He reassured himself the entire way through thinking, "You have got to be in it to win it."

Plenty of pretty women to choose from but who they really were seemed to get lost due to the process. There were few that actually knew how to use the profile to accurately convey who they were and what they really wanted. He was starting to remember all the games that people play in this arena. He had so many questions. Can you really tell if someone has a good sense of humor from a posting? How about a poor attitude to go with that humor? It was a crap shoot and he was starting to figure it out real quick. So he focused on creating his own profile.

He posted his picture first since it seemed that is the way people were meeting - picture to picture. It was not much different than the bar or club except for the fact you didn't have to leave your home. He tried to be as detailed as possible about creating a clear picture of who he was deep down in his soul. He was searching for a mate for his soul, so he did the best he could to reveal it without seeming too vulnerable. He was a complicated person who harbored complicated thoughts and feelings. Nothing was as simple as black and white, even when it appeared to be. Therefore, he needed to be around someone who understood that; someone who would not need to change that about him. Once he felt he had done an adequate job at the little show-and-tell game he was about to get involved in, he went on back to the photos and sent little hello messages to about ten different women. He thought of it like the lottery. The more tickets you buy the better chance you have of winning. He was excited about his chances and the responses he might get. He could see his life changing no matter what and those kinds of odds brought more than excitement, but hope. He closed out of the site, feeling accomplished, and went back to his studies. He could not stop his mind from thinking after such a process.

He was also in the midst of pursuing his Masters degree at the same time he had started law school. He had done any and everything to stay active so he did not have to think about his bleak existence. He was lonely in that apartment he had rented with full intentions of another kind of life. And each night he picked his son up from the day care and drove home alone, each time he prepared yet another meal for him and his son, he felt it; the stinging loneliness of being there by himself. In addition to diving into his job as a school teacher with plenty of needy young children who could use his guidance, he also dove into his own school work. But during those few lonely hours at home with just him and Angel, he could not deny his emotions and where they were threatening to take him - to a life filled with disappointment and despair. So during those hours, he poured every ounce of his love into his son and caring for him. He hugged and kissed him, tickled and played with him, and spoiled him rotten. He finally understood how so many single mothers had lost their life pouring them into their children, doting over them like they were all that existed. Most never saw the choice they made to give up on life in favor of that child. Sadly, he, too, was completely unaware of what he was choosing but once he figured it out, he did it anyway. Love is stronger than pride, and he was finding out that he was no different than those single mothers he had always criticized, and he was certainly not any stronger. He had resigned to this defeat in love until he could find a foothold on another level that would hopefully be his love supreme.

But right now he had just finished looking at a bunch of strangers that were trying to look hot in order to hide the cracks in their personalities. It was sad really, the length some go through to shelter themselves from hurt; the ultimate lie in the illusion of control provided by the distance in the World Wide Web. The truth is, the moment you speak for the first time, or you meet but for that brief moment, you and all your flaws are on full display, like it or not. So he figured he would always try to be as honest as possible so as not to set anyone up for disappointment in hopes that others would be kind and think the same.

"We'll see," he thought to himself, as he closed his laptop with a still hopeful feeling.

*   *   *   *   *

The next day came and went without so much as Tony even checking the site. He was engaged with school work, lesson plans and Masters degree assignments that kept him far too busy to even notice just how lonely he really was. The plan was to go about his day as if all the shadows of his subconscious no longer existed. This afforded Tony some semblance of normalcy - more of that illusion of control. It was becoming more and more difficult to hold the thoughts together that begged him to abandon all the things that held his life together like the goals he set for himself around his career. All the things that made the world feel safe, that made him look employable and more confident. It was all just an extension of the mask that kept his world together. It was getting more difficult living down here so far away from any and everyone who loved him, or he loved. He was constantly reminded by the distance and isolation that the Deep South provided for him, that he was indeed alone.

25

With each passing breath he was reminded of the life he did not have and he knew he was in too deep. He leaned so hard on his parental relationship he worried if he was ruining his son, making him the equivalent of a momma's boy, but from the other side. He reminded himself all day at work to breathe in and out, so he did not drown in his sorrow. There was a teacher at his job, Ms. Cruz, who he considered to be picture perfect in every way. He viewed her in such a way that she intimidated him to the height of his fears that he was not good enough to actually have something so, seemingly, perfect. He knew that despite all of the things he was able to accomplish since leaving the discomfort of home, he was not the man he used to be in his twenties and his self-confidence in the single market was the first to take a hit. If his shallow single life had taught him anything, it was that women love confidence, even if it was fake. He knew without it you were useless and the chances of landing someone you wanted as badly as he wanted her were slim to none without it. He simply wanted it too badly. Sitting where he was, asking for something he didn't feel able to give put him at a serious disadvantage and killed whatever confidence he had in his looks. After all he was not a bad looking man. In fact, he was quite handsome and never had a problem in his youth approaching or having the women of his choosing. The problem was today he was older and wiser and through the years of digging through his own inventory, he came to the place he was taught about from the time he was a boy. That place that said beauty was only skin deep and you were only as beautiful as who you were on the inside. Looking honestly at his history and the things he had been through, correct or not, he didn't feel half as beautiful as Ms. Cruz was. So each day he resisted the urge to speak even though his heart wanted to jump out of his chest for merely being in the same room with this woman. He could tell she noticed him and maybe even felt what he did but knew she was not the type of woman that would ever pretend to notice. He also knew she was not the type of woman who had to; she was far too attractive. He spent his lunch hour watching her in the play ground with her students, while he dreamed about a relationship with her and what that might be like. He felt safe knowing just how far off that really was. These humble but hidden thoughts usually were enough to give him enough hope about his romantic life to drag him about the business of the day. He knew he wasn't hopeless although he was not where he wanted to be.

As the day ended, he was feeling hopeful about the day's good work he had completed. Teaching the third grade made him not only proud of his chosen profession, but about his life in general. He was an, above-and-beyond, type of individual, so he left having accomplished more than he set out to, which brought him a lot of pride and again gave him one more thing to smile about at the end of the day. As he pulled his car off campus, he was beginning to feel hopeful about what might be waiting for him at home on his PC by way of the dating service he had become a member of. Maybe he had gotten a response from one or more of the women he had contacted the night before. As he drove home with his music up and singing, he imagined any one of those women looking in on his life at that moment - feeling happy and full of pride and confidence.

"Leaving work having accomplished so much on such a pure agenda, who wouldn't want that?" he thought to himself. The time flew as the blocks whizzed by on his way to pick his son up from the daycare that looked after him. He was usually late due to traffic or one of the many clubs he started in order to provide remediation to children whose mentality would not allow them to show up for anything called "tutoring." He taught at a school in what they called a "high risk" school, where he taught "at risk" children. I'm sure you know what that really means? He had taught at other schools of the same sort, but this one was different. It was in the middle of two city housing projects, one on each side. Not only was the expectation in the school low but it dropped sharply once you left the safety of the school doors, where there wasn't a lot of value placed on education. So he found himself being very creative with the students and the parents to get them to participate in educational clubs and programs. It was like giving children gummy vitamins; they taste good, look like candy but give you all the nutrients you need for the day. It was a tricky tight rope, but he walked it like he always did. The problem was most times this demanded far more time from him than his work schedule allowed. But he knew that the children and parents wouldn't care about what he had to teach them until they knew he cared about them. So he gave.

Today, however, was a good day and he was headed home relatively on time and arrived early to pick up his two year old. He was still in a singing mood when he walked in but decided not to subject any innocent ears to his loud acapella. Humming, as he walked in and spotted his pride and joy, he surprised Angel as he turned and gave him the biggest hug like it had been a lifetime since he had seen him last. Tony heart swelled as picking up his son was honestly the greatest part of his day. He never realized, although he had other children, just how rewarding transferring all his love to that child could be. Other than the romance, there was no let down.

He took pride in the fact that he was a single dad with physical custody of his son. He had both of his sons until his older son's mother went off the deep end and split his boys up. This was a never ending source of drama and pain but today he was just focused on how proud he was to be where he was. He wasn't where he wanted to be, with both his boys but at least he wasn't where he was with his daughter, no contact at all. Most days he didn't even open up that bag of pain. So today, like all others, he thanked God for, and stayed focused on, what he had by way of blessings instead of what he did not. At that moment, life and everything around it was good, never mind the lack so evident in his day to day.

Once home, he and Angel settled into their normal routine and played for the remainder of the time he was awake. Tony knew Angel usually fell asleep within a few hours of him getting home and always took advantage of that open eye time as soon as they got home. Within forty five minutes of laughing and playing, now about seven thirty, Tony knew if he didn't get Angel to eat now that he would fall asleep and throw the entire night off. He had lost track of time with all the good feelings and getting off early.

He turned on the Backyardigans, Angel's favorite show, in the den next to the kitchen and began preparing something for his son to eat. As he waited on the stove's temperature to rise to cook the food, he began to multi-task and opened his laptop and began the booting process, while the loud Windows chime sounded off, letting everyone in earshot know the computer was just about ready to be used as it was intended.

"Pewter Daddy."

Even Angel knew what was going on as he called out to his Daddy in the kitchen.

Tony could feel himself becoming more and more anxious, then eager, to log onto the dating website so he could affirm all the good feelings he had been riding the coat tails of for most of the afternoon. He did his able best not to get his hopes high but by the time he sat down with his plate and began to log onto the Internet, he could already feel the butterflies in his gut starting to flutter. With each key stroke, the nerves and excitement increased, only to be calmed by the reality that NO ONE may have answered his request for a response.

"It is what he did. He called it the all-or-nothing. Either he was all in and believed wholeheartedly that the woman of his fantasies would be there just waiting on him, or none at all. He had learned that this was a part of him, but had yet to recognize just how much harm this thing would cause him. At that moment, it felt like safety. He opened his email first as a sort of prelude to what he really wanted to know. He opened up his Hotmail to find exactly what he was looking for. He had been responded to, but it gave no real details and asked that he visit the site. Immediately his butterflies had turned into a full on stomach churn and he began the necessary clicks in order to get to the website.

Logging into the site, he saw that there were hearts and alerts directing him to his Inbox, letting him know he had messages from some of his matches. The entire process fascinated him. It involved all the excitement of meeting someone new without nearly as much fear of rejection. If you got rejected it was in the privacy of your own home and no one would know unless you told. So he opened his Inbox eager and expecting. There were about sixteen responses to his photo, which immediately brought a big smile to his face.

The opposite of rejection is to feel wanted and he was feeling that in a big way. He noticed that only about six or seven of the responses he received were from women he had sent a message to. The rest were women who had spotted his photo like those he had contacted. Most of the messages were sort of generic with some cute or clever way to let him know they were interested. He was flattered by all of the attention. However, out of the sixteen, there were only about seven or eight he was actually interested in, and only about five or six he was feeling up to meeting. He responded to those he was interested in, seeking to move this internet dating thing further into the real world. He had sought out mostly Latino women. He didn't know if it was his feeling for Ms. Cruz or him seeking his own roots, but he felt like he had given every other type of woman a chance and now needed to find out for himself what all the fuss was concerning Latinas. He had dated Latinas in the past but he always felt the shame of not knowing his culture and it usually kept him from diving all the way in. He always felt they were the most attractive women in the world, next to light-skinned black women. To him they virtually were the same. They usually looked very similar but he identified more with black women, having been raised by one. So ultimately they were the most attractive but he had denied himself those thoughts since the last time a light-skinned woman had broken his heart. They say you are attracted to yourself, so the woman that most looks like you is the woman you choose on a subconscious level. He didn't know if it were absolutely true but could admit that those he had loved did remind him of himself in many ways, which was usually the primary reason he never went all the way to the promised land with these women no matter how much his lips professed to desire it. So there were no light-skinned women in the photos he chose. NONE. He was not willing to gamble with his heart so soon after having his hopes dashed by his last relationship. He wasn't exactly playing it safe as he did want a real relationship that would lead to marriage. This was his primary desire. He wanted a woman he could feel love and passion with but someone who wouldn't... couldn't... rip his still beating heart out of his chest, as had previously been done by what he believed was the true love; and yes she was a light-skinned woman. So he would take it slow and walk his fears down one by one and deal with all that mess and walk into a loving relationship with a mature woman who wanted what he wanted, a marriage, a family and life with him forever. This is what he desired most - til death do us part. He was so ready to finally enter into that part of his life. He had thought he was previously but was so blind to so many things that he had ruined it each and every time. This last time though, he had proven to himself that he could stay and love beyond the bullshit; even despite himself, he knew he was ready.

He pushed on past all of the demons in his closet and lost so many things that had burdened and weighted down his soul. He was on that path towards forever with someone he was sure he had proven himself to and earned every bit of her love. He was certain that this was not only a relationship that he deserved but he would be showered at some point with all of the love, affection, patience, forgiveness and latitude to be his imperfect self. But she couldn't see past her own demons and refused to take the leap beyond where she was ready and he knew it would never lead to that forever he sought. So once again, he packed up his heart and headed back out toward his destiny. All this sounded far greater than the twenty-four dollars he spent to become a member of the website that would bring him the love that would fulfill his destiny. He knew it was grand so he never put that much on it; only that this is where he would start.

Chapter 3
Blue Head

There he was knee deep into the largest bottle of Blue Head Tequila, drowning his troubles in his favorite fire water and feeling a lot like that Indian on the front of the bottle. He, too, felt like screaming. His life was caught in a place where there was clearly a disconnect between reality and what he wanted. The question was how was he going to get there? Tony believed strongly in the power of the mind and prayer. As with about everything else in his life that he had managed to be successful with - he dreamed. All his life, folks mocked him for being a dreamer and for keeping his head in the clouds; never concerning himself with where he was at the moment. To him, it was but a temporary circumstance to be moved with his will; never to quit until he moved into the life he had dreamed about. Each year, for as far back as he started, he was getting closer and closer. He had failed in the past, but THIS TIME he was certain he knew where to go to find the answers to the questions. It was all going to have to start and end with HIM. He knew that there was something in this thing he was carrying that kept him from reaching that last rung. That last step in the ladder that held all his hopes had always been elusive to him. But why? After some time he figured out it was he who either backed away, got scared and ran away, or put himself in impossible situations so he would never succeed. He was indeed afraid and had been running not only from his happiness but from the destiny he sought year in and year out; blind to the fact that it was HE who was his greatest adversary. It was he that let his fear drive Sensimone away. It was he who had not committed to the marriage he promised his ex-wife, and God, he

33

would love forever. It was he who had chosen all the women who had let him down time and again.

After he searched out each and every situation, he had discovered somewhere deep down in the crevices of his decisions - in the bowels of what was real - that it was he who had brought each and every imperfection, every crack in the armor, the stench of death to his life. That is not to say that these women, those that would dare to love him, didn't have a part in it. Oh, they had their issues and they did their deeds but it was no more than he allowed them to do or be in his life. It was he who had chosen them after all. So they could do no more to him than he had brought them there to do. Anyone with eyes could see who they were from the gate. He was no fool. He merely pretended to be one for the purposes of HIS OWN deception; and even that he pretended to be unaware.

This thing ran deep; deeper than he ever allowed himself to dream. If he had known, he would have prevented himself from taking such nasty falls time after time as he wandered the halls of the unknowing and, more importantly, the unforgiving. He had become a master of weaving the truth into the color of his thinking as he made excuses for those who hurt him; but moreover, for his existence and their place in it. It was not that he was merely a victim, because he also had a major part to play, just as did they. There were no innocent parties in this torturous game; only fools and the lonely. Forasmuch as he thought they were different, they turned out to be much the same, just fools.

Now as he hit the milestone of his mid-thirties with the scales beginning to drop from his eyes, he was finally beginning to look at this manhood thing and what he truly wanted for his kingdom. He found it severely lacking. Not just in those things he wanted, but also in the leader who was to rule this realm which always started in his mind. So he set out upon a journey of self discovery to find out if he was truly the man inside that he actually believed himself to be. He knew for certain

34

that the outward was nowhere close to what he thought of himself. That is when he got honest with himself.

This was a secret mission, one he could not let anyone in on. But once again, he was playing the fool because just as easily as he spotted those who were not there, it was folly, or maybe pure arrogance, to even think that they would not spot his mountain of bull a mile away. But still he did try. He had to save some dignity, if you can even call it that. This was not about beating himself up about all the things he was not but finding out for starters who HE WAS. So he started out with this idea in mind as he sought out his mate and knew he would instantly see his reflection of himself in her eyes. It made him afraid, fearful to know that for the first time, probably ever, he had to admit to himself the truth about what he really thought about himself. With the invention of the Internet and this whole cyber dating, this made the process at least a bit more bearable. He only had himself to look in the eye and not those he was sure he would disappoint. He could feel himself and his esteem slip to the bottom of his thoughts, but again, refused to give into the enemy that told him he deserved to be where he was; and who did he think he was to even seek higher if he himself was not higher. Where would it land him to put his entire burden on some unsuspecting "good woman?"

Again he pushed past the enemy and his sullen words knowing that he was hitting on truth which is why it stung so badly; though he knew it was a lie. He did deserve better and despite his attempts to grow and get it from where he started, with the mother of his children, the woman he asked to marry, it appeared it was not to be. She was too wrapped up in her own denial about her life and all the shadows in which she remained hiding from herself, her past and whatever future she was going to have, for fear he would see her for what she really was and leave her flat. Truth was he saw her from day one because she was a reflection of himself, and they both knew it.

But he wanted to grow and move past the co-dependency and past the hurt and depression that bonded them into this place of crutches and reasons why neither of them could do, nor have, more. She threw herself into her job, her friends, her education and even her son. He had done the same. At the end of the day they both were lonely. They had each suffered much to get where they had grown although it wasn't nearly where they had set out to be. Honestly, it was a miracle that they had made it that far. With all the demons and ghosts of life's past that they both dragged around like old luggage, it was a feat to be able to say they had managed to move that far. Both of them holding one another's skeletons as well as their own was enough to break any mere person, let alone a relationship. They not only managed to push past those things, but after ripping each other to shreds, inviting, begging and challenging one another to leave, they made it all the way to a proposal of marriage and a child before it finally got to be just too much and they both silently quit.

****

She stopped caring about her appearance and let herself go completely - gaining weight, looking the part of a frumpy old house wife at barely thirty years of age. She stopped trying to please him in any way. Hell, she had already stopped trying to please herself. She had begun to care about nothing but her son. With Tony being such a capable father, she could even afford not to care too much about that. He had it. So she could fall as far as she wanted and her son would be safe; this she knew. Tony was a solid father. She was sure of that. She had chosen him for many reasons, this being the paramount one. Her children, however many or few she had, would have a solid father, unlike the one that raised her. He would be everything she didn't have and everything she couldn't herself be. He was stronger than her and she knew it; but again this is why she had chosen him, so she let go. They were both living in a home divided not just in their stance as to their relationship but in their pain and progress.

While Tony had taken the step to talk to her about his pain, what he wanted, and why and where it left them, she in turn would not, or could not, pay that shit any mind at all. She had come further than she ever thought she would with a man she dreamed of and knew that this thing could not be over as he stated. He had just taken her to the top of the Eiffel tower and asked her to marry him. She had just bore him a son, the pride and joy to his life and she was sure that no matter what he said, that he was not going to merely leave her behind, no matter how far he moved himself away from her. So each time they talked, she cried but when she woke up the following day and looked around her, their home, the pictures and all the elements of his love, she was driven to this place of resolve that this was merely him protesting to her quitting on herself. But in her mind she never quit on him, just herself, so she would be able to hold on to her family and her man once she pulled herself up off of the floor. It was just a matter of time for her and as long as she pushed on getting busy about the common task before her, she would be fine. She would get to those other things when she got to them as long as she could go about the quick fixes that bothered Tony so much, they would be fine. So she worked hard to bring home the money they needed to take and keep the pressure off of him as the bread winner. She knew that no matter what he said, it mattered to him. She had to work on pleasing him more (i.e. give into him more sexually). She had been stunted this way and this is what first clued Tony in that there was a problem with her and her growth. Part of those skeletons were sexual in nature and they had begun to haunt her hard since she gave birth and became a mother and she didn't know how to run them out of her life so they were more successful at running her out of hers. So each time she offered, or made advances unsuccessfully, she told herself she was doing her part, and in her mind that was enough. When he finally came around he would see her effort. For him it was too little too late and he couldn't bear another wounded, half in/half out moment of broken sex in that house. His moving Angel into their bed was the final step to ensure that she no longer even had the opportunity to make such advances.

This was a clear symbol of everything that was wrong with their life and an even clearer message that he wanted no part in repairing it. He decided that this was his time. It was time for him to grow. Time for him to heal. Time to figure out all of the answers to all of the questions he was afraid to ask, or even try. He had to look at himself in the mirror, at the man he was. He could not just remain fixated on the man he intended and worked to be and see who flinched first. He needed to know, who he was. Was he even built for this life he kept asking for? Or were his choices not only indicative of the fact that he wasn't but that he never would be? Was he destined to follow the footsteps of damn near every man he knew and end up grumpy, bitter and alone? He watched even the women in his family, one by one going down to pride and a multitude of sin to a place that only, and always, ended in being alone. Was he destined for just such a fate or was he cut from a different cloth as he had always believed?

There was only one way to find out the answers. He had to push himself beyond what it was he only thought he knew. And that was scary on more than one level. It was scary because anything we don't understand and are pushing into the unknown is never easy to face down. But more than that, it was scary because he knew that once he pushed into these waters, that there would be no one to help him. No guide. No one to lean on for advice or support. It would be what it always was - him against the world. The same troubled waters he took on when he was young and full of piss and vinegar didn't quite look like the same challenge. Hell, he wasn't the same young man. He had seen some things, buried his first son, already been through a horrible divorce and lost more loved ones than he cared to count. So he knew first hand that things didn't always work out or go as you expected. Sometimes things got away from you and sometimes things didn't always work out and one rogue wave could capsize this dingy and put him on the other side of the earth if he wasn't careful; and these waters were mean. He needed a navigator, so he turned to books, inner peace, and thought. He had dabbled in Buddhism in college but it never jived with his Baptist upbringing. So it never stuck.

He had read a myriad of self-help books and his education was the spark that lit the flame to pull him out of the ghetto he had risen from. But none of this was enough. He needed an anchor. But more than that he needed a port he could bring his ship to in times of trouble to find shelter and peace from the storm because if he was certain of anything, there would be storms. Then, of course, there was the matter of advice. After all he barely knew any real men, let alone any that were successful at what he wanted, and had tried to build.

So he blew the dust off that bible his grandmother had given him back in junior high school when he first found the Lord. Then he went about dusting off that faith that he lost to the world and all the things he thought he knew when he had decided to become his own god and stopped following the one in heaven. It was time to come on home and walk into the life he was intended to have. Come on home and step into the man that God had always intended for him to be. Yes, God's will be done!

"And damn this bottle!" he shouted out loud with eyes full of tears he had held back for what felt like his entire life.

He slammed the bottle back onto the bar and with tear drawn eyes he took the pad on his desk and scribbled on it, in an attempt to start a list. This is something he always did as he started his march toward whatever goal he set before him. He was most definitely a list guy.

Find out, WHAT IS GODS WILL?

He bent his knee and finally opened that book he had been running from for so long and began to seek out his kingdom.

Chapter 4
It's Over

Tony woke up with a full blown headache that pounded like a jack hammer first thing Monday morning on a fresh construction site, with a foreman determined to finish his project on time. He could barely open his eyes as the sun shone through the small cracks in the blinds that it was indeed morning and time to go to work. He had sworn last night that this was it. And now dragging himself off the mattress, he thought to himself how he wished he had come to that decision about ten to twelve shots earlier. It would have made this morning a tad bit easier as he steadied himself on the footboard trying to make it to the bathroom.

As he rounded the corner of the bed, he almost tripped as he kicked Sharon's leg as she was lying on the floor in their bedroom. They had been fighting pretty much nonstop and it was clear that he had made his decision to make this relationship over. They had already had this monumental conversation but it didn't seem to have the desired effect nor did it seem to change things in the house very much. Actually things pretty much went right back to their normal routine. She ignored him. He ignored her. And in between they both went to work and loved and raised their son. He refused to believe, or buy into, this idea that this is what his life would amount to; that this is what his life was supposed to be. A loveless existence that said the only thing that mattered was the children, and whether or not we worked and paid the bills on time. Could this be a life?

He had another image in his mind; one that actually resembled who he and Sharon started off to be. He had loved her hard, through all the doubts and fears. But his patience had worn thin throughout the process and he was tired of waiting for her to follow him out of that place that said her abuse was greater than their love. She had been horribly abused in her childhood and it shaped her thoughts and actions in just about everything she did. So was he, and it bonded them at first in their subjective place of codependence for a long time but he was ready for something else that she was not. So it was clear, it was time to move on. It was time to make this real. As the warm water ran from the shower head down his weary body, he thought to himself how he would have this conversation with her again that night once she got home. He imagined all the words and things he would have to move in order to make this thing real.

What would that mean for her functionally? Moving her things out. Her finding another place? When? Where? And all the details therein. He thought about if that meant his son would be going as well or how all that had played out. They had already had pretty detailed conversations about how things would go if and when this thing ever happened. But neither one of them really believed it would ever come to this. Deep down they both believed outside of all the realities that laid before them that no matter what they would love each other more and would ultimately end up being together for life. But now, lonely and beaten down by those same words, things looked as if they were going to be very different than what he had imagined since that love at first sight meeting that day they met in college so long ago. He was quiet, deep in thought the entire way through his morning ritual getting dressed and grooming himself.

As he exited the bathroom and grabbed his bag for work, he went back to the bedroom door to look in on his family one final time. Sharon had crawled into bed with Angel now and they both lay there asleep and hugged up tangled up with as much love as exhaustion. He watched them sleep for a moment, their chest's rising and falling, and he walked into the room and placed a gentle kiss on his son's cheek and leaned back and turned for the door when it hit him, that this may be the last day he saw them that way in that house. He turned

41

back around and placed another gentle kiss on Sharon's forehead and before he got emotional he turned and headed for the door.

Still half drunk and full of all the things he needed to do for work and the mess his life was in, he drove to work in the same fog he got ready in and headed out the door with. He barely noticed the fact that he was able to get to work a full half hour ahead of his usual time because traffic had been so light. He was just grateful that he would have the extra time to get his mind on work and out of all the drama that surrounded his life. As he pulled up to the building and saw the gates to the school were still chained, he was shocked. He knew he wasn't that early.

"What's going on?" he said out loud, as he pulled into the driveway.

It was then he took his cell phone out of his pocket and realized that it was Sunday and he was early for work by a full day. He just sat there looking and feeling stupid to have gone through so much and never even noticed his surroundings. He sat there thinking for another thirty minutes when he started seeing some of his students walking around in the projects that were just across the street from the school he taught them in. He witnessed them noticing his car and didn't want any of them seeing him in the shape he was in, still a bit tipsy and full of emotion. In fact, he was sitting in his darkly tinted car crying. So as he saw the children begin to point, he slowly pulled out of the driveway and rolled his window down far enough to push his hand out and wave to his students as he slowly dove away.

"I told you it was him!" one child shouted.

"Hi Mister Alfonso! See you tomorrow!" The small brown-skinned boy shouted as Tony slowly drove down the street on his way back home.

As Tony drove the long way through the city, and hit each traffic light that accompanied just about every corner, he was in no hurry. He was thinking about all the times he had been hurt, all the times he had been disappointed and Sharon's response to it. He was

42

thinking about how much time she was missing with Angel and how he would end up being better off with her moving out because she would more than likely end up overcompensating for her absence in their home by spending more quality time with him. He began to rehearse the conversation they would have to make this thing official. By the time Tony got home, he was in full frustration mode and felt as ready as he ever was going to be to have that conversation. As he made his way up the stairs he could hear Sharon and Angel playing and laughing and genuinely enjoying each other's time. As he reached the top of the stairs, he could see big smiles and more laughter and quickly had doubts about ruining the moment they were sharing. Angel ran up and grabbed his hand and pulled him into their little game of playing hide and seek and then peek-a-boo. He would have had to be heartless in order to rip apart this moment. Soon minutes slipped into hours and he and Angel had fallen back to sleep on what ended up being a lazy Sunday afternoon. Tony was awakened by Sharon who was on her way back out the door to work for the evening. He heard the door lock and knew that he had missed another chance to talk about the life he hoped to have one day and the fact that it wouldn't include her. He once again closed his eyes and allowed the little rest to come back to him and he rejoined his son in a plate of ice cream dreams and Barney and no talk of such adult things that only hurt and wound.

Soon they both got up and were into the rest of their day, which for Tony included grading papers and school work, while Angel enjoyed more playing and Barney. Eventually, it was time to put the little man back to bed and for Daddy to finish the household chores that it seemed he alone was always responsible for. Once done and finding himself restless after such a long nap earlier in the day, he stayed up watching television and waiting for Sharon to return so they could have the conversation he intended to have earlier that day. The late show turned into the late, late show and then to the late, late movie. As Tony's eyes once again got heavy,

43

he turned in with Angel already in his bed waiting to be held on his way to soothing Tony to sleep. It was three in the morning when Sharon finally walked in hours after her job at the restaurant had been closed, again smelling of cigarette smoke and loose women. Tony, who was a light sleeper, heard her on her way up the stairs. His heart began to race as he was getting himself ready for the confrontation, when her cell phone rang out and she quickly quieted it. She stepped back outside the door for a moment to take the call then right back in the door and headed back up the stairs. Tony laid in the dark fuming and waiting to get himself together. He didn't want to yell and wake up Angel and he didn't want to have this conversation as an angry one so he was trying to pull himself together. She clumsily stumbled back into the dark room giggling a bit for stubbing her foot on the stand that held their television. He could hear her struggling to get out of her clothes quietly thinking he was asleep and not wanting to wake him. She laid herself on the floor on the opposite side of the room from him and let out a big sigh. Tony lay there still fuming at Sharon's choice to come home not only so late but what appeared to be drunk, or at least having drank, while her family lay at home wondering and waiting. Tony tried to control his tongue and his breathing as he could feel his blood pressure rising with each breath. He could hear Sharon's breathing change too.

SHE WAS ALREADY ASLEEP! He sat up on the bed and began to whisper her name when her cell phone rang out loudly. He jumped up and grabbed it off of the dresser where she had left it when she entered the room.

"Hello?" he answered, curious and annoyed at who could be calling her at almost four in the morning.

"Hello? I want to speak to my baby! Who is this! Put my baby on the phone! Where is my Sharon poo?!" A man's voice replied with a tone that hinted that he had been drinking as well.

"What!? Who the hell do you think you are calling my home at this time of night on a phone in my name that I pay for?! Calling to speak to someone who is supposed to be MY woman! Who the fuck is this?!" Tony was now screaming and not giving a second thought to Angel sleeping just feet away.

Sharon woke up and sat up on the floor watching Tony now on the phone at a full yell and questioning someone on her phone.

"Who the fuck is this?!" He yelled.

"I just want to speak to my baby! Can you put my baby on the fucking phone?!" The strange voice yelled back.

Tony, catching himself, realized he was making something out of nothing because his relationship with Sharon was over and this just proved it. He took the phone away from his ear and looked at it in disbelief. He looked up to see Sharon staring at him and just handed her the phone. Sharon took the phone and put it to her ear.

"Hello? Pete? You need to go lay down and sleep it off. Everyone is asleep over here and you just woke the entire house up," she said as Angel also sat up in the bed.

"Pete, Pete?" Sharon began to try to talk on the phone when Tony asked her to hang up because they needed to talk.

Sharon did, and as Tony laid Angel back down he motioned for her to go out to the dining room so they could talk, which she did. Once Tony got Angel back to sleep, he came out behind her. For as upset as he was, he had managed to pull himself together in the brief moments it took him to lay Angel back down to sleep.

"It's over," he said as plain as day looking Sharon in the eye so she could see there was no hesitation in his words.

"I know that Tony. We have already discussed this. Which is why I don't know why this whole thing has got you so upset?" she answered.

"Listen we have got to make a plan because I can't live like this anymore. I need you to get your things and move out," he said.

"Where do you expect me to go? I haven't saved enough money to be able to get my own place? I already tried to get a place in this complex and they won't accept me? Where do you want me to go?" she shot back.

"I don't know, maybe you can stay with Pete or one of your other friends but you have got to go. And I am taking my cell back tonight. You have already run up a $1,400 bill in my name and haven't paid a dime. I'll be damned if I'm going to pay for one more conversation between you and your new boyfriend," Tony snapped back.

"Ok you're right. I'll make some calls and be out tomorrow," Sharon replied and just sat back in the chair as Tony got up, having had enough of the conversation, and walked out.

He went back into the bedroom and closed the door, sending the message that she was no longer welcome to sleep in the same room even if it was on the floor. Sharon received the message and didn't even try to re-enter the room and the house finally fell peaceful as the morning approached.

The alarm rang and Tony jumped up having slept maybe an hour the entire night. He went into the bathroom to get ready for work. After he finished his normal routine, he walked out to the living room where Sharon had not slept the entire night, but stayed up packing and getting herself and her things ready for today's move.

"I spoke to one of my friends and I'll be gone today. I'll wait for you to get back from work but I'll be leaving when you get home as you have asked me to," she said to him very matter of fact.

"Good," he replied as he barely looked at her and headed down the stairs and out the door to work.

He really didn't mean it that way and was just as hurt as she was at how this thing had played out; but was also angry and feeling disrespected at the moment. So he wanted to put on a good poker face and make for this final push to get his life back. He figured in his mind he could always mend fences once she was gone and they both had some time and space to heal from a very hard situation. After all they would be in constant contact with such a small child to raise and deal with on a daily basis. He knew they would have plenty of time to talk. This was just the beginning. With this, his final thought, he felt confident that he had made the right decision for all involved, and he began to think about his work and the job he had to do once he got there.

As the end of the day came upon him and with each passing minute, he gave less and less thought to the home life now behind him, so much so that when he returned home and saw his apartment door open and Sharon putting things into the trunk of her car, it was as if he had almost forgotten the drama going on in his home. He walked inside to find Angel in the den watching television with some boxes at the bottom and top of the stairs. He didn't think much of it and didn't even lift a finger to help. He just waited for her to be finished and asked if she wanted to talk. When she said no, he allowed her to leave her keys and walk out without saying a word. She didn't look hurt at all. She looked angry. You could tell by the look on her face that she was not happy at all about leaving Angel behind but she could not argue with the fact that she didn't have a safe home of her own to take him to. So she agreed and knew it was best to leave him there with his dad in a room and place he had known his entire life. She didn't even argue the fact, or point, but anyone with eyes could tell she was hurting about it, far more than how she looked about moving out. So there it went, months in the making, if not years. As quickly as the conversation began it was over and she had moved out. She was gone. IT WAS OVER.

Chapter 5
Now What?

Waiting. It seemed like Tony spent his entire life waiting. His mind was always ahead of his time, or position. He had come from very humble beginnings, to say the least. Growing up in the projects of Brooklyn, no one, including the family who loved him, really expected him to go much further than the neighborhood he came from. He was constantly encouraged to become a civil servant or military enlisted man. He had to have some serious mental toughness in order to overcome so many doubters. So his mind was always in another place. More often than not he lived in his future and the world he could see ahead. He imagined himself completing college and leaving Brooklyn; and so as each day passed, this is how he walked. This is how he behaved and this is who he saw himself to be.

Now the world, however, only saw the young man before them who had so many things lined up against him. They saw the slim chance he had to reach the dreams he had for himself. But his determination and drive could not be denied and he got as much credit and opportunity as that would allow. As it turned out, it was enough. He had maneuvered himself out of the battlefield of his past and now sat where he intended to be at this moment in his life. Facing forward and headed toward a better future for himself and his children. He never let his imagination go. He possessed an ability to dream, see and believe in things you could not see. Some call it faith; others determination. He had always thought it to be a bit of both, and depending on when you checked him, one would be greater than the other.

Today, he was sitting on faith with full confidence that he would indeed be soon walking into his future and the family he wanted all his life, despite the fact that he was, once again, for all intents and purposes, walking further away from the family he wanted so much. He had two sons to this point in his life and knew all too well with the birth of his first son that things don't always go as you planned, or the way you wanted. With his first son, he was unexpected and had been conceived during a one night reconciliation, so it shook up his world a bit. The most difficult thing about the situation was that, in his mind, it could not have been further from what he wanted.

Although he loved his son very much, he knew full well that he and the mother would never be a couple, or the family, that he dreamed of. They could not have been more different. He was a dreamer. She was a realist who had no idea about dreaming and no faith in anything other than the bird in her hand. She was harshly critical of Tony and his desire to be something more and the method he had chosen to get there. There was always more than one way to do something and Tony was often denied upon first attempt or request. But if life was as easy as just making a request then there would be no poor in the world. So as he reached, she doubted, and quickly lost faith in him and his dreaming ways. When it came time to put in the work to build the family he envisioned, she could not see past all of the holes she saw in his character.

In her eyes, he would never accomplish the things he set out to do, or become, because she couldn't see it. Therefore, he had to let her go. On this tough road, this hidden path, there was NO ROOM for doubters. No room for non-believers. If he was going to build that family, if he was going to reach the reaches of the world he had dreamed of, monetary and beyond, he needed a supporter. Someone who would get behind him and his dream and support him no matter how it looked on the surface and she was definitely not that. So by the time his son was born, it was already understood that although they would be parents, they would never again be a couple.

Sharon had been different. Their relationship started out as a friendship that later turned into a romance. So she had always believed in him; choosing to see his progress and looking deep for his vision instead of only what lay in front of her by way of proof. They were very similar in personality. They had both been athletes who liked to work out and take care of their bodies. They both loved watching sports and were fierce competitors who didn't know how to quit in life. Although she came from a very different background than Tony, she too faced adversity in her life and had to dream to overcome it. Having had a bit of her own success in that way gave her a clearer window to Tony's soul and where his heart and intentions lie. They appeared to be the perfect couple. The child that they made was the child they both prayed and asked God for. He, too, was another one of their dreams and he could not have been more perfect. He was born almost ten pounds with the baby build of a linebacker if you ever saw one. He had dirty blonde hair and the brightest blue eyes you ever wanted to see. He was the perfect looking child.

As he grew, his personality rivaled his looks and he melted hearts and minds wherever he went. People stopped them in the street to pass out compliments. Once while Tony was pumping gas, Angel was laughing and flirting with the women at the other pump across from his car seat, and he was given a modeling spot in an agency. He went on to be in several modeling campaigns, including one for Ralph Lauren that went national. The photos were taken on the beach and he looked like the perfect child to the perfect couple headed towards the perfect life. Everyone who laid eyes on them and their child immediately urged them to have another to the point where it was almost intrusive and embarrassing considering what they both knew inside. The love they had when they produced Angel was long gone and they didn't know how to get it back.

There were so many differences now and so little patience to settle those differences that were broken. So after all that life had thrown at them and all the obstacles they had to overcome, it was this happiness, this assent towards something greater, that finally brought out the quit in them. They had silently agreed to the terms that they would silently fade off into the night; and he was completely sick and tired of it, and was screaming to be freed.

And now that she was gone, the slight hesitation he held about moving forward was gone and he was now indeed free to move forward with his life and dreams. He once again began to seek out the life, and wife, he wanted by continuing to throw his hat in the ring via the Internet and the dating site he had joined.

He spent hours looking through pictures and reading profiles and interests of women who appeared to be like-minded people. Some were more attractive than others, but mostly he looked for people who, in his mind, shared his vision. He was not searching for the picture perfect one but a reasonable recollection of his now broken dream. For weeks, he responded to and sent out invitations to his life. He had even managed to go out and meet a few people; none with much potential but at least he was trying.

He met one young woman with a body to die for and the face of an angel but the more they spoke, the longer he listened, the more twisted she sounded. Her words were controlling and shallow. He was certain that she would never understand a man like him. The only thing they had in common was that she, too, wanted children and had grand visions of being married in the near future. He absolutely loved her body and on the one hand couldn't wait to taste the nectar. But Tony had learned a really funny and simple truth.

"Sex makes babies," he would say to himself, all the time, and laugh. Reminding himself of the one night reconciliation that bore a son he never intended to have. This is how he pushed his self-control and true agenda to be married with a family before his primal need to conquer and have this beautiful woman before him.

51

She cooed and fawned, making it plain that she was buying whatever it was he was selling. But he did his able best to remain strong. They had met for dinner and sat and talked for hours over dinner and then drinks. They now sat in her car still talking. She began begging with her eyes for Tony to reach out and touch her with his strong hands, as she pulled him towards her and reached for his kiss. In a moment of weakness, Tony succumbed to the calling of his flesh and leaned in and enjoyed the passionate kiss driven by lust, and she grabbed his shoulders and pulled him closer. He was as close to the stick shift of her car as he was to her. They both reached for each other in a way that said only one thing, they were headed for her place in a hurry. She reached around his back and took a hand full of his round, firm buttocks and then rubbed his lower back again pulling him closer. He instinctively reached for her hips, and while squeezing her hip bone, he ran his hand up her toned abs towards her firm D-cup breast.

As he reached her breast and gently squeezed her large nipple, she moaned and pulled his head towards her breast. Understanding the language their bodies were speaking, he, all at once, raised her blouse, exposing her firm supple breasts. He pushed his tongue out, licking and swirling her breast, savoring the flavor as they sat in the middle of the Hooters parking lot. He leaned back a bit and took in the vision as he squeezed her two breasts together and murmured, "Mmm, mmm, mmm," as he admired what beautiful breasts she had.

She reached for his package and repeated to him, "Mmm, mmm, mmm," as they both caught themselves in that speeding moment, and shared a laugh.

He removed his hands and she began putting her body back into the very sexy bra she was wearing and they both sighed as they once again took notice of their surroundings. They looked around the dark parking lot and knew they were not in a place safe to be doing the things that they had started and she looked at him with serious intent and bedroom eyes.

"I want you to stay with me tonight Tony," she said.

"I can't. I have to go get my son. He is at the sitter," he replied, having second thoughts.

"Please don't go. Don't leave me. I think we were just getting to know one another," she pleaded.

He was thinking to himself that the only thing they were getting to know were each other's body. And although she was right and they were making a connection, it was not the type of connection he wanted to make at this point. He was fighting all the lustful thoughts his body was calling him to do. Twelve play had already consumed his thoughts and would not stop playing in his mind. She was so damn sexy, with almond brown skin and "chinky," bedroom eyes. She was sitting on a five-foot-five frame with measurements that looked like 36-24-36. She had tight, smooth skin and shoulder length dark brown hair. She smelled great, was well groomed and had the perfect French manicure. Firm in all the places she needed to be and soft in all the places men desire a woman to be.

He and Sharon fought about sex the most. The fact that they had stopped having it was a major point of contention. The moment they started fighting the sex stopped, and they had been fighting a long time. So Kisha was looking extra savory tonight for all the wrong reasons.

"Sex makes babies. Sex makes babies. Sex makes babies." He just kept repeating this to himself. Remembering that he had worn a condom the night he conceived Lil Tony. So he couldn't let the monster in his pants convince him that it would be okay, as he had done that night. With this in mind, he began peeling Kisha off of him and his mind off of her body by saying all the right things. He explained to her that this would not be their last chance to be together, that there would be other nights, and they needed to take it a bit more slowly and that their flesh may have been clouding their judgment. She completely agreed with Tony and both their mouths said the right thing but their bodies still longed and called for one another.

He began exiting the vehicle. She again grabbed him and begged him not to go. She reached out of the door and pulled him closer once again and planted another long hard kiss on his lips that told of deep intentions for their night. Tony's radar was not off as his manhood again shot straight to the sky and was now poking his navel and throbbing to no end. She grabbed it again and this time pulled it towards her and he could feel his manhood drooling all over his belly. She knew it as it began showing over his belt line. He sat down again and sighed louder. This time it was harder than before and he didn't really want to leave the car. But as he felt himself start to tremble down under, he managed to once again pull himself out of the car as she petted and stroked his manhood. This time he walked to the other side of the car to say goodbye keeping the closed door between them while saying goodbye through the window.

She continued to plead as he continued to make excuses as to why he couldn't go with her tonight. She offered to go to his place and stay as long as he wanted, but he once again found the perfect excuse as to why that, too, couldn't happen. They finally parted as he walked toward his car in the parking lot. As he unlocked his car door and began to clear his mind, she pulled up alongside his car and he sat down and they again talked for another fifteen minutes. Once he finally said goodbye, he was feeling uncertain about the choice he had made, still being super horny, when the phone rang. It was Kisha. She was calling to plead her case yet again. She was making it tougher on him than he thought possible. He had never imagined that their simple dinner date would end up here. Funny, he should have felt flattered that she wanted him so badly but all he felt at this point was pressure. He began to see Kisha as too desperate, that there almost might be an agenda for him that she maybe wasn't communicating, outside of sex. One that may have included the same fears he had about unplanned children or maybe roping him into a relationship the wrong way. Or maybe she was simply in it for the sex. In any event, he was glad he made a good decision.

He had a pretty tight schedule this week with work, school and three more scheduled meetings. He was certain he would meet someone who would be better suited for his dream. She was short-sighted and he needed someone who was looking a bit longer than tonight and where all that lust would lead. Her profile said she was a Christian. She said that she wanted to take it slow and she wanted a real relationship; one that would lead to a marriage and life. She spoke a lot about God on her page and her resistance to one night stands and men trolling that site for sex. This was one of the main reasons why he felt so safe meeting with her. There were no expectations and he felt good about that and the chances of meeting someone real. She was about thirty three and damn fine for her age but she absolutely seemed conflicted and wounded; something that said she wanted more but just didn't know how to go about getting it. It was something he wanted to avoid. He needed more clarity, not more drama. In all, he was satisfied with his decision, the conclusion of his date, and satisfied that this was the beginning of, at the very least, a good adventure.

Chapter 6
The right approach

Night after night, and day after lonely day, he spent them watching and waiting, wishing and moaning to the moon. He had since doubted the decision to have turned down Kisha, but was happy to be living drama free for the first time in as long as he could remember. He was once again on the dating sight looking through photos, responding to others who had spotted his picture and responded likewise. He found himself drawn to those who had reached out to him. He almost seemed addicted to the compliments and it hit him, that this had been his pattern. This had been his "M-O" of sorts. He went after women he found attractive and was never shy in that way. But if he was being real with himself, he had to admit that he always ended up with those who pursued him.

What this meant in his mind was that he wasn't as involved in the process as he thought he was. He had been taking the easy road, the path of least resistance, and something about that disturbed him. Yes. He ultimately had to say yes to the advances and reciprocate the interest in him. But it didn't hurt to know that he had an edge, or even better, that the win was in the bag. It had always given him the confidence that he needed. So the women who spoke up, the ones who paid him the most attention, were the ones who got his attention because it was easiest. But those supposed easy wins were never what he wanted, they were always something to compromise with. By the time he realized that he and the women of his affection didn't have much in common, they were usually knee deep into a relationship and a history that said they were far more entangled than a couple.

Thinking back, this had been his history. Summer, Sensimone, and all the major relationships in his life were forged when they pursued him. In fact, most of his relationships were formed by advances from the women in his life. He got lucky with Sharon. In fact, she shot him down at first. It took her a full year to come around and show him interest. He had never ended up with the type of woman he wanted - what she looked like, her views in the world and even her favorite music and foods were always like a pot luck type of thing. None of these things were a deal breaker for him but he never got what he set out for. This was a disturbing thought, so he decided that this time he had the unique opportunity to do just that. Choose from a ton of women, the woman he actually wanted, and pursue her over and over again until someone said yes. So he sat down and began to think about all the things he wanted.

He thought about all the things that were important to him - his deal breakers and the things that made someone supremely attractive for him. Everything from her personality, sense of humor, to her body type. It was easy to objectify women. The whole world did it, but he was brought up a little better. While body size and type were always important to him, he knew there were some things that were more important and non-negotiable. He was a list guy and needed to get through it all, but most importantly, he needed to get really honest with himself and what he liked. What was most important to him?

Before he could get to his wants, he had to get to his needs. In order to get to that, he had to go inside himself and figure out who he was. The honesty that he avoided didn't stop with the things outside of himself and what he wanted, but also all the things he avoided within himself. The first thing he had to think about was the identity crisis he had to acknowledge he was going through.

Tony was of mixed decent; his mother being black and his father Puerto Rican. This was not his problem in itself, but the fact that he hadn't seen his father since he was a small child and never got the chance to know his Hispanic side. He sought it out but always carried the shame that came from not being able to speak a word of Spanish. His birth name was actually Antonio, but when he was small, he changed it to Tony so he wouldn't have to answer as to why he didn't speak Spanish. He had dated Latina women when he was younger and honestly, they were who he felt most attracted to. It wasn't a curiosity of what he was at those times. It was simply who he thought was most attractive. Today, however, there was more to it, which included not knowing the Hispanic side of his culture. They always seemed hot, hot bodied, hot blooded and full of passion. He always wanted to date and settle down with a Latina woman on some level but it was his fear of rejection - his not feeling Latino enough - that kept him from really reaching out for what he wanted.

He decided that this is where he wanted to start - dark hair and dark eyes. It made sense that the women he was always most attracted to and fallen in love with were fair-skinned with dark hair and eyes. Well truthfully, in his heart of hearts, he believed the love of his life had been that, the only true and pure love he had ever known. All of the rest were guarded. He had been wounded and it was not until just now did he realize that he had avoided that type of woman up until this point, thinking he was keeping his heart safe. However, he was starting to think all he had saved his heart from was true love.

He decided he was going to step outside of his fears and get out in front of this thing and step into his destiny. It was time to stop living in fear.

His mother had told him time and time again that beauty was in the eye of the beholder. She had taught him to look for something deeper than just how a woman looked. She had trained him to see past the eye lashes and full lips for something deeper. She was the first to call to his attention his affinity for fair skinned women. On the other hand, his family - the family, and women - that raised him were all dark-skinned. She didn't make it any secret what she thought of that. To his mother, anyone who could make a decision about what they liked and disliked before they got to know what it, or who, she actually was had a bias, a prejudice, and this she never took lightly. This put many women in his spectrum who were great people, yet he just didn't have it for them as much due to this secret prejudice he hid, and the shame it brought him.

He was finally stepping out of this shame and fear, and acknowledging that he was not just black. Despite all the dark skinned women he dated, he was also Hispanic, and also wanted fair skinned women. He had just as much right to say he wanted this kind as that. He wrestled with these thoughts for years and was determined to put these thoughts to bed once and for all. So this part of his mind was settled. He would explore this avenue. Next he asked himself what else he wanted in a mate. He made a list and he would be looking at features like he did in picture after picture on the dating site. This is where he would start. She had to be:

Pretty
Beautiful eyes are a must, preferably dark
Long hair
Full lips
Nice body but didn't have to be perfect, something to hold on to
Tall- no one under 5'8" (He wanted tall children)

Since he had learned that you couldn't really count on what people said, he would have to actually meet with these people to determine the rest. But he made a list of those things too. She had to have:

-A sense of humor (This is a must)

-A serious side but doesn't take herself or her life TOO seriously

-An open mind about life and willing to learn more as I'm not done growing and want someone to grow with.

-An artistic side

-A love for poetry and reading (My dream girl would be a writer and we would love to read each other's work.)

-A sensitive side but a drive to have something more of the world.

-A love for travel and a real desire to see the world

What he didn't write, and wanted more than anything else he had written on that paper, was that he needed her to adore him. If he did indeed find his dream girl, no matter how improbably, he would need to be her dream guy. He wanted to be her everything, as he was certain she would be to him. To find her at this point in his life, to him, could only be destiny; something he believed in whole-heartedly and deeply. For him, he needed her to believe it too. Not only believe that there was such a thing, but that he was her destiny too. He was a strong man that believed in the romance of love. Some might even call him a hopeless romantic but he needed to be loved. He needed passion and without it, in his mind, there could be no love. It just simply couldn't exist. He had ideas of grandeur about changing the world through his work, or his art, and she needed to have a similar vision if not for him but for herself.

She didn't need to be perfect. In fact, with all the flaws he saw in himself, it would be better on him if she weren't because this would give him room to grow, and even more room for them both together. He had been hurt and was still working on pulling back the scabs to start cleaning out the scars so he could really heal and be ready for this dream of love in his life. One thing he knew for certain was that he wasn't certain of what she would be, but he was certain she would not be perfect because no one is. If she appeared to be that he, knew she would not stay. He was willing to accept her flaws and all because he knew he was pretty flawed in matters of the heart too. So the plan was to start with the photos and work his way through the beautiful women until he found someone who he could fall in love with and see if she led to his destiny. He was certain that there was something out there for him but unsure if it would be his forever. Nonetheless, he was most definitely on a journey of self-discovery and could only hope that it would be one that would build him and make him a better, stronger man without leaving him broken and still wondering.

There was one other thing he was certain of - that sex would not be primary. So any woman he met that came on too strong, and sex became, or was a major part of the conversation, no matter how fine he thought she was, he would leave her alone. He had had enough sex in his life to know that sex was not what he was seeking. Besides, for him, sex began in between his ears and not his legs. She needed to stimulate his mind before they got to their bodies. She needed to have sex appeal, but not
be over-ridden by the need to have sex.

He knew it was not a normal position for men to sit in, especially men who are looking to date on the Internet. Through this process, this was made really clear to him, at least two women had already questioned his sexuality because of him being so neat and fit. He was the sort of man who paid attention to his appearance. He was also sensitive, a writer, and loved to enjoy the beauty of things. To not be outwardly interested in chasing tail in this day and age only meant one thing - gay. He was very aware of the stereotypes – down-low brotha, keepin it in the closet, etc. It was offensive to him that he could not be sensitive and care about his appearance and not be a whore without being gay. Even the word metro-sexual offended him, so he made it a point to go a little left so this would never be questioned. He didn't like pretending but he didn't like to be judged either. It was easier for him to alter his personality a bit than to have others question his sexuality just because he didn't jump on every loose piece of tail thrown at him. So his game plan was set and he knew what he was looking for and also what he needed to unearth within himself to begin this journey anew.

61

He got real with himself and only introduced himself to those who he could see himself going all the way with. If he couldn't see himself in a serious relationship with her, he didn't even respond to any messages. Night after night, he got messages from plenty and he sent plenty out himself; but none peaked his interests more than a medium flame.

There was one Latina named Rosie. She was beautiful - a real knock-out with a killer body. She was as close as it ever got. But after about a month of talking and courting, he found her still wanting to party and be in the club; this with five children was confusing to him to say the least. But she had been recently divorced so he figured she was still trying to lick her wounds. This, to him, meant that he was possibly a rebound and he didn't want to be that. So ultimately he hung back and waited to meet her although they talked every day. He had finally agreed to meet her out at a local club. Although he really didn't want to be in a club, he wanted to meet her more and knew he could no longer stall her as to why they hadn't met.

She was beginning to think he was a farce and was maybe married, playing games, and not what he said he was, or wanted. Although she was beautiful and he really wanted to meet her, he also knew he was lying to himself and her when he agreed to meet her. He agonized over it all day and into the night up until the club closed and he still sat in his living room wishing he had the courage or the stomach to show up to that club that night. He had called Rosie's phone and made excuse after excuse but none of them made him sound anything other than lame, or a liar. He emailed her with no response. She had indeed been at the club waiting and left him several messages from the club with enough loud music to prove it. Out of desperation, he checked the dating site for a message from her of reprieve for his unwillingness to meet her at the club. There was nothing from Rosie, but there were some other messages.

He quickly looked through the pictures to find that there were no surprises. There were messages from women he had written and none of which were too exciting; merely tentative messages feeling him out. But then there was a message from a woman he hadn't written that had no photo at all. Now usually this meant that the women had something to hide and was either unattractive or cheating on her significant other. But he was intrigued so he opened up the message. It was short and to the point.

"Your picture keeps popping up although I put in different information in numerous searches. I took it as a sign and decided to reach out. I think you are attractive but figure you must have already found someone because no one who looks like you has to be here looking for a mate but for so long. It seems we may have a lot in common and I would like to get a chance to know you a little better. I have been told I am attractive but have no current pictures of me at this time which is why my profile photo is missing, but I can assure you I'm not ugly or disfigured in anyway. I would like you to contact me but if you chose not to that's cool too. I just wanted to reach out because it seemed like maybe we were fated to meet." Signed DD.

Tony's heart was leaping in his chest as this simple message had hit on so many things he said he was looking for and he was shocked. The irony in this message for him was that the one thing he thought he could count on - her image - was the one thing that was missing. He was very interested in talking and meeting DD but didn't want to seem too over-eager. He wrote her back in the same sort of nonchalant attitude and approach she wrote him in. But the truth was he was more than excited. He was once again looking fate - destiny - in the eye, or at least in the screen. Rosie would most definitely have to wait.

Chapter 7
Let there be light!
(Enter Crucible Steel)

It had been weeks since he had virtually met his mystery girl DD and she really did seem to have plenty in common with him. She too was a writer and loved reading and writing poetry, she seemed well rounded with a real interest in the arts. She seemed very interesting and cultured for someone her age. She was only twenty-six and as he was thirty-five himself. He was nervous about jumping into anything with a young girl, someone who still didn't know about herself or life. The last thing he wanted to do was to end up raising another girl, dragging her into womanhood, scared, kicking and screaming. Oh boy, been there, done that and he had bought the t-shirt to prove it. He in no way wanted to go through that with some young chick, so he pressed her about her life and thoughts about the world and found her to be quite mature for her age. He was pleasantly surprised and really happy that she seemed to possess a really open mind. This meant, as he had hoped, if they were to move to the next level, it left them room to grow together. Considering the fact that she was twenty-six, it seems crazy to even be considering if she had an open mind or not. But you would be surprised how many people, especially young people, think they have the world all figured out because they have had some measure of success. He wanted to be certain he was not getting involved with someone who was beyond listening and learning even if she didn't always agree.

If Tony knew anything, it was that they wouldn't always agree and he didn't want to end up with someone who was stubborn as a mule. He didn't want to waste his words and time on someone who had already made up her mind not to change in the face of a challenge.

Change is constant and he was willing to bend upon the wind to reach this world he dreamed of and he needed someone to see things the same way. It was a far leap but it gave him hope in that he was headed in the right direction. He felt better about the dialogue he was having with DD than any he had been having with any other woman he had met to this point. In fact, he felt better than he had with anyone in years. He was more than enthusiastic about his chances at this point, although he was doing his able best to curtail his words and actions. The last thing he wanted to seem was too eager, or needy, so he did most of the listening and asked questions. As it turned out, she was an awesome conversationalist and she had as many questions about him as he had about her and he was all but too happy to get off into that conversation. It was one of substance which is what most of this Internet dating lacked. They had been talking for weeks and other than the initial conversation where she expressed her concern about meeting someone who was only interested in sex, the conversation had never sunk to the talking about sex, not even jokingly. This first conversation set the tone and made it a lot easier to be himself, without worrying that she would think it strange of him that he was not pressing the issue of sex. And because he hadn't so much as seen a picture of her, he had nothing to imagine, nothing to lust for and this made for authentic conversations and he really liked that; and by all accounts so did she. It ended up being really awesome for the both of them that they met the way they did. He didn't know if her not sending her picture was genius and a planned exercise to ensure that she would be genuinely liked before she was wanted or if it was exactly as she said it was. Either way, he was very happy it had worked out this way. Now the only thing that remained to be seen was if she was a troll or not. He laughed to himself.

Truth was, he just didn't believe she was and there was just something about their conversations and the way they talked that spoke to him and said there was nothing for him to worry about. So for the most part he didn't. Their conversation gave all good and left very little room for bad. It had Tony floating on air and walking amongst the clouds. There was a hope in his life again that he had thought he lost for good and this was a major thing for him and his dream.

DD was very insightful and stood for many of the same things he did, like politics and religion - two major obstacles in any budding relationship. She had told him when they met that she, too, loved to write. Although she hadn't yet shared any of her writing, they had discussed in full some of his writing and some of the classics. They enjoyed many of the same authors and had plenty of conversations about all sorts of things and he was more than delighted. It was supremely important that he was able to connect to someone on an intellectual level and not just a physical one. There was no way he was going to be able to look at anyone's picture and get all that? And in his mind, it didn't matter what their profile said. He still didn't believe he could learn these types of things on a dating site with contact.

At some point, he was feeling like meeting her might only dispel the myth of this almost perfect woman he was building in his mind. He knew he was going to have to breach his little fantasy and find out what this awesome, cyber-girlfriend looked like. She was now starting to hint at wanting to meet up and he didn't want to walk into an unknown situation. She wanted to meet him and know what he looked like. Although he had told himself that it wouldn't matter, because the part of the new him that said he was going to ask for what he wanted knew this was not the truth.

He wanted, and needed her to be fine and if he mouthed anything else, he was lying. He was going to press her for a photo this afternoon, even if it was an old photo, so they could finally meet. But before that they needed to actually TALK. For all the conversations they had shared, they hadn't even spoken on the telephone yet. So he grabbed his sack and sent her the message that contained his phone number. She, on the other hand, had already done that, but he hadn't called her. He wanted to savor the flavor of the neat, little, controlled fantasy. But, he knew once he gave her his phone number, she would call him that day and they would no longer have that little gate of safety. He asked her to call him about four in the afternoon, as he would be off work and would have time before class. It was about one o'clock, so he had a few hours to get his nerves together. The time pushed on without Tony giving DD, or the phone call, a second thought. Right around 3:30 pm, his nerves kicked up seeming to know he was going to hear the sweet voice of his angel in thirty minutes. Every minute after that was spent agonizing over what he would say and how he would sound saying it. With all the conversations they had had, he was now suddenly worried about if he would have anything interesting to say. He was always a good writer and never lacked the skill to make something sound interesting once he put in on paper, but he didn't have the same confidence in his conversation.

It was an irrational fear since he really did know better but it never stopped him from worrying nonetheless. So he rehearsed the conversation they might have, at first in his mind, then out loud, while he was driving home and waiting for her call. He figured he would be driving when she called, which was better than him being at work, or even at home with his son. That way, other than driving, he would be able to focus on her. He was about a quarter mile away from home when the phone rang with DD's number showing on the caller ID. His nerves were jumpy and he hesitated on picking up the phone. He pulled the car over into the Pet-zone parking lot, which was only down the road from his house, and basically stared at the phone and the number until it stopped ringing. He took a deep breath and after the second ring he picked up the phone.

"Hello," he said.

But it was too late. Dead air. She had already hung up. So he let the phone drop down to his lap and let out a sigh. He then picked the phone back up, scrolled through the call log and pushed send on the last dialed number and pressed the phone back to his ear. Before it even rang he heard a woman's voice on the other end of the phone.

"Hello? Hello Tony?" she said.

"Hey DD?" he replied.

"Hey mista. Finally, I got you on the phone!" she exclaimed.

Tony was floored at the voice he heard on the other end of the phone. It was a rough gravelly voice that sounded very raspy and COUNTRY. She was using street slang combined with serious country slang. She had told him she had a daughter but he wasn't prepared to hear her yelling at her little girl their first conversation.

"Kayden, you betta go on with all that mess! You see that I'm on the phone! Hello? I'm sorry. She is trippin' right now," DD said.

Tony was astounded at her lack of tact in their first conversation. She hadn't said anything too far out of the way but it was just her tone and how she sounded. None of the messages she had written sounded anything remotely like this woman he was now talking to on the phone.

"Wow, you really sound so much different than I imagined," Tony said.

"What did you imagine?" she said giggling. "What, you weren't expecting this much sexy baby?" she laughed and said.

He laughed out loud, which allowed the tension to be broken, and they shared a loud laugh from a good, healthy place. They went on to have a good conversation which ended up being a lot easier than he remembered courting being. He had forgotten that a conversation goes both ways and that the other person had a part to hold up too. Sounds simple but you would be surprised how many women leave this sort of thing squarely on the man's shoulders. He had felt the pressure of having to carry a conversation too many times, almost as if it were an interview of sorts. This didn't feel anything like that.

It was a breeze, which made getting past his expectation of what her voice was supposed to sound like much simpler. He felt really comfortable about talking to her and being able to be himself without putting on airs. They concluded their conversation with the intent that they would talk more, later that evening. They had spent the last hour or so just talking and losing track of time as he sat in that same parking lot. By the time they got off of the phone, it was time to go and pick Angel up from the day care center. On his way there he thought about their conversation and all of the things he liked about it as well as all the things that worried him.

He loved how it flowed and she was so easy-going and easy to talk to. However, he was concerned about her ghetto mentality and wondered with all the intelligent conversation that she and he had shared if that was really her or if she was putting on an act for those around her. She lived at home with her father, step-mother, and their family. From what he gathered they were pretty abrasive. She may have felt compelled to put on this attitude as a form of protection. He decided to give her the benefit of the doubt and allow her the opportunity to show him who she was instead of judging her for what he thought he was seeing.

As he went on about the remainder of his day, he couldn't stop thinking about the leap his virtual relationship took into the real world. He prepared dinner for his son and laughed to himself about some of the very funny things she had said during the course of their conversation. She had an awesome sense of humor and he loved the fact that she didn't have a little dainty female laugh. It was a grand, full-belly laugh that said she was not afraid to be herself. In truth, there was a lot about her voice that sounded and felt like his mother's voice. His mother had a loud personality just like DD did and at times he had thought it was too much, but it always felt like home. Ironically, his mother had the same type of laugh, which he now loved and could

69

remember, as a child, it being a sign of approval for him. He worked hard during his childhood to make and keep his mother laughing. There had been so much sadness in her, and their life, that laughter was always welcomed. He had worked hard to become a consistent source of his mom's laughter and happiness.

His personality was always a bit shy. He was naturally an introvert, but when he was home and around her, he was different. He was the extrovert she needed and wanted him to be. This was their love language and how he got the love he needed from her. It was an unspoken, yet existent form of communication they shared. So hearing DD's laugh and sense of humor, was not new, or strange, but to the contrary. It was all too comfortable. It took him a minute to put it all together and realize just why their relationship and conversation felt so familiar. But once he had, he was sold on the fact that he may be entering into a relationship with some version of his mother. He thought to himself that if this relationship resembles that cheerful version of what he shared with his mother then he was okay with that. It was actually funny to him when he thought about it. He laughed admiring God's sense of humor, as he considered how folks always said, "You seek out, and end up with, some version of your parents." Girls sought out their father; and boys, their mother.

"Wow this is crazy," he said to himself and laughed out loud, which got Angel to laughing too.

These types of conversations went on for weeks and things went from good to better. He had gotten the picture he asked for and she looked much different than he thought she would. BETTER! She seemed very attractive with a beautiful face and athletic body. She didn't have the D sized breast he had hoped for, or big ole booty he imagined- at least not from looking at the photo she sent. She had a great body, which was very muscular and toned and what looked like great skin. Although, in her photo, it looked a bit darker than she described, but at that point it didn't really matter. It was not as if this was a determining factor as to if he would be able to love her. That was just a starting point for the photos and not a deal breaker. It never was.

She had nice full lips with jet black hair and dark eyes. She looked Hispanic, although she wasn't. She had told him she was a product of a bi-racial marriage just as he was. Her mix was white and black, but there was another common thread. This was something she understood instinctively without him having to ever explain it to her. She was him in that way. The more he thought about it, the more he realized that she was turning out to be all the things he had always wanted in a woman. The list - item by item was being met through no influence of his own. This HAD to be a God thing? He was curious if this was really true or if he was making this all up in his head. He pressed for more photos. She explained that she didn't have any photos because she had recently lost her apartment in Atlanta which is why she was back living with her dad. This was a really complicated story that TONY figured would work itself out in time. He went within himself to try to understand her story.

She had a job with a local credit repair company in sales. She was so good at her job that she was asked to move when the company decided to expand to another location. She had spent her childhood and high school years growing up in ATL and had a lot of family and connections there so it made perfect sense for her to make that move. She worked with her sister Lisa at the same place since the company opened. In fact, she claimed that they helped found it but never got the recognition they deserved. From the sounds of things the company would collapse without them there. Tony didn't pay this kind of talk any mind because everyone likes to feel important and needed on their job and figured it was her insecurity of becoming jobless that pushed her to talk like this. In any event, he felt he understood she was in a rough patch in her life and probably didn't need any more judgment than she had already heaped on herself if she was anything like him. Eventually the business dried up and the company

71

couldn't afford to keep the newest branch of their business open so they closed down the Atlanta office without so much as a warning. She was very upset about this to say the least, mainly because she had taken her daughter there to live in what turned out to be an unstable situation.

While she was in Atlanta, she had become friends with a woman who she allowed to move in with her to share the bills as she needed the help at that point. Eventually, the money ran out and so did the girl with most of her things. She came home from job hunting all day, picked her daughter up from day care and returned to an empty home with just about all of her possessions gone. The story sounded sort of dramatic and farfetched but he had been through some rough times himself and had some things happen to him that may have sounded similar to this story to anyone on the outside looking in. After she opened up and talked about this she made another part of her available to him, beyond the laughter, that said she was indeed vulnerable and in need of a good and loving man. She finally located some other pictures of herself and sent those as an attachment to his inbox. These pictures were better in terms of showing her in different poses and angles that said the others were indeed really what she looked like. Her photos were with some other ghetto looking dudes, which Tony didn't appreciate at all but again considered the circumstances of which she was currently in and after all he did ask for more photos. These photos showed a different side of her, a softer and more vulnerable side. She was wearing this big, Sunday morning church hat that he figured women wear in the south and she didn't make eye contact with the camera for most. The ones she did make eye contact in her smile just looked fake, like she was hiding some sort of pain beneath the surface that now that he knew a bit more about her made sense. In fact, the entire situation she was currently in was sad. She had just lost everything but a few months ago and was not only living with her dad but she and her six year old daughter were sharing a room and a full size bed.

And with no job, it seemed like her situation was going nowhere fast. The more she talked about her home life and the circumstances around her life, the more Tony's heart strings were tugged. It seemed like she had had a very difficult life and wasn't given very many chances and she was once again in another tough spot.

He was more than familiar with those types of circumstances as he felt like he had been fighting them off himself his entire life and knew in his heart of hearts that all she needed was love and someone to support her. He found himself wanting to be all the things in her life she never had. He felt more needed than ever after hearing the details of her life. It was exactly what he wanted. Every man wants to be needed, but to Tony, in particular, who wanted to be everything to his wife as she would be to him, it meant there was a little something extra in this for him. He was seeing her as more and more the perfect fit for this ideal dream of love. Granted she wasn't perfect and needed to get herself up off the ground but then again he didn't want perfect. And isn't that when you actually show and prove love, when someone is in need and doesn't look or have their best to give? If we only gave our hearts to the perfect person at the perfect time then how would they ever get to know you loved them past what was perfect? He believed that if he could love her from here then he would always love her because this was surely the worst of her life to this point and surely she would see this as him truly loving her and not whatever she could do, or be, once she got up off of the bottom of this thing life had dumped her onto. So he did not let her setback scare him off or keep him from moving forward in their relationship although his life looked stark in contrast. His success didn't scare her and her setback didn't frighten him. They had pushed past a major point of insecurity without even having to talk about it. This was an awesome sign in Tony's mind. He had two jobs making great money, was finishing his masters degree, was attending law school with an awesome apartment, drove a Mercedes Benz and an additional Benz same

73

model a couple of years older which he had taken back from Sharon just sitting in the garage and the income that afforded him the ability to pay for it. He also owned a nice motorcycle and mountain of stuff that made up his life.

Although she had nothing but the room full of used things in her father's home which she shared with her daughter, this never scared him away. He believed in his heart that if he could stand by her during this time, she would have to see that she meant more to him than all of the things he owned and wanted to share with her. Again, it was fated that he have the opportunity to prove his intentions for her and his budding love from the onset of their new and growing relationship. This had to be a God thing. He was convinced that although things weren't ideal, they were lining up in a way that should help with all the doubts people usually enter into relationships carrying but never admit. What they were looking at wasn't perfect or ideal but it was most certainly real with real problems and real people. This held significant weight when placed in contrast to the falsehoods that people typically created initially, only to have the truth destroy all the false expectations.

Some might have looked at DD's situation and run for the hills like every other man in her life seemed to do including the men in her family and Kayden's father. But he made a promise to himself that for better or worse, he was going to see this thing through and not let his fear run him away from finding out the truth about her and himself. For the first time in his life he was going to ignore the murk around him and walk into the light and believe in something he could not see OR CONTROL. Something outside of himself.

This is what he had always lacked in other relationships; the very same thing that made him so strong and the very thing he relied on in himself. He always took himself out of the game instead of learning that final lesson, before the love was lost, before there was too much water under the bridge, before you said all the things you couldn't ever take back. He was going to stand firm, without flinching from minute one, thereby building on a foundation that would be unshakable on this issue for ever more. At least he hoped. There was light and he could see it. Like his old football days, he was running to daylight WITH the pill in tote. And the pill wasn't that same old pig skin to be fumbled or smashed against some line. Today, however, the pill represented far more than six points. Today as he marched forward on this gridiron of life, he did so with the pill of HOPE.

Chapter 8
THE FULL MONTE!

"Time to get real," he thought to himself, as he went through all of his fears as to why he was afraid to meet with DD in person. It had been a full four weeks since they started courting through the dating service.

She was everything he could have wanted at this point and they were becoming really close friends no matter what. He figured his real fears were that maybe he wasn't good enough for her at this point. He was about six feet with a football player build about two hundred and fifty pounds of weight lifting muscle. He dressed well and smelled nice but he knew beneath all of the good looks and hunky exterior, he was hiding the rotting stench of fear that had dragged every relationship he ever had to the bottom of the abyss never to be heard from again. His inability to trust put him into more relationships than he could count with women who were totally untrustworthy because at least in his mind he knew what to expect from them, which made it easy to at least fake trust, knowing his little secret was he would never give them his heart. And the fact that they both knew he couldn't made it a ready-made, easily available reason he could pull out from time to time as to why he didn't have to. Keeping his heart tucked away safe but what he didn't realize was it had kept him from love too. He was so ready to shake off this fear; but to be honest, he didn't have the slightest clue as to how to do it. But what he did know was the first step toward taking this issue down was to step into it, and face the fear.

At this moment, his fear was being transparent and letting DD know that just like her he had his problems except his weren't so easily discernable. This meant that he was no better than her and he put them on equal footing. Honestly, looking at her life, this scared him, too. So after some self-talk and encouragement from DD, he agreed to meet with her at a park around the corner from his house since this was sort of a halfway point for the both of them. Tony would leave Angel with his mom for the evening and meet with her today. They had decided that they would have a shot of tequila to take the edge off since they both liked tequila. It was their favorite drink and they often joked about sitting down and getting hammered together over a nice bottle of Patron, no lime and no salt, just the hotness of the real. Well Tony was bringing tequila and two shot glasses and although it wasn't Patron, it would do. It was a good fifty dollar bottle of tequila but he was still feeling a bit insecure that it wasn't what everyone agreed was the best.

He was wearing the exact same clothes he wore in his profile picture complete with the fitted navy blue New York Yankees cap, button up blue and white striped shirt and white uptowns. He was sharp, smelled good and felt more assure of himself as he pulled up to an open spot in the parking lot of the park with his jet black sports Kompressor shining in the fading sun. He turned the car off and sat there facing the entrance and waiting anxiously for DD to arrive. With each passing minute, his nerves were getting the best of him until he decided that he didn't need to wait for her arrival in order to crack that bottle. He quickly filled up one of the two shot glasses he had in his glove box. He was a native New Yorker and very proud of that and ever more proud of being from Brooklyn as most Brooklynites are. He brought shot glasses which both said New York; one glass for the Yanks and the other for the Giants. He turned on some Jay Z and took the first shot, then immediately poured another and sipped this one slowly and waited for the calm to arrive. As long as it got there before DD arrived, he was good he laughed to himself. He drank the second shot with intention. He wanted to taste the drink, savor it, feel it start to course through his veins and wash away all the fears he was cultivating while he waited.

Soon two turned into three and three turned into relaxed. He didn't want to be noticeably tipsy so he stopped there; he wanted to be mellow, not sloppy by the time their night turned into whatever was in store. She told him she was driving a black Saturn so he kept his eyes peeled. He was starting to feel warm all over and that began a little perspiration beneath his hat. He was sitting with the windows open. He could have turned the air on but he figured he was going to be out of the car soon anyway so he might as well get used to the evening air. So he stepped out of the car and sat the bottle and glasses on the trunk and went back to close the door. Just then he heard a loud car that sounded as if it had a busted muffler, or none at all approaching. He looked up just in time to see a black Saturn flying like a bat out of hell. The car bent the corner hard, with what sounded like some southern rap blaring on a cheap stereo system. The car was an early nineties model with faded paint and bald tires; it had definitely seen better days. The car sped into the parking spot next to him like an Indie car racer coming in for a pit stop as Tony stood there with his mouth half open trying to get a glimpse of Ms. Mario Andretti. But since the driver's side was on the opposite side of him, he was going to have to wait until she got out of the vehicle in order to see who and what the speed demon looked like. The music was still blaring and the car was rocking but no one emerged. Out of curiosity, Tony began walking towards the car door to see if it was indeed DD or someone else driving crazy and he needed to move his car. He chuckled to himself. He peeked around the corner at the back of the car and could see a large female moving her head and body so hard he could see why the car was rocking. She was in a white wife beater tank top with shoulder length curls like a poodle that sort of looked chopped and half done. As he made his way towards the front of the car, approaching the door, she finally turned and acknowledged him and laughed as she turned down the stereo.

"I love that song," she laughed, saying with the biggest smile. She was giving him the once over and he could feel it. She began smiling bigger now without the laugh. So much in fact she began to cover her mouth hiding her smile. She turned towards him more and he could see she was hiding her teeth. She was staring at his teeth that were really straight and white which must have made her feel self-conscious. She must have believed her teeth weren't as nice as his, and this made her continue to hide her smile. It did not stop him from noticing that she had an awesome smile and he was bothered by the fact that she was trying to hide it. Feeling like he understood why, he began to move closer to her so each time she did it he moved her hand away almost like Shug did Celie in The Color Purple. She was very rough around the edges, literally. Her hair was un-kept and she was wearing clothes that not only looked too small for her but had stains on them. She had told him she lost all her clothes in this robbery but he didn't know she was this bad off. Honestly she looked a little butch, like the male equivalent in a lesbian relationship. In fact, she was so aggressive in her speech and body language that she moved this way too. She cursed and used more street language than he did, but he kept down playing it in his mind. He was looking for the woman who had written all the beautiful words to him online. He was looking for the person who understood his poetry and seemed to understand his soul. He kept searching for this gentle side she had allowed him to see when she was a stranger. But it was hidden beneath a dirty terry cloth baby blue sweat suit about two sizes too small, a loud laugh and sex filled eyes. She stood about five-foot-seven inches tall with shoulders like a line backer, almost as wide as his were, and thighs as thick as running backs legs, no hips, not so much booty but killer legs.

She wasn't wearing any bra beneath her wife beater which highlighted her B-cup. Although she lost some points for leaving the house with no bra on, she had what appeared to be extra large nipples that were on full display once she took her jacket off. He thought it was vulgar but couldn't deny that he liked them, so she got at least some of those points back. Her body, or at least her breasts, told a story of multiple pregnancies as they bore the tell tale signs which only added to the butch look. Tony was beginning to wonder if this was even the same girl. She had on no makeup, not even lip gloss, nothing, she spoke to him out of the side of her head almost like she didn't want to look at him. So he kept moving within her gaze so he could get a good look at her as she kept shifting her eyes each time he moved or made eye contact. Finally he was able to coax her out of the car with some minor shit talking about her, saying she wanted this bottle, he had brought it, and now she was hiding in the car. Seemed she liked a challenge.

"You ain't said nothing but a word man," she snapped as she jumped out of the car.

She slammed the door behind her and finally looked him square in the eye. He could finally see her face full and he was all at once finally staring into the eyes of the woman he had contacted. He could see the vulnerability she tried to hide. He could see the insecurities she was doing her best to make diversions for with loud talk and aggressive body language. But it was too late. Her eyes could not lie although she tried. He could also clearly see she was high. He knew she had told him she got high from time to time but she was doing it far less frequently and was actually ready to quit all together. He being drug free, never having so much as touched a drug was definitely put off by her coming to meet him high, especially with meeting him for the first time and knowing how he felt about drugs. He did his able best to block out this fact as he continued on in the conversation. He thought to himself how much courage she must have had to work up in her current position to come and meet him knowing how far she had fallen from who she really was.

Standing here before someone who she hoped to court, someone who by all appearances had it all together, she too must have needed to take the edge off. He did the same before she got there, so while he didn't agree or approve of her being high, he did understand. He knew within himself that this was a deal breaker for him, but he had never told her so, therefore, he could not hold it against her. She was just being her and he needed an honest look at who she was. Later, after he made himself clear as to what he was looking for, he would make it clear that if she chose to continue to get high, he would have to leave her alone. But for now, he decided not to judge, although he was taking a mental note. They went on talking and drinking, laughing and joking for hours until the entire bottle was gone and the sun was breaking dawn. They had managed to stay in that little park the entire evening until the following day. Still tipsy, he was taking account of her and who she presented herself to be. She had hinted throughout the night several times about and around sex and maybe fooling around at the park. She even indirectly challenged him to take her but he, being in a different frame of mind, decided to ignore her and her notion as to where this thing could possibly lead. Besides he had been down that road far too many times before. He had been there more times than he had done anything else. He was older now, no longer a twenty-something year old punk kid, far past the point where this type of thing was cute or even remotely interesting or intriguing. It was lustful, fast, hasty, vulgar, cheap, petty, and leading nowhere and everywhere away from his dream; none of which he wanted or found desirable in himself or a mate. Maybe later they could play around that way; he wasn't a prude or beyond a little kinky, not at all. But this time he had to put first things first. So, after all the questions had been answered, when he knew it wasn't just cheap sex and held a meaning other than satisfying some primal need, then it would be possible. He needed to get these thoughts straight and not just to protect her virtue but for himself. There had been a time in his life where sex ruled the day for him. The last thing he wanted to do was to slip down that rabbit hole again. It was hard enough getting out of it the last hundred times. Sex is a powerful thing and when you have been abused that way, it is hard not to abuse it and everyone in your path that will allow you to.

81

It had become so easy with women today losing their virtue with all the rap songs and movies that told them they were nothing more than that thing between their legs. That told them they had to PROVE it was worth a damn to be loved. Seems like every song you heard blasted, and sang in the car, or club, these days was something that objectified women. The craziest part is when they sang along; it's with their own approval. Things have changed and women have forgotten that they could never be pimps or players because, unlike men who have no virtue to protect, they were built for something greater. It's why God saw fit to give THEM the ability to carry and grow a child, and not men. Men just ain't built the same.

And here he was looking directly at a prime example of a beautiful woman who he could tell intentionally made herself small to please others, especially men. Like her covering her smile- she had a beautiful smile that she hid behind a raised hand simply because she believed she had yellow teeth, all so Tony could shine. He knew there was something going on with her - the way she moved, the way she reacted and showed herself to be. There was something up with her, he just couldn't put a finger on it. If truth be told, it smelled like a whore but in this world of denial and benefit of the doubt, he let it slide. No, no that's not the truth either; the truth is that Tony knew in his heart of hearts that inside, behind all the Sean John he was wearing, the seventy dollar cologne, past the college education and professional career, he was not that different from her. He just hid it better. He gave himself goals and work. This would keep the world from knowing how broken he had been on the inside. He was finally ready to stop pretending and needed to get in there and dig whatever was inside of him out. That thing that refused to allow him to be happy. That thing that each time he found his way to success, found a way to sabotage it for him. Because somewhere deep down, he didn't believe he was good enough. He didn't believe he was worthy of his accomplishments, a good relationship, a great wife, an awesome job, nor did he deserve to be a star collegiate athlete or pro-ball player, even though his talent said so. Whatever it was, he was going to find a way to trash it. He was tired of working his tail off time and again to make it to that top rung on the ladder, only to nose dive off of it in search of the bottom, unaware until he felt the final snap of bottoming out. With all sorts of questions, "How did I get here AGAIN?" "Why?" and his personal favorite, "When does this stop happening TO ME?"

Yes sir, it was time to come out of the darkness and into the light and there was only one way to do that, face his demons. In order to do that he would have to go down deep into the darkness of himself, with all things he was and was not, and all that made him afraid. Who would want that guy? Who could look at him and say he was worth anything? Deep down, Tony never believed he was his degrees, education or any of his many accomplishments. He believed he was that same thing he had been taught over and over again. It had a name but he could not bear to call it.

Looking at DD, he could see himself in her in a very BIG way. She was actually quite pretty and far more intelligent than she wanted the world to know; this he got from their conversations. She got high and drunk to keep herself from her demons, just like he dove into his work to hide from his. She would not run from him. She would not shy away from the pain if he pushed her from it. She would embrace him and they would be able to hold each other in a place that he was certain the world would not understand. The world couldn't even see people like them. To them, people like Tony and DD were simply a product of their own circumstances; either slackers or over achievers, even perfectionists. Tony knew the world missed this obvious flaw with success draped around your neck. But he knew there was no real difference, you just had to know how to spot it. It's always one extreme or the other. Energy was a powerful thing; it could be rage or sorrow, depending on which way you bent it. It can make you CEO or a crack whore.

He wanted above all else to show her how to bend it in another direction. He wanted to teach her how to build herself up and overcome the horror as he had done for himself. He wanted to find a safe place in this love and acceptance within her. So he could finally believe he was good enough and he wouldn't have to break the pretty picture by leaving because she wouldn't.

He had been abandoned by his father at a young age and later by his mother when he was older and those feelings stuck with him more than he was ever willing to admit. DD and Tony, both handsome and beautiful, both disgusting and vile, it was again destiny. He smiled at her advances and laughed at her jokes and again at her advances, never tipping his hand that he knew full well what she meant, more so, the sorrow behind the words. Oh he absolutely knew far more than he would ever allow her to know he could see at this point. He knew exactly what she wanted and whether she knew it or not it had very little to do with the actual act of sex, but what it held for them both at this point. He did his able best to never tip her off that he wanted the same things and was still like a junkie fighting for his sobriety seeking to run from that place. Eventually the sun rose and they parted, still laughing and damn near drunk having finished the entire bottle of tequila. As they left the park, he went left and she right as they both headed home with smiles of happiness for the first time in a long while. They had plans to talk again later and maybe meet, and although the plans were tentative, Tony knew he wanted to jump in with BOTH feet. He also knew that this thing was dangerous and needed to be tempered. He could not just walk into the darkness without a plan. He needed a solid exit plan from this dark place he knew they would have to come out of, or he just might end up engulfed in her pain and never emerge. It was so deep that he may never find his way back to himself from demons so powerful. So his plan was to take it slow, without pushing or having expectations outside of himself. He would use his relationships with others to fill that needy void within himself that could easily spend his life devoting all

84

himself to someone without a thought of himself. He had gone down that road before too and lost a lot of himself without finding very much once he got there. He was well aware of this weakness within himself to please others without care for how or in what position it left his life. So he knew he was going to have to move slowly into this thing with eyes wide open if he was going to get to the things he needed to for himself and not just fall into her arms and land wherever she was going to take him. He had always done the taking in his past relationships, so he knew how to make sure he didn't get taken if he didn't want to. The problem was that he desired to be taken as much as he wanted to take. So before he would allow himself to let it go that way, there was some house cleaning to do.

DD's life was a mess and she really needed some direction. He felt strongly that if she was willing to listen to him, he could help her clean up some of her messes. He knew that if indeed she was anything like him, they were all messes that she had created and imposed upon herself. Therefore, she could lift them off of herself when she was ready. It was a simple matter of choice, but he knew she would have to be ready. He wanted to give her something better to choose. The only question was whether or not she was ready. Fixing up appearances and the outward was an easy fix, but dealing with the mess we all hide on the inside was another story completely. So as he planted his feet firmly back in his world, he once again tucked his slip back beneath his clothes. He had no time to be weak. He needed all his time to be all the things Tony was. It took a lot of work being "perfect." Trying to appear to the rest of the world that you, or your life, didn't have any cracks in it, was hard work; especially for someone who had so many bags to carry. Bags of guilt for things he had done. Bags of false guilt for things he had not, but felt responsible for, nonetheless. All the things his mother did and the things his father had not. The things his step-dad had and had not done. They all added up to plenty of imperfections that burst at the seams of almost every part of his life. He knew those demons were there. All those bags were pretty heavy. He was finally ready to sit them down. He would rest his heart in a home called DD.

She did not look reliable but he remembered a time when he wasn't that either. She did not appear to be clean or without her bags of bullshit.

He thought to himself, "Neither am I. If she could see who I really was, it would be she who would not stay." His vision was that he would slowly walk them both to a place of healing. He was so confident in all the work he had been doing in waiting on the Lord that, God willing, he was going to be able to finally HAVE the love of his life. It had been written and therefore it was. His destiny had finally arrived and he was not afraid as he had been in the past. No, he was not afraid; not afraid to look her deep within her eyes, shameless. Not afraid to walk her to his path led by his father God. Most importantly, he was not afraid to walk WITH HER and her name was DD.

Chapter 9
No Stopping

For all the not so good things that Tony had seen in DD, he had to be honest and look at, and deal with, all the things he had seen that attracted him to her. Those things that were outside of their dysfunctions; things that made them a strong couple and him attracted to her in a way he had not been attracted to any other but those who had broken his heart. He called it his "Denise Huxtable heartbreak attraction." Of course this was something he made up when he was a kid and not really old enough to understand his identity crisis.

One day, as he was watching the Cosby show for the first time, he laid eyes on Denise, and fell in love. She was black but had fair skin and for the first time in his home, and family life, a girl who he was infatuated with was accepted. So he had no inhibitions about having to hide the little fantasy and he ran with it in his mind. Soon after he was able to spot a million Denise's everywhere and he found himself attracted to them all in some strange way. It was not until later- much later- did he surrender to the fact that this was his type; the kind of woman he had a real weakness for. As his mother used to say, a woman who had his "nose wide open." He had his first experience with this type of woman when he was about eight or nine with a distant cousin through marriage. She was fair-skinned, tall with straight hair and amazing legs, and she was as pretty as a button. He was always smitten with her but had not figured out why until he was old enough to really like girls. But she lived a far distance away and their love was never realized other than the small amounts of time they shared at family gatherings flirting and finally kissing once they got old enough.

The last time he saw her he was about fifteen. She had saved her virginity for him all those years and one night at a family barbeque, they finally found their way to adulthood together, hurried and full of emotion in the coat room. Then again, in the hallway and again behind the garage. They were madly in love with each other, as in love as teenagers could have been but their love was not meant to be. He was heartbroken that this distance was the thing that kept him apart from his first love. Two years later he would find out that although she was his first (what they call puppy love), the real deal was way deeper.

When he met Stacy, he was in the eleventh grade and she was all that and a bag of chips. Five foot five inches tall, shoulder length hair, thick full lips, light skinned with a body no sixteen year old should have. She was the type of girl who you would imagine with green or light eyes except that she had deep chestnut colored eyes that went far deeper than any light color would allow. She was smart and accomplished. She was funny, interesting, and so very fine. Denise Huxtable had NOTHING on her; in fact, it was at that time he gave up his Denise fantasy all together. They fell so deep in love with each other that they couldn't tell where one of them ended and the other began. Sadly it would be distance that kept them apart as well. She went off to Spain to study abroad ripping his heart completely in two and he swore off all women who even looked like she did.

A full five years later, after a stop in Uncle Sam's Airborne Rangers, he returned to college to spot a young co-ed who looked almost identical to Stacy, even their names were similar, Cassy. She was slimmer than Stacy but just as bright and equally as funny. She had the same shoulder length hair and awesome smile. He knew at that moment no matter how much he lied to himself, he would not be able to keep that promise to himself to never again fall into the arms of a woman that looked like she did. His first day on campus, he spotted her and told himself that he would not date any other woman on that campus except her. He approached her several times and struck up polite conversation, doing his able best to get to know her but she was a bit younger than him and had lived a sheltered life. She had never dated much as a teenager. So he gave her the space she needed in order to choose him if she wanted. He wasn't offended because at this time she wasn't dating anyone.

They had lived on the same campus, so he wasn't worried about losing her to distance. He had three or four years to walk her down. They talked and got to be friends. Never did he press or push. Never did she even notice that look in his eye that said he wanted something more. He wouldn't allow it. So somewhere at the end of their second year, she finally came around and they began to talk in a way that said she too wanted more than they had been. He had waited a full two years for her without so much as dating another woman on that campus. He had committed to her with her being completely unaware.

He was on the football team and hung out around a group of guys who behaved more like frat brothers than school mates. They were a pretty popular group and most of the guys got around, sleeping with whomever they fancied at the time. He worked hard to keep his nose and reputation clean so he would be easy for her to choose once she noticed him. She was a woman with virtue. She had not given herself away to anyone. In fact, she had told him she was a virgin. Not that this mattered to him but it said what type of woman she was. This in turn told him what type of man she might want to have. A woman with virtue he assumed would want a man that would protect that virtue. So the last thing she would want to settle with is the campus male whore. So he stayed clear of loose women as to protect her virtue and show his interest. And after all this time she was finally coming around. They dated, went to movies, took long moonlit strolls on the beach, and shared candle light dinners. It was an awesome time, completely worth the wait. She had far surpassed all of the expectations he had placed on what this could possibly be.

One night while walking along the sand, they stopped in the moonlight to look at each other. While looking deeply into her eyes, he began to confess not only his love for her, but everything he had done in trepidation of their relationship. She was shocked at all the thought and preparation that Tony had put into making this time and place possible. She realized that what he was saying was not just some mere moment of emotional weakness where something you may not mean slips through the cracks. She knew right there on that beach, as the waves broke around their feet, that he was already deeply in love with her and had been maybe for a while now. She was confused but ultimately flattered that someone had thought of her in this way and went through that kind of effort. They shared a long kiss and embrace that told him he had done the right things and his heart sang and opened up in a way he had refused to open it before that moment. The next few days Cassy was in finals and difficult to reach. Tony didn't take anything away from it because he knew she was serious about her school work. Eventually, around day four or five, they had made plans to have a candle lit dinner as a little break from all the hard work she had been up to. He showed up with the candles and the take out Chinese food full of smiles and hope. As he waited at the end of the hall in the common room, moments became minutes and minutes ran into a half an hour before her roommate came out to tell him that she was not going to be able to make it. She had too much studying to do. He left heartbroken, knowing something had happened and he missed it completely. It was not long before she told him that it was over, providing the final grain of sand in the hour glass of his heart that said, "Closed for business."

Now here he sat, more than ten years later, looking at the very thing he swore he would never open up his heart to again, willing to delve back into that place. He was full of fear, but more than that, full of excitement for where this love might take him untamed and unimpeded. As DD and Tony spent more and more time around each other talking, discovering and sharing who they were, and wanted to be, they fell deeper and deeper into a love without limits. He had listened to all the things she said she was and believed. She was fiercely loyal. When she had your back, she went all in. She had gone through great lengths to show him this in all the stories she shared. She was a very blunt person who seemed to delight in giving you the raw uncensored truth, so he took her at her word.

He believed her stories to be true as most of them usually included something embarrassing, humiliating or unflattering which would make one believe that these things must be true, otherwise why would someone tell you something so negative about themselves? These endings seemed to serve to prove the idea that she was honest and loyal to a fault. She was a woman of virtue who cared what others thought of her too and would never shame him by going behind his back in the streets as others would do and had done to him in the past. This was a relief and although skeptical, the length she went through to tell Tony about it, and the way she spoke about "those" type of women seemed to disgust her, so he once again believed. Now he was no fool. He had seen some things and had been around the block a time or two. But he was more like willingly ignorant.

There were things he thought he saw in her that he just blocked out, choosing instead to give her the benefit of the doubt. One of those things was all the late nights she was out with him, leaving her child at home with her father and step- mother while she roamed the streets. He rationalized this behavior because, in his mind, it was for a purpose. They were building a relationship that would hopefully become a family so in his mind it was an investment. But many nights, she was out with "friends" getting drunk, high or in the club.

He knew that despite what she was telling him, she was getting high just about every night. He also knew that she had many male friends but again chose to believe what she was telling him, rather than what he thought he knew about the type of woman he was seeing her to be. It was a decision to believe her and not his eyes; one he was sure she would become once she realized that he had made this leap of faith in her.

She was growing everyday and looking at the changes she needed to make in order to move her life. It was always moving to Tony to see someone sincerely trying and even more so when they got it. She pushed herself even when it was tough. For example, she had a hard time opening up and became silent often when she felt the pressure to disclose. The first time she ever mouthed the words "I love you" was just a few weeks into their budding relationship as they spoke on the telephone. She had left a message while he was at work. He had seen the call but couldn't take it at the time. When he heard the message, he was touched at her effort. It sounded sincere and heartfelt and it made him smile.

She still had a way to go but she was progressing. She was still unemployed and spent her days around her father's house playing maid and cook waiting for her daughter to get home to do the mommy thing. She had even mended some fences with her sister who still worked at her old job. She was not only attempting to reconnect with her sister but also trying to get her old job back. Things had gone well but she hadn't gotten her job back as of yet. In hopes that she would be able to see the God in him and the progress he was making on a personal and emotional level, Tony had been consistently talking to her about getting close to God and his walk and where it would take her. He had begun disclosing about himself and all of his young life.

He shared with her about his childhood and the abuse he endured and overcame to escape the worst of situations and how he knew that it was God and his protection that brought him through. This seemed to open up a new leaf in her life and he could see she was making a noted effort to open that door between her and God again. She had even allowed some Jehovah's witnesses in one day and began taking weekly meetings with them to discuss God. He was very happy for her that she could meet with someone to talk about the love of God, even if was them. She, too, seemed excited to meet with them as she was sometimes meeting with them a few times a week.

Now Tony was a Catholic but was not about to discourage any attempt she made to get right with the Lord, no matter which path she had decided to take. It disturbed him that she didn't trust him enough to worship with him but he knew that was his issue, so he never pushed her. He himself had issues around how other's had used God against him in his own life in the past and for all he knew she went through something similar. It seemed like she and God were on the outs for a minute and their new relationship was on a probationary basis so he didn't want to do anything that was going to turn her away from that light. He prayed with her every day. He led her to some verses he thought might help her through where he thought she was, and even tried on occasion to do some bible study with her. She was unwilling to follow him and the bible study became more like a battle than a study so he didn't push it. If she was studying with the two old women as she said she was, then it was good enough for him. He was just happy to have had the Lord use him to bring her back to God in any way. This would surely help them as a couple as they walked through life together hand in hand, intertwined with the Lord and his laws.

For the most part, he could see from day to day, she was making small progresses, thinking about the things that would get her life back on track. The truth was that this entire ordeal with her losing her apartment and job had weighed heavily on her mind and she was severely depressed. She would walk amongst her friends and family smiling and pretending she was fine but when she finally started to open up to him she was full of depression and even suicidal thoughts. This should have disturbed him, but he knew he had delivered her into the best hand possible, the Lord Almighty. What was far more disturbing to him was her aggression in attitude and demeanor, and the sexual tension she put on

93

him and their relationship. She would put pressure on him almost as if she were addicted to sex, begging and tugging at his pants. She would reach into his pants and grab his manhood, tugging at his zipper trying to give him head. She knew full well, as they had discussed the possibility of sex many times, that this, not unlike many men, was his weakness. She tried in vain many times to give him head. He was determined to not let this ship get off track and to put first things first.

She always seemed to get pissed as if she was insulted, like he didn't want her or thought he was somehow better than she was. This only made her push harder and talk more vulgar because she was hurt by the rejection, and she needed to pump herself back up. So she would talk about other men she had been with, and how they had always loved her and her body, her sex and how great it was and she had given it to him.

Maybe she thought it was a turn on, almost like a sales pitch, but it made him jealous and question if she was the woman she said she was. She even went so far as to talk about sexual encounters with her past lovers; how large they were and how they "beat the pussy up" and loved the "pretty pussy she had." This never had the desired effect she wanted. In fact, all it did was push him further and further away from the day he would give himself to her. In the past, he knew that this was about sex and he would have happily partaken in this sexual delight, giving her what she said she wanted or needed only to move on to the next. But he knew that she really didn't want what she said she did; only she didn't know it. She was moving like a common whore and after awhile, even she could feel the shame and embarrassment that came along with the realization.

All the stories she continued to tell were now for the purpose of hurting him the way he was hurting her with his constant rejection. He could feel that there was no real connection between them yet. There was no genuine love and therefore any sex they had would be just that - sex. A futile exercise in physicality, and he was not interested in that any more than he was interested in "a hole in his head." He tried to explain his intention to her; that he wasn't just turning her down and he thought she was very attractive, beautiful even. A word she was unfamiliar with.

"No one has ever called me beautiful before. I'm not sure I believe that I am," she said to him.

"You are, far more than even you can see. But you have to trust me, allow me to show you where it is. And it ain't between your legs, love," he said, as he pointed to her head.

"Right now you still feel sex and get aroused by touch. If you let me I'll show you how to make love all day and it starts in your mind. Foreplay starts in your mind. Most women know upon meeting a man if they want to have sex with him or not. Some just need him not to mess it up. But when you really love someone you will take the time to get to really know and love them, so when you MAKE love to them, you will know just where to go within their mind to please them completely. No more fumbling around like a lost school boy. Or 'beating it up' gorilla style in the pussy. No it's not about how long you can go, or circus tricks you can perform in bed. It's about a connection that no one can infringe upon. When you are there, you will know it. Then we will go down that path and find where love lies."

He told her this with a real look of love, fighting back the mist in his eyes that said he was emotionally connected to what he just said to her. He had decided that with this much aggression, they could never get there and that he needed to calm her down and show her a slower track.

He told her a joke he had heard in an old movie he watched when he was a teen.

"So there were these two bulls on top of this hill looking down upon a field of cows. There was one old bull and one young bull. The young bull says, 'Hey pa, let's run down there and fuck one of them cows!' The old bull just looked at him and said, 'No son. Let's walk down there and fuck 'em all."

He recanted the joke as they both laughed.

She said she thought the joke was cute and they got a good laugh out of it but he could tell she was not satisfied with the situation. That night he could tell she had taken their conversation as yet another rejection of her and who she was; not the loving conversation that he had intended when he spoke true words of love from his heart. He left it alone as she seemed to bite her tongue, and they parted once again with her seeming distant and off, like she was holding these times against him. He was getting the sense that she was starting to think that he was not attracted to her. This was the furthest thing from the truth but he had no idea how to make someone who was so steeped in the physicality of the thing understand that there was something more there - something way deeper. If she never experienced it, how would he make her understand? He didn't know the answer at that moment. What he did know was that he could not sacrifice himself at this moment to give her what she said she needed, and harm himself.

What he wasn't talking about yet was his own wounded past, which included sexual abuse by members of his family and his mother's so called friends - women who had preyed on him and his young body. The advances from DD brought up far too many horrible memories to even go there with her at this point. So even if he wanted to do it, she was so rough that it would have put him in a bad way now that he was being honest with himself and was going to God with this thing in a major way. Until now, he had hidden this thing from everyone including himself, but he was tired of keeping everyone's secrets. It had cost him far too much. He was going to have to tell her the truth if he was going to convince her that this is what she needed to do. He had to let her know that this thing wasn't just about her but him too and he needed her help on this matter. Maybe his honesty would bring her in as an ally and they would make it through this thing now that should, or would, have someone else to blame. It seemed like she needed that - someone to blame. It couldn't be her, so now it could be him.

It wasn't that she was no good and he didn't want her so now it could be him and some weird dysfunction that he had. But the more he learned of her despite the little hints he was dropping on her, he felt very strongly that she had some of these same demons lurking around in her closet. But she was fast to deny as he began to talk a bit about what was going on with him. But soon and very soon he was going to have to tell her the truth so she would know where he stood from a completely transparent place. This was going to take some serious courage and he knew only one place he could go to get it, tonight he would begin his prayers and tomorrow his fast to ask God to give him the strength to talk about these things he had kept from everyone for so long. His fears were simple: that she would see who he was and run for the hills, or somehow see him differently; he feared it would ruin their relationship.

It took him weeks of prayer and meditation to work up the courage to break the capsule on this conversation, but one night as they were on their nightly walk, he did. She was completely silent and in shock as he mouthed the words of his deepest secrets and ultimately his deepest fears. She listened intently as he recounted year after year of abuse and how he had heralded from the horrible situation he was in and how now he was fighting the good fight not to fall back into patterns of that same abuse and keep it from being reenacted in his life in any dysfunctional way. By the time the conversation was over she was in tears, a far greater reaction then he could have ever hoped for, but it appeared she understood completely. She was silent for all of his conversation and after he was done remained so. She only hugged him with a face full of tears to say she understood, furthering his inclination that she too was hiding some of these same demons of abuse in her past. Clearly she was hurting but not ready to share, maybe she wasn't even ready to remember for herself but whatever the deal was, he was happy that he had found an ally in her to deal with the very real problems that he was seeking to face. They cried, they hugged and left one another that night with a deeper understanding of each other than either one of them knew was coming or would have hoped to have found this early on in their relationship. This gave Tony a whole new level of trust and respect for DD. The fact that she accepted him and stood by him was major and he would do anything to give her that measure of love back.

Chapter 10
Tested

It had been weeks since Tony opened himself up to DD and told her the truth about his past in an attempt to explain who he was and why he made some of the decisions he made. Sometimes he could seem hard, distant or even uninterested, but he wanted to be sure that she knew that it was not so much her as it was his past. This was something that he knew he had to do for her to bring her some much needed understanding as to some of the decisions he was making. The main focus was helping her understand his decision to wait on sex, so she would know it was not that he didn't want her but that he had a greater plan. But he also needed to do this for himself, maybe even more because this was affecting his life in no small way either. Once he had done it, they both shared an understanding that brought many good things to their relationship and life. Unfortunately, it was short lived. She was at once compassionate and didn't push when she could see the truth in what he had confided in her. But, after a while, she slid back into her former position. It was one of suspicion and mistrust, since sex had been used as a means of control in her former relationships; she seemed to think he was up to the same dirty tricks. She had confused sex with love all her life and this relationship was not different for her. In the past, she loved her daughter's father and he withheld her love, chose instead to belittle her and pick her personality apart, stripping her self-esteem and robbing her of not only her dignity, in the end, but her self-worth too. This much she had shared with Tony up to this point but not much more than this; she was still very guarded. He could tell that she was becoming more than annoyed with what she must have considered his stall tactics and attempt to control her through sex or the lack thereof.

Tony had no way of knowing this but she had begun to flip the script on him and put his theory about the speed of their relationship to the test. It would be the beginning of a terrible game and time in both of their lives. She was about to start a major battle for control that she had to have known in her heart of hearts was wrong and would probably end in nothing good, but it was all she knew. Conversely, what she should have been able to figure out, had she not been so steeped in her own denial, was that he, too, had been victimized by the same abuser of sex, life and love that used sex as a weapon in this battle for his soul. He, too, was familiar with this form of control so this thing was about to get ugly for certain.

It was a Thursday evening and Tony was returning home from a week long visit back to Brooklyn, visiting family. He was returning with his friend Jason, who had decided to move down to Florida permanently, seeking a change since he was just coming out of a nasty divorce. He and Jason had talked about this for months and now the time was finally here for Jason to strike out on his own in a new place, using Tony as the launching pad. Jason would be staying with Tony for a while until he got a job and saved enough for a place and could strike out on his own. This would help Tony out with a second household income he had not had since Sharon had left. DD knew Jason was coming, so as she picked them up at the airport, she wasn't surprised to see that Tony wasn't alone. She was, however, surprised at how handsome Jason was. He was a good looking man, six foot, two inches tall with low cut hair, sporting the same wave hair style as Tony. He wasn't as built as Tony actually, but he had a basketball player build. He too was fair skinned with brown eyes and strong handsome features with a charismatic personality. DD behaved strangely the entire drive home. She was flirtier, laughing at all his jokes and smiling at him a lot. DD was a horrible flirt in fact; this is why Tony didn't like going anywhere with her, as it was always an embarrassment to him. But he never imagined that she would do it with one of his friends, right in his face. He continued on in their conversation, trying to figure out if he was being overly sensitive or if it was going down like he felt it was.

When they finally arrived back at Tony's place, he sent DD home as he didn't want to be around her in her current state. He couldn't tell if she was high but she appeared like she might be, and maybe this was contributing to her flirty behavior. She seemed again annoyed with him for not allowing her to come in and keep company with him and Jason. Tony promised they would hang out tomorrow after work, so she fell back and went on home. He was embarrassed by what he perceived as flirting and hoped his boy didn't notice it or at least wouldn't ask him about it, making it worse. Jason wasn't slow, so he knew the chances of him not noticing were slim to none. As they walked into the house Jason burst his bubble,

"Yo, your girl smokes?" he asked.

"She claims she doesn't but I think she still does," Tony replied.

"She was definitely high just now son. Did you see the way she was looking at me? I can see why you say you don't trust her. If she could do that with me right in front of you, then…?" Jason looked puzzled.

"Yeah I know," Tony replied, completely humiliated and not knowing what to say.

After all, this wasn't one of his flings like back in the day when he didn't care what she was or who she gave it to. This was someone who he like and cared about; in fact he was sure he was falling in love with her. So until Jason changed the subject, there was an awkward silence that said Tony just didn't want to talk about it. She had embarrassed him like this before, but not on this level.

Just a couple of weeks ago she had met his son Lil Tony for the first time and something very similar marred that night. Tony's son, Lil Tony, was visiting from New York, where he lived with his mother. Tony was both nervous and excited to introduce him to his potential new found love. He didn't make a big deal about it. He figured he would allow Lil Tony to draw his own conclusions based on how they all behaved around one another and if he had questions, he would explain the rest. That evening they had planned on taking Lil Tony to the movies and a huge arcade in Ybor City that Tony knew his son had never seen the likes of, because they just didn't exist anymore. Lil Tony was excited to be out so late on a Friday night. The energy was amazing and the promise of the arcade and movie was just over the top for him. So needless to say, he was very excited to meet DD, as she was the one who suggested this night of fun. Upon meeting each other, she too, was excited to meet Tony's other little man and things seemed to be going better than Tony had hoped. But things turned quickly once they arrived at Ybor City and parked the car.

Ybor City was a long strip of bars and clubs and since it was Friday night, the place was crowded with adults and would-be club hoppers. DD hardly waited for Tony to park the car before she was out, walking ahead of them. She was dressed as if she was headed to the club herself which was strange, but Tony didn't consider it odd since he knew the area they were headed to. However, he did wish that she had made some better clothing choices around his son than the high heels and tight clothes, although he was old enough to have seen mildly provocative outfits of people walking down the street. Tony didn't make a big deal, so he figured Lil Tony wouldn't either. However, now walking down the street looking at DD walking at a brisk pace in her high heels, a full fifteen to twenty feet ahead of he and his son, he began to wonder if her clothing choice had another purpose. As she sprinted towards the main street where the arcade was, Lil Tony looked up at Tony and asked,

"Why isn't she walking with us dad?"

"I don't know son, you just never know what is on people's mind," he answered laughing trying to make light of the situation.

As they arrived at the arcade, she didn't wait for them as she entered the doors. She didn't even wait for them once she got inside. She walked on into the back where she waited for them and waved them in. He walked into the back of the arcade looking confused. She stood there looking as if there was nothing wrong and asked if he wanted her to go get Lil Tony some tokens for the arcade so he could begin playing. Since there was a bar in the arcade, she wanted to send Lil Tony off to the games so she could have drinks with Tony.

"No he can do it. It's only a few feet away," Tony said as he handed some cash to his son.

As Lil Tony walked off with ten dollars in his hands, he headed for the token booth looking puzzled by the upset look he saw on his father's face. Tony forced an awkward smile as he sent him on his way.

"What is going on with you? Why did you just walk off like that?" Tony asked DD, now looking visibly upset.

"What do you mean? I was just walking at my usual pace. I really didn't think anything of it," she replied looking like she could care less.

"Ain't no way you didn't notice how you left us behind like you didn't want to be seen with us? Even my ten year old noticed!" He snapped back.

"No I didn't," she shot back, looking even more aggravated.

"Well I don't see. . . ." he began to say as DD grabbed his arm to alert him that Lil Tony was back, knowing he didn't want him to hear this conversation.

Tony, realizing that his son was back, bottled up his concern for the moment and chose to save that conversation for later.

"So do you want me to go and get us some drinks?" DD pointed towards the bar.

It was a good thing she just got that job because there was no way he was going to be paying for her drinks tonight, he thought to himself. She had finally gotten a job after almost six months of dating. Tony had finally shown her the way to the confidence she needed to strike out on her own to find a job. That plus the fact that he wouldn't play sugar daddy for her no matter how hard she tried to rope him into that typical game she played. She had no problem showing her disdain for him and flaunting her new found independence as she coldly turned and walked towards the bar. He had told her that he did not intend to drink around his son and she just walked off. Truth was, he wasn't opposed to having a drink to be social but he was feeling like he wanted to be alert around her, and how she was behaving made him sure he had missed a lot already. She had gone to the bar and came back with a drink and quickly downed it again looking aggravated. They stood there not talking, although Tony tried to break the ice for his son's sake, with no luck.

"I'm hungry. I'm going to the front to order something to eat. I think I'm going to get another drink too, you sure you don't want anything?" she asked Tony again, with the same obvious bad attitude.

"No thank you," he replied, happy this time to see her walk off as he was certain the night was turning down a bad road. He was embarrassed enough but didn't need his son seeing him in this type of light. He was mortified.

After she left, Tony did his best to re-engage with his son and his video game world, but after about fifteen minutes, Tony's mind began to wonder about DD and why she had not returned. So once Lil Tony finished his driving video game, Tony suggested a two-person shooter video game close to the food area so he could check in on her without being too obvious that this was his intention. Once he got up to the front, he spotted her at the counter laughing loudly and flirting with the guy behind the counter. He stood there watching her for minutes as she leaned on the counter whispering and laughing. It took her a moment to notice he was standing there with his son, who was watching her every move at this point; since she had taken all of his dad's attention. She looked startled as she turned around and saw the two of them standing there. She turned and walked towards them with the same attitude she had left with, although she could see the hurt and disappointment in Tony's face.

She still had a look on her face like she was angry with him for catching her in a compromising position. She was acting like he had ruined her mack. She walked back into the arcade without saying a word as Lil Tony tugged on his dad's arm towards the video game they had come to the corner of the arcade to play. They played and laughed, although Tony couldn't get the vision of her betrayal out of his mind. Eventually the food that she ordered was ready and DD headed back up to the counter. It wasn't long before she was again smiling and laughing with the guy behind the counter. He was completely humiliated and decided he was going to have to block her out and focus on his son if he was going to save the night at all. She sat and ate her meal while he and Lil Tony got into as many video games as he possibly could before their movie was due to start. She left her empty food box and walked off to the bar a few times as they played games.

Once they finally left for the movie theater, she once again took off without them. By this time, Tony was prepared for it and kept his son's attention by engaging him and pretending not to even notice she was not walking by his side. They watched the movie on opposite sides of his son, basically ignoring each other for the rest of the night. It was clear that DD was not playing fair and had something or someone to hide. He knew from that moment on that she was either dating other people or seeking to date other people. He wasn't sure but what he was certain of was that she was a flirt he couldn't trust as far as he could see. They argued about that night for three full days before she finally admitted that she had done something worth apologizing for. Tony had to convince her that if she intended to be with him, she owed his son an apology too as Lil Tony was totally turned off by the thought of DD now. And if she wanted to be in his life, she needed to get right with his son. She did so almost a week later.

He knew what type of woman she was but also knew that anything worth having was worth working hard for. For some reason he was convinced that there was something great inside of her. At the moments and times when they were alone, she presented such a different picture to him. She was soft. She was vulnerable. She was beginning to take some of the walls down that kept her in this place that made her the woman the rest of the world saw.

So Tony had no answers for Jason as he brought up this uncomfortable conversation about his lady's promiscuous ways. He had no answer for Jason because the truth was he had no answers for himself. He couldn't figure out for the life of him why he was walking into this place for this woman. He had plenty of opportunities to date women with far less work and more to offer him but he could not pull himself away. He knew all of the twisted reasons in his head but none of them made any sense, especially at times like this one.

The following day was Friday and he had plans to take his boy out for a drink instead of his usual hang out date with DD and she wasn't too happy about it.

"Well can't I come out with you and your boy? With work and school I hardly see you outside of the weekends. I don't want to be a third wheel but I really miss you. What, you have a problem hanging out with me and your boy? You and him have some kind of special night planned? Maybe y'all going to find some loose ass?"

She was questioning his character as she liked to do when she was pushing his buttons. He was already embarrassed from the night before and couldn't bear the humiliation that would come from having to admit to her that he knew she was attracted to Jason. Like somehow if he didn't say it, he wouldn't have to hear the lie in her voice as she tried to deny what he already knew was true. She pressed and pushed until he agreed to allow her to go. She was always good for a fun time and maybe she would be on her best behavior if he made his point.

So without speaking about last night he would state his case.

"I know my boy is handsome but try not to smile in his face too much," he said laughing, trying to make light of the situation.

"Whatever Tony. Now you know I ain't interested in your friend," she said, also laughing trying to keep it light.

That night, once Tony got off and Angel was dropped off, they all went out to a local bar less than a quarter mile from his place. DD met them at the bar and they sat and talked over their favorite drink, Tequila. Before long they were laughing and joking. It didn't take long before they all were a bit tipsy and moved from the bar stools to the patio and got even louder. It also wasn't long before DD stopped being polite and got familiar with Jason, and no time before she was leaning into his face, smiling and laughing.

Tony was sitting there, outside the conversation, just watching as he could see where this thing was headed. Just at that moment, as it was clear where Jason and DD were headed, she realized that Tony was not talking and looked up to see him staring at them both. She got up and excused herself and headed for the bathroom. As Jason and he sat there and talked, Jason once again downplayed the obvious attraction and flirting that was going on, embarrassed for his best friend but too drunk to have that conversation at the moment. It would be another twenty minutes before Tony got concerned about DD and went looking for his flirtatious companion. She was sitting at the piano in the bar talking with yet another man. He didn't want to make a scene and walked by her towards the bathroom as if he didn't notice her flirting again. He played it off as if he had to go to the bathroom. As she looked up, he shot her a look like he wanted to slit her throat for embarrassing him. She chuckled out loud, ignoring the guy standing there talking to her and walked off back towards the table.

Tony went into the bathroom and headed directly to the stall; he needed privacy as he walked in and let out a deep sigh. He made water and stood there staring at the wall wondering if he could pick up the pieces of his heart if he did what he knew he had to do. He had to let her go but he knew it would be hard. He could feel the emotion building up in himself and the Tequila wasn't helping. He wanted to be angry at Jason but knew it wasn't his fault she was behaving like a whore. He wanted to be angry at her but realized it would be a waste of energy and thought that it was better to deal with how he was really feeling, which was hurt. He pulled himself together as he could feel the tears building up in his system. There was no way he was going to allow her to make him shed a single tear, not one.

As he walked out of the bathroom, he sat back down at the piano she had left, partly to pull himself together and partly to watch DD from a place she couldn't see him as she sat talking to Jason with her back to him. They continued talking closer and closer and the personal distance that comes with strangers was gone and she was now close enough to him to damn near touch his lips with hers. He was not about to wait around for that shit to happen. He walked out of the side door and jumped into his car which was but ten feet from where Jason and DD were sitting. He sat there waiting for them to notice. They did not. He started the car, drove off and got all the way home and they still hadn't noticed he was gone. Within minutes of Tony pulling into his driveway his cell phone was ringing. It was DD calling. He forwarded the call to his voice mail, embarrassed and hurt by what he was sure about to happen. She called time and again about ten times in a row before Tony picked up the phone.

"What the fuck is going on? Why did you leave me there?" she yelled, sounding as if she wanted to cry.

"I figured you and Jason were having a good enough time without me," he replied.

"What the hell are you talking about?" she yelled.

"You were all in his face, smiling and flirting, fuck that! You can hang out with him!" And he hung up the phone.

She left several voice mails crying and yelling at him, calling him paranoid and telling him how fucked up he was for leaving her there with his friend. She was turning this thing around on him but he never took her call, so her efforts were wasted. Within ten minutes Jason was knocking at the door with DD still blowing up Tony's phone. She begged him to let her come inside so they could talk but he refused and demanded that she not only stop calling but go home to her dad's house and leave him alone and once again hung up. He opened the door for Jason who immediately apologized, claiming it wasn't what Tony thought but admitting that she was indeed flirting with him. Tony retired to his room too tired and drunk to even finish the conversation. He took the bottle of tequila he had on the bar in his bedroom with him to make sure his mind wouldn't be keeping him up tonight with all the fucked up thoughts he was having. He drank and drank until he passed out.

When he woke up the next day, he not only still had all of his clothes on but was laying in bed with Sharon holding him from behind. She too was fully dressed and asleep. As he stumbled to the bathroom, he was searching for his phone as the first thing on his mind was DD and if she had called. His mind was still reeling from the events of last night. He pulled his pants off and relieved himself of the serious pressure in his bladder that woke him up from a sound sleep. He woke Sharon up and asked her why she was there. She told him of a tearful man who woke her in the middle of the night begging her to come and hold him. She had come and held him all night as he had cried himself to sleep. Jason had let her in as she and Angel had stood outside pounding on the door for about twenty minutes. Tony was completely embarrassed, especially since in his drunken state, he had told Sharon about what happened that night. He was so ashamed, he just climbed his still drunken self back to bed and again allowed Sharon to hold him as he fell back to sleep. He could feel the tears coming again so he sat up and hit one more shot and passed out again.

Tonight his relationship with DD had been tested and there was no need to grade the progress, it was what it was. And more importantly DD was what she was, and he had to let her go to be what she was going to be. It could no longer be with him. He had to cut his losses. DD was even more than he was ready for.

Chapter 11
Love Is Stronger Than Pride

It had been three days since DD had ruined their relationship with her promiscuous ways and Tony had decided it was best for them to part ways. She had left many tear filled messages and they had done what they were intended to do, tug at his heart strings. He had heard that song, *Love is Stronger Than Pride*," so many times but had never really felt or paid very much attention to the words. But this night as he played Angel's favorite CD to put him to sleep, he could feel each and every word. DD had opened up in a big way and bared her soul to him, now that he wasn't interested in it. She pleaded and begged him to forgive her. She sent flowers, bought chocolate and wrote him letter after letter, which she left at his door and on his car. Although he didn't want to admit it to himself, she was starting to break down his already weak defenses. He was drawn to her from the sickness that still lived in his soul that begged him to love someone that he knew couldn't love him back. It was more than a challenge but he wanted her so badly and she was doing everything she could to convince him to follow his heart back to her. She knew if he came back to her that he would be hopelessly hooked into her web and she was right; but he knew it too. And even this couldn't stop him from walking back to her with his heart and nose "wide open." I guess love really is stronger than pride; if this was love.

DD had figured out a long time ago if she could get a man to show his emotions, any emotion, even if it was anger, he would be open. Each time Tony got jealous, each time he got angry, he was being drawn into her web tighter and tighter. So it was no surprise that once she began to cry, he was drawn into empathy, his male ego and his need to rescue this broken woman. She was far more manipulative than he could ever have imagined and she played him to feed his ego. Each time he had class, she would make herself scarce. She would be out with her friends at the club or getting high at their place. She made new friends at her new job and got drunk and high with them too. She also spent countless hours away from home and her daughter getting high, drinking and partying at her new friend's apartment. Tony never did know who her friend was but between this new friend, and her old friend, Tonya, DD was hardly available when Tony was. She was always conveniently busy, or out, blaming him for not having the time for her. This drove him crazy as he spent his days trying to keep track of her and their last relationship. He was sure that he was losing her and she had to be seeing someone else. This went on for months until Tony was faced with the ugly truth that neglecting his school work had taken. He was pursuing his Masters degree in education while, simultaneously, attending law school and was now so far behind; he had to make a choice to save one or the other. Both could no longer be done at this point; at least not with chasing DD too. He knew he did not have the will to stop chasing DD nor was he ready to lose her yet.

Once Tony made this decision, he and DD began to spend a lot more time together and it was clear that she had manipulated him. They fought for weeks before she admitted the truth and stopped using her friends as a barrier between them and their relationship. It was about this time that Tony began to notice more and more the way she dealt with her so called "friends". She dealt with them more like they were her lovers; talking to them like she was a jealous man and it struck him like a bolt of lightning as he listened in on a phone conversation she was having with one of her friends.

The butch appearance, and feel, he got from her upon their first meeting was more accurate than he knew. He began to question her on their walks, about her sexuality, encouraging her to open up and talk about herself and past; each time disclosing more and more about himself. After weeks of talking, badgering, and even arguing, she told him the truth. She had been involved in lesbian relationships. She explained it as threesomes she had with her ex that she was forced into. It was nothing she liked, but she did it for him because he was sexually twisted. He felt this wasn't all she had to say on the matter. He felt she was hiding something deeper but wasn't sure he was ready to hear it. Knowing that he, too, had been involved in threesomes with two women, he accepted her explanation. He felt to himself that he couldn't judge her because he, too, had convinced a woman he was involved with to delve into sexual deviance with threesomes. For all he knew, she could have felt the same way about him and their sexual deviance as DD did about hers. He was certainly not ready to share that with her, so he stopped pushing her on the matter. His guilt played no small part in his decision to let the conversation go. He couldn't stop envisioning her with another woman and the measure she was going to for her man at the time, knowing what he had done and where they had gone. He did all he could to block it out, but the flood gates had been opened and since Tony hadn't judged her on this matter that she was so ashamed of, she felt confident to share more.

Night after night as they went on their walks, she finally opened up and began to really share about herself and her former life. She talked about her childhood and how rough it was on her, including the abandonment she felt when her parents divorced. She spoke at great length about how angry she was at the extreme verbal, mental, and sometimes, physical abuse she suffered at the hands of an angry mother who put so many expectations on her but never even tried to live up to the same. She went on and on about a family who just wasn't there for her. This is why she had struck out on her own at such a young age. She basically ran away from her entire family the first opportunity she got. This is also what ultimately put her in such a horrible position with the men she ended up going with, who took advantage of her young mind and abused spirit.

They got closer and closer upon each level of, what Tony thought was understanding. She had reached out in the same trust as he had and told him some things about herself that weren't at all flattering. Her mom had even accused her of prostitution. It was horrible. Her shameful truth was that she ended up being a stripper for a time in her life. Having not pursued an education, although having great potential to do so, she was left in a position that didn't give her very many options. Therefore, the jobs she was able to get either didn't pay that much or were sales jobs where she couldn't rely on the salary to support her and her child. She felt like she didn't have any options, so she did what she had to do. By the time it got back to her mother, the translation portrayed her as not only a stripper, but a prostitute.

It hurt her greatly that her mom could even think she would do such a thing. At her lowest, she could never imagine herself doing that. This drove an even bigger wedge deeper between the two of them. Now telling Tony this had quietly pushed his wig back. But in an effort to not only be supportive, but nonjudgmental as her family had been, he reached inside himself so he wouldn't freak out and run off as everyone else in her life had done. She didn't need judgment. What she needed was help and someone to support her and show her another way. Someone who would stick by her long enough for her to get the courage to go outside of what she thought she knew to try and do something else.

The sales job she had did not provide much money but it was what she knew and she had done it all her life. Although she hated it, it was easy to get and plenty of jobs were available. She was certain that if she just kept pushing her techniques and kept a positive attitude, things would come around and she would start making good money. With each passing day and subsequent week, she became less and less confident in her abilities to turn this thing around at her job.

Digging into her past with Tony had opened up some memories and thoughts she hadn't faced or thought about in years and it was making it difficult to function in her usual place of denial, which in turn made it difficult to do her job. She began to worry constantly if she could cut it on her job and if she would ever make the money she needed to support her and her little girl. In her mind, she was certain that even though Tony wasn't freaking out, or saying he was going to leave her, that the things she had disclosed to him, in addition to what he didn't know about her, would be the reason he would eventually leave her. She viewed him as the man she was seeing as well as her future, and had expressed ideas of marriage and a family. She kept telling Tony how afraid she was that once he knew who she really was that he would leave. It was a challenge to him to stand up for her and stay. He was feeling deep down in his soul that if no one had ever broken that idea and just loved her for who she was, that he would be that guy for DD.

She finally broke down and told him that she had used her friends to hurt him while she felt he was "too busy" for her. They had literally spent every Friday night fighting with one another over the phone about her being at some club getting drunk and high with her girlfriend, while he was home with his son looking for his would be girlfriend. She finally confessed that she was secretly insecure that she could never be the type of woman that Tony would settle down with. It wasn't just her past that made her feel that way but her present; who she was today.

She had barely been holding onto this little piece of a job; the first one she had in the entire time she had known him. She had no education or ambition to do anything except make money and she really had no idea on how she was going to do that, which usually led her down the wrong paths. She watched him and how he dealt with his children and found her parental skills lacking; not by anything he said, because he had never judged her or spoken ill of her in that way, but in all that he did for his. She knew she didn't measure up. All the lies she knew she was telling him about herself and the drugs was constantly pulling at her heart and if she wanted to keep playing this game with the only man she had ever met who wanted to give her the world and take her as she was.

She couldn't believe it was real. She couldn't trust him long enough to find out the truth about it, or herself. Was she woman enough to withstand a man who wouldn't just take, who wouldn't just use her up and leave? In fact, he had never asked her for a single thing. But what frightened her was that at this point in her past relationships, she usually had the man eating out of her hand and he was giving her everything she wanted. Although she wore what looked like second hand garments, she always spoke of high priced designer clothes. She kept dropping hints about what she expected. She spoke all the time about her financial needs. But up to this point, they had fallen on deaf ears as Tony had always given her what she needed but never what she wanted in that way.

To this point, she was also able to work her mojo on her past lovers through sex and all the dirty little physical things men crave and desire. But because Tony was on the spiritual journey to find himself and where love laid, she was unable to reach him that way. Until then, they hadn't even had sex, which also weighed in on whether or not she was the woman for him, or if she was the woman she thought she was altogether. It was all working in a slow walk backwards towards insecurities instead of the confidence she should have had in him at this point. He explained that he was comfortable knowing that she knew he wasn't using her for her body or sex. This brought her no real comfort as she thought to herself that if he had been using her for her body then they may have been further along. He pointed out time after time how he had supported her and brought her to what real love and support was, even opened up the bible and prayed with her and had her talking to and about God for the first time in years.

This entire conversation should have brought her some much needed evidence as to how much he really loved her but it didn't work like that in her mind. Since she didn't trust him, or anyone else for that matter, she viewed all he had said as measures of control, the way her ex had used sex to control her, and her life before. She thought that Tony may just be doing the same with everything - his money, his life, access to his children and even his home - as he hardly took her there. Truth was that he hardly trusted her either. He knew that she was lying about some major things. He was certain she was trying to use him but couldn't be sure if this was the extent of the relationship. But what he was certain of was that this was her modus operandi. She was used to using men and it appeared to him that she was doing the same with others. This meant that she more than likely had several other men on the side to provide for the things he would not. He wasn't sure if this meant sex or not since she was so crazed for it but now seemed far more under control about it and rarely pushed him or put the pressure on him for it as she used to. He didn't know if this was something he needed to be worried about or if he could feel safe that she was coming around.

Most of the time he was tight and waiting for the other shoe to drop, knowing in his heart of hearts that she was a whore and stepped out on him every chance she got. But the whore in him refused to judge her, refused to let that be the reason she was unlovable because this meant that his true self, was also unlovable and not worth staying. If he left her for those reasons then he would never find the love he sought, because he knew that the love he REALLY sought was of himself.

She was so much of him, he could only take her in parts at times. He recognized the little slick shit she did with her phone like, the sliding off to talk, the "oh if you're busy, go ahead and do what you have to, I'll be here waiting" talks, all the while filling that time and space with other partners. He had done all of those things and recognized them all too well. He didn't want her around his boys. He felt it was too obvious and he didn't want them to get the wrong idea about her but most importantly what kind of man he was - his true inner self. The one he chose to hide away, choosing instead to show them the him that he wanted to be - full of goals and accomplishments, degrees, work and honor, all the things he expected of them. She recognized that as long as he kept her in this position that nothing he had said, or had done, was real. Additionally, he knew he could never be what she wanted him to be until she got real with him and stopped doing all the little shady shit she was doing. They were playing an unspoken game of chicken with their lives, their children, future and love. It was a game where she had unspoken expectations that she would just be given the trust, respect and all the things she needed without ever having to change herself, or life, because to her that was complete acceptance. She sought this unconditional love and that is what her subconscious stuck to no matter how crazy it sounded.

What her conscious mind stuck to was that she was a grown ass woman with plenty of financial needs who was living in one room with her daughter, in her father's house. She had needs that this man who said he loved her was not providing for. When, and if this man stepped up to do those things he kept talking about, including all the things she could see he was doing for Sharon, all the things she was in the photos and stories he was for his ex-wife, then and only then would she stop being who she was. Other than that, he was full of shit.

For him it was impossible to give her the financial support from a place where he KNEW she was lying. He KNEW in his soul she was cheating on him and had other men in her life, which made him the worst kind of fool - a willing fool - and he could not be that. So it was no wonder with all this stress and worry, having opened up all these doors in DD's life with her not having any answers - a ton of questions, a ton of needs and no certainty as to how they would be met - she began to have panic attacks. They happened at home when she took a look at her life and where and who she was. More importantly, she began to have them at her job and it was affecting her performance. Finally she had a full blown panic attack that she and everyone around her was certain was a heart attack and the paramedics were called. She was laid off the following week once she returned. This only added to her stress and anxiety.

Tony decided that day he was at the hospital with her father and family that he was going to have to step up and do some of the man things that were expected of him at this point in their relationship. He knew it was going to be hard. He also knew it was not going to be one of those things he could do without expectations of his own. He knew he was going to need some assurances from her. He was going to need her to stop doing the things she was doing. He also knew he was going to have to step up and tell her what he saw and knew about her, and that things were going to get worse before they got better; but if he was going to stay with her, he could not continue to allow her to take the lead in their relationship. He knew that if they were actually going to make it to marriage and family, he was going to have to be the lead in this dance, and cover her as God had intended him to do. And as the priest of what would be their home, he was going to have to say some things that she didn't want to be said. At a time and place where she was already stressed out and having panic attacks, they prescribed her medication that took her out of her personality. She was there but hardly seemed present and the things he was trying to talk to her about were lost on her, so he just tried to support her the best way he knew how.

Despite the fact that he, too, had needs, he never imposed upon her. He knew the roles were different for their genders. He was a single father with four children. He needed help with his house, the cooking, the cleaning, and the day-to-day tending to the children. He had gone down to only one job now since all of the clubbing and cheating along with all the men and women he imagined in his mind. It was keeping him crazy, so he gave in to her and gave her the time she needed.

Things got harder with only a single income, as Jason had moved away several months now. He was receiving no child support from Angel's mom and was, in fact, still giving a third of his income to child support for his son back in New York. All of the bills were solely on him and he needed support too. She couldn't even keep a sales job to support herself and her daughter. He knew he would be taking on another two mouths to feed but he was making a commitment, at least in his mind, to do so in order to get to what was the next level of their relationship. He was going to open up the doors to his home and invite her in and try to get started on this family, despite the fact that things were not ideal.

He was going to accept and meet her where she was with the hopes that she would rise to a family level with he and his children. Months went by and she had been coming and going in his home, never picking up a broom or dish, despite the fact that he was now providing for some simple but needed things in her life. The piece of car she finally was able to get kept breaking down and he kept helping her with that and little things for her daughter and bringing them around him and his family. They stayed late, never spending the night but he was trying to create the feeling that this is what it could be if she would jump in on the next level, but she never got it. Eventually the bills, two car payments, the rent, the utilities, the insurance, the food, the clothing, the gas and everything you could imagine got to be too much. DD never got a job, still dealing with her anxiety, so Tony had to make a choice.

For months, Sharon was moving from place to place not able to hold it down by herself either. Finally she and her roommates lost their place to live and she was homeless. Tony's heart went out to the mother of his children. But more than that, when she asked about moving back in under roommate conditions until she could find another place to live on her own, he remembered that she had always kept a job and steady income. That was the one thing he could always count on from her. She was a slob and he hated cleaning up after her all the time but she did pull her share of the bills. He knew that DD wouldn't like it but there was no way he was going to leave the mother of his son out on the street.

He would not add any more pressure to her already fragile state by telling her that she had contributed to this decision in all the things she refused to do. He decided instead to step up and start talking, start demanding the things he knew needed to be addressed if they were going to be able to move on to the next level. He was going to start speaking the truth and in that truth he was also going to have the resources now to provide for her more than he had previously. He was hoping this would encourage her down the correct path. When that car finally broke down and could not be repaired, he gave her the key to the Mercedes Benz he kept in the garage. He had bought that car for Sharon but she didn't keep up the payments and it was repossessed. He paid to get it back but not before he gave her three thousand dollars from his savings to help her buy another car of her own so she could get to work and back. It was after she bought her new car that the finance company came back and offered to allow Tony the chance to get the Benz back and repair his credit. He paid the two stacks and put the car in the garage paying the five hundred dollars a month it took to keep his promise to the bank and credit clean each month.

The car cost him seven hundred dollars a month just to keep it in the garage collecting dust. He had never considered giving it to DD before because he just knew she would be driving her "friends" around in a car he paid for and couldn't bear those thoughts.

"Willing fool," kept playing in his head. The car was only five years old, a far cry from the thirteen year old POS she had been driving that had just kicked the bucket. The car was fully loaded with power everything. It needed some new tires but that was about it. She had always claimed while riding in his newer model Benz that she wasn't a Mercedes type of person, she didn't need all that luxury excess. But everything she said otherwise, told that this was a lie. She wanted fine clothes, a big house and plenty of money. Why not a Benz? He had always ignored her words, choosing instead to watch and believe the actions and OTHER meanings behind her words. He gave her the car and she was nervous because this meant that there would be an expectation of her and she knew it.

"I don't have the money to pay this car note," she said.

"It's ok. I know that. Just give me what you can, when you can. And if that is nothing, then it's nothing. I want to help you, and you can't get a job without a car. I have been paying this note all this time. It will be ok," he said lovingly, trying to be as supportive as he could. Hiding his fears beneath the confidence, he needed to show he loved her.

She took the car and drove it, trying to get used to being supported without being expected to sell her soul in the process. She had been taken advantage of by men who had been kind to her and she never saw their evil ways coming, so she was suspicious of Tony and his kindness. In fact, she tried several times, unsuccessfully, to refuse the car. Even after she was driving it, she began to love it and became comfortable with it but she wanted to give it back. She did not want to become spoiled with it, making the disappointment greater once he took the vehicle back as she was sure he would do. Before getting it, she would say little things to downplay its luxury and her obvious desire to not only have the vehicle, but the life and lifestyle someone who drove that sort of car was usually afforded.

"I'm just not a Benz person. It's nice, just not my style." After driving it for a day, she had to admit she WAS a BENZ PERSON. Her being able to admit she found comfort in something she could not afford herself played a major part in her anxiety. This made DD really nervous, so the more she felt herself liking it the more she offered to give it back. It did not make matters any easier that in addition to the car, Tony began buying her little things, like a blouse or some shoes. Heels. She loved heels and Tony had figured a way into her heart. And the heels didn't make her half as uneasy, so he was sure to buy her some each week as he could afford.

If she had a bad week – heels. If she was upset with him – heels. If she wanted to feel pretty - a nice pair of seven inch heels usually got a big smile. He started taking her out more against his fears of the things she had done to him on the few occasions they had gone out. He had also increased buying things for her little girl that he knew she needed. Once he started giving, he could see a million and one needs and things he could do for, and give her. She had stopped going out with her friends. They were still there but he was now showering her with not only attention but things and now he was getting her full attention.

It didn't hurt that the one new girlfriend that she made at her last job had stolen her purse after a night of getting high. He was certain. So now they stopped speaking. It was of no consequence because Tony was happy to have her. It didn't matter how he got her, only that he did. Each week he started this thing called date night, where he took her to a show, or to dinner and things were starting to look like real progress in their relationship. They were the happiest they had ever been with one another. As long as Tony turned a blind eye to his needs, they got along superbly. He was in full husband mode without asking for anything, which was a hard thing to do especially with all the thoughts he still had in his mind as to what she may or may not be doing. Yet still he pushed passed these thoughts knowing that, "Scared money don't make no money." He knew full well that he had to give of himself in full faith if he expected anything to happen. Through his journey he was studying the bible everyday now and he came to a cross roads where he had to admit he understood very little about God's will for his life and even less as to how he was to get there. So he had decided to follow the Lord and this is where the Lord had led him - a place of little knowledge and asking of the Lord.

Tony understood from the time he was a small child that faith without work was dead. He had grown to know that he couldn't just show up to God at the level he was at with his hand out without the work necessary to receive the blessing. He had to put himself in position to get the lesson in order to receive the blessing. Why not? He had tried everything else. He tried sin. He tried the ways of the world in any and every fashion, but like the bible said, it was time to, "try the spirits." So for him to ask, to seek the answers to the questions was more about doing than just merely uttering the words. He decided to ask God to show him and deliver him his wife. He stepped out on faith to receive it. He knew this was God's will. The bible told him in James 1:5

> *If any of you lack wisdom, let him ask of God, that giveth to all men liberally, and upbraideth not; and it shall be given him. But let him ask in faith, NOTHING WAVERING: for he that wavereth is like a wave of the sea driven with the wind and tossed. For let not that man think that he shall receive anything of the Lord.*

These were powerful, ground breaking words for him. To not waver. Tony could not remember the last time he did not waver in love but he knew that this was the answer to his question and it was staring right at him

124

in the form of DD. And if he was ever going to get right with himself and the Lord, this is where he needed to start. Not so much asking her to be these things for him but asking himself to be these things for her and, more importantly, himself.

Chapter 12
All Fall Down

God's Will
Romans 12:2 And be not
conformed to this world:
but be ye transformed by
the renewing of your
mind, that ye may prove
what is that good, and
acceptable, and perfect
will of God.

Day after day, he tossed and turned on this one verse. The will of God and yet even that wasn't good enough. THE PERFECT WILL OF GOD. Wow, that was lot of pressure. But he had studied the word long enough to feel like he knew the perfect will of God for his life and that concerning DD. So he was going to stick to his guns no matter how tough this thing between them got. He had always considered himself the sort of man that stayed. He didn't run from commitment, didn't run from his responsibilities, not his four children, not his relationships and certainly not his problems. But the more he learned about himself, the more he learned the truth in that belief. There was absolutely some truth in that statement which he had poured all his belief. He did not run. He could remember a time or two in his young life when threatened by thieves who came to rob him and others back in high school, he did not run but stood his ground while everyone else ran. It was his courage that allowed him the presence to stand against the wolves as they came and took what they wanted that day and never be touched. He remembered staring down the barrel of a gun on more than one occasion - unmoved. It is why it was so tough leaving his family behind at a time he knew they needed him to go off to college. Even knowing that one step back would propel him twelve steps forward, it was still the toughest decision he had to ever make in his young life. With these types of memories of his character at times when it was called upon, it left little room for him to question if he was indeed the man he believed himself to be. The fact was, during most of those times when he stood up and looked his fear in the face, it was in a sort of survival mode. He did what he had to do in order to make it through. He knew when they came to take the winter coat off his back he could not afford another and could not go to school without it, so he stood, and fought, and won. He knew about his resolve to fight and he called on it today as he thought about his personal life and the all the fighting he would have to do now against his greatest adversary, himself. With all the people he had chosen to love, he had always thought he was loving and living this life for them, in some weird way. With Sharon, because she was so jacked up emotionally, and had no real family to speak of, he had convinced himself that his staying through all that crap was more about his love for her than it was about the love he needed, or the family he needed to build. So when things got tough, he didn't leave or walk out physically. No, he stayed right there. But emotionally he checked out the same way he had done with his wife years earlier. She had stopped being intimate with him. No sex and no disclosure due to her lack of trust in him and his cheating ways. He could see how his behavior was building the cycle he was in. She had stopped coming to him as her husband and outsourced her need for interpersonal communication to her sister and friends and this made him seek others as well. He sought company and sex with other women outside of his marriage which made it an easy decision for his wife to stop trying.

When it came down to it, this made him wrong on all points because it was he who was the adulterer and it never mattered that she was the one who abandoned him. They would never even get to that behavior because NO ONE got past the obvious. He was a cheater and a liar.

New love, new life, new relationship. This time he would not cheat. He would decide to leave instead because he had learned that stinging lesson that cheating only leaves YOU hurt in the end. But the bottom line was that when things hit rocky roads, he would stay physically but always left emotionally and left it entirely up to HER to fix, no matter how much of it was his share. Until she came around completely, he was gone. It had been to the point that by the time he left the relationship completely there was no doubt that she was wrong. After awhile he started to figure out, "Who cares who is right or wrong?" The only thing that mattered was the fact that he was once again alone and without a wife, partner or the family he was seeking to build.

This time, right here and now, he had decided that he would not only stay with DD no matter what came but he was going to stay invested, stay locked in emotionally and otherwise, not just because of what he saw in her - the light, the life, the love - but FOR HIMSELF. He needed to learn to stay and persevere through these tough times if he ever hoped to find God's promise. So far it was he who had done the wavering, so he could not reap the promise. He realized that it really didn't matter what Sharon, or his ex-wife, Joy, had done, but only what HE, himself, had done. After all, it was himself that he was stuck with? So after all is said and done, it is only his part he could answer for, to himself, his children and to God. He was tired of losing relationships. He was tired of losing jobs and most tired of losing children. He had lost his daughter in a bitter battle for parental rights, once again seeking to be right when DOING right should have been enough. Ultimately his daughter's mother died and he did get custody halfway through her childhood but even then it had been, and still was, a bitter battle at times to pull his little girl and her probate mind out of the dark places her life had taken her in his absence - being right. Now he was reduced to a part time father with his first son little

Tony and he was looking down the barrel of yet another decision that could very well lead him back to the same path with Angel. He had always mocked all those "baby daddies" out there who spread their seed all over the place. He always thought he was and would be *smarter* than that. What he figured out is that he really didn't know that much about life and adult choices and how naive his harsh judgment was. He had to make some changes, not just for himself but for his children; for his legacy and for all the dreams of life he held for all those around him. With all of these factors considered, he had made up his mind that this was the horse he was going to ride out on no matter what came.

Funny thing was DD represented so much of himself; he knew this would be the greatest challenge to his ideas about life and love and he was as scared as the need for oxygen in his lungs. She held the potential for the greatest love he had ever seen, in the one hand, and the greatest defeat and pain in the other. It was completely and totally going to be up to him to stay and see what she and God had in store and since he had stopped believing in coincidences a long time ago, he knew he was led here with purpose and would be in for a long ride. How long he didn't know; only that he was buckled in whether DD knew it or not.

*   *   *   *   *

It was Friday night and Tony and DD were headed out to the Forum to watch a live boxing match, Ronald "Winky" Wright versus feared welterweight Ike Quartey. It was billed as a grudge match following Winky's loss to Jermaine Taylor. Big fights rarely came to town and anyone who was a sporting fan could feel the electricity in the air. Tony loved the fact that DD was a sporting fan, and was looking forward to going to the fight just as much as he was. She was also a big time football fan. It was like the family business in a way. Her family got into it in a way that most only talk about and she being the oldest child was all in first. Although she didn't really get into boxing before they got together, the physical nature of football made it an easy leap to boxing. It was Friday night and this boxing match fell squarely within their standing Friday night dates and this one was the best yet. They mostly did a night at the local bar, dinner and drinks or they would do what Tony called, "chicken and beer night" where they went picked up buffalo wings and a twelve pack of beer and headed up the drive in movie and watched a couple of new movies. They enjoyed having drinks and laughter, so from the bar to the drive in was more fun than one might imagine.

They both were full of smiles on the way in as they arrived at the fight with a street full of people and all the buzz of a major fight. They got to their section, stopped at the bar and picked up a cocktail for DD and a tall brew for Tony. They took a seat near one of the big screen televisions that was playing a Gators game. Tony was a "Noles" fan (Florida State), while DD was a "Gator," so watching the game was extra exciting for her especially since they were winning. They sat and watched the "Gators" trample someone before they went in and took their seats. Just like him, she was always happy when her team won and they liked to pick at each other about which sports team was best and who would beat who since their two favorite college football teams were major rivals.

"Well I hope you got all your jollies out and happy feelings this week because next week when dem boys meet my NOLES, y'all are GOING DOWN!" Tony said as he began to laugh.

"Whateva! Y'all going down in the same way. HARD!" DD shot back, as they both laughed.

This conversation went back and forth until their glasses were empty while watching all the pre fights. Tony got up and went for a refill, as the night just rolled on in a fun filled adult evening that far exceeded even their usually fun "date night." Their spirits were high and he could look into DD's face with no trouble at all and remember why he loved her, why he had chosen her and why he could lay down his old life in search of a new beginning with her. She was starting to appear more and more beautiful with each smile and passing pleasant moment. He could not remember a time in their entire history that he had seen her so happy. He had to take that moment and pinch himself. They had finally arrived at that place. You know that place where it feels like you two are in a bubble, smiling and laughing at things only you two can hear or appreciate on the level you're on. They were so much alike that even talking crap to each other was more fun than usual because they were often finishing each other's sentences. The fights were good but the company was awesome! And as the night rolled on, they felt more and more of that connection that made their relationship special.

As the fight ended and they began to walk back to the car, it really felt like the night was just beginning for them. They were laughing just as hard on the way out as they had on the way in. They got to the car happy and full of each other's love and Tony couldn't help but wonder where they were going from there. As each street passed and they continued to talk and laugh, he thought to himself that he really didn't want the night to end. But it was already past closing hours for cocktails, which meant in a small city like Tampa, there really wasn't much else to do. They still hadn't reached that point in their relationship that Tony trusted DD, so he had yet to open the flood gate that lead to the pathway of their desires in any sexual way. In fact this was a major point of contention between them. She often pushed the envelope, while HE was the one resisting. Having been a former whore himself he recognized in her some serious whorish behavior and that when she called out to him and his body, he knew although his head was firmly fixed in place, anybody would do. Not saying it did not matter to her at all, he was sure she wanted it with him but he felt he was interchangeable for any man in his position at this particular time and place in her life, whether she knew it, or wanted to admit to it, or not.

131

He never called her on it or made her seem like she wasn't good enough for him or anything like that but in his heart of hearts he knew he wanted something more than hot sex. He wanted the passion that came with intimacy and commitment that only came with someone you love. He was in his thirties and had done enough jumping from bed to bed and now wanted something serious, something different. He knew the only way to get it was to save DD from herself and stop her from tainting something so special with cheap booty calls and back seat lust that comes with all the guilt of sin and none of the height it was intended to have. So once they had made it to the car and she had already started with her sex talk and flirting, he knew where it was headed. With each passing street light he could not only feel the night's laughter and fun start to fade but the pressure from this woman he loved that refused to value herself. He could hear it in her talk and see it in her body language and movements that she really believed that this was the only way to please a man - the only way to keep his attention and get his love. He was stricken with an instant sadness that he fought off as he laughed off her advances as jokes. He knew that there was much truth in her jokes about cheap sex and flirtation that broke far past aggressive. As she began to grope him and he resisted, it was now clear his resolve was being tested. He didn't know if it was conscious or subconscious but he was sure it was a test to see if he was the man he had put himself out there to be. It mattered not to him because this was one test that was a no brainer. He did not want her in that way. As they got closer to his place she pressed him harder and harder with no results. This led to her feeling rejected and exploding.

As she screamed at the top of her lungs, he could literally SEE the devil in her almost like some sick exorcist movie. It was like literally witnessing some old demon crying out within her to be satisfied by tearing him to shreds with her wicked tongue. Tony was becoming more and more defensive as DD slung insults towards his manhood and ability to perform under the type of pressure she could bring to bear with her "hella" sex. The more she spoke, the more he was certain he wanted no part of it. As they pulled up to his apartment and it was beginning to become real to DD that Tony was not going to submit and she was indeed rejected, she again began to curse, scream and holler. Tony didn't say a word, but instead allowed her to vent and express herself, however inappropriate he felt it was. He knew her ego was bruised, as well as her feelings. He left room within himself for her words to pass through, somewhere with the cap off so he wouldn't retain that muck. Tony withstood this onslaught of foul words and bitter temper until even with the cap off it boiled over to the point he just couldn't take it any longer and he began to jab back.

"Are you SERIOUS? You're not going to have sex with me tonight?" DD shouted, for what had to be the tenth time.

"Yes DD, I am serious. This is not something I take lightly at all. I am standing firm on my decision. This is not something you can push me into," Tony replied, now beginning to shout.

"This is some bullshit Tony!" DD shouted. "What kind of fuckin' man are you? I played nice all night and we have gotten along fine until this moment. What the fuck? Tell me what the fuck is wrong with me why you refuse to touch me? Hell! Tell me what the fuck is wrong with YOU because I know what I'm holding and ain't NOTHING wrong with it!"

DD was now panting like an enraged bull and you could clearly see the fire in her eyes. Tony wasn't sure if it was anger and she was just going to explode, or torn feelings of rejection and she was going to just burst into tears. By the way she was beginning to shake, it looked as if she didn't know either.

"Listen I have already told you, this thing between us has got to be more than physical. I want more. I don't just want a good night, a glass of beer and some tail. Those days are over for me. I have grown as a

133

man and know this is not the way to a wife. I have prayed on this thing, long and hard and feel very strongly that this is not the path. Furthermore there isn't anything wrong with EITHER one of us. Nothing is wrong with you. I think you are fine as hell, my dream girl, everything I always imagined I wanted INSIDE and out. But what you are holding inside, you are hiding and that is who I want to be with. HER!" He said firmly, as he put his index finger in the center of her chest.

"She is who I want to lay with, wake with, eat with, fall asleep with, work for, give the world too, marry and have children with. HER! Your outer is fine but who you are hiding inside is beautiful and if you stop being so damn afraid and leaning on sex as a crutch you might find your way to her sooner than you think. And there is most certainly NOTHING wrong with me either! I like sex, WANT it, DESIRE it like any other man, there is nothing wrong with it. But it has got to be under the right circumstances, with someone I love and intend to be with, not some quickie or hit or miss even after a great date. I WANT MORE! Can't you understand that?" Tony now also had fire in his eyes.

All the fire, all the pain, all the disappointment of so many years of seeking and not finding, asking but NEVER being answered was all coming to a head, and he was being moved emotionally. He could feel his emotion about to pour over as his tear ducts began to fill and all he could think was, "I will not allow this woman to make me cry. For what? HELL NO!"

And just like that all at once the pain, hurt and disappointment was turned in for a heap of anger and fury. Now every word that went between them was angry and full of sarcasm by the very definition of the word. Ripping each other's flesh to shreds until there was nothing left between them but hard breathing, silence and hurt feelings. There they sat, the two of them still in the car in front of Tony's place, staring off into space in opposite directions, panting and fuming at each other, until DD broke the silence.

134

"Fuck this shit!" she said as she flung the car door open and began to step out.

Tony wanted to call out to her but knew he only had hard words left on his tongue so it was better he let her go. She slammed the car door shut while Tony watched her as the click clack of her high heel shoes took her further and further away from him and he could see she had made it to her car. He restarted his car and pulled it into the garage knowing that no matter how angry he was, he couldn't bear to see her go away. He pulled into the garage and just sat there, trying to pull his mind together. He was hurting and he could not let it go down like this. His pride refused to allow himself to lose in love again.

She would not just walk away from him this way. This was the setting of his resolve to not bend on any of the words he had spoken that night. They would not be in vain. He would not only be heard but respected and this would be the price he would pay to have his character clearly recognized, not just for DD but for himself as well. He walked into his place with but a glance towards where DD's parked car used to be. She was gone and so was he mentally, and emotionally. He closed the door that night on what should have been an awesome night. Yet he was in misery and once again alone. As he closed the door, it was symbolic of the closing of his mind and heart to DD and her games. He had stood his ground and she hers, now what? This was the beginning of their first "cold war." The power struggle that couples usually can't verbalize full of stubborn, selfish pride. It would be two weeks before they would even speak again.

Once they finally started speaking again DD had changed. She was a little harder and TONY could tell she was keeping things from him. He didn't know what, but he had a feeling it wasn't good. He questioned her on it repeatedly but after many denials that there wasn't anything wrong, or being kept from him, he finally resigned to leave it alone. But his gut was telling him something wasn't right. After all, having played the

135

field, and this game before she even knew it existed, something told him she was still playing. After all the sneaking around he had done, he could see her form a little more clearly now that she was hurt. And in this horrible game, it most definitely takes one to know one.

Chapter 13
Game Recognizes Game

Tony and DD had spent months taking long walks at night, working out and spending a ton of time building a trustworthy relationship with one another, all to be torn apart in that one night after the boxing match. It sounded dramatic but that is how it was feeling to him. He was questioning everything now. She felt different. She moved different and she had even begun to look different to him now. She had begun to show some of her inner beauty to him before that night but now it was like she had locked it up again. He couldn't tell if it was due to the shame she felt in the rejection and all the why's that followed for her in her mind, or if it was still her pride and anger that was forcing her hand, thereby causing her to still seek to prove she was right.

It might even be fear. Now that she had been hurt, they say once bitten twice shy. She may be trying to protect herself at this point. None of the reasons to him seemed to matter. He believed that while any of them could be reasonable, none of them were acceptable. Furthermore, he viewed them as excuses. If you are serious about wanting love and the life that they stayed up late dreaming about, then he knew they both were going to have to step beyond their fears and comfortable positions which absolutely included dropping even the HINT of pride.

So often he had been in relationships where he felt he needed to prove something; who he was, that he was right or had something better to offer than what appeared outwardly. He had finally come to a place where he was confident in the man he had become. For so long, Tony had prayed that God would walk with him and mold him into the man that he would have him to be without really understanding what or who that man was.

It was becoming more and more clear that this was the path he was on and DD would play no small part in it. This one thing he was certain. He was tired of losing relationships and never truly knowing if it was he or them, or better yet, never really understanding why. He was determined to walk through whatever challenges lay ahead to find out, because he realized that this thing he did with his love life was pretty much what he was doing with every facet of his life. He did this with his career, his family and children, all of his friends and acquaintances, and basically everyone, and everything, that passed through his life. He knew he didn't trust. This was a product of his childhood and his feelings of abandonment, not to mention abuse. He was abused, physically, mentally, emotionally and worst of all sexually, but was always determined to never let this be the excuse as to why he never did anything meaningful with his life, including making a better way for his children and family. But as certain as he was about the fact that it was their issue and the mistrust for damn near every human being on the planet, it was a huge part of his inability to maintain meaningful relationships in his life.

He was equally sure that once he got down into the bottom of that box, that there would be more. He had a sinking feeling every time he thought about it too long that there would be far more. He also knew the only way to get to it was to dig down in there and sort through the mess and all those bags. Which ones would he destroy, pick up and dust off and renew within himself for the betterment? And which ones would he simply sit down at the doorstep of which they came, filled with lies and untruths? Oh, he knew they were in there, just waiting on him as surely as they had lurked in the shadows of his life, twisting the knife deeper and deeper in the wounds of his misery. Tugging at him and his character to once again self destruct, lay waste to anything good through the path of emotional reaction and over reaction. He was sick of it all. All of the symptoms and false hope that came along with the belief that a cure was as simple as dealing with this one behavior or another.

The mirage of betterment without the fortitude of true work. Something for nothing had always been the fool's gold of content. Keep you blinded in denial just long enough to take anything in your life that could be any damn good and again he was sick and tired of it more than he was of DD and her games. He recognized that within her, laid not only him and his heart but the path to his final level of self discovery, where he learned not to run but face the devil and all his lies. In her, he found the motivation and he would drag her across the finish line if he had to. It meant that much to him. On her better days, when she was being completely honest with him and herself, and she stepped beyond her constant companion – fear - she could admit that she too wanted a life filled with honesty, love, commitment, fulfillment and God.

She had no clue as to how to get there. In fact, she had even given up on praying or talking to God, convinced that she could never be forgiven for the things that she had done. Her fears ran deep and for good reason. But to think that God couldn't forgive you was beyond Tony. He had seen some things in his life enough to doubt the goodness of man, but never God. So this was beyond him. He knew if they were to have a chance, he was going to have to slowly walk her back to his Father before she would ever hear or understand his words. But at this point she seemed further than ever - even further away than she was when they had met. She had always lived a thinly veiled existence between them where she never volunteered any information that wasn't asked for. But now she was like the CIA, "I wasn't there, so don't ask." She had become super secretive about the simplest of things. Tony was never the one to pry because he believed he understood everything he needed to know about DD. He figured he could see clearly she was shady and he needed to guard his heart because she would more than likely put it in harm's way. But he also knew that trust was a major obstacle, so he also understood he needed to put himself out there. So this meant that he would take everything she told him at face value. This meant no questions, even on things that struck him as odd or things he recognized as game. He told himself that if he wanted her to be more trustworthy he had to show her that he already trusted her and this may give her something she may want to keep. He had always operated previously, in a place where all things were questioned and trust was earned and not simply given. He didn't figure this was a mistake since he thought he had a handle on who he was getting involved with, so he accepted her words, her promises and even things he felt were lies, as the truth or partly thereof. The rest she would work on, he thought to himself.

Now more and more often she was unavailable for those late night walks and talks. She was often unavailable for the evening they shared after he was done with work and graduate classes. Things had begun to completely change and he could feel the shift in the air as a power struggle continued under the guise of a busy life that otherwise was non-existent. DD still had no job but never considered going back to school, although she only had her high school diploma, and was clearly far more intelligent than some of the graduate students he knew. He would pray on it for her day after day that she would realize that her talent and her gift was not only perishable but decaying as each day passed. This was one of the things for which he had quietly planted a seed within her thoughts, but never pushed.

This was also one of those things he was certain fell on deaf ears and only his Father would be able to move her towards in her own due time. First things first. He had to get her ear for her to see his vision of God and her life. Now with her new schedule filled with games and deception, it was going to be tougher than ever to find her amongst all the muck she had re-immersed herself in. She was spending all her free time either with her sister or her best friend Tonya. Tonya was a single girl who still enjoyed club hopping and the single lifestyle and according to DD had put their double digit years of friendship up accusing her of turning her back on her for a man. The way she explained it to Tony was like she had no choice in it if she wanted to keep her friend. So Monday through Thursday he would see her maybe once instead of the every night they had built up to and Friday. Saturdays were spent club hopping with Tonya. Now Tonya didn't like Tony from the beginning for this exact reason and she had made this no secret, nor did DD as she had relayed Tonya's ill feelings back to Tony. DD spending so much time with Tonya didn't bring Tony any comfort at all, not to mention the kind of time they were spending. Michael didn't see any reason why DD needed to be out in the club doing the single "thing" with her running buddy, if she was indeed in a committed relationship with a man she claimed to care about so much. It was a question he put to her the first night DD stepped out.

It was a Friday night and she had been MIA since he had gotten out of work that afternoon, as he entered class and again after calling once he was out that evening. He hadn't spoken to her since his lunch break at the job. He was trying to play it cool and give her the space and trust that he had promised himself he would give her but this missing in action business was starting to push him over the edge.

He KNEW without a doubt that this was her intention. Games, plain and simple. There was no other logical explanation for this type of behavior. The whole club idea was a power play; maybe to hurt him like he had hurt her in his rejection of her sexual advances. It could simply be to get him to react emotionally and suck him into her world. Once there, perhaps she would toy with him and his emotions thereby gaining the upper hand in their relationship. At a minimum, she would then know all his weaknesses; those in his personality and character, such as if he were a jealous person and how far would those behaviors move him. Would it move him to snap and curse or become a stalker? If this was in him this sort of play would bring it to the surface, especially if he were the type of dude that liked to put his hands on women.

At a minimum, this would at least let her know just how much he was invested in her; how much he cared. And again, at a minimum, it would be an ego stroke for someone who may be insecure and needs that type of thing. Tony had been around manipulative women his entire life, having been raised in a single parent home. Being the only man in a home with not only a single mother and her two sisters along with a TON of girlfriends; but add that to his three sisters, and he was like the fly on the wall in their womanly world. He would sit and hear all sorts of things whether he wanted to or not. The plotting, the games, the lies and deception. Oh yes, he had a front row seat from day one. So outside of his desire to do something different and trust someone who didn't appear trustworthy for his own personal growth, his pride refused to allow himself to be played. He would not get sucked into her games. This was going to be difficult because if he ignored it, then it could be perceived as participation in the game because this is the move if you are to flip the game. If you show TOO much concern then you are back to square one and whether it's true or not the belief is, YOU'VE BEEN PLAYED.

So he decided upon the fourth back-to-back call, as he could feel his temperature rising, that he would have to play it completely straight, go against the grain and hit her where she would never expect it, then leave it completely alone. One last call and this time he would leave a message and that would be it for the night.

"Hello," a voice spoke, as DD finally answered the phone after about the fourth ring.

"Hey, what's going on? Why haven't I been able to reach you?" Tony asked calmly.

"I have been running all day. I'm so aggravated right now. This is the first time I noticed that you have called. I'm sorry," DD said, trying her best to sound sincere.

Tony recognized immediately with the obvious effort she was feigning, that the games had indeed begun in this conversation. So he cut to her quick.

"Well I have been trying to reach you all day. But I'm sure if you looked at your phone you already know this. Although I am upset by this I didn't call to argue but to simply say this. I have no idea why you need to be in that place when you already have a man in your life. I want you to know that I love you and want to be with you in a committed relationship. This is what I thought we had? But your behavior says otherwise when you are out in the club with your single friends, especially ones you know don't like me. I can only imagine what she may be encouraging you to do," Tony said, again calmly.

"She can't encourage me to do anything. I'm a grown ass woman!" DD shot back.

"Well I don't know DD. She encouraged you to put our relationship in jeopardy by getting you to come out to the club tonight like you're single as she is?" Tony shot back.

The phone went silent. Tony had made it clear that this was no game to him.

"If what you say is true about how you feel about me and what you want with me, I would think a club would be the last place you would want to be. But if this is what you think you have to do I will not argue, fight or chase you. I am entirely too grown for that. When you are ready, I will be here. But while you are out with your girl, I want you to look at her and ask yourself if you would trade places and want her life. I'll be home and we can talk when you're ready," Tony said, and then fell silent waiting to hear DD's response.

At first DD, too, was silent with nothing to say. He could tell he had given her food for thought since she seemed like she did not expect this reaction. After a moment she finally spoke.

"Tony you know I think you're right and I don't want to trade places with her. I hate it here and wish I had never come. But Tonya's brother died not too long

143

ago and I feel like I abandoned her at a time she needed me the most. She has always been there for me and I feel I should be here for her at her time of need."

"But how far does this go? If she is truly your friend she wouldn't want to come between a relationship she knows means so much to you. And is the club really a place to show support? Even if it's against everything your life is supposed to be about at this point? We aren't twenty something kids any longer and you need to make some better choices otherwise you could very well end up where she is," Tony said, sounding like he was done with the conversation.

"Yes, I think you're right. I apologize for you not being able to reach me earlier today and I promise that won't happen again. I am going to take some time to think about what you said and call you once we get out of here," DD said, again sounding like she was ready for round two of her games.

"Okay," Tony said, sounding puzzled. Thinking to himself, "Thinking, in a club? Yeah right?"

But he was done with the conversation so he kept that final thought to himself. He was determined to push through this and get her and all of this foolishness off of his mind. So with Angel with his mother, he stepped out into the cool night air to begin his jog. He would come back that night for his lifting routine with DD and her games heavily on his mind. This type of thing went on for weeks with DD being MIA and Tony doing his able best to stay focused on his school work and job. He was graduating from Graduate school in two weeks and still uncertain if he was going to the graduation ceremony. With all that was going on in his life he was feeling a bit overwhelmed and couldn't press himself to make such a decision with so much on his mind. He eventually decided that it was too much to add to his plate and passed on walking the stage. Instead he bought himself a very nice frame for his Masters Degree in Education certificate. He was very happy and proud of his accomplishment on the one hand, but on the other, he was afraid to celebrate it because he knew he was in the middle of his law degree. He needed to stay focused and he felt with Angel, his full time job and the drama of DD, if he let up for one moment his dream of law school would slip through his fingers.

After a few more conversations like the one they had at the club, Tony was completely frustrated with the situation and having only seen DD maybe three times in the last month decided that maybe he needed to consider if he had been too rigid in his choice or how he communicated it to her. So he reconsidered his approach to things, maybe he was too harsh in his treatment of her and that type rejection was too much? After all, every relationship is supposed to be about give and take, and some measure of sacrifice. He was not prepared to make the ultimate sacrifice, but maybe he could have dealt with it better.

Somewhere in his mind, her whorish behavior had offended him in a deep personal way that he was starting to realize was mostly due to how much of himself he saw in her and her actions. Was it fair to have judged her so harshly having been in that same position not that long ago having narrowly escaped himself? He had enough doubt to question himself and reconsider DD's position. So he threw up the white flag and decided to call DD and ask her to change her plans to be at her sister's house tonight and come and meet with him so they could talk and straighten some things out. There was a huge "Pink Elephant" in the room and he no longer wanted to pretend as if it wasn't there.

She agreed to meet with him that night and they hung up both nervous and a bit excited to see each other. The truth was they both wanted to see each other more than either one of them would admit to each other. Sadly this emotion would not be the ruling factor that brought these two together. No, each arrived with not only the fondness that comes with absence but also an agenda to push. Each of them was right but because they had gone about it in a wrong way, neither of their points really mattered more than the fact that a relationship that was born out of an intimacy neither one of them had come

145

across in a very long time, was beginning to fade away. By this time DD had gotten a job doing phone sales for a company that sold a little bit of this and a little bit of that and a lot of nothing all at once. She had managed to obtain an old Buick that was about as long as the old Cadillac and got about the same miles per gallon. It was a serious POS but she was proud that she had been able to afford it on her own although it only cost her 500 bucks. Never minding the fact that looking at it you could never guess where or why it was ever worth that kind of money.

From this position, DD, who had been pretty much unemployed since the time she had met Tony, felt pretty confident in herself as a mate. In fact, she showed up with the attitude, speech and body language of someone who felt she was above all of the pettiness she felt from Tony and their relationship, or lack thereof. DD had given Tony his Mercedes Benz not long after their last night out had gone so badly. She returned it out of fear, as she didn't want to owe him anything. The truth was she couldn't bear to keep something so luxurious and wonderful knowing full well she not only hadn't committed to Tony but her treatment of him didn't match this level of a gift. She deemed herself unworthy and pushed it away from her as she did him at that time.

In her mind she was beating him to the punch by giving it back before he got fed up with her crap and took it back from her. This would not only have hurt but been completely humiliating and she was not about to give Tony that sort of power over her. The Saturn she had been driving belonged to her step-mother and now that she had her own car, she was even more free to be out and about. She had just received her second check from her new job, and with steady income added to the mix, you couldn't tell this big headed woman she wasn't an independent lady.

She had completely been in denial of the fact that she was still living in her father's house in one room with her now six year old daughter, sleeping in the same bed for two years now out of necessity. No, tonight she was clearly projecting an air to Tony that said she did not need him or anything that he had to offer. This was her way of entering the conversation with the emotional upper hand, with the idea, "I can't lose what I don't put on the table."

Tony saw this as sure as he could see the nose on his face. He knew, based on DD's tone when he had called her to meet, that there would be some attitude to overcome. He was prepared for it in no small way. He too was upset about the way things had been going. But the moment he saw her, he could see her vulnerability and all the direct, maybe even cold words he had gathered for the occasion just fell from his head. All he could do was to sit there and stare at her. She had changed her hair color and style. It was not to his liking at all. It sent the same message of availability that the rest of her attire sent. One that said, "I am not to be taken seriously. I'm still playing and if you want to play, holla." His heart was sinking the more he thought about it because he knew that her pride was not the only thing preventing them from continuing on with their budding relationship. He asked her to speak first and address her concerns with him so he could recover his mind from all the hurt emotions he was feeling having seen what he least wanted and most feared.

As she spoke many words were coming from her mouth but she was saying a whole lot of nothing. Every word, every movement, every gesture and facial expression was full of pride and a cavalier attitude that she no longer gave a damn and "it was whatever" as far as she was concerned. The more she spoke, the more her words just floated on out the car window they sat in to talk and Tony heard nothing. Her body language and tone was doing all the talking, no matter what her words were saying and he was getting the message loud and clear. He was glad he had allowed her to speak first because with each passing minute he was coming to a good understanding that his words would have fallen onto deaf ears. By all appearances DD was no longer interested in coming to a resolution. Actually, if Tony had to guess he would have said that she had the feeling that she had already moved her heart. He was beginning to feel as if all this time she had been spending apart from him she must have been spending with another. So he packed away all those words he prepared. He also packed away all those emotions he had built up over the time they were apart as well as that fondness they always attribute to absence and prepared himself for what he assumed would come next.

He was waiting to hear in some form of words from DD that it was over. As he waited and waited, his eyes faded beyond the car they sat in and he wondered if there ever was anything he could have done to prevent this. At some point, DD realized that Tony was no longer in the car but his mind was a million miles away. So she stopped talking and asked him to speak.

"I really don't know what to say. I didn't realize things had gone this far. It feels as if you're saying this relationship is over and if that is the case I can only respect that decision. I wanted something more for us but it seems like that wasn't meant to happen. A secret part of me, one I have never really dared to tell you of had always looked at you as the dream girl I had always imagined as a kid growing up; one I would want to be with forever. I spent a lot of years in my young life dreaming about and putting together in my mind what she would be. And despite all your flaws, hang ups and growing to do I have, since the day we met, felt that she was you. You see I know I may have it together today but I wasn't always this way. And I too, come from a sorted past; one where I imagine I have made many mistakes similar to the path you are on now. I can't tell you that I know everything but there are some things I do know and it is those things that said to me that you aren't as unlovable as you might think. I know my spurning your advances felt like rejection but I promise you, it wasn't ever that. I want you, but not this person you pretend to be. The one who showed up here to meet with me tonight, filled with the bitter attitude that tells her she had to put on in order to be loved. Somewhere inside her head she thinks the only way to please a man and keep him is if she pleases him physically. I don't want to sleep with that woman because I no longer desire to have sex. I have heard you use a term far more vulgar, one I have used plenty of times prior to now but today, right now, from where I am, where I feel my journey has brought me, I can no longer do that or move in that way. I have fallen in love with the woman who wrote me those sweet words when we met. The same woman who opens up to me to tell me the deepest darkest part of herself with the freedom of heart and mind that allows me to love her where she is. No airs, no attitude or extra effort to be liked or funny. Just you. She is who I look forward to see, kiss and love each time I call your name. But the closer we get on an intimate level, I can feel your uncomfortable spirit at times when your brain moves in fear of losing something so special and you go into this automatic pilot place. You become this person I not only don't know but honestly don't even like. She is forward and crass with the mouth of a woman without virtue. In my heart I have always wept for her and prayed that one day you will put her away and go with me because you no longer need her. I will love you, no matter if you don't like your body. I will love you, even if you don't think you can be funny tonight. And I will love you when I am finally able to look you face to face in a real place and see all your scars and imperfections. Because believe it or not, that attitude you put on like armor to keep me out is a greater tell than any I have ever seen. Again I don't say these things boastful as if I'm some know-it-all, but I can only tell you this that I see having been where you are today. If you would just allow me to show you where love lies, I think you will find my love is easy. I can love you through these rough times you know are coming because you know who you are and have been. I know I can, not because I'm so great but because that love I spoke of comes from another place deeper than even I can call up. And I know the way if you just allow me to take you

149

there. As I said I don't know everything but there are some things I do know and THIS I KNOW. People can teach you two things, what to do and what not to do. Let me love you and I don't believe you will ever regret it."

Tony closed his mouth and looked away as he caught the last of his fallen tears. He had tried to fight them off but those words he had spoken came from this deep place that not even he was prepared for. He wasn't ready for her to leave, not now, maybe not ever. He knew he had no control over that but what he did have control over was whether or not she left without knowing his whole heart and where it lie. When he was finally able to bring himself to look at DD she too was in tears. He couldn't believe that his words could touch her heart this way. There was some deep part of DD that had longed to hear those words her entire life. Someone who would accept her unconditionally and this was the closest thing to that anyone had EVER said to her. The "cool as a fan" act she was carrying fell to the wayside with the quickness, and as she opened her mouth to speak and with her face drawn, yet again tightly, she began to cry.

She pounded her fist on the dash, "Damn it! I can't believe I'm doing this shit! No one has ever seen me cry."

As those words left her mouth it was like a flood gate was opened from a place that she had indeed been holding down for probably more years than she cared to count. Endless heartbreaks and countless misfortunes all ending with the same cool and collected caricature that showed up here to meet him tonight.

Tony reached across the car and pulled DD into his chest.

"It's ok baby, put it down. Put it all down. I'm here now DD and won't let you fall with it."

With that came another wave of hot and emotional tears that came from a place mixed with just as much desire and passion as fear and rage and just as confused. Tony was all but too familiar with this place having been there at a time when he could not stop the

150

love of his life from walking away. Too cool to stop her and too angry at himself and his history to do anything else but play the fool up to the bitter end. Today he made a different choice and hopefully helped DD not only see the wisdom in it but the love he held and spoke of too. Like he had said, he didn't know everything but out of all the things he hadn't figured out yet, he absolutely knew what NOT to do. So tonight as he dove all into a place he felt the Father God himself asked for him to go, he did not go half hearted. He jumped in with both feet as he opened his mouth and this is the love inside of him that came pouring out. And it was good.

Chapter 14
The Point Of It All

Weeks had passed since that late night DD and Tony had met that night in her car outside of his place. Tony had laid it all on the line that night and it really appeared to pay off. It almost instantly brought them back to a place of far more honesty than they had been sharing since the night of the fight. It's almost crazy to think that something so hard could have been born of something so seemingly good. But Tony had finally figured out some things about DD; one of the primary things he figured out was that there was something deep within her wounded heart and mind that just didn't believe she deserved to be happy, nor did she deserve a man as kind and loving as Tony was. Furthermore, he also believed that this intense subconscious belief was similar to many of her emotions, confused with this deep desire for it, followed by the fear of accepting anything so wonderful she was afraid to lose it. All of these factors made it simple to understand some of her odd behaviors and why she tried so hard, unwittingly, to push him away at times she should be seeking to get closer.

In the beginning, he was at a loss as to what he should do. She didn't know how to stop the pain, or the bleeding, as she had obviously been hemorrhaging her own love for years before she ever met him. If she knew how to stop it, she undoubtedly would have done so by now. So he knew that this road meant to their bitter end. He had prayed for so long that he would come to understand God's word in the land of the living and not just the supernatural.

Throughout his life, he had been tested regarding his character and work, and many other things he had been able to overcome, at one time or another.

But the thing that had avoided his understanding for his entire young life had been his ability to discern God's law and understanding further into his love life. He was beginning to see God's vision for man and his role as leader and priest of the home. He could see that this was his responsibility to lead them out of this dark place. And only his submission to God and his word would bring him to this seat of power in their relationship.

DD was a hard-headed individual to say the least, not unlike how he was during his days of youth and ignorance. Therefore, he understood full well that someone who had been led, in most of her intimate relationships, down the wrong path, would not simply allow herself to be taken once again, no matter how good the presentation. She would need time to, not only know his heart, but see it in full and living color, as it breathed and moved things in his and their life.

None of these things would come easy, as all of them, on various levels, made DD very uncomfortable; although, she did desire them. While they had poured their hearts out that night following the tearful moment they shared and come to a place of better understanding, things still weren't ideal. They had agreed not to give up on one another and they had promised to stay and fight for a love they both believed in. But Tony knew what this meant, more so than he even pretended to know what she meant since DD still hadn't made any real move to even appear committed to their relationship.

While she stopped spending as much time away from their relationship, and he did get more of her time and attention back, she still hadn't committed to seeing him everyday as they once had. She was still spending a ton of time between Tonya, her sister and some other friends that she talked about, of whom she never spoke their names. Each time it was someone else and they were doing something else.

She was a master with word play, with an advanced degree in being vague. He didn't sweat it, just pressed on and took her at her word. He began to spend more and more time with her when she was available.

This came at all hours of the night which disrupted his tight schedule. But Tony viewed this as the sacrifice that needed to be made in order to build something better. He was slowly but surely disrupting his graduate school studies and was beginning to fall behind in the writing assignments. He would have to make a push this weekend if he was going to catch up.

All the rearranging of his work, life and school assignments was finally starting to catch up with him. He was starting to bring that wall down from between DD and himself so he was confident that things would eventually get better and he would once again be able to get back to his academic pursuits without the worry of DD running the streets to curb her lonely heart. This was already a constant distraction, since he had met her at the tail end of his Masters degree. It was the thing that made him hesitate on jumping straight into his doctoral studies but he was confident that he would get there.

When she finally arrived today he would tell her his plans for the weekend and hoped she didn't take it too hard, or the wrong way. This came at a bad time since her girlfriend was going to be out of town this weekend in Atlanta with her new boyfriend. She would surely be aggravated that he suddenly got busy after agreeing to spend more time. Ordinarily this should be no problem since graduate school should have been a priority. However, Tony knew that DD lived in a world filled with games where everything was coded and meant something. He was certain she would see it as a brush off, especially since the entire reason she gave for her spending so much time with her friends was that he was "too busy." She had actually used the quotation marks as if she had not gone with him to one of his classes and really didn't know he was in school.

Between finishing his Master's degree and working on completing law school, she said she didn't feel like he had time for her and didn't want to make any. She said she felt like a convenience to him and unimportant. It was not the sort of thing he ever expected to hear from a woman who was serious about him as he thought that law school would have been a priority to her as well because after all if they were headed down the same road in life together, his life improving meant hers did too. But DD lived in this world of upside down sort of thinking where nothing made much sense to anyone outside of herself. The frightening thing was that when Tony went deep into himself, he got it.

It was still majorly twisted and his acknowledgment of it didn't make it right but he had to admit, he got it. It made it hard to just move forward and do what he thought was right because he empathized with her greatly again seeing so much of himself in her. This weekend however he was going to have to do what he needed to do, come hell or high water. He could not afford to do poorly this coming week at all. This meant he needed to be prepared. He had already dropped the ball in class once before. It seemed to go unnoticed; but in a world filled with the most critical people, he highly doubted it meant as little as it was spoken of.

When DD finally did call that night she said she had something that she needed to talk to him about. It sounded pretty important, so he decided that what he had to say could wait. They agreed to meet for their nightly exercise, a three to six mile walk around Tony's neighborhood. DD arrived late and Tony was a bit agitated since time was beginning to become a serious concern considering the situation he was now facing with thoughts of this weekend, and more importantly next week, looming. But he held that down since DD looked even more stressed than he did.

"What's wrong boo?" Tony asked.

DD barely looked up at him as her gaze continued off into space. She walked over and kissed him on the lips without saying so much as a word.

"You look real heavy. What's going on with you that is making you look so stressed?" Tony asked again trying to get DD to open up.

She just let out a sigh and shook her head. Still looking stressed as if she were trying to muster up the strength to talk about a thought she had no solution to.

"I don't even know where to begin. First off I wanted to say I'm sorry because I know I put myself in this situation. And not communicating about it has only made it worse," DD started to say.

Tony's stomach did a little turn not knowing what DD was about to drop on him. A little dark space in the back of his mind was expecting the worse and his heart began to race. He took a silent, deep breath trying to control his breathing and slow his heart rate so he would not appear rattled by the start of the conversation. After all she hadn't said a word, why was he already panicking?

DD continued, "Well I lost my job almost two weeks ago now and I was embarrassed to say anything to you. I have been letting you think I was still going to work thinking I would have gotten another job by now. I planned on telling you only after I got another income. But that hasn't worked out yet and I honestly don't know when it will so I figured I had better come clean with you."

DD paused and most of the tension in Tony's body fell away. He thought to himself, "Losing your job I can do. Nothing we can't handle."

Then DD began to speak again.

"Well you know how I have been spending all this extra time with Tonya? Well her man is a musician who works with India Arie and they think that some of my poems would make good song lyrics. Tonya is going to Atlanta this weekend to visit with him and they suggested I go along and pitch it to India herself. What do you think? It may be a good opportunity for me as far as money and me having no job right now. But more than that, it is a chance to get my poetry out there to the world. What do you think?" DD asked, as she stood there looking nervous and waiting.

All of what she said hit Tony square between the eyes as all of this was so sudden. The bad news about her losing her job, the horrible news that she was lying to him about something so big, combined with such great news that she may have this huge opportunity. He didn't know exactly how to feel. He was silent for a moment thinking it over. He didn't want to crush her dreams by coming down on her for not telling him about her job situation because it may end up overshadowing what should be the point of the conversation which was this great opportunity. After a moment, he decided it wasn't such a big deal for her to go since he had so much to do this weekend anyway. This put him in the perfect position to get what he needed to get done without having to be the bad guy.

This also opened a door for her and this whole music thing. It was a win-win. The one exception, however, was that she was still lying to him and this again showed him by her actions that there was yet another reason why she shouldn't be trusted. He had to make a decision, what was more important. He decided not to make a huge deal about the lying and accept her reasoning.

"I think it is a great opportunity if it works out for you. I don't really like you going back to Atlanta so much. I know it's your old stomping grounds and I am concerned with what you might get into. But if you say it's about work, then I am going to trust you. I am, however, disappointed with your decision to lie to me about your job situation. It makes me wonder if you are lying about something like this, something I was obviously going to find out about sooner or later, what else are you lying about? How did you lose your job anyway?" Tony asked.

"They are on some bullshit up there and I just got tired of it one day and snapped on my supervisor. After that, he had it out for me and it wasn't long before they found a bullshit ass reason to fire me," DD said, as she stared at the ground looking embarrassed by the whole thing.

"That's jacked up. You couldn't have taken your concerns to your boss's boss?" Tony asked.

"Nah by the time I even saw how it was going down, it was too late." DD said. Then she changed the subject like she was again embarrassed by the conversation and wanted to move away from it.

"Listen I know I have not always been straight with you and have made some bad decisions and I'm sorry for that. I am working on it and know going to have to do better. But this is square business as far as this music thing goes. I won't have any free time to be doing any hanging out, let alone finding my way back to my old stomping grounds. Besides there isn't anyone I would want to see from that time in my life. Those days are gone. You are my future now and this is where I want to be," she said, looking him directly in his eye.

Her eye contact made Tony feel comfortable about trusting in her words. He needed that because if he had to go by her actions, he would never trust her to go to the corner store much less to Atlanta. She was still maintaining male "friends" who she continued to receive calls from at all hours. Tony hadn't made it a fighting point since he, too, had female friends who he would not let go if she asked him to. So he was just going to have to eat that until he was ready to take the next step.

Although things weren't ideal by any means, they had been making decent progress with their intimacy as far as being open and sharing about their past, their fears, challenges and dreams. All the things one hang a dream upon. But as far as DD's present situations, she was still tight lipped, requiring a rigorous Q and A to get any information out of her. She never gave up any information he didn't already know about, so there was never any questions. Mostly it was just a feeling about all the things she wasn't saying. All the things she wasn't doing and things that left huge holes in what she said versus what she did or didn't do.

He had some major doubts about this trip and who she was going with but what could he really say? His only choice was to allow it to go down or put his foot down, which would only result in what he thought would be another break up conversation. But he knew even that wouldn't stop her from going. Doing that would free her up completely to do whatever she wanted; free from any guilt she may carry knowing she was still in a relationship with him. Reluctantly he let it go and spent the rest of their workout time talking positively about this opportunity.

Friday morning DD and Tonya were headed to the airport when Tony got the two-minute phone call that she was indeed on her way out of town. They exchanged pleasant words and all the "be carefuls" those that love one another do when they leave each another's presence. This entire thing was sitting on Tony's chest and he was wrestling once again with this idea of playing dumb about something he felt like he knew and had a front row seat to so many times in his life.

He knew full well that her inability to be transparent with him concerning anything was a much larger issue than he was willing to deal with. He was hammering himself as to why. Why did he need to go through this? Why was he risking his heart this way? If he was going to be in a relationship this way, why didn't he just stay with his ex? At least he KNEW she loved him for as messed up as she was. And with her, came their child and potential family unit. They say it's better to stay with the evil you know sometimes. All of this was running through his head a million miles a minute on his morning commute to work.

Tony had a deep desire to go for his Doctorate in Education that he put off in pursuit of this relationship. He was feeling cheated by life to have to put off this dream of his in order to have what he thought was a larger one. One that meant more to him. But it was looking more and more like he was the only one with this dream. This was the first time he considered putting himself first and what he felt he needed and not just his desires and those of the ones he loved since he began his relationship with DD.

DD had gone through great lengths talking about how committed and loyal she had been to all the men in her life before him. At the time, he thought it was kind of odd to say things like that about yourself; almost like she was bragging about herself. He was a humble person who always felt you didn't have to brag about yourself. If you were the man you said you were then others would do it for you. But within the context she had brought the conversation up, he understood it and didn't think much of it. She had told him how her loyalty had left her vulnerable to others to take advantage of her and that those she loved had done so time and again.

It sounded not unlike some of the bad relationships he had been in throughout his life, so none of it really sounded out of place. It just felt wrong. He couldn't put his finger on it, but it did. It was almost as if she was trying too hard, like she was trying to convince him of something. He couldn't see that far then but he was absolutely seeing it now. She didn't seem to have a sliver of loyalty to him on any accord. And while he didn't like it at all, it made it easy to do the same with her.

In the past, this was ideal because he would at that time be out in the streets doing the exact same things to her as he imagined she was to him. The difference being he knew positively what he was doing and to what end. He would never be certain about her, mostly because he didn't want to know. He turned that blind eye to it, with her, as he was doing now. The problem with that old thinking was that it only left him with old options and since he wasn't living that life any longer he was greatly dissatisfied with the outcome.

He had no inappropriate friendships. He had no secrets to keep and he had nothing in or around his life he didn't want to invite her to be a part of completely. He knew she would dive right in which she had each time he offered it to her. This, however, was never any influence as to what she was willing to, or shared with him. She was just as vague and closed which only left him feeling foolish and ultimately resentful. He had stopped opening up so much, not because he didn't want to, but because he knew she wasn't ready and it was leaving him with something on his heart he didn't want to carry.

This was what worked for him at the moment. Until he figured something else out, this was how he would handle it. This never quelled the HUGE elephant in the room. For the most part DD was a breath of fresh air in his life. In his last relationship, he didn't feel wanted or desired, but with DD he felt completely wanted and desired. Even her sexual advances, as they came from time to time, made him feel desired. Although he wasn't ready to take it there yet, he felt that there would be a great deal of passion there once they opened that door.

For the most part, she made him feel like she listened to the things he said and considered important all the things he did. They talked for hours and both loved reading and writing. They were more friends than lovers since that part of it had yet to be explored. They shared their enthusiasm for sports and love of the arts although they did possess a split in musical tastes. She tolerated his music while she actually liked some jazz. Once he really introduced her to it she actually liked it more than she thought she could and even that became the source of countless hours of great conversation.

She was more intelligent than most people he came across day to day, which was really saying something considering he was an educator working with young minds. We always want to believe that great minds are at work molding our next generation but sadly this is seldom the case. She was a ray of light in his life in that way, especially since he had moved to the south. She was hardly ever at a loss for words and had an opinion on just about anything, which also provided hours of entertainment at a minimum. She had big dreams and grand ideas about her life and the vision she had for herself and the world she intended to live in. This was the thing that enthralled him, because he believed that he needed to be with someone who was not only a dreamer and risk taker but someone with faith who could see beyond what was before their eyes.

161

He, too, was a huge dreamer and even bigger on faith and walked into his dreams completely on faith. Only he didn't view it as taking risk, he had at a very young age witnessed the goodness of the Lord in the land of the living as he was moved from harm's way into the loving arms of God's grace more than once in his young life. He had, with the help of God, and this vision he had of himself, along with all those grand dreams, managed to work his way out of the housing projects in Brooklyn. On welfare, and with nothing but his ability to think and willingness to work, pulled himself out of a horrible situation into a now middle class lifestyle complete with multiple cars and living in the suburbs. He possessed an education that no one believed he was capable of and told him so as often as he ever dared to utter his dreams around them. He knew firsthand what kind of effect negative people around you could have. Having those you love, not be able to see your vision is frustrating; but to have them not believe in, or back you can be devastating.

His ex was a dream killer. She called herself a realist. But in his mind, too much reality is only something someone told you that you couldn't do and you ended up believing them. So this is where you obtained this reality. He never allowed anyone, or anything, to define him so to be around someone who believed in him and his ability was refreshing and felt awesome.

Other than the obvious trust issues and what appeared to be some hang ups about sex, she and he made a pretty good fit. Feeling he was in no real position to call anyone on their trust issues, as this had been his major issue his entire life, as well as knowing he had his own hang ups about sex due to his past, he just dealt with things as they were. He would work on himself and hopefully she would work on herself, and they would find their way together. It was a wonderful concept and when it worked, it felt like the best relationship he had ever been in, barring NONE. This is why through the frustration, through the pain and all the mistrust issues,

162

he stayed. Besides the fact that he viewed this relationship as a necessity to his own personal growth, he valued all that DD was while appreciating what she wasn't, as this gave him time to correct all those years of bad habits and denial he too, lived in.

If she had arrived at his door already adjusted and ready to have this life they both dreamed of, he knew in his heart of hearts that she would have been the one in his position, waiting on him while he was messing it all up. He viewed his position as one of a seat of power as well as blessed and filled with anointing. He felt it was one filled with power because as he was a lifelong learner and educator, he knew knowledge was power. And in this circumstance, what you don't know could kill all the love in you and all the love around you. He had never looked at the mistakes he had made and horrible history he survived through as an asset at any time in his life. But he was beginning to realize that all these things had brought him to an understanding about life and most importantly, about himself. It was because of this, he absolutely knew, without question, who he was, what he stood for and could answer honestly, if he was indeed doing all that he could to be the man that he said he was.

There was very little about himself that was lost on him. Therefore he could see all of the turns, where they may be headed, or how to avoid pitfalls having been there before. Also, he could see the value in the lesson this position and relationship provided. He could readily see how much he was going to learn, if done right, within the will of God. THIS would be the experience he prayed for daily - to finally be the man God would have him to be. The father, the husband, the brother, the son. The man he had left Brooklyn at age seventeen searching for. He never found it in those streets or broken home and family. He only found pieces in the Army and his travels around the world. And with each relationship, he lost almost as much as he gained. That, in itself, could never build the man he desired to be.

163

But this walk he had begun, as he waited on the Lord each day, with all the prayer, meditation, bible studying and his commitment to the church was the one thing in his life that was pure and incorruptible. So when he had questions, he leaned on the Word, and the Lord, in prayer. He came equipped with a ton of faith but he had always lacked the work in seeking out God's face.

Each day as he sought his kingdom in Christ, he could see revealed to him, more often than not, a man that looked a lot like him. He was awakening the God within himself and it was not lost to those around him. This gave him the feeling of not only confidence but POWER; the power that comes with the certainty of knowing who you are and your vision of your destiny. And this relationship was the missing piece to that puzzle. He could feel it in everything that he did and every part of his life it touched.

This is why he felt strongly that it was anointed by God himself. Each time he wanted to walk away, each time it hurt, he was able to find yet another measure of grace within him that he didn't know he had. He had a wisdom that was seemingly beyond his years, since at this point, he was out of his depth in this relationship. He would have run out of this union long ago in his former years and went and found someone who was a bit more put together, never minding the fact that he wasn't.

Continuing to hide from himself and his fears and never dealing with all he needed to in order to have an authentic life. He knew it was time to let those things go and man up, grow up and deal with all the things that prevented him from having the life he knew he wanted in his heart. He could hear God's voice in his own and feel His pleasure in the choices he made and knew absolutely through His word that he was doing His will; living it through his life.

He felt he was blessed because so many times in his life he was the victim of bad timing. More often than not, he was more a part of all the things that were wrong between him and the person he was in a relationship with than any part of the solution. From this vantage point, God had given him someone who needed him so he could become part of a solution. Someone who through all her flaws and mistakes she would make, he could understand and empathize with. God had given him someone he could still love after she hurt him, which meant through the rain he would still be standing, holding heaves of mercy and grace bestowed upon him through all the work he had done within himself with and through the Lord's help.

After all his journeys and the things he had managed to do in his life, it had all come back to this one true place. This was the purest thing in his life - his faith in God. Within God's approval, he could see and, more importantly, feel his life changing and had no doubt he was on the right path. Sure there was plenty left to be done but he felt assured that if he remained faithful to God, he would not be led astray. In this, he felt the authority and responsibility, for the first time in his life, that came with the idea of taking a wife, and having a family. That is what this was for him - a blessing.

The word says that he who would find a wife, finds a good thing. He felt blessed to be able to find this good thing while building their kingdom in God at a time that presented the least amount of risk of really jacking this thing up. This was indeed the point of it all.

Chapter 15
Broken Wings

It was two a.m. on Sunday morning and Tony could not sleep. He is out on his workout walk having left Sharon at home with little Angel. She had been spending a great deal of time in his home, as Tony had been spending so much time with DD. She is around more than when she was living there. They have been getting along so much better than they ever had. No arguments or harsh words, yet still they seem a little better than cool.

Sharon is watching as DD rips Tony's tender heart to shreds with her games and lies and remembers back to a time when she, too, had done the same. She wished she could do more for him. She wished she could take back all the heartache and pain she caused; give him the love she stole from his life, and heart back. But this was impossible. You cannot un-ring that bell once it's been sounded. The least she could do was try to bring his life some peace as far as his son and the worries of a single father. She was becoming a good mother and the more time she spent at home with their son, the greater Angel blossomed.

A child needs both parents in its life to flourish and it goes both ways. Tony always knew this though it took a minute for Sharon to figure out. She made so many mistakes that she had started to believe that Angel might be better off without her around to screw up his life as she had always done hers. For now she was grateful for the progress and the opportunity to have her family back intact again but if only for the brief moments.

She knew it was a farfetched fantasy, but in her heart of hearts she prayed that through Tony's journey he and his heart might swing her way again. So every chance she was given, she tried to show him the love she only wished she had shown him when she had his attention. All those nights she had left him alone and wondering, she agonized over again and again. She had stopped beating herself up over them but the memories were hard to fade.

Tony was a good, strong man and she knew it now more than ever. He had always been a provider with a gentle soul and a kind and generous heart. He was also a hopeless romantic who was spontaneous, which added so much to life. She realized now just how much she had taken him for granted once she got out into the single world. My Lord, the 80-20 did apply. She knew she had lost a good thing. But now that Tony had gotten so much more serious about his walk with God, she could literally see the light around him. He spoke differently, moved differently and even looked more attractive. You could see the God all over him.

It softened her heart and made her want to be a better person too - a better mom for Angel and better woman for herself and God. She, too, had found her way back to church after all this time. Tony had invited her to church with him and Angel so many times and she never made the time. Another in the long line of regrets she now had to live with. She just never truly believed he would go. Now she was at home in that same rocker singing to her son as he lay in bed asleep as she dreamed of what days may come.

Tony and his thoughts were far removed from the look backward that seeing Sharon that way would require. At the moment, his mind was consumed with DD and why he hadn't heard from her since she reached Atlanta. She didn't even call him when she landed to say she arrived safely. She was supposed to be staying with family once she arrived to town but he didn't have any contact information and she was not answering her cell phone. She was supposed to meet with those music people today and pitch her stuff, but he was starting to feel like this was just another one of her lies. As he walked around the neighborhood taking in the early morning air, he had thought about all the holes in her story.

Her poetry never sounded like a song to him. Most of it was filled with sexual thoughts and words. He found it vulgar. It fit who she was at the time. She had softened since then and they didn't quite fit any longer. They had spoken about her work many times and had pretty much decided that she, too, didn't want those words to represent her to the world. He hadn't read anything new from her in awhile so what was she presenting? Had she changed her mind about how she felt about those poems? Or was she simply placating him to keep the peace and never felt the same way? Lies! All lies! There were so many lies and the worst part about it all was that he had sold himself this bill of goods so she never had to. It was like he was doing the work for her that she would have otherwise needed to do in order to blind him this way. This unwavering faith and trust, he knew it did not lie in her. But his trust lay in a belief that God would not lead him somewhere that he did not have a plan for him or his heart. He could not see it from where he sat today.

Was God protecting his heart? Then why was he hurting so awfully right now? He was back to neglecting his work in a constant battle between following his heart and his head. All of this only added to the feeling of being foolish, WILLINGLY FOOLISH. He knew that God protected children and fools. In his mind, it had always meant those that were ignorant and had no clue. This was not him so was he still covered in His grace, or His mercy? Oh how he needed it right now to bring him from this place. He wanted to beg God to release him from this hell but he had promised to follow Him. No matter where it looked like it was going, he would follow Him. It was so difficult to walk in the spiritual all the while seeing the worldly. But he believed in the core of his being that THIS was the path God asked him to walk.

He had so many questions of love and very little answers. If he never stayed through the though times, he would never know that "until death do us part" he had sought his entire adult life.

"Love is patient. Love is also kind. It is not filled with judgment, for that is not my job," he thought to himself.

He scoured the Bible for the answer, looking for the romance of and in his heart. There was very little talk of romance that he could find so he held onto those parts and ran them through his mind over and over again. It was odd. He did find the word love a lot. It just didn't fit into what he had always been taught about love or romance.

"Love is patient. Love is patient. This is all for you Lord. I will not turn away from your will," He said in a silent prayer. "I will wait on you. I pray you protect my heart. Amen."

He opened his eyes and he could feel the emotions coming over him as his eyes clouded with the familiar warmth of tears that had often fallen during this journey. He could not remember a single time in his life he had cried so much. He did not cry for DD. He did not cry for his dream deferred. He did not even cry for what felt like a broken heart. Those tears he shed were filled with love for God; a love he had never felt before. Each time he thought about it, it touched him in a way he had never been touched before. He could feel God's love in him so full. As he cried feeling forsaken, it filled him.

The more those lies tried to fill his head, he could feel the heat, the joy, the love. It was overwhelming. He had to stop and sit down for a moment on the bench by the bus stop just outside his community. He could feel God's hands reaching down from the heavens and embracing him and filling him with all the love he would ever need. This love he longed for was not from any mere woman. He could see that now.

His mother, who left him long ago, and his father who had left him even before that, had left a huge hole in his soul that was constantly hemorrhaging all the love he could build up. So no matter how much someone

169

showed him love, it was never enough. It made it so much easier to see all the wicked in them than the love they provided. It was never enough because it was almost as if they couldn't love him fully. Then he couldn't love himself fully either. Rejected by his parents and molested and abused by those that remained, he had believed himself unlovable. He could see that now. Without this understanding of God's love that he never got all his years in the church, he could never face those thoughts.

"Oh my God,I too have been living in denial! Praise you Father. Praise you. Thank you," he said, silently, as he continued to weep.

It was amazing. He was filled with more love than he had ever felt in his life and there wasn't a single soul to be found in the darkness of the early morn. He looked around and there wasn't a single car moving; not a solitary light on in anyone's home in his vision. There was no one walking the streets, on a Saturday night? It was surreal as his eyes burned and his emotions continued to overflow. Then he could feel the peace washing over him that said,

"You are loved and no matter where you go from here. I will be here with you, holding this love for when you need it. I will be right here. I will never leave you. You are my son and I will never forsake you. Now stand up and walk with me, I have some things I want to show you."

The feelings he was experiencing, the voice he was hearing and the hands he actually believed he saw from the sky felt so real to him. He knew that there was no way he could, or would, ever tell a soul about what he saw or had happened to him on this walk. He was right in front of his community entrance but knew he couldn't walk back into his place looking like this with Sharon still there. He had to get himself together. He could not explain something like this to her. It is not that she wasn't a believer but she wasn't on that same walk so he didn't believe she could ever understand it. It was better that he didn't have to explain about the tears at all.

He decided that he would walk the extra two and a half miles around the neighborhood that it would take to get back to his entrance. This would be plenty of time to get himself together and think more about what had just happened to him and how he would apply this to the rest of his life. Surely this had to be the key; the answer to some of these questions. Deep in thought walking down the darkened street, his thoughts were interrupted as his cell phone rang. It was DD's ring! At three a.m.? "What the hell is going on?" He thought to himself.

"What the hell is going on!" He answered.

"Hello? Tony?" DD's voice said on the phone.

"Yeah, where on earth have you been? You arrived in Atlanta yesterday morning and I haven't heard a word from you since you left. I wasn't worth the time it took to pick up the phone to push one button to call me and let me know you arrived safely?" Tony exclaimed.

"I really apologize for that but we were rushing from the moment we got off the plane and I have been running all around everywhere since our arrival. I have no excuse why I didn't call you, I apologize," DD said, waiting to hear what he would say.

"I don't believe a word out of your mouth. You aren't sorry at all. Every time you make one of these bad decisions you hit me with the "I'm sorry" game. If you were truly sorry you would make better decisions," he snapped back.

"You're right Tony. I'm ashamed that I am here again and don't have any words for how disappointed I am that I hurt you once again."

"You know I was apprehensive about you going there and all the people I have in my mind you could be hooking up with given your fast past and this is how you ease my mind? You were so busy you couldn't call for two days? What the hell?! And you were supposed to have that meeting today? You didn't even call me to tell me how that went. I would have thought that being someone you love so much, as well as someone who has supported your dreams to be a writer since I met you that I would have been the first person you called? Especially

171

since you're always talking about how much you love me and want this life with me? Is this how you treat the man you love and are supposed to be in a committed relationship with? This is insanity!" Tony was so excited he was now out of breath.

He was a long way from the touching moment God had filled his body with. The phone was silent and he could hear himself and the anger in his voice. He realized that this is not where he should be at this moment having had such an experience. In fact he was doing himself a disservice by allowing ANYTHING, or anyone, to steal away the joy he had just found in the comfort of the Lord and knowing his love. He took another breath and reset the counter on his tongue and remembered what the Word said about communication. It should be to edify. This conversation, however, was missing the mark a bit.

He again reminded himself of the role he was seeking in his kingdom - one of husband, father and leader of his family and the Word says you must also be the priest of your home. He knew he had better not only understand his role but be practicing it if he hoped to master it well enough to be entrusted with such a responsibility. Jesus' instruction was to love your wife like you love the church, and at this moment, he was not. He could only hear his pain and fear speaking and knew immediately he was failing the mark. So he set down his fear and pushed past the pain.

"Ok ok, maybe I am overacting here. I'm emotional for sure. And I know this is my pain talking. I apologize for that having to be the first thing you hear from me. Are you ok? It's three a.m. Is everything ok there?" Tony said in a much calmer voice, now concerned.

The phone was silent but he could hear she had the mouth piece covered with her hand. But it didn't help. He could hear she was crying.

"What's going on DD? Why are you crying? Talk to me! It's three a.m. Something is obviously up. Talk to me! You called me remember?" Tony said, now trying to coax her to speak to him and knowing her shame may very well be the thing moving her to tears.

"Talk to me DD. What's up baby?" Tony pleaded again.

"Things aren't ok," she said, with congested sinuses as she was fighting back tears so that she could speak.

"What's wrong? What's happening?" Tony asked now even more concerned.

"I'm out here walking all alone and don't know what to do. I made a bad choice and feel like I'm being punished for it," DD says, now crying harder than ever.

"What do you mean out there all alone? I thought you were staying at your family's house? What bad decision? What are you talking about? Talk to me. You are really getting me worried."Tony said, emotions beginning to build as his voice again began to climb.

"I tried to reach my aunt, the one I was supposed to stay with from before I left, and I haven't been able to reach her since we arrived. Tonya and her man went off seeking some alone time and didn't want me around. So I called an old friend I used to hang out with and he said it was fine for me to stay there so Tonya and her man dropped me off. I never fooled around with him or anything. He was just a good friend, so I figured it would be ok.

But once I was there and we were hanging out after awhile he pushed up on me for sex. And when I refused he put me out of his house. So now I'm walking up this dark ass road towards the Waffle House. I have been trying to reach Tonya but neither she, nor her man is taking my call. I'm going to sit here and eat to stall for time until I can reach them. I just needed to call you to let you know what was going on and I felt so alone. I'm sorry. I can see now that this was a horrible decision," DD said, as she began to cry again.

Tony didn't believe a word she was saying. He knew now that this woman was a liar to her core and didn't know anything else but that. He wanted so much to take her at her word but his life had shown him so much it was almost impossible to turn a blind eye to this. There just wasn't any way what she said was true. He played the scenario in his mind and this is "the truth" he deduced.

She had been planning to hook up with an old flame who she was very much looking forward to hooking up with, and missed. In his mind this is where all the excitement in her voice about the trip came from before she left gushing about leaving. This made sense to him. She got there and slept with dude and things didn't go as she thought they would. Either he slutted her and tried to do her like he used to and she didn't receive it the same because of where she was at this point in her life, or he used her up like a Kleenex, got his and had no further use for her and put her out. Either way, he felt she was lying about not having slept with this dude.

Tony's ears were ringing and he needed all that prayer he had just asked of God to cover him where he was at that very second. He had made his declaration to God, the Father and here was the enemy showing up not a second behind him to test that faith and strength without a moment to rest on it. As DD continued to cry and explain this sad story to him, he recounted in his head all the times he was that person on the other side of that phone. The slut, the whore, the liar and cheater. The heartbreaker and back stabber who didn't know anything else or better yet who didn't know how to CHOOSE anything else. He still wanted someone to love him and accept him. He still needed God's grace and cover, even when he didn't know how to ask for it. He imagined her in a million and one compromising positions where men had abused and taken advantage of her. There was something about her and this pain, something about the familiar sound in her voice that was more than his loose history.

He could hear abuse. He could hear someone TAKING her virtue away from a tender age and all at once he understood. He had thought this a few times before when he looked at her behavior and heard some of her stories. He had even brought it to her like, "Are you sure you weren't the one molested? Your behaviors sound so much like classic abuse history?"

He would say it laughing and half joking but really wanting to know the truth. She would always deny it right away saying, "No all the decisions I made are on me. I don't have any reason why I did the things I have done. I was just a bad seed I suppose." Her response was often why she questioned if God could ever forgive her for some of the things she had done.

He knew there was something there but never pushed her to talk about what he saw or felt about her past. He knew now that she was a victim and was still playing one and maybe this was why she was never satisfied with him? He didn't put her in this role, so she had to. Each time he treated her like his wife and loved her, her history told her that she didn't deserve it. That she should only be tortured and treated badly or that good treatment was only a set up to let you down. It was some sort of manipulation. No one had ever just loved her for who she was and not what she could do or give to them and here was a clear cut case of that.

And now she was calling him to see if that God in him was real. Did he really possess the unconditional love he professed to her? Was he truly a reflection of God's love for her? Could he forgive her even when she was obviously dead ass wrong? Because if he could then she might be able to see that God could too. He could hear it in her voice. She was asking the question and she hadn't said a word. His eyes were all at once opened and his heart burst free with the love it was just filled with and he was indeed ready with the answer to that question. For God loves you so, he will provide you with the perfect mate. One he built JUST FOR YOU.

"Baby I'm so sorry you are in this place. It sounds horrible. I wish I was there to help you. I would come to you right now. You should have called me when you couldn't reach your aunt. I know you didn't have any money and would have gladly used my credit card to book you a room. If you had told me this before you left

I would have taken care of it before you ever got on that plane. I am the man in your life and I want to take care of you and that includes providing for you when you can't make a way on your own. This is my role. It was given to me by God himself. I'm here to help you baby. But you have got to let me in to do it.

"Give me a chance, I can't promise I will be perfect or won't ever fail but it won't be for lack of trying. I love you so much baby and we have got to do better with this sort of thing. Do you want me to book you a room now? I'm almost home I can get online as soon as I walk in the door. Just tell me where you are and I'll find somewhere near you so you can lay your head down and get some of this worry off of you. I got your back boo and I love you. Don't ever be afraid to call me and tell me anything. Do you hear me baby? Tell me what you need baby. Tell me what you want me to do." Tony said softly with as much love in his heart as he had been filled with.

He could hear her still crying even harder at this point in disbelief at what she was hearing. He had forgiven her and she hadn't even asked for it. What manner of man is this? She cried until she was weak and ready to collapse. She stopped walking and just sat down on the curb where she was and wept uncontrollably as Tony continued to tell her how much she was loved and wanted. Mouthing the words of this dream she had and always wanted to hear. How much she was desired and wanted not only as a mate but a wife and she would never have to go through anything like that again in her life if she did not choose to.

"Damn Tony!" She sobbed again. "I just so wasn't prepared to hear that. I was expecting the worst. I had fucked up and was looking for the worst. I feel like I should be punished right now for what I have done, TO YOU, TO ME. Hell I'm even bringing drama to Tonya and her man's life right now. I don't deserve this, I should be punished for what I have done," she said, still sobbing.

Then Tony hushed her quietly, "Shhhhhhhh, baby please. Stop. Haven't you been punished enough?" And she broke down and her words were now unrecognizable as she tried to speak. She sounded as if she couldn't catch her breath. She was having a full blown panic attack. Tony recognized it from the wheezing and huffing and again tried to soothe her.

"Shhhhhh, baby come on. All that is over now. He is gone. You are gone from him. Now you're here with me my love and I got you. I am going to take care of you, if you allow me to. I really would like for you to calm down and take some deep breaths for me, please," Tony said.

He could hear over the phone she was starting to calm down and did take his advice and took those deep breaths. He could hear her emotions start to come down and she had begun to rein herself back in.

"Ok keep breathing my love. I want you to get up and keep walking to that Waffle House and get in off of that dark street please. Please love, I'm already worried to death about you baby."

He could hear that she got up immediately and brushed herself off and was now walking again.

"I will take your help if you really want to give it to me Tony. I am sorry I am putting us here. I need to find out what is around me so we can figure out what we need to do," DD said sounding a little better now.

"No need I'm walking into my community now. Just tell me where you are and I'll find you a nice place to sleep and arrange a cab to get you there," Tony said, on top of his job.

"Hold on, it's Tonya calling me back. One minute baby,"
DD said.

Tony sat on the phone listening intently for DD to return to the phone. For a split second, he considered if it was dude calling her back to reconsider, but washed that thought out of his head as quickly as it crept its way in there. Just then DD clicked back over.

"Ok I just spoke to Calvin, her man, and they know exactly where I am and are on the way to get me. I don't want you to spend a dime of your money baby. They are coming now and I'm just going to tell them to take me straight to the airport and I'm going to sit there until my flight departs this afternoon," DD said sounding serious.

"But that's like twelve hours from now?" Tony said questioning.

"I don't care. I have brought enough people drama with my bad decisions and if I left tomorrow I would still be going there right now. No one should have to put up with bad decisions I have made least of all them," DD said. "Hold on, that's them again," DD said, before Tony could answer.

"They are just around the corner. I'll call you as soon as I get to the airport. I will not let you down again. I love you." She said softly.

"Ok my love, be safe and please make sure you call no matter what you decide to do. You don't have to go there but either way I understand. I just want to know you're safe so please call," he asked, calmly.

"I will. I promise," she replied.

They hung up and Tony was blown away by the love in his heart. Even at this very moment, although he was certain he had been betrayed, he was not angry or bitter. Sure it hurt if he thought about it or focused on it but that was only the selfish part of him that only considered his feelings. That part of him that didn't believe that he could be loved either and wanted to say, "See I told you so." But oh no, he was not allowed a voice, not tonight and if he had anything to say about it, not ever again. He was a bit saddened that within DD's plan she still managed to find a way to punish herself even if Tony wouldn't. And make no mistake about it, over twelve hours in an airport with no shower, or money to feed yourself, has got to be punishment. But what could he do but wait for her call and again tell her how much he loved her? And so he waited.

She kept her promise and did call him as she was arriving at the airport. She stayed on the phone with him until she was through security and at her gate. They talked for hours about anything and everything until he could once again hear the laughter and something pleasant in her voice. He knew he had walked her home and out of the darkness. They talked off and on until she got on the plane. He caught a quick nap during her flight so he could be bright-eyed for her arrival, as they made plans for him to pick her up once she arrived.

And still . . . he waited.

Chapter 16
Through The Eyes of An Angel

It had been two days since DD had come home. Tony had done his able best to show her the love that he felt put on his heart to give her, at her time of need. Although he had no regrets, feeling as though he had been obedient, he did, however, feel as though it was time for some straight talk with some real answers. He had the faith that he was asked to have in moving as he was told to move. Although, he could not see clearly, the place he was to set his feet. It was now time to be about the work in this relationship that should always follow behind faith. He planned on breaching this conversation when they met later on this evening after he got out of his Contracts and Torts class at Stetson University School of Law.

He went about his day as he did just about every day. He lived with purpose, therefore he moved with purpose. He questioned everything and believed that anything worth doing was worth doing right. In a world where you never have enough time to get to all the things you would like to, if you don't have time to do it, you most definitely don't have time to do it over. He took his life serious without taking himself too seriously. It was a fine line to walk, one with confidence in himself and his ability but didn't look like arrogance or pride. He believed in humility and knew it to be the key to keep him from too much pride.

By the end of the day, he should have been mentally worn out; by all accounts he probably was. But for the conversation he had been anticipating all day, he would have been at home on his couch watching the most mindless of television shows. His stomach turned all day as he thought about the prospect of having this conversation with DD. She was an all or nothing kind of person who only knew two ways, fight or flight. Either she was going to fight you to the death, whether she was right or wrong, or she was going to quit immediately and say whatever she needed you to hear so that you would back off and she would leave.

There was another method she liked to handle during these times too, one where she simply didn't show up. That, too, was flight in a different form. This is why he hadn't mentioned it to her at anytime throughout the day as they spoke. He had a strong feeling that, given too much time, she would have convinced herself that it wasn't even worth trying. He knew that having this kind of conversation was going to be difficult, as well as one that would go deeper than they ever had. It almost seemed unfair as if he was ambushing her with something so heavy. But he didn't know any other way to guarantee she would show up for this kind of conversation. There really was no telling how she would react so he prepared for the worst and hoped for the best.

Just moments into the car, he had made the call that he was on his way home so she would be ready to go by the time he got home. Shortly upon his arrival, she showed up to his door. He was once again free for the evening since Sharon had Angel. He had just finished tying his shoe lace when the knock at the door came. He looked out of the peek hole and saw DD standing there smiling; happy to be coming to his open arms. He opened the door with a reciprocal smile, from ear to ear.

"Hey baby!" he said to her, as he planted a juicy kiss on her full lips.

"Hey daddy," she replied.

"You ready to go boo?" he asked.

"Yup," she answered.

He grabbed his keys from off of the coffee table and they headed out of the door. As they began their walk, they started off with the usual small talk about the weather, their daily events, the kids and things like that. The entire time they were having this conversation, Tony was completely zoned out and could only think about all of the questions he had for her about this past weekend. His stomach was in knots and he could barely contain himself with all of the pleasantries he and she were exchanging.

DD noticed the tension in his face and body and she, too, began to get tight, anticipating what may be coming next. She knew at some point he was going to want to have this conversation. After all, she had gone to Atlanta for a purpose and hadn't even mentioned it upon her return. In an effort to show her she was valued and loved, he was supportive and kind and had made sure to give her all the love she needed upon arrival. She knew deep within her that this was the least that she owed him. An explanation was the very minimum she could do for him. Although their lips were moving and there did appear to be a light conversation at hand, no one was mentally present for it between the two of them. Their words seemed to just fall off in mid sentence and float away, like some sort of dream scenario. They both took a moment looking into the full moon, wondering where those words were going. DD would have liked to be riding them wherever they were headed at this minute.

"You seem like something is on your mind Tony, what's up?" DD asked, letting out a quiet sigh.

"I can only imagine at some point you would expect me to ask you about what the hell happened with you in Atlanta. I have held off asking about it knowing how upset you were about it. But I need some answers. I need to know how you ended up there? Who this dude is? And how you know him? Why was he the man you turned to instead of me - the man you say you love and want a life with? Doing this thing the way you did it with your friends in tow makes me look like a fool, and was more than disrespectful. I need to know why and that something like this will never happen again."

Tony paused as he could feel his emotions starting to rise. He did not want to come off angry or bitter but he was hurt and it was very difficult to talk about this thing without that coming out in some way.

So he decided to stop speaking and give her an opportunity to answer the questions he had put to her and give himself the chance to pull some of those negative emotions back in so that this discussion didn't turn into a bunch of hurt feelings and a shouting match. He had not looked her directly in the eye until this point, afraid of seeing any doubt or uncertainty in her eyes. If there was one thing he was certain of it was that he could not deal with any more lies. If he looked at her during what he had just said and saw any attitude or negativity, he was afraid he would have just lost it. Since this is her way on a regular basis, he figured it was a safe bet. He now looked over toward her and stared directly into her eyes. It was now her turn for her eyes to find something other than his to look at out of the shame that the night in question brought her.

"I honestly don't know where to begin. I want to start by saying that I will never do something like that again. I realize now more than ever that that night was the biggest mistake I have made during the course of this relationship and you know I have made more than my share. I am so sorry for putting you through this. I know you aren't lying when you say you feel like a fool but I challenge that notion, not to say that you don't feel that way or that I don't understand. I challenge it with the truth, which is that you weren't a fool that night. I was. I was the one who made a fool out of myself. I lied to you and I have got to live with that and whatever fallout that comes along with it. Whatever it is, I deserve it. But please believe me. I feel more foolish than anyone. I was the one walking the streets in the middle of the night with nowhere to be, acting as if I were still single and did not have a loving man to support me the way that you did that night. It was a major mistake and I will do just about anything to make it up to you."

DD said this last part with conviction, as she looked up at Tony. She may have been expecting some form of punishment but instead he just had more questions.

"I appreciate your apology and I have already forgiven you. I realized you also played the fool that night. However, this still doesn't sit right with me. I need more in order to know that this thing won't happen again. I need some history. Who is this guy? And please no more lies. I feel he was an old lover who you planned on going to see and be with all along. If so, I really need to know this. And even more than that, I need to know if you slept with him. I know you said that you hadn't and I didn't press you that night but what you said honestly doesn't make any sense to me. I used to run these streets harder than anyone. I have been out there and known a woman or two and none of what you said rang true for me as to what I believed could even be a possibility. I need you to start at the beginning. Who is this dude?" Tony said, now looking DD in the eye the entire time he spoke.

Whereas before he didn't want to see the possible deception in her words for fear of the conversation going south, he was now searching for the truth. He watched as her lips moved and her eyes fixed in on his and waited for her to say something to him that made sense in his world.

"Ok, again, I really don't know where to begin? He is a dude I used to know back in the days. There was a bunch of us who were friends who used to hang out and. . ." As DD spoke, Tony decided that this was avoidance and not going to work for him. He interrupted.

"Alright, see this is what I'm talking about. This is that bullshit. You are being vague and I need some real answers. He is 'someone you used to know and hang out with' does not answer my question. How do you know this guy?" Tony snapped, starting to show some cracks in his patience.

"I knew him back in the day from Atlanta," DD said.

"No shit? How did you meet him?" Tony snapped.

"I met him from Kenny," DD said, now backing down.

"Your ex Kenny?" Tony asked puzzled.

184

"Yeah," DD responded, hanging her head in shame.

"How the hell does that make any sense? Why would your man be letting you hang out with some other dude? Why are you lying to me DD? I am giving you a chance to come clean here." Tony said, still looking directly into her eyes.

"I'm not lying. I swear. Ok, ok. He was more than just a friend. Remember I told you that I had been involved with selling dope back in the day? Well it was with Kenny and this dude was one of our customers," DD said, with shame once again falling in on her.

"What's this dudes name?" Tony snapped, interrupting her again, feeling she was still attempting to be vague.

"Rob. His name is Rob," she answered.

"So this is your friend? A former customer? Why on earth would you hang out with a dope head? I don't know anyone who dealt in that line of work that hung out with their clients?" Tony said.

"Nah, it wasn't like that. We sold this dude weight and he was cool with us. He helped make our 'connect' on the other side of town. He liked me, so we all hit it off and became friends is all," DD said, sounding nervous.

"What? He liked you? What the hell does that mean? Your man was alright with that?" Tony shot back.

"Yeah, Kenny was like that. Whatever kept the money coming in, he didn't really care," she said.

"So he didn't care about you either then? How is this your man, if he didn't care about you? And why would he allow you to even so much as be in this man's presence, knowing this man 'liked' you? I'm confused. None of this is making sense to me. You have got to break this down for me. Make it plain, because I'm feeling like you're lying to me. I am feeling like you're making a fool out of me right here and now.

"So I'm supposed to believe what? Your man 'pimped' you out or some shit? Seriously DD I have dealt with you straight up the entire time I have known you and never have I ever tried to play you or treat you like you were slow. Never did I try to treat you like you were stupid. But seriously, I am from one of the largest cities in the world. I LIVED in that world you are talking about and don't need to tell you that what you are saying doesn't make any sense!

"I remember you telling me that your moms had stepped to you once about someone telling her you were 'hooking,'" selling yourself on the streets, and you denied it then, and to me. So what you are saying really doesn't make a damn bit of sense. You really need to stop treating me like I'm stupid and explain this!" Tony was visibly upset and she could see the veins popping in his forehead.

"Yes! Yes Tony Yes! HE WAS PIMPING ME! IS THAT WHAT YOU NEEDED TO HEAR? Damn this shit man! I'm tired of hiding these things. Fine, you want to talk about it? I'm going to lay it all out. If when we're done having this conversation, you never want to speak to me again, I will understand. But you're right. I do owe you the truth. I owe you at least that," DD said, suddenly looking confident. In fact, she had the stone cold look of the hard truth that she knew in her heart she was about to speak.

"Right, so tell me about this. You never told me any of this before. You mentioned the drugs but never went into any detail. Explain this for me. He was your pimp?" Tony said, now feeling a bit of the shame she lost for having to drag her through this obviously difficult time in her life.

It was a time he was certain she wanted to put behind her and NEVER tell a single soul about ever in her lifetime. But it was too late now. She had opened this door when she dragged him down into that place with her and now he needed to know the truth about what he had gotten himself into.

"Here's how the shit went down. We were slinging dope out of the apartment Kenny and I used to live in and we lost our 'connect,' thereby losing our income because of the fuck-ups he was partners with.

When Kenny tried to get back with the 'connect,' we had from out of town, he didn't want to do business with Kenny because he really didn't know him like that. He only knew his boy.

"Since Kenny wasn't messing with old dude, or his boy, anymore, he was trying to figure another way in with Rob, who he knew could change the game for him. At the time he sold it to me, he said it could change the game for us. But ultimately he was the connection to Kenny going solo and cutting out other middlemen, thereby not only increasing his/our take but also solidifying our business relationship with dude so no one else would be able to fuck it up again.

"Rob dropped on him that he saw the 'little light-skinned thing' he had around the crib and liked what she was working with. He told Kenny that if he would let him take me out, he would consider doing business with him. We were broke and desperate so when Kenny came to me to ask me to do this, it was hard to say no. But there was no way I was going to just go out with some dude I didn't even know. I didn't trust him worth a damn. Hell, this is how chicks come up missing, you know? Kenny begged and pleaded and told me that all I had to do was go out with this dude and we would be good on the 'connect' and everything would get back to normal. He swore he would never hold it against me.

"The kicker was, I loved him and wanted to please him. What was even more serious was that the rent was due in three days, and I knew if I didn't go out with this dude, we would have to find somewhere else to live in like three days. I finally agreed to it after him pleading with me for another day and dude showed up to pick me up that night. Kenny talked to him and told him he cared about me so there shouldn't be any funny business. He also said I didn't have to do anything I didn't want to. Dude agreed and we left.

"He drove me to the complete opposite side of the city, which was too far to make my way back alone. It was also outside of the train or bus lines, and Kenny didn't even own a car so I knew something was up. He drove us directly to a hotel and I got tense. Once there he pulled out a bag of weed and we just smoked until I was so high it didn't even matter anymore. Once it was done, he brought me back and told Kenny how good I was and how he was straight from then on. We got our 'connect' back and the business got back to normal. My relationship with Kenny immediately got worse. He stripped me down once dude left and inspected my body and made me get in the shower and questioned me the entire time. Did I like it? Would I want to do him again? What positions did I lay with him in? Was his dick bigger than his? The whole nine.

"By the time I was done in the shower, I was numb and felt horribly guilty as if I had just betrayed him somehow; like I had cheated on him. So when he started punching and slapping me, I was numb to that too. By that time, I felt like I deserved it. He took me in the room. Although I fought it, he forced me to have sex with him. I was now angry that after this bastard kicked my ass he wanted to stick his dick inside of me. Because I fought so long and hard, he raped me anally. He ripped me open and I bled for a week. After that we were never the same.

"From that point on, the only times he was remotely nice to me was when he wanted me to meet with other customers. He started messing with some other chick that would come to the house whenever she wanted and I had to fight for his attention. I was the one who always came through for him in the clutch so I felt the most wanted and loved. I know now it was all manipulation and in my mind. But for me, at that time, it was real. That is how I met Rob. That is how I know Rob." DD said, now running out of steam.

Tony didn't say a word, still taking it all in. He was shocked at how much DD had disclosed to him. Not so much that she did it, but how she had done it. He was also shocked at the things she had told him because she had presented him with so many other things; none of which sounded anywhere close to the things she had just told him.

He realized it was, once again, this cool persona that had sold him that bag of goods. In this journey to believe and trust, at any cost, he had bought into it, hook, line and sinker. If he had not put those goggles of denial upon his head, he could have seen this thing for what it was and kept himself from so much pain. But he had not, so there was no one to blame but himself. He had more questions but was afraid of coming off like Kenny and his questioning session in the shower. He fought within himself for a moment, then against his better judgment he went in again.

"So you met this man during a time you were selling yourself to your best customers, which he was one of? So does that mean you slept with him?" Tony asked, falling silent, waiting for the answer.

"Yes. Yes I slept with him. But it wasn't like that. I wanted to sleep with him. As I told you before, I have always been a very loyal person which has always been my one of my faults. Kenny was out of town and I was hanging by Rob's crib. I had never slept with him although I had thought about it. We were getting high, he started to push up on me and I wanted to. But I was so loyal to Kenny that even though I knew he had another girl in his life and was out of town with another one of his chicks, I still called him and asked him if I could do it. He gave me the go ahead and I did it. It was a one shot deal because dude's sex was trash. I just chumped him off every time he tried from then on." DD said, now sounding as cold as the streets.

But Tony knew just as DD did, once you ring that bell you cannot go back and unring it. " Yo, hold up, if dude tapped that then ain't no way you are over there hanging out, chilling or getting high if you ain't upping no tail. That's a lie. Come on DD be real?" Tony shot back.

"No really, it wasn't like that. He was there for me after something major happened and helped me through it and we were never on it like that again," DD responded.

"Something major? Like what?" He asked.

"Whew!" She let out another really loud sigh. She stopped walking and started pacing back and forth. "You really need to know all this? You can't just take me at my word at this point? I have given you so much truth. Isn't that enough for you to believe me? Do you really need me to go here?" DD asked with cold, yet sad, eyes.

"I think I do. I need to understand something that makes sense to me. When these doubts come into my head about what is real and not, I will have something I know is real to quiet all the lies. The ones you have told that rest on the devil's truth and all the ones the enemy comes at me with. I do think I need you to go there." Tony replied, not knowing exactly what to expect.

He had already heard what sounded like a nightmare. How could this thing get any worse? He knew in this deep dark place that it could indeed get worse; a hell of a lot worse. He had seen it firsthand. But this was not a thought he wanted to acknowledge at this point. So he did not. If ever denial had a use, this was it.

She began to speak again. This time her voice got lower and she seemed to take more moments of thought between each word. He knew she was about to share something with him she more than likely hadn't shared with anyone.

"What I'm about to share with you I have never shared with anyone who wasn't there and knew first hand. And when I am done telling you this story, I will not answer any questions, so please don't ask. If I can handle it, I will give you as much detail as I can muster but please just listen. Try not to talk.

"One night that same dude, the original dude who took me out on that first date, came back to town. He called the crib and told Kenny he wanted to take me out. Kenny agreed and told me. I got myself ready and was actually feeling kinda good. I hadn't been out in a while. Kenny and I were hardly speaking. I hadn't had sex in weeks. Kenny didn't touch me anymore. He only let me give him head. He used to do the shit for hours, making me give him head until my jaws were falling off my face. He called it training. He did this while he watched porn.

"Every now and again he would stop me to let me watch some chick on the TV screen giving some guy head so I knew how to do it better. He was teaching me how to give head and this was my education. Anyway, it made me feel less than human, like a dog jumping through hoops. I knew this dude coming to get me really liked me. We always had a good time. We had been out about five or six times by then. Each time it was about the same thing. We got hella high, ate good and screwed for about twenty or thirty minutes. It was decent sex but I was more looking forward to the opportunity to become human to someone even if it was for a brief moment.

"Dude came and got me, Kenny met him at the door, no speeches or words, he just called me and I came downstairs and we left. I jumped in the Jeep but dude felt off. I could just tell the way he was looking at me and how he was talking, his whole body language was off. It was like he was trying to distance himself from me. And that human connection, even if it was through meaningless sex was instantly lost. He started heading towards the wrong end of town. We were deep in the hood by the time I spoke up. He told me to just chill. Things were good. He just needed to make a pick up. Knowing the business he was in, I sat back and tried to play it cool so he didn't see the panic in my face.

"When we pulled up to the corner store, he told me he was just running inside to grab some condoms and would be right out. I always used rubbers and never slept with anyone without them. He knew full well that I traveled with them so it seemed strange that he would come all the way out here to the hood to get them. Again, I kept my cool but I, honestly, was so shook. When he came back out of the store, he had two of his boys with him. As they jumped in the car, they looked at me like I was raw meat and they were hungry dogs. The dudes in the back were like 'Yes sir, this one is right.'

"As they began to paw on my body and breasts, I spoke up. 'Oh hell nah! It ain't that kind of fucking party dude. Pull over and let me out right here. I'm good I can make it from here.' Just then dude in the back slapped me in the face hard, with the side of a forty-five hand gun. 'Shut the fuck up slut ass bitch! You aint going a fucking place.'

"The other two, including the dude who had brought me, started laughing like he had just told the funniest joke they had ever heard. I began to bleed from the side of my face; cut from where the gun had hit me on the edge of my eye brow. It was flowing like an open stream. One of the dudes took off his shirt and told me to hold it to my head and stop bleeding all over his boy's ride. I did what I was told.

"When we pulled into the motel, my stomach fell from the lump that was in my throat into the bottom of my belly. As I walked up to the room, I was trying to convince myself that this wasn't real. As they got to the door, it swung open without anyone even knocking. Standing in the doorway was the craziest looking dude I had ever seen in my life. I had been around some cold blooded people in my life on this side of things; I mean some real killers. This dude scared me worst than any of them had ever done. Behind him were three other guys.

"As he snatched me into the door and to the middle of the room, the door closed and they began to rip my clothes off of my body. Seven sets of hands, drugs and guns everywhere. I could already see them pulling out erect penises. I knew then that this was no dream. But for the life of me it was like it wasn't real, like it wasn't me. It was like I was having an out of body experience, looking down at them pawing at me and ripping my clothes off.

"I was standing there completely naked just holding onto shreds of what started out as my panties. I was fighting and screaming at the top of my lungs. The dude who had bought me there stopped them and told them to chill. I thought he was going to stop this thing from happening. 'Hey, she is being way too loud. Y'all gotta chill out. Li'l mama is gonna take care of all of us. Ain't ya li'l mama?'

"As he looked at me waiting, for my approval, I was so frightened I just shook my head. My entire body shook. He went on, 'We just have to give her a minute to get her head together. Hold up.' He took me from their grasp and pulled me into the bathroom. 'Na here. Get your head together. When you come out, you know what time it is.'

"He passed a sack of weed with some blunts already rolled inside. I took it and sat on the edge of the tub. As the door closed, I began to cry. I could hear them talking outside. They were whispering. I could overhear them plotting out my murder, Tony. Where they were going to dump my body and the whole nine. I knew it was real because shit like that happened all the time over there. I lit the blunt and inhaled deep. I knew shit was about to get worse for me than it ever had. I smoked that blunt faster than I had ever smoked in my fucking life. Dude always had the best weed.

"This was one of the reasons why I was looking forward to messing with dude tonight. It was taking me out of my head and away from there, when the door flung open. I pulled out another blunt with my hand still shaking, as I was pulled from the bathroom. I did not fight this time. I was puffing hard on that second blunt and had it half way in when 'Crazy eyes' said, 'Fuck this shit.' He punched me in the back of the head and I fell forward on my face. And it began." DD stopped. She looked as if she had seen a ghost. She just stopped talking.

"And once it was over I laid there on the floor, bleeding from my goodies and my ass. I had blacked out more than once and was coming to. I tried to get up when 'Crazy eyes' grabbed me from behind and started to choke me. I could feel myself once again start to black out when I could hear some of the guys say, 'Ah fuck this. I don't want to be here for this part of it.'

"As they started to break for the door, I felt his grip loosen. I fell to the ground and just laid there doing my best to pretend I was knocked out, praying he just walked out and left with them. But by the time everyone had gone, he, and two of the others had stayed behind. He picked me up from the floor and threw me on the bed. I didn't move even as he pushed his erect penis inside of me.

'I'm gonna fuck you to death bitch.' As he started to screw me again, he began choking me at the same time. Once I realized that this dude wasn't bullshitting and actually meant to kill me, I tried to fight. But he was too strong. In the middle of this mess, someone was pounding at the door. It sounded like it was the police. I was thinking, 'Thank God.'

"I heard this other dude screaming through the door. I figured it must have been his boy. He got up, pulled his pants on and opened the door. Dude at the door was extra angry. 'This is what the fuck you're up here doing when I told you motha fuckas to lay low!?' He screamed. Ya'll motha fuckas get the fuck out of here! We are here to get money! That's it! And all this extracurricular shit is dead!

"He must have been their boss because the two other dudes who were there just watching, got up immediately and bounced. 'Crazy eyes,' however, stayed behind like he wanted to try dude or something. But once dude pulled out his heat and got to screaming on dude, he got his clothes together and dipped too. Now I wasn't sure if I was still going to be murdered or not, but I felt safe for the moment. Before dude came, I was certain I was moments from death. He threw his coat at me and told me to cover up. Then he took me down to his truck. He gave me an old pair of sweat pants he had in the back of his truck. He then handed me an old tee shirt that smelled like he used it to wax his ride, and dropped me off on my side of town.

"He didn't take me home but got close. I was actually closer to Rob's crib and out of shame, I went there. I begged him not to call Kenny. I was sure he would make it worse with his questions and implying that I somehow wanted this to happen to me. I couldn't take that at that point. But he called Kenny anyway. Kenny told him to keep me. He didn't give a fuck about no run down whore.

"This is what he saw me go through and this is why he never wanted to mess with me again. I don't know if Rob felt sorry for me or was just grossed out but he never pushed up on me again."

And just like that she was done with the telling of this horrible story. Not another word. She got up from the bench we had stopped at and began to walk again.

Tony didn't know what to say. He was paralyzed with shame for having made her relive what had to be THEE worst moment of her life. They walked home silently and all the way Tony kept looking at her for cracks. He wanted to comfort her, hug her, tell her how sorry he was and love her. But there was no place for that now. She was gone. Stone cold. Hard shell. DD wasn't home any more. Her body was present like that night in the room but she was long gone.

There were very few words spoken once they arrived back at his place. DD went to her car and stood there for a moment before she told him she had to go. He did not want to keep her from it, as he could feel the emotions welling up in her and did not want to stand between her and where she was about to go. He knew it was a private hell that he was not welcomed to; especially having been the cause of it today. He kissed her lips yet again as he had when she arrived. They were cold as ice. She didn't even look at him as she returned the kiss. She turned away from him again as she jumped in her step-mother's old beat up Saturn and started it.

The loud muffler broke the silence and reminded Tony to get the hell out of the way. Her tires squealed as she backed up and then pulled out. He could hear her screaming and crying as she got to the exit gate and turned the corner. Tony's heart sank as he stood there dumbfounded and feeling like the worst jackass in the world. Had his pain driven this conversation? Could this have been avoided? At what cost though? Would he always be last? Or was this a necessary evil in order to move forward with more understanding and honesty. Only time would tell. At this moment, there was nothing he knew for certain except it was going to be a long night for the both of them. He was certain that NEITHER one of them was in for any sleep tonight.

Chapter 17
What Lies Beneath
(Forming)

It had been days since Tony had heard DD's horror story. He had yet to shut his eyes without seeing those images. Therefore, he hadn't slept a wink in days and his mind and body were starting to show the signs. All this time he had been blocking out the obvious truths. All the things he did not want to see or know about her and the pain he saw her lugging around every day. Things that she just didn't want to face herself and things she most definitely didn't want him to know about her. But as he said to her at the start of that wicked conversation, you cannot unring that bell. Those images and faces were stuck in his head more than likely for life; and deservedly so, for his part he considered it his penance, like a true catholic.

This entire relationship, he had thought it was DD's hard head and stubborn demeanor that had kept her from committing and giving over her life to him as he was so willing to do for her. The bible talks a lot about submission - to God and your husband - as he submits unto God. It is a difficult concept for those of us who are whole, and haven't been ruined by the wicked things that men do. Now knowing at least part of DD's truth, it had now become clear why she was so difficult.

All this time he was begging for submission, he had no understanding what he was really asking DD for. To him it was a concept. To her it literally meant death. He was asking her to walk willingly back into a hell she had narrowly escaped from the first time. The last time, and every time thereafter, that she put her trust in a man, this had been the result. They beat, abused, pimped out, burned and cut her flesh and soul; leaving her to rot like a filthy piece of meat. It made him think of the book of

Psalms in the bible which said, "For my love, THEY ARE MY ADVERSARIES."

All she wanted was love. She gave herself onto them and they took up and ate her flesh by the bucket full, until the only thing that was left was the shell of a woman he met. It was a wonder she was still alive. And no wonder at all where her virtue had gone. He, ignorantly, thinking that she had given it away, could not have been more wrong. It was ripped from her bosom like her innocence ripped from her chest - still beating. Now here he was demanding that she go back there without her having what she would need to do so. She needed absolute PROOF that he was more than just words. He needed to be the living embodiment of the love he wanted and that had to start right here, right now.

He knew, first hand, what it was to be victimized and what state it left you in. Yet, for him, this position was still unimaginable. He had rushed to judge her foolishly like all the others that had come before him and she never so much as sought to correct him. Why would she? She had never been worth it in her entire history. Why would she believe she was now? He had given her nothing but demands. Sure he had given of himself, but it was restrained because he didn't trust her. How could she trust that? She could not. She would not. He knew he wouldn't.

If indeed he wanted to be with her, he was going to have to be all in. There could be no other way. He absolutely knew that now. He could not be like all the others that came before him. He could not even have the appearance thereof. Not even the HINT of those iniquitous people. He had to be in the complete opposite direction. Again, he was put in mind of the word.

John 10:10 The thief cometh not, but for to steal, and to kill, and to destroy: I am come that they might have life, and that they might have it more abundantly.

He knew that although this was a tall order, he was going to have to be the walking embodiment of this idea. He was going to have to be a clear example of

God's love - the LIVING WORD. Because after all she had been through, he might just be the only bible she would ever read again. He had prayed every night for DD since he heard that terrible story and was now praying for that those awful things would fade from her mind, and life, like the sands of time. But this time, while he was down there, he prayed for the strength to love her completely and more whole. He asked that God enter both their hearts and heal them together, to let them become allies in healing and walk.

"Let us walk those hallowed halls together Father, hand in hand. I will care for her and not fail to show her my whole heart. Amen."

For the first time in days, he was feeling some comfort and could feel what he recognized as approaching slumber. He did not fight it even as his mind fought his body with thoughts swirling from every corner of his imagination. There would be another day to mourn the loss of DD's innocence. Perhaps once he rested his weary heart and mind. As he closed his eyes, he fought back yet more tears, feeling angry and helpless. He wanted so badly to hurt those that had hurt this precious woman he had grown to love so much. But, alas, he was years too late. Upon his final waking memory, he could again feel the rogue, disobedient tear drop that ran warm, full down his face as he faded off to a well deserved slumber.

*　　*　　*　　*　　*

It had been days since DD had dropped the bombshell about her life on him and he still hadn't caught his breath. From the time he had met her, he knew that there was some serious grit and grime all over her. You could see it all over her. It was throughout her persona, meshed seamlessly to her personality. There was no avoiding it. If you wanted any kind of relationship with her, it was a huge part of who you were going to get as well as who you were going to have to deal with.

If she had just been a fling, he could have simply tolerated what looked like a mess until she had left his spectrum. But she was not that to him. From the moment he first opened up to her online within those hours of conversation, he knew. Even when he was still trying to downplay it, that she was damn near everything he wanted. Sure she had flaws. Who didn't? He certainly had his own share, and more than a few. So how on earth could he judge her?

He had hinted at DD during some of those long nights they spent walking and baring their souls to one another that he could see some of the things she ended up confessing to the other night. She, of course, denied it. He understood that. She was in denial within herself and couldn't face those thoughts nor deeds. How could he expect her to do anything differently with regards to him? If she could do that for him, she would have, more than likely, done it for herself first. It was obvious to him, and anyone with eyes, that this was the cracking of her capsule. He didn't take it personal. However, he was secretly harboring a heap of guilt for being the one to open that door that she was working so hard to keep shut away from him and the rest of her life.

She knew in her mind that everything behind that door was pure evil. He had heard her allude to it many times. She also knew that everything it touched that was worth a damn was either ruined or taken away from her. This is why before she even started she offered him the door. She provided a readymade excuse to leave her once he knew her "real worth" - her "real shame." At the very minimum, this was a real possibility for her. It also said that she had bought into it on some level, which meant that she, too, didn't believe she deserved anything good.

From the time he laid eyes on her he KNEW, after so much talk and getting to know the DD who was on the inside that the DD that she projected and put out front, was a lie. That DD, the one she wanted everyone to look at, was the low expectations she wanted the world to accept. This way neither she, nor anyone else

200

for that matter, would be disappointed once the "real" DD showed up. It was like leaving herself no place to fall from because you can't fall from the bottom. If she managed to reach any height, then there was only praise for something she never showed you she could reach. But it was all a game and he knew it the moment he met her.

She had told him about her dreams, her love, where her passion lay and all the things that made her world go around - the real her. All this, he understood, never having laid an eye on her; never having heard her voice on the phone. There were no airs to put on, and no expectations to adjust. Maybe he would show up and wouldn't be anything like he said he was, his picture, job, personality, nothing. She opened up to him in a way she would have never opened up to him had he met her in person. Showed him the deck and then he showed up and was everything he said he was and it shook her up. She wanted him which meant this now gave her something to lose. This required protection from all the dark places in her life, so that they never had to ruin this new thing she had grown to love and desire.

He was getting a full picture, with more than he wanted. But he, too, understood that this was not something that he could afford to continue to run from or deny any longer. He also had lived in denial. Not only with her and all the things he saw in her that he didn't want to see or believe, but all the bags he had snuck into the room for the ride as well.

For days, as he had been haunted by the images she had planted in his head, he was disturbed by them and all they meant for her, him and ultimately their relationship. No, he was taking the time to dig up some old bones of his own. Why had he chosen yet another woman who was emotionally unavailable and broken? Had he purposely done this on some subconscious level? He was no less committed in his thinking with his last relationship and the woman he thought he was going to marry. So what was so different now? Why was his NEW declaration so different? Why would this one stick? Or was he just fooling himself? Hopelessly in love with this romantic idea of love conquering all and unaware of the truth it would take to actually get there? With him, never so much as possessing the tools to get such an ambitious job done, how did he manage to end up here again? After all, he had chosen her. He could clearly see all these things surrounding her. So, why?

Spending those days in thought, he figured out that the ingredient he was always missing was the literal knowledge in order to advance to the next level. He hadn't witnessed it on any level with any real reliability in anyone he knew personally. So he had tried to do it as he had done with everything else in his life, with determination, passion and hard work. He had learned the VERY HARD way that this was no substitute for the lack of knowledge. If you were building a house and had no understanding of carpentry, no matter how hard you worked at the end of the day, THAT HOUSE WAS DESTINED TO FALL DOWN. But he had found something that he was positive would help him with his understanding when he started to go to the word of God for all of his answers.

He remembered the bible said in Psalms 127:1 Unless the Lord builds the house, thy labor in vain that build.

He most certainly hadn't used the Lord in his building process at all until this point. He had put him all around it, almost like art work or a constant theme. But he never put him in his life. Not like now. HE WAS ALL THROUGH IT. Now each time he picked up a brick, it was covered in cement that had been mixed in the Word. He then prayed over the brick and asked the Lord to bless it. He then placed it, and thanked God for providing that brick and future shelter.

"*Matthew 7:24 Therefore whosoever heareth these saying of mine, and doeth them, I will liken him unto a wise man, which built his house upon a rock: 25 and the rain descended, and the floods came, and the winds blew, and beat upon that house AND IT FELL NOT: for it was founded upon a rock. 26 And every one that heareth these sayings of mine and, doeth them not, shall be likened unto a foolish man, which built his house upon the sand: 27 and the rain descended, and the floods came, and the winds blew, and beat upon that house; and it fell and great was the fall of it."*

Although he tried with the purest intentions, he had always been the previous and was now seeking the latter. He had finally come to the very real understanding of the two schools of education and who the headmasters were. He had dwelled and walked the halls of the school of consequence his entire life. This school isn't difficult at all. There is, however, a heavy penalty at the tail end when the bill comes due. When you live your life in a sort of trial and error way, not set out to do harm but also not understanding in which direction you should be pointed, sometimes you do more harm than good. And in this school, when that bill comes due, the price is usually pretty damn high. You can owe so much at the end of some lessons, that you can't repay them during your entire lifetime. You can lose your life completely, be dead and gone and still owe. These are hard lessons to learn.

Then there is the school of wisdom. This school is different in that you pay on the front end. In order to PREPARE TO DO IT, the first thing you have to do is drop your pride. So most folks immediately don't qualify, and never get accepted. But ultimately it's their choice because everyone is welcomed. The bible said, "He who have need of wisdom, let him ask me." So the doors are always open but the cost is OBEDIENCE! And this too is a hard row to ho. Tony was seeking the answers for certain. But it was not easy. Obedience is hardly ever easy, especially when you are as hard-headed as he had been. Out of all the things he felt that he was driven to do, he NEVER, in all his years, EVER felt so compelled. On this thing between DD and him, he felt compelled. Like the Lord had opened the sky and spoken him directly and said,

"You, you there son, YOU MAY NOT GO."

The price for disobedience is of course consequence and he had paid that bill far too many times. Those four children spread throughout four different mothers was a harsh reality of his failure as a man, and at times, a father. A bitter pill, but one necessary that he see those faces of the very ones he loved, disappointed and hurt, to be moved. He was set and everyday he did seek Him.

Proverbs 25:2 says, *"It is the glory of God to conceal a matter; to search out a matter is the glory of KINGS!"*

He was most definitely seeking his kingdom. He studied his bible each day as if it truly were a manual for his life, and how to obtain the ultimate goal, salvation, eternal life and love. He was beginning to understand why there wasn't any real mention of the romantic love. He was starting to see that this other love that is mentioned so much was making far more sense. He was almost to the point where he had figured out that they just may be one in the same. He wasn't certain, so he kept his head down, ears open and chin tucked. He knew in order to get what he had been praying for, he was going to have to fight.

"Proverbs 18:15 The heart of the PRUDENT getteth knowledge; and the ear of the WISE seeketh knowledge."

Yes, today he felt he was on the right path and this is what made his journey and his promise to DD so different. He already made her his wife in his mind and sought constantly to cover her in what God had revealed to him and blessed him with. He wanted to give it all to her; from the beginning, on the spot. He was eager to submit from the start. It was DD that took pause and he had no choice but to respond. She would not allow him to take her. She had no idea where she would be taken and he understood that all too well at this time. She needed to see it for herself and know God's love. Accept it. Believe in it, so that she could see where he was going to take her out of.

When he looked at her, he did not see the torn down, shattered frame of a woman. He saw the glory of God's promise. He could see so brightly in her future and he needed her to see it too. His heart burst with all of God's love when he thought about God's promise. He could hear him saying to her so very loudly,

"DD, for I love you so I have built the perfect man just for you. I know you believe you are not worthy and unlovable. I know you believe you cannot be forgiven for all you have done against my word and desire for your life. Even you with all your perceived problems, bags and hang ups, if you would just set them down long enough to look, I have placed him before you at this very moment."

With all the horrible things that she had thought that she had done, there he was showing up with the love she had at one time in her life prayed for diligently. In fact, although she had stopped going to God, stopped asking for forgiveness and lost her faith some time ago, she admitted to Tony that she had indeed prayed for him. The very night ,she found his picture. She told him how his profile had popped up and she passed it by once, twice and then three times. It just kept popping up until she had it on her screen more than anyone else. She laughed. "It must have been a sign," she said, as she made that first contact. There was a powerful lesson in it for DD, only if she chose to see it.

There was a powerful message in what lies beneath this denial. He had been meditating on it and studying the bible ever since DD came home and shared her life with him. Through those efforts and prayer, this is what he found. Denial wasn't merely a coping mechanism which kept them from overload and shock. Because once they were past that point, they remained there seeking to avoid the pain, work, penance, and sadly even avoiding the joy and happiness they had both prayed for each, feeling undeserving.

This last couple of weeks, Tony had learned, right along with DD, a major lesson about denial from the school of consequence. Once the bubble was burst and denial was no longer an option, the truth arrived. And that truth was incredibly painful. It tore his heart so violently that he would never again seek the false shelter of denial. He realized it threatened the very existence of God's promise.

The bible says, "Luke 9:23 *If any man will come after me, let him DENY himself, and take up his cross daily, and follow me."*

Each time Tony had turned a blind eye to DD and her loose ways, not only was he not covering her, he was seeking to protect HIMSELF from the pain that came with dealing with his jealousy; from dealing with his need to run and escape the pain of the rejection he was certain would come if he pointed out all the things he saw that were against any relationship in the physical realm, let alone all he saw in the spiritual one. With him living in this place of denial, it left him an easy out. He was leaving his cross - his issue - on the ground daily. Like his little secret, his subconscious kept this running tally in the back of his mind. Even as he willingly gave her the trust she sought, and he promised, each day, he knew in his heart of hearts that she wasn't being truthful or honest.

This would be his readymade excuse, so when it was time to quit as he had done so many times in his life, he would have this truth to fall back on. He would throw it on the table and push it to the center and feel righteous with his decision. And it would never even be disputed because, just like him, she dwelled in that place but she too knew the truth. She was denying her fears and living in that place full time too; and rent free. At this point, she was doing it so blatantly that even she wouldn't try to pretend it wasn't what it was. He was just as much at fault as she was if he didn't ask for better, out of fear. Maybe even more.

After all, it is in the word that HE was to be the "Priest" of their home. It was also HIM that was to cover her, as God covered him. He was the one who was responsible to deliver the law of the Lord to her as well as tenderly wash her in the Word "to make her holy, cleansing her." Nowhere was this more clear than in,

Ephesians 5:26 *That he might sanctify and cleanse it (her) with the washing of water by the word, 27 that he might present it (her) to himself a glorious church (woman) . . . holy and without blemish. 28 He that loveth his wife loveth himself.*

He finally understood that in neglecting his responsibility to sacrifice, he had left her – and himself - uncovered and unprotected. It was no wonder that this thing came home to hit him right where it hurt. He had been stuck in a place where he could see DD's value and fixated on all those things HE WANTED, but didn't understand the cost.

One of the most important components of one's integrity is the ability to follow through with a commitment, no matter what the cost. *"Many a man claims to have unfailing love, but a faithful man who can find?"* Proverbs 20:6

Had he been faithful? Had he been faithful to his ideals; loyal to his character? Had he been faithfully attending her virtue, watching her as the church she represented? He, too, was exposed, FLAWED! This was all hitting him like a lightening rod. As he was reading the Bible, he began to question himself out loud.

"How do I cultivate her trust or garner her respect when I have not committed to gaining it by accepting my responsibilities as a man and leader? How can I blame her for not committing to me? Better yet, how could I expect her to accept this atmosphere of dishonesty that I have been helping to perpetuate? After all I know about her and her history of men who betrayed her trust?"

Honesty is minimum, one of the basest things you can do for your mate and he hadn't even been that. How could she trust that? Now that he was fully aware, there was no more room left to shuck and jive. He was no longer ignorant to this sin of omission he was knee deep in, with the good understanding that:

"To him that knoweth to do good and doeth it not, to him it is sin."

Thinking about it, now that he had come into a better understanding, it was a romantic enough idea and shouldn't take a lot of motivation. When it was ideal, it read like a love note.

"When I looked at you and saw that you were old enough for love, I spread the corner of my ferment over you and COVERED your nakedness. I gave you my solemn oath and entered into a covenant with you . . . and you became mine." Ezekiel 16:18

It was a beautiful notion if ever there was one. One that came with responsibility that required he face his demons and deal directly with all the issues and fears that he had been avoiding. This meant he needed to step outside of his fears and walk into the light of faith, trust and belief, FIRST, without the safety of a net; no guarantees or assurances. This was HIS charge. To sacrifice for the things he said he wanted. It could only be one way. He was the man and this was God's asking price. When God called for SACRIFICE, he spoke to Abraham NOT Sarah. (Genesis 22) It was his responsibility, not hers.

It was time for Tony to MAN UP! His avoidance left the bill unpaid and his sacrifice unfulfilled. Each time he let his fear tell him that he wasn't worth asking her to stop disrespecting him, to stop running the street, to stop getting high, to stop CHEATING, or at a minimum stop, what appeared to be, cheating behaviors, he was denying his cross and ultimately denying his happiness. What he learned this week, was the thing that put God's promise to him, and DD, in jeopardy.

Matthew 10:38 *He that taketh NOT his cross and followeth after me, IS NOT WORTHY OF ME.*

That was it. If he wanted this position in her life, this was his duty as a husband, father and leader of their home; one he could no longer refuse.

"Make it plain brother. Make it plain," he thought to himself.

He had to drop the wounded act with the quickness. All those hurt feelings about what she may or may not have done were dead. There was no more room for those emotions. He bore equal shame and burden in this thing and had no right to hold it over her head or shame her with it. He had to let this thing go and put it behind them. He knew this now. No more time for hurt feelings and petty emotions. He had a job to do and up until now, he had been asleep at the wheel. It was going to be difficult, but he had to accept some of the responsibility in this. Knowing full well that each time he didn't cover her with the wisdom he had sought which God had bestowed onto him, he was taking the easy road. And ANYONE with even a BIT of sense knows that this is not, could not, be him picking UP his cross, nor covering her with a minimum of honesty. After this week, if there was one lesson he was clear on; one that he would no longer learn from the school of consequence, it was this one. How could God bless him if he wasn't willing to do the work?

He had failed miserably and knew he owed HER an apology too. God had revealed that to him. It was going to be up to him if he would drop his pride and do the right thing. After this week, he didn't see any real use for pride, so it would come easy. Barring the shame would be another question altogether.

He knew exactly where to begin, forgiveness would be first. Next, LOVE. It seemed too simple but the answer was, again, right there in the Word.

She is programmed to respond to love. It is in her nature. Loving her lets her know she is special. In all his seeking out his kingdom, it seems that he had not actually prepared to have it. There was a protocol to how things were to be placed. He needed to open his heart and deliver the love he held for her in the way the Almighty had required of him to do it.

"In love, a throne will be established; in FAITHFULNESS a man will sit on it --- one who in judging seeks justice and speeds the cause of righteousness" Isaiah 16.5.

"A throne is established through righteousness" Proverbs 16:12.

Walking in righteousness had to be the first step toward keeping their life, and future household, on the path of God. And forgiveness was a righteous first step. His heart told him that his love was ready to crown her today, make her feel like the priority in his life that she was. Make his intentions plain, for the world to see. This should go well towards the work necessary to garner her trust and will let her know that her heart is safe in his hands. Esther 5:2-7 was his plan. Love, it was a good place to start.

*   *   *   *   *

It had been a solid week and Tony and DD had both remained in their neutral corners. They had both been licking their wounds from the heavy pounding they took in their most recent lesson learned. He had turned to his bible and prayer, while she, not yet having re-established that line to God, ended up turning to depression and despair. She had resigned to spending her days crying, and her nights getting as high as she could to forget all the things that had been tormenting her about her ordeal.

As they slowly walked back towards one another, Tony had no way of really knowing how badly DD was hurting. She was an expert at concealing her pain and making others believe she was always fine. He knew she was hurting and through their conversations, found out about the drugs. In the state she was in, he decided not to push, for the moment. Through his church, he found a Christian-based counselor that DD could go and talk to about all of the things that were pulling her to the bottom of her dark places. He also found her a church-based support group and they both started to attend. He was stepping up and out into his role as leader - King of their family - and assuming his throne. DD also agreed to attend his church a few times. She even began to attend the same church her support group was in. She, too, was ready for her new life and crown.

She had stepped up out of the darkness of depression without the benefit of medication in order to do it. They had a long talk where he had explained where he thought he had failed her, and their relationship, and apologized. She didn't say much. She looked amazed and said she really didn't know what to say. He knew that conversation would sound crazy to her because, at times, it sounded crazy to him. But he felt compelled to do it, so he did. Obedience was the payment for wisdom.

Although he didn't see God's plan completely, he did what he was told. She was back in church. She was praying, and they were studying the bible together! He was so excited and relieved because her depression was being lifted with each passing week. She still hadn't obtained a job and he found a way to help her with that as well.

About a year into law school, Tony decided to take a job as a paralegal at a corporate law firm, so he could get some experience in law; sort of like an apprentice. Once there, he caught on very quickly and soon he was the top paralegal. He held lengthy conversations with attorneys, discussing everything from his school assignments to his future. This was a great point of pride for him. In fact, he was so good at his job he handled most of the work the attorneys signed off on.

He had been contemplating starting his own paralegal firm so that he could share in some of the profit that all his hard work had benefited so many attorneys already. So with DD's job situation in mind, he started this business and made her manager/ administrative assistant. He also gave her a partnership share whereby she was in complete control over the credit repair part of the business. Every penny of that money went to her and she was paid a salary for the other position. After they established advertisement, which he paid for out of his side of the business, ensuring her portion was pure profit, business was good

- really good. Soon DD could afford the things her life required and wanted.

He, again gave her the Mercedes Benz she had previously returned to him. This time she didn't have to give him any money for it, at all. He took care of that car note too. He took Kayden, her only child, shopping for new clothes when she asked him about a sweater she had seen. They hadn't really had the opportunity to establish a relationship yet. DD had kept Tony and her daughter Kayden apart; partly selfishly and partly protecting her from what she thought may only be a temporary relationship. He understood her position. He had done the same with his children. All that was about to change, now that he was accepting his responsibility. He would no longer let this slide. He started looking after Kayden after school when DD had to work. They began spending time together on a regular basis; going to movies and shows. He even got her some guinea pigs she really wanted, when she came home with her first honor roll report card. Things between them were going well.

DD still had a lot of free time on her hands, but they were working on that too. At any other time in Tony's life, something that would have had him running for the hills, or at the very least backing off, ended up moving him forward. He had weathered this storm and learned a very valuable lesson. He vowed to remain obedient and in looking at how this worked out. It made it look and feel easy. He was more than encouraged. Beneath it all, isn't that the point?

Chapter 18
Surrender

Tony had finally come to a safe place, a new plateau; one he had never seen before. He was more enamored with DD than ever before. He was able to see past her flaws, past his pain and the things she had done to him out of her own pain and doubt. He was seeing DD with all new eyes; with an honesty that she was momentarily unable to give him. But with that, there was just so much she simply couldn't hide from him, even if she wanted to. At no time in his life had he ever felt the way she was making him feel.

He was so certain that all the things he was going through with her - all the things he had, and probably would endure with her - would be for a purpose. All the things he had gone through in his own personal life had all been a staging ground, getting him ready for this. The love to end all loves. The final time he would have to endure this uncertainty. Walk through the fearful place. Bare all his pain, secrets and fears to a stranger. From this point on, he would know exactly where she was in his life and where his love lied. Just like he knew the moment he put his eyes on that pretty brown eyed girl, she was his soul mate, his destiny and every road, every path, every thought and change his life was going through, all lead to her. It was so clear, if it had never been before.

It was impossible to ignore any longer, all of the clarity, all of the transformations he had gone through. All of the things he had been able to endure. All these things, he never even considered with so many. He was flying through them on wings of an angel with her and he knew this was no coincidence. There was no such thing. He simply didn't believe in them. No longer could he overlook these things. Her beauty, her effort, her strength, in all the places he was weak. All of the things she held down in a solid way, like her ability to pull him out of all of those dark places he had been so afraid to go into, was amazing.

He remembered how his entire life, he had dealt with all of these issues around sex and its attachment to love so much so that it became love in his young life. Those feelings eventually grew into some sort of addiction whereby he was collecting women like trophies. He had been exposed, far too early, to a world he should never have known, by all the wrong people. This brought him to a place where something that should have been so beautiful, had become reduced to mere satisfaction. He knew that this was not what it was intended for.

This could not be what our Father, God, had in mind when he created such a wondrous act. No, this was human perversion. It had touched him from a very young age. This was something he had been dealing with his entire life. He had come through so much, but most of it looked more like discipline than it did healing. So by the time he met DD, he was no longer that dude who used and abused women, and their virtue, for his pleasure. He was far from it. He was, steadily, on the other side of that equation.

He was now a gentleman, far more concerned with coming into the light with this act, and far more interested in the real and pure emotions filled with LOVE that lead to, and came out of, this act. This, however, still wasn't healing and he knew it. Right now, it was the best, and all, he had. This was the reason he had been so careful with DD and her virtue. This was the reason he needed to walk so slowly with her; not just for her, so that she could save her own virtue, but also so he didn't fall back into a familiar place that said her virtue was nothing to protect.

Since that first date, he had begun, ever so slowly, to see her true and real beauty revealed to him. It wasn't in her "look," her features, or her body. It went far deeper and he thanked God each day for that vision, as frightening as it was. Some days, it literally scared him into wanting to go back because he could see in her a future so bright, it made him feel unworthy. She hadn't even gone down that road yet. He knew, if she could see the person that he saw in her, then she may be able to see the real him as well. The real him, was just as broken, only with better coping techniques.

He knew, in his heart of hearts that she deserved so much more, especially coming out of the hell from whence she had marched. She was standing before him, in this life, a walking miracle. He knew he needed to be better so he pushed on that old door inside of himself to go in there and throw out all those ill things that would keep him from accepting DD completely on this level. This was the same level that wouldn't allow DD to touch his face, and needed to control her hands when they got close.

On this level, he only allowed her to kiss him so far. It most definitely didn't allow them to walk into any sort of sex. She craved his touch, his kiss and his embrace now, far more than she yearned for his sex. She had finally come down and found her way out of the shelter of protection that the safety of sexual contact provided through the physical world. It was something he understood all too well, having lived there so long himself.

But now she stood there, working out her own salvation, with fear and trembling. And there he was, the head that God had promised he would be, yet still afraid of the very things he was walking her out and away from. NOW WHAT? He was praying for a healing. He was looking for freedom from these issues for DD. For his life. For himself, because he too deserved more. After a long day of meditation, he was really disappointed because he had tried to face all of those old things that he faced before that had brought him to so much healing. He eventually realized that maybe he had some more of that work to do. He had done this with the highest hopes, and the deepest fear, that this thing would, again, bring him to his knees as it had the last time he had to claw his way out of that hole, to find his life.

When he got there, he was anew. But today, even as he tried, he found it dull, un-enlightened and nothing had changed. That night, he was on one of those long walks where he had listened to her bare her soul - a trail laden with many of her tears. He had shared of himself and never been ashamed to share. The problem was unseen by him as he started this walk but it would soon be revealed.

He was looking pensive and upset and DD started in concern, "What's wrong Tony? You look really upset tonight, like there is something deep on your mind. You want to talk about it?

"Honestly it's a difficult conversation but I just don't know if it will change anything. It has everything to do with my past, most of which I have shared with you. So I'm not sure it's even worth rehashing," Tony said, sure as he always was that he possessed all his own answers.

"Well just as you have been there for me, so am I for you. Two is better than one, remember? You taught me that," DD said.

It hit him like he had never heard those words before. She was absolutely right. She had brought that to him and he realized now that he needed to jump in and trust his love, and more importantly, his God, and this woman He had put in his life. He needed to allow her to show up for him the way he had shown up for her. He was confident that the conversation would be fruitless, as he was certain he had already thought of all the angles and looked at everything inside out already.

He was overconfident as he started in on this road. DD, however, was now the one with the pensive look on her face as if she was afraid that she would find out something she may not be able to handle about her love that she didn't formerly, know.

He began, "It has all to do with the things we have been going through lately around our physical contact. I'm not talking about sex. You have gotten

216

much better about taking this walk with me and have quickly come back into your virtue and found the worth I have always known you possessed. I have come to realize that the things you are asking me for as far as my reluctance to allow you to touch me, and my resistance to allowing myself to touch you as you have asked, has made me look at this thing in an entirely new and different way.

"I have always viewed these things as a matter of discipline. I needed to learn to control my emotional self so that I didn't become needy to the point where I needed to use sex as my only method of safety, healing or way to feel love. I am realizing now that you have taken up your part and started down this path I have asked you to go, and that I, too, have some much needed work to do. You have pushed me as much as I have pushed you. I will admit to you now that I have not only been afraid, but also unwilling, to delve into that part of me I needed to, in order to heal so I could give you this thing that you have been asking me for.

"You have not been unreasonable. I have deflected and blamed you. I have run and avoided the conversation. Hiding behind you, it became easy to avoid what was real and going on with me. Today I want to man up and get real with you and tell you what I KNOW you already know. I want to apologize and tell you that I truly desire to touch you and hold you the way that you want to be touched. I have never wanted to do that for another as much as I have for you.

"I think about you constantly in this way, longing to touch you, to kiss your face, to rub all of your body the way you have rubbed mine. I desire to do the sweetest things for you but I realize I can only do them under my terms and conditions. This means that any time you move or add your input, all those little things that make you, you, I immediately clam up out of a serious fear I KNOW could only come from my past and all the pain back there I have refused to look at. I just don't know how, at this point… I don't know how to let

217

go," he paused as if he was looking to her for advice but really he was only seeking mere acknowledgement.

"You have to let go and resist the urge to fight me and fight it. I only want to love you. I would never want to hurt you through those trails into your past. Let me love you baby. You have to let go," DD said, with the look of love in her eyes.

"I know baby. I know. I have tried. I have laid there and allowed you to touch me against my instinct; against my nature. Each time I am only counting the seconds until you have gotten your fill and will stop. I'll be honest and tell you at those times, my skin is crawling and I am jumping out of my body and doing everything I can think of not to push you away or just tell you to stop. Sounds crazy but it's like I can't bear to be touched at all. I know that this hurts you, just as I knew it then. If I was to tell you to stop, it would hurt you just the same. And I swear I am so sorry DD," Tony said, feeling himself becoming emotional.

He could also feel himself starting to close up and become fearful like he wanted to run away from this conversation. At any other time in his life, it was a good place for a joke, or saying something clever, to take away from the focus of what was really going on inside of him. He could hardly face it. He could hardly accept it. He knew with all certainty that he would never accept what it was he was holding onto from another so it was a no-brainer that his fear in telling her these truths was that she would run from him like the plague he felt he was. He was hesitant to speak as they were walking silently and fighting back tears from double-digit years of buried pain and emotion, wondering when God was going to show up and rescue him from himself.

Just as the first tear dropped, DD began to speak, "I understand Tony. I swear I do. I know where you have been. You have told me about all that horrible shit you went through. I just don't know how you have made it this far, to be honest. But you are stronger than you think. You have come out from those things and have managed to make a life apart from that, virtually untouched by that world. You have a beautiful home and have become a world class father. I see the love in you for your children and I know that it could not come from that place. It is this very thing in you that drives me, gives me hope, let's me know without any doubt what kind of father you would be to Kayden.

"It has brought me to a place of desire to give you my whole heart against all of my fears and the things I THINK I know. It is these very things that have helped me to see, and finally face, all the thoughts I fight each day not to tell you out of fear that you will leave me. Things I, too, think that no one will stand by me through." And now DD was beginning to tear up as Tony was already silently feeling ashamed for allowing himself to be opened up to the point that he was crying.

Imagine two people in the south within the midnight hours walking down streets barely lit. It is just dark enough for one to think that he could get away with tears from such a deep place that he may believe that he was alone on this road. As he listened to DD's words, they all struck home like the million dreams he had dreamed of someone - damn near anyone - to come into his life and speak those words. He had always secretly wanted this. Although, he sold himself on this never happening so many times that he no longer believed in it. He was now faced with those words. He was now faced with that reality of all the things he had dared to dream and never dared to truly believe in. It was weighing in on him like nothing he could ever have imagined it would feel like. He had asked for it, prayed for it and truthfully never even seen it coming, even as the love of his life had FINALLY shown up.

It was a pressure he had never experienced and he wasn't at all ready for it. His greatest fear was that she would see that all over him. It was for this reason he could not stop these tears. He knew he had to talk. He knew it was time to let it go and talk about all the things he couldn't dare utter to another soul. Those things he had denied to himself, pretending they never happened, or existed. Things that only happen to other people. He started in on it and saw it playing out in his head as if this were a movie and never happened to him. He lost his breath, inhaled deep then spoke with the honesty he only wished he could maintain with her for the rest of his life.

"I know I told you about my childhood abuse but I didn't tell you everything. When I was a child, and my family fell apart, I ended up going into a foster home. It was there I was re-introduced to a world of sex and wanting. In order to eat and continue to live in Ms. Percy's home, I had to service her. She made me give her head each day after school before her own children arrived home. If I refused, I didn't eat. I got beaten and she made my life hell. She controlled everything in my world.

"I was taught that I wasn't even allowed to enjoy all the twisted things she had brought me to unless she gave me permission. I became afraid of my own shadow. I couldn't use the bathroom unless she game me permission. I would be in school and stand at the urinal with my eyes closed, trying to block out her voice - her picture - just so I could go pee. She was a dominatrix and she practiced her skill, what she called her art, on me.

"By the time I left her home, I was broken of anything remotely my own and was completely lost of any identity of what it was to be me, let alone of what it was to be a man. So as I stand today, the last thing I want is someone touching me that I can't stop. Someone touching me in a way that even pleases them because it takes me to a certain place. I freeze up and go into this sort of auto pilot thing that only I seem to understand, where I am not myself but a performer. Where the only thing that matters is her orgasm, her pleasure and my expression of pain." At this point he could no longer control his emotions or pretend he could ever have done so.

For him, the cat was out of the bag and he had spoken the words that he himself swore he never wanted to think, let alone hear. So he was falling - falling with no net - trusting that she would be there to catch him with some sort of magic words. He had prayed to St. Daphnia, the patron saint of the emotionally disturbed, and the sexually abused. Honestly, he didn't believe in her, or her ability to help him through this thing he was experiencing.

He did, however, believe in God. He waited patiently for Him to come in and take this pain, and shame, away as he lay there naked to the world, and the love of his life. Where was God? Where was St. Daphnia? Where was their protection? He waited on it as he had waited on his mother to arrive and take him out of that hell that he knew only Satan could have delivered him into.

DD began to cry at his honesty and for all the things he had never told her. She realized her contribution to a world so wicked and twisted and she, knowing a little something about shame, pain and guilt, spoke from that wounded place with words that only God could have put on her tongue.

"Maybe we should back off of this for awhile. Maybe we should go slower into these places if it causes you this much pain. Honestly it causes me pain too. But hearing all you have said, it puts me in a position I have never considered and it hurts me in a way I cannot explain. I think we need to take a break from our physical side altogether," DD said, as she fell, face first, into a pool of tears.

All at once, it was like Tony had fallen into a vat of fire and his flesh was engulfed in the hottest flames he had ever experienced in his lifetime. All the very things he feared about telling anyone his fears, was realized. He had always believed that this thing made him unlovable. Anyone who knew a hint of this thing he had gone through would run from him like the hell it was. There she was in the midst of the hardest thing he had ever done in his life, like a puppet playing out the very villain in his worst nightmare. She was leaving. She was running. She was leaving him like the wretch he was. This was all too much for him. It was like the entire world was closing in around him. He could hear the demons howling at the moon as he begged God, and the saints, for this very thing to be untrue. He could not control his emotions. He could hear the demons taking over his spirits in the form of words and the form of needing to rip and tear the flesh of another.

He tore into DD, "Well fuck you then. If you can't handle what's real about me after all I have stood through for you then you were never meant to be with me. You are nothing but a common slut anyway. You are a whore and I never want to see you another day of my life. I hate you DD! I fucking hate you for getting me to believe in you! For getting me to tell you all of my secrets while you, yourself lied, hiding behind all the shit you wouldn't tell me. I hate you and never want to see you another day in my life, FUCK YOU!"

He screamed at the top of his lungs in a way he only wished he could have done at his abusers all those years ago. The devil had stolen his heart and replaced it with one of stone that he now controlled. He did not have the will nor did he want it. His pain seeped through every pore of his being and he spewed every foul thing he could thing to say.

He was experiencing emotions that he literally felt like was taking him outside of his mind into a place where he could not control his words. Eventually he could only hear the howl of the demons that had always inhabited his body and soul in that place. It was truly like that movie *The Exorcist*. While he was howling at the moon, DD remained silent. At first her heart was pierced by his foul words. Then, as if God himself had touched her, she turned her head and refused to listen to a single word he had to say.

"I know this is the devil. I know these are those very demons fighting to maintain control over your mind, body and spirit. I pray unto Jesus that you leave this man I love. I pray that you leave our lives and never return. I rebuke you in the name of Jesus. I call down from heaven the archangel Michael and the Almighty God himself to drive forth this evil spirit that is now controlling my love's tongue. I know this isn't you talking Tony and I refuse to listen to these words. I refuse to respond to these words. I know this isn't you." DD began to sob uncontrollably as she continued to speak.

"I see you Tony. I see your shame. I see your pain and heartache. And I say whatever guilt you are holding onto, IT IS NOT YOUR FAULT. I love you. I will always love you. I will never leave you so you can ask me to go but I will not." DD said these words at the top of her lungs. If this had been any other city, at any other time of day, the world would now be watching. They would be seeing what appeared to be two nut bags ready for the asylum. Truth be told, no one would ever believe this. They were in another place that people can only see a psychotic break in.

As she sobbed, those demons continued on, "I swear it doesn't matter what you say. I hate you and will never be with you again. I hate you!" Tony screamed out.

He could only feel DD in the deepest, darkest, worst parts and spaces in his own personal hell. If she could see all the hate and self-loathing he had held and hid from her then she would never stay. He had left himself at the worst possible times, so he knew that she could never stay. So he pushed. The more he pushed the calmer and more collected she became.

"I refuse to listen to you Tony. I want you to know that when you are done, when you come back from this place, I will have not lost a single thread of respect, honor or love for you. I am holding it right here next to my heart for you. I will never hold these words against you. I will never recall them or remind you of them. I love you with my whole heart and will not leave you; and least of all, will I leave you here."

She continued to sob in a loud way that said that even if those people who would have committed them were there, she was ripe for the picking because she no longer cared about appearances, or who saw into their little shop of horrors.

"Let me take you home Tony. Allow me to get you home and I'll leave you to what you and only God can get you through," DD said.

She had met him at their usual walking spot about a quarter of a mile away from his home. He refused to allow her to drive him home and decided instead to walk the remainder of the way home. He vowed to himself he would not cry. He would not allow her abandonment of him to cause him a moment's pain as he knew, within his cynical heart, she was not only capable of this, but she had this planned all along. The moment she found out who he truly was, she would leave. The moment they arrived back to their meeting spot, DD jumped into her father's car and, without so much as a kiss or wave, she drove off in tears. Tony turned to that dark lonely road that he knew only he could face as he thought about his long walk home alone.

As he began this walk towards his apartment, he could hear the demons around him. He could all but see them and he was more than afraid. He began to pray and ask God to walk with him and help him make it home in this pitch black environment. This place was devoid of light; not only His light, but the actual physical light it required him to see his nose before his face. With each step, he focused in on fading out the loud voices that begged him to kill himself. The voices that told him no one would ever love him and that he may as well give up. He could see the saints coming to his rescue and knew this would not be the end of his world.

Once he got home, he was speechless, but no longer felt like his life was worthless. He crawled into his place and cried until he could no longer keep his eyes open. With the freedom of closed doors, it was far greater than he ever imagined it could be and he let loose the cries of a grown man that had been holding in such pains and secrets. It was all that anyone could ever imagine. He tore his living room up. Tore down every prayer and picture in his place. This went on until he was spent and out of energy; until he could no longer keep his eyes open.

As he felt the last tear his body had left to offer fall down his face, and he felt the last bit of bitter energy leaving his body, he heard his phone ring. It was DD. She was still sobbing.

"I want you to know I love you Tony. I want you to know I am here and know that this isn't you. I will be here whenever you're ready. If it's tomorrow. If it's next week. If its next month. I will wait for you. You are a good man and I love you. You are worth waiting on and I will not give up, or quit on you. Call me when you're ready," DD finished saying, then fell silent.

Tony was stuck in a place where he couldn't acknowledge her words and refused to believe, or hear, them. He didn't say a word. He broke into, yet another, hard cry that simply didn't have the tears left to provide for, but had plenty of screams and emotion. In this spirit, he fell asleep in the middle of a living room that had seen better days. DD's world finally faded to black and amongst the very same tears, she did so in prayer. Something she could never manage to get through for herself, she was now praying harder than she could ever remember for the life and sound mind of this, the love of her life.

She dared to utter those prayers against all that life had given her. She was praying for support against all of the horror that Tony was yet to see or hear; against all of the horror she still wasn't certain he could handle or deal with. He was in a place where some of those same fears ruled her and told her that he couldn't stay. She knew unto herself that she loved him the way she needed him to love her. She needed him to be a man who stayed so she would stay. She would stand by him through this and any other thing that came his way.

Then, she not only prayed for God to lift this thing off of her but him. She asked God to continue to mold them both into the love he desired to see of them. Most of all, against her own fears that said she too didn't deserve it, she prayed. Through his fears and strength to share, Tony had shown her that this could be done. Now she needed to show him that he, like her, could be accepted and loved. She closed her eyes, hurt but still hopeful. He had already affected that portion of her brain and she leaned on God for the rest.

She said in a low voice, "Good night my prince. I love you and will be here tomorrow and the next day. Whenever you're ready, I love you. Good night."

Although he couldn't hear that silent prayer, Tony was sleeping beneath the miracle of love she had afforded him, beyond anything he ever thought he could be, or deserved. She remembered as he had pointed out in God's word that "two is better than one" and she pulled hard on that third strand for God's sake.

Chapter 19
Unthinkable- I'm ready
(Forming Complete)

The sun came up on a day that, neither Tony nor DD thought they would ever see after a night like last night. Tony knew that he would have never survived a night like the last one without the kiss of death to seal him into the safety that he imagined only death could bring. He couldn't think of another way he could look into his reflection in the mirror. As the alarm went off, he knew it was time to wake up to get his son back from Sharon. He knew he had to pull it together. All those things that held him and his soul, captive last night, fell to unfertile ground this morning.

Sure, he still carried a heavy heart but it wasn't filled with the scent and full content of despair that last night's dialogue ensured him would follow as long as he took wind into his thick chest and lungs. Today he was filled with a hunger for knowledge and he knew exactly where to head for it. Before he opened his eyes completely, he went directly into a silent prayer and started off his day much like he had ended it, with some more silent tears. As the gentle greeting of his human frailty greeted him at dawn, he was reminded of his weakness and his strength alike. He could not shake what DD had said to him. It did give him strength, whether or not he could say it out loud. Those words she spoke were powerful. Honestly he never saw that kind of love - that kind of strength - in her. He knew he loved her but it was something he honestly didn't believe ANYONE could love him through - let alone his dream girl.

By the time he finished his prayers, he was filled with an overwhelming feeling to call DD and tell her that he was alright and that he loved her. Even if he couldn't say another word, he knew he had to at least do that. Once he made it off of his knees, he hit the number two button that was programmed on his speed dial. As the phone rang, his feelings of love and what he wanted to say to her just increased. She picked up.

"Hey baby," Tony said.

It was silent for a moment as DD was shocked to hear from Tony so soon after such foul words just hours before.

"I'm here Tony. Are you ok?" DD asked.

"Ok listen, I don't want, or need you to say anything, just listen. I heard what you had to say last night and really needed to hear that more than even I realized. I am going to ask you to give me some patience and time to come through this. Honestly I don't even know where to begin. But I do know wherever I'm going and whatever it is, it's mine. I am indeed sorry for all those horrible things I said. You were right. It wasn't me. I can't explain why, or what that was. I can only thank you for understanding and standing by me. I'm sorry," Tony said, then fell silent to hear what she might have to say in response to his comments.

She, on the other hand, still felt her duty was to listen and had very little to say. "I'm here for you baby if you ever need to talk. But I feel like I should just be falling back to give you the space to do the thinking you need to do to come out of this measure. Whenever you call me I will come. Whenever you say you need me, I will be there. Until that time I will be here waiting on you. Faithful and waiting. I love you Tony."

Tony again began to allow those silent tears to run down his face as he thanked her and allowed her to go back to sleep.

Once off of the phone, he did his able best to tuck all that beneath the surface so he could get his son without issues from Sharon. He rushed into the bathroom to hit the shower, thinking maybe he could wash all of the misery off of his face and body. "Just send it down the drain where it truly belonged," he thought.

For one more time in his life, he wished he could follow all that filth right on down the drain to wherever it was going. Somewhere he could hide away and no one would ever have to see him this way, not ever again. But just as those thoughts crossed his upper story, he could feel the sting of the internal question he could hear being asked of himself.

"How would you deal with not being able to see your son's face everyday? Would you be able to know the pain you would bring him? Having been there to watch him suffer through the absence of his mother, you would take his father away too? Selfish!"

He could hear what he assumed was either his conscience, or God. Honestly, he believed them to be one in the same. It brought back, yet again, those warm streaming tears. There was hardly anything that didn't cause them to flow. He was super emotional and extra sensitive. He could feel it through every part of his being. There was no way he was going to be able to hide that, especially from Sharon who had lived with him and knew him for so many years. She was a good woman who had always tried to take care of him. That was the one thing he could say about her, she had always cared.

They met one another at a time and place that they became each other's shelter from the world. It was during his first time of trauma which he relived through exposure to all of his past skeletons. She may very well recognize this look in itself, the moment she walked into the place. She was intuitive even when she pretended she wasn't. During those long hard years with one another, she had always been good for that. He knew, as always, if he needed her, she would show up for him in that way because he had been exactly that to her their entire existence. He also knew that there was only so far she was willing to go and he needed more than just a shelter. He needed a home and she wasn't ready to be that, although it appeared that way.

He had spent those long, lonely nights and knew better than to fool himself, even at this time of need. If he wasn't going to share this with DD, he wasn't going to share it with anyone. This was truly going to have to be between him and God. He was going to go to him and ride the rest of this mess out. As he toweled off, he was deep within those very thoughts when he heard the doorbell ring waking him from his haze. He threw on his undershorts, tee and bathrobe and hurried down the stairs to grab the door.

That was it! He would seem rushed and run back upstairs and into the bathroom. If he avoided eye contact and kept focused on all the little things, then she would not have time to even notice, he thought to himself. As Sharon entered into the apartment, she too was in a rush as she was running late. He quickly jumped in to appear helpful and preoccupied. She would hopefully stay here and never even notice his tear drawn eyes. As he went to the car and grabbed the rest of Angel's things, she had already headed to the driver's side of the car. When she turned to look him in the eye to say goodbye, he quickly looked away and at Angel. He could feel her peering into the side of his head, straight into his heart strings, as she stood there staring at him. She knew something was wrong and had stopped rushing for just a moment. She stood there waiting for him to make eye contact. As he headed back to the apartment door pretending, once again, to be too preoccupied to look at her, she called out to him.

"Hey you? You're not going to say good bye to me?" She said.

"I said goodbye, Sharon," he said, smiling and playing with Angel in his silly daddy, baby voice.

"Mommy is so silly, isn't she Angel?" He said trying to make light of the situation.

"Look at me for minute Tony. Tony, look at me," she called out to him, as he almost made it back to the apartment door.

He turned around and looked at her. He already knew she could tell something was wrong, so he went to plan B, which was denial. She was good at that and would recognize it immediately. Because she viewed it as a sign of strength, using it as her main coping mechanism, she may just let him slide for now.

"What's the matter Tony? You look like you have been crying. What's going on with you?" Sharon said.

"It's nothing Sharon. I'm fine, just got some shampoo into my eyes. That's all," he replied.

"I know you're not telling me the truth. Something is up but I won't push you. When you're ready I'm here, like I've always been. Don't let DD steal the best parts of you Tony. You're a great man, no matter what she does to you, or tells you. She is a fool and will lose you just like I did if she doesn't see who you are. Maybe you'll be ready to talk later. If so, please call me. You don't have to suffer through this alone," Sharon said with the look of love in her eyes.

He knew all too well how this would go if he let her back into this part of himself. Again, he knew if he intended to go forward he could not go backwards. He was feeling like shit boiled over, but he could not fall backwards into his past for safety. This new plateau required something different from him in order to start that ascent to the next level. This much he could recognize, even if he wasn't quite able to pick himself up off the mat.

He smiled at Sharon and hugged Angel as those warm tears once again started to build up in his eyes, promising the same slow roll down his face he couldn't stop just a few hours earlier. He waved goodbye to her and made sure to look her in the eye to let her know he would be alright, as he stepped into the apartment and locked the door.

Once he got to the top of the steps, he knew he was in no condition to drag himself into work and deal with a rowdy group of third graders. He picked up the phone and called his job and told them he was ill and would need the day off. He had plenty of days on the books and always left lesson plans in case of his absence, although he never used them. He would today. He then took his little man out of his little clothes, and

231

he and Angel crawled right back into the shelter that his warm, comfortable bed would have to provide.

As he lay there on his cool pillow, thoughts of his childhood trauma refused to give him any peace. He was remembering things he had blocked out for years. Why he didn't like to touch. Why he had lost his faith in God as a child. Why he had lost his ability to trust. He was realizing now, for the first time that he faced those demons, why he didn't like to be touched unless he could see every detail and have complete control. He could remember the physical pain inflected. He could remember the cries he held in due to the promise of a worse punishment. He wasn't allowed to cry. He wasn't allowed to show pain and he was NEVER allowed to say no. He began sobbing for all the days he wasn't allowed to. He sobbed and cried for all those times he wanted, and needed to. He took some of his power back from a place that said he was unprotected from the horror provided by those who said they loved him and came with words and promises to always love you but always broke your heart.

He was left exposed and stripped away of the ability to protect himself, which was the ultimate poisonous seed. It told him that he was worthless and there was nothing inside of him worth saving besides his body, which was only to be used and abused. So they came, and they took of the fruit - his only bounty - as they wished, and as it pleased them. They left him with NOTHING! He was falling quickly into a tailspin of anxiety and fear, one that said he would always be giving of himself in that way on some subconscious level, unable to protect himself from all of those who would come and take of his flesh, leaving him but with the bone. He was just a child who was so full of love. They stole all of it to the point that he couldn't even recognize it as it stared him in the face so many times. He was feeling more hopeless than he had ever felt in his life as Angel sat on the edge of the bed watching his favorite program on Nick Kids. He looked up and saw Angel and thought of his innocence. He thought of how he would die before he would allow anyone to take that from him. The tears flowed again as he cried, considering those very questions he uttered so many nights in the dark.

"Why wasn't I worth loving like that? Why wasn't I worth protecting? Saving? God why? Tell me pleeease."

His world fell silent. He could no longer hear the television as it blared *Wonder Pets*. He could no longer hear Angel or his laughter. He could no longer even hear the sound of his own voice, or weeping. It was as if he were underwater, holding his breath. All of the noise and crying stopped. As clear as day he could hear, "For my love they are my adversaries."

Emotion flooded over, but no tears. He could feel the heat on his head as he still felt his tears running, along with the emotion running through him. All of the physical components were missing. He was no longer shaking. He was no longer panting, as he struggled to breathe. In fact, he was still and continued in silence. He had studied the bible for so many months, read the verses, chapter by chapter and so many he had marked. Those words sounded so familiar, but not any he remembered marking. He jumped up and walked into his office and took up his bible and began searching for those words. Psalms 109. It's called A CRY FOR VENGEANCE.

"109:4 *For my love they are my adversaries.*"
And the next line blew his mind away.
"but I give myself unto prayer."
He continued on in amazement.

"They have rewarded me evil for good, and hatred for love. Set thou a wicked man over him and let Satan stand at his right hand. When he shall be judged, let him be condemned: and let his prayer become sin. Let his days be few and let another take his office. Let his children be fatherless, and his wife a widow. Let his children be continually vagabonds, and beg: let them seek their bread also out of their desolate places. Let the EXTORTIONER catch all that he hath and let the

strangers spoil his labor. Let there be none to extend
mercy unto him: neither let there be any to favor his
fatherless children. Let his posterity be cut off; and in
the generation following, let their name be blotted out."

Tony was frozen in notice of this part of the
bible and God's word he had never previously seen. He
was amazed. When he thought of God and all his
goodness, he never did see this. He knew about patience
and mercy, turning the other cheek, letting the Lord fight
your battles and the vengeance should be His. He had
read about the Lord sitting him upon rocks. He viewed
DD as one of those rocks; even Sharon, at a time. But
this, he had never seen. For so long, he had such a hard
time understanding fairness in the world and he was just
now realizing why he never wanted to open up these old
wounds. Somewhere within his mind he never felt like
he had vengeance for all that happened to him which
made him a perpetual potential victim. No justice, and
no sense of fairness, makes faith hard, and trust
impossible.

"LET THEM BE ASHAMED; BUT LET THY
SERVANT REJOICE!"

As he hit those words, he could feel the chains
of bondage breaking free from around his brain, and
from around his soul. All the fear and anxiety that held
him in this place was losing its power. He could see how
these things had stolen his innocence in an entirely new
way. The ability to allow someone to touch you on the
shoulder, or touch your face, without feeling your skin
crawl was extreme and didn't get any more innocent!

All at once the tears just dried up, and his
emotions went calm; not numb, but calm. He could feel
the love, safety and God accompaniment. He no longer
felt alone and he stood, and praised God. He thanked
him for his strength and held his bible close to his heart
as he walked into the bedroom and lay down. He closed
his eyes, still clutching the Word and began to smile.
Thinking intently about God's promise, he called Angel
to him on the bed. As he came, Tony wrapped his arms

around him. He was holding the Word, his son and what remained of his heart as he fell asleep still smiling.

Chapter 20
Melding Complete
(Birth of an Eagle)

It was coming upon a full week since Tony had gone into his wounded psyche, and soul, to battle the enemy for his emotional health, and ultimately, his life. He had spent countless hours in meditation, and reading scripture. He felt like he was on more solid ground than he had ever been. He spent just as much time talking over his process and all the feelings it brought up, with DD. She was amazing for him; far more than he thought she could have ever been. She was strong for him without feeling presumptuous or arrogant. She was vulnerable without feeling sorry for him, or herself, which was just as important as the first.

For the first time in their relationship, she was equally as soft as she was hard and he could see more of her beauty than he ever had before. With each passing day she became greater. They walked. They talked. They prayed. They discussed the Word and all their clarity and confusion. She was just what the doctor ordered; and exactly what his soul needed. She and God restored his hope in an area he never believed he would be whole in again. His desire to be close to her in a more physical way had returned; but this time, with absolutely NO FEAR. He couldn't explain it. He was slowly opening up to the idea that he could take the brake off and allow her to touch him as she pleased and he would do the same.

It sounded simple, but for him it was like asking him to use a Chinese calculator. It took time and you needed training. He noticed it one night as they walked. He watched her in the moonlight and felt like he wanted to touch her face. Without so much as a second thought, he was thinking about what it would feel like to have her touch him in the face. It was nothing short of a miracle, in Tony's eyes. And he knew, without a doubt, that God had brought him to this healing place. He also knew that DD was the catalyst, as she was the reason he wanted to be whole again.

Since his childhood abuse, he had purposely chosen relationships with women where he could maintain control during those types of situations. He knew he would never have to face himself, or those feelings, if he didn't want to. But it always got to a point where this thing came between them and he either fought like hell against it and they left, or he did. He was tired of ignoring the truth. He was absolutely tired of running. But more than either one of those, he was tired of choosing the same woman over and over just to have the same relationship repeatedly. He wanted something to keep - a real love he could grow with. She was so perfectly suited for this. She was smart and intuitive. She was attractive and becoming more and more beautiful with each passing month. Reclaiming her covenant with our father, God, she was once again recovering her virtue and protecting it as well.

While things still weren't perfect, he was indeed encouraged by the woman he saw DD working to become. Each time he looked up, she was more beautiful than the last. For the first time in his life, he didn't have to carry around this dirty little secret. This thing that came from the deepest, darkest part of hell that told him that he was worthless, was on the table in full display and she stayed. She accepted him for who he was and still loved him. She was patient and kind. In fact, now that she knew the truth about his past, she didn't feel nearly as rejected as she had when he was encouraging her to slow down. In her mind, all the onus was on her. Now that the truth was out of Tony's bag, she had an ally in healing and she wasn't alone with her bags. She knew he was just as human as she was. This perfect fellow she had thought him to be was dispelled and he became human and once again attainable. He was someone she could walk side by side with - no longer

237

someone to measure up to. It was a reality that they both needed.

So she stopped pushing and started allowing him the space to desire her, and it had turned his world on its ear. Men like to pursue, especially a real man. He likes to hunt what he eats and love; and making love is usually no different. One of the worst parts about what today's women had become wasn't that they had lost their virtue in a world filled with pimps and hoes with how young people look at their music and culture. No, the worst part is that they had traded the word allure for sexy. Sexy is for the night. Allure is for a life time. Allure, by its nature, requires mystery and begs one to repeatedly ask the question, while sexy is out there for the world to see, allure tempts you to go deeper; deeper than you have ever gone before. You simply can't ignore it. It calls for you and beckons you out of your shell; all the while with that same burning question on your mind. It cannot be quenched because if you are protecting your virtue it can never be given entirely away. Moreover, that desire can absolutely never be quenched by another; unlike sexy, which appears everywhere.

DD had not only found her lost virtue but unbeknownst to her, she had also stumbled back into her allure. Before long, she found *that it was her now being pursued.* And it was a wonderful thing. It changed around the entire dynamic of their relationship. It put everything back into its perspective and place. They had talked endlessly about their roles before God; those given to each of our genders. It was almost as if they were talking about jobs or duties. This forgotten art of courtship was totally lost on them. By simply including that third strand that is tied to the Father God Almighty, they found their way, seemingly by mistake. They just stumbled upon it. They were both firm believers in the fact that nothing happens by mistake. Everything is for a reason. We can learn from it, or suffer through it; sometimes both. There is always something in it for you. You have just got to swing your perspective around far enough, sometimes deep enough, in order to see it.

The ultimate in their understanding was one night about three weeks after Tony's revelation. They were sitting on a bench at a bus stop on a dark street. In the south, the buses don't run all night, so after a certain hour, these benches effectively become places to sit, and rest, rather than what they were intended for. Once again, Tony was looking into those deep, chocolate eyes, hanging on her every word, but marveling in this new beauty he had found in her. He just reached out and ran his hand down her face, slow, soft, and full of intention. This almost shocked DD, as Tony rarely, if ever, did this sort of thing. She blushed and immediately stopped talking and began to stare into Tony's eyes, trying to figure out where this was going. He leaned over toward her and kissed her gently on her lips. It was a slow, closed-mouth kiss. Then, again and again, until they were kissing full on. As he stopped and pulled back, he looked at her again with his gaze of love. Once again, he took her face and pulled it toward him and allowed her to kiss him the same way. As she stopped, he leaned in and gently kissed her on her lips once more then leaned in towards her ear and asked her, "Now which one felt better? The first or the second."

She stood for but a mere moment and softly whispered, "The first."

He looked her deeper into her eyes. This time with the most serious face and said, "For me too."

They stood there silently for a moment realizing what they had just said and what it all meant. He then took it a step further and asked her, "Why?"

"It made me feel desired and wanted," she replied.

"Isn't that how it's supposed to be? What was intended?" He said.

"Yes," she said, as her eyes began to fill with tears.

He chose that very moment at the height of her emotions, just as that warm tear hit her cheek, to kiss her again and hold her, while rubbing and caressing her. He wanted her to feel his desire, and how much he loved

239

and wanted her. For all those days and lonely nights that she had gone home wondering if he wanted her the way she had shown him that she had wanted him. He wanted her to leave tonight without a single doubt left in her head. He wanted to dispel her fears as she had done for him. He had always wanted her but it took them to come to this point of healing for him to be able to show her this place where he absolutely knew she would not only adore it, but feel like the woman she was intended to feel like. As men, we were charged to love our wives as we love the church. This is a place of worship, where we commune with God and praise him; show him our living embodiment of our love for him manifested in our worship and praise. Tony could think of nothing less in regards to DD. It was becoming time to go to the temple and his thoughts of resistance were far less reserved than earlier. He wanted to give himself to her completely; moreover he wanted her in a way that he had not previously thought of. Having recovered her virtue, she actually had something to give him other than the only thing that sexy affords our young, lost women.

They left that night having touched one another in such a loving way that they both knew that their relationship had changed in such a way that things between them would never again be the same. The greatest part about it was that this type of touch never required hands that went beyond anything you could do in public. It was not what they touched, but *how* they did it. It said they were ready.

*   *   *   *   *

"I'm thinking this Friday night after work we'll get a nice room down town. We can go dancing, have a couple of cocktails, a few laughs and spend our first night together wrapped up in each other's arms. What do you think?" Tony asked.

Being submissive and maintaining her allure was so brand new to DD, and beyond being quiet, she really was out of her depth on this thing. All she knew for certain was that she felt more desired at this moment, in this relationship with Tony than she had ever felt her entire life. She didn't want it to end. In her mind, all she had to do was not mess it up. This made her hesitant to say anything that was beyond agreement with him, as it may be perceived as too aggressive and coming from her past. She had to be honest with herself and admit that she honestly couldn't tell.

In her mind, it was better off left in his hands. Hell, he had been doing a great job up to now. All the things he had promised to show her to this point, he was not only right about, but spot on. She did feel better about herself, about her worth, her life and her relationship with him. It all looked far different than it ever looked, or felt, before. Deep down, she began to believe she was worth it. All those nights, all those men she gave herself away to, begging them to stay and love her. At the end of it all, all they did was take. She could never have guessed that less was more and all she had to do was wait to be GIVEN. She remembered her favorite bible verse. Tony had inadvertently lead her to it through a conversation they had about a different verse. Being the type to always read everything around whatever she was lead to, she stumbled upon it and it stuck with her for this very reason.

It was from Proverbs 28:1 which said, *"The wicked flee when no man pursueth: but the righteous are bold as a lion."*

It was how she looked at him, thought about him, felt about him. Although she never said so, she could never mouth those words to him because her fear was still too great. In her mind, every man she ever put up that high used his position to tear her down and take, once again. But in his stance, where he held fast to his ideas about God and his intentions for her and her virtue, he was unwavering. He played no games. Although she looked at this thing from every position, she couldn't see any angle beyond what he had said he intended to do.

She never took anyone at their word. Action always spoke far louder. She waited for him to show himself a liar, a cheater, and a thief, as all the others had been. Those who, at first, stole her virtue, stole away all of her life and those things she called dear and precious. It was for this reason she never allowed another man around Kayden. She would never allow those thieves to steal her away too. He had walked her to another verse that she was slowly beginning to believe about him too.

It said, John 10:10 *"The thief cometh not, but for to steal, and kill and destroy: I am come that they might have life, and have it more abundantly."*

At first, she thought him arrogant, as he shared this verse. What was he trying to say about himself? That he was God? And how did he know? How could he guarantee he had the key to abundance? She was immediately put off by this until he spoke on it.

"I believe I know you. I understand you and where you are today. Where those who came and took as they pleased from your life. I believe I know because I have taken the time to truly empathize with you and walked in your shoes through your own personal hell that you have shared with me.

It many times broke me down completely, keeping me up full nights at a time, making me unable to sleep because I couldn't get those images out of my head. I struggled to remove the anger and hatred for those who hurt you out of my heart. I prayed long and hard throughout many a night.

I was lead here, myself, in regards to you. And I couldn't imagine either one of us in such a great position to be able to make either one of us such a promise. But the way I looked at it was all those others that came into our lives for their own selfish reasons, didn't they steal our innocence and your virtue? Didn't they KILL our spirit and for a time our connection to God? Our faith? Didn't they destroy our lives, in that, we couldn't see past our bottoms?

If we believe in God and destiny, then we also believe that nothing happens without purpose or reason. Therefore your presence in my life, and mine in yours, is not a mistake either. I am walking in the spirit of the

Lord and am responsible to Him. Therefore, I am His direct representative of the love He intended for you.

I am human and fallible so I don't always do it right. But, as long as I'm checking in and working hard to stay in line with His word, it is I that will fulfill His promise of a husband and full family, and you that will be my wife in a life of abundance in our Lord."

She liked this idea that she would be a part of someone else's abundance and not the curse she so often viewed herself. She couldn't lie, as she admitted to herself within the conversation, that it made her feel safe, loved and wanted. To know that someone was working so hard to be that for her as well, was overwhelming. She was absolutely ready to walk into the next phase of her life and this relationship. So while she didn't know everything, and had not yet walked that path, she was slow to speak and eager to listen as she allowed him to be man and she woman.

"That sounds really nice my love. I'll leave all the arrangements to you," DD said.

"Do you have a preference for dinner?" He asked.

"Not really," she replied.

"Ok, well I'll make that a surprise too," Tony said, as he laughed.

"That sounds wonderful Tony. I can't wait," she said.

She had to laugh to herself. "Who the hell was THIS chick?"

She had never met this girl within herself; someone who could submit to her man without feeling like, less than, or uneasy about where he was taking her. It was funny, but the fact that he always made his intentions plain and always mapped out their course, gave her a sense of security beyond her fears, at the moment anyway. But then there were other things like the fact that she never had to question him to find out what was on his mind; or about plans for himself, or them. He was really transparent. He seemed like he made an extra effort to do so. She didn't see it mattering, at first, since others who sought to fool her had done something similar to her so she had her guard up.

Week after week, and month after month, as she waited for the other shoe to drop, a funny thing happened. First off, that other shoe never did drop. The very next thing that happened was that she had gained some serious insight as to who this man was; the content of his character and she found she loved him. It too made her want to be a better woman, beyond what she was currently able. Although she did try; more so than she had ever tried for any other relationship in her life.

She was bred to mistrust and this thing was so hard for her to do. At the moment, she could relax and allow Tony to do all the heavy lifting he was so very eager to do so. She had never had a man so eager to just be good to her without an ulterior motive. Something that would cost her much more than he was willing to give. This was a whole new world to her as everything else in this budding relationship was. She decided to allow herself to let go and give him the ability to lead.

The remainder of the week seemed to fly by and neither one of them could keep their date on Friday night off of their minds. They had waited so long for this - the right moment. Their moment was fast approaching and Tony couldn't be more confident. DD couldn't be more nervous. She had always used sex as a shield to mask her real and true emotions - being a freak was far easier. She was really going into this thing naked in more ways than one. Unlike the start of their relationship where she was the aggressor and the most confident, these tables had completely turned around. The funny part about it was, although she was nervous - just as nervous as she remembered as a teenage lover - she was just as excited.

As these thoughts consumed her mind Tony called, "Hey baby, I'm on my way. Are you ready?"

"Yes, I sure am," she replied nervously, trying to sound confident.

Man, he had even taken away her cool card. This had been the second best weapon in her arsenal. As he pulled up in his car, she walked out the door in a long black dress with a slit up the leg, a bit past the knee. It looked very nice on her as it flattered her figure, one that Tony completely loved. She had no idea about that since he hadn't spoken those words yet. Choosing instead to focus on all the other wonderful attributes she possessed, she could rest assured that at the end of this night, she would know all his desires for her and her lovely body.

They arrived at the restaurant and ordered. They made pleasant conversation through the meal, laughing and joking as they usually did. They ordered a slice of thick, deep, dark chocolate four layer cake, to go, for later. He had a feeling that although she said she didn't want any, by night's end, he would change her mind. They chose a chic new night spot not too far from where they had decided to stay the night. They entered and had a few cocktails. He was careful not to overdo it or allow her to let her nerves get the best of her, and be tempted to do the same.

They danced a few songs. But honestly, by the third song, the sexual tension was so thick that neither one of them was having a nice time. They were just bidding their time there, waiting to leave and to explore their love in their relationship after having waited over a year's time. This was longer than either one of them had ever waited before. Ironically, their interest and desire was higher than either one of them could remember it ever being for another. As they danced to an Usher song and the crowd moved to the upbeat tune, the world seemed to slow down as DD had pressed her body against Tony's, as she moved her hips from left to right. At first she moved fast, but as she could feel the heat on her behind, she knew she had his attention and she decided to slow down and get a better feel for this manhood she had waited so long to realize. She could feel him tremble with anticipation as she swayed back in the other direction. He grabbed her right hip as he guided her even slower, as she whined against his hard body and she let out a sigh she had been holding for months, that today, felt like years. He grabbed her by the waist and pulled her towards him firmly and ran his left hand up her back to her head and grabbed her firmly by the back of her neck and opened his fingers running them into her long, jet black hair.

As he reached the crown of her head, he took a hand full of her hair. At first gently, then firmly pulled her hair until her head leaned all the way back and they could look each other in the face. Arching her back to the hilt she could feel him stiff and lodged between her soft bottom, rubbed against the soft fabric of that long black dress. She was doing everything within her power not to just grab his hand and swing that man around and drag him the hell up out of that nightclub and back to their room.

He then took his right hand from off of her hip and ran it up the side of her body until he reached her breast and slowly guided his hand around her breast and along the contour of her neck until he reached her throat. His touch sent chills up her spine and she could feel the hairs on her body raising. He clutched her throat in his strong hand and pulled her yet closer and then he kissed her on the mouth. She felt her knees getting weak as the upbeat song came to an end. They never even noticed since they were already dancing to the beat of their own song, and hearts. He turned DD around to face him and spoke

"Do you want to get out of here?" He asked.

"I'm ready," she replied.

They both headed to the door and straight for the car as if they had somewhere to be. They pulled into the hotel parking lot without a word and remained silent all the way to their room. They opened the door to darkness and immediately began to undress without a word. He had imagined a world where he would slowly undress her and caress her body but that would have to wait for now, as they were undressing themselves. They met at the bed and she kissed him passionately on his mouth. He could feel her aggression begin to rise and he immediately recognized her going into her comfort zone, and what may have been her auto pilot, when it came to these matters.

He had a very similar way about him. It was how he hid from himself and also hid his heart. Presenting his body as the sacrifice, as he hid his heart from those he perceived would hurt him. He froze and waited for her to feel he had vacated their plight towards reckless abandon. It took her a moment but she did catch on and stopped herself and waited in silence. He started in again, this time, softer, more gentle, more deliberate and intentional. As he kissed her gently, he began setting his hands free and touched all of the body parts he had dreamed about. Behind her ear, her knees, and the small of her back. He gently kissed her neck and her collar bone as he allowed his tongue to taste her flesh. He took a handful of her breast, first gently then firm. She, again, let out a sigh that said, "Take me." But he wasn't quite ready.

He placed his body on top of hers, moving their flesh across one another so she could feel all of him in a sensual way until through all the kissing and touching she was drenched in her own juices and her place on that bed was soaked and waiting.

"I'm ready daddy. I'm so ready. Make love to me baby please. I want you so badly," DD whispered.

He continued silently to caress her skin and moving his body up and down her legs until he could feel the tip of his manhood tap, tap, tapping her clitoris; until it eventually breached the plain of her goodies. He teased her slowly with the tip of his erection until she began to quiver and he knew she was about to orgasm. As she continued to shake violently, he slid more and more of himself into her until she had driven her nails into the back of his arms.

"Now you're ready baby," Tony finally whispered back.

He then pushed himself into her more completely and began to slowly introduce her to himself and this place he called love. Tony was an excellent lover and never had a problem in this area. But tonight, he, too, was out of his element. He was seeking another and finding this far more passionate and filled with more

247

desire than any he had ever sought previously. They made love for hours. This slow love went on until the sun broke the morning clouds. Each time he would feel DD start to get too aggressive, he would stop and allow her to calm down and allow him complete control of her. She didn't think she would like it but it actually turned her on in a more complete way. He had his body pressed hard against hers and he opened her mouth and laid his lips on top of hers. As she lay there with him moving in and out of her, his lips and warm breath moving back and forth, and both of them panting for their love, she eagerly awaited his searching tongue into her mouth. It never came. Only his lips pressed up against hers. It was so passionate and hot. She had the first multiple orgasm in her life.

Before it was over, they had changed positions many times. She had more orgasms than she could count while she still waited on him to have his. It was daybreak and she was feeling a little insecure about him not getting there for as many times as she had taken. It was just then, he turned her onto her back and began to slowly build up to one of the most intense releases either one of them had experienced, all the while looking deeply into one another's eyes, without shame, without fear and full of love. He collapsed alongside her. They held each other tight as they both quickly fell into a deep slumber they had waited over a year to feel.

Smiling and pleased, he threw his arm over DD's body and pulled her tightly into him and she let out a moan. Then spoke, "I'm so glad you decided to buy that cake. I'm starving." They both had a hearty laugh on their way to meet the sandman together for the first time.

Chapter 21
Family Ties

For the duration of Tony and DD's relationship thus far, it had been, at best, up and down and, at worst, tumultuous. You could almost set your clock by the drama. If they had a great week, even a good one, you could count on the following week being filled with some trying moments. This is what made the past few weeks of Tony and DD's relationship so note worthy thus far. They had finally hit a plateau and there hadn't been so much as a cross word between them in weeks.

It felt amazing and Tony spent a great deal of time trying to figure out how to bottle this particular genie. DD had, after all this time, finally landed a job and was actually happy about it. The only problem in this equation was that Kayden needed to be picked up from the bus stop each day and looked after each afternoon until DD got off that evening. As the second half of their duo, he recognized that this was his responsibility and it wasn't a problem with him at all. Although she had spent the majority of their relationship keeping Kayden apart from him, he never took it personal and looked at this as the next rational step in their progression. He understood all too well how important it was as a single parent to protect your children from your adult world.

Barriers had to be put in place to keep them from harm. Children are innocent and love freely. Therefore they get attached easily, which is awesome as a parent because it bonds our children to us quickly and most of the time effortlessly. All we have to do is show up, smile, love, interact and play with them. We will subsequently have happier children and little friends for life. But the same awesome place that is set aside for us as parents also can be made for those adults we love that don't know how to stay or love completely.

So we shelter our children from fleeting relationships and those who we may not be sure are going to stay or may not show love in the appropriate way. These attachments cause more harm than most might think. So Tony didn't hold it against DD one bit that he had been on the outside of that relationship between DD and Kayden. After all, he was also being careful about having DD around Angel. He needed protecting too. From all he could see of DD, he wasn't quite sure what kind of parent she was. So he let time do the telling. It had finally come time after almost two years of ups and downs, backwards and forwards, that they had finally arrived here - the family line. Crazy that it only came about because of necessity and a job. Even more crazy is how long it took in their relationship for her to get a job. Nonetheless, here they were and however they got there he was content with it. As they went over the agenda, he got out of work at 2:45 and would rush home and to be at the bus stop by 3:30 for Kayden, then to the day care center to pick up Angel. It sounded like family life.

It started off well. He would pick the kids up, make dinner, go over preschool stuff with Angel and help Kayden with her homework. They would eat dinner and be at home waiting for DD to arrive. At first it felt just like it sounded but after about three days it began to feel distant, DD would pick Kayden up and rush out the door on her way to take care of this or that. Eventually it became customary. He would meet DD at the door with Kayden and they would simply leave in preparation of her taking her home and to ready her for bed and their next day. It stung to be treated like the help. It didn't feel anything like he had figured it would be like. Add to the fact that he and Kayden were having a pretty rough time getting to know one another.

Kayden was a pretty quiet kid who didn't speak at all, not even if she wanted something. She would simply stand there and cry; it was the strangest thing.

250

She was in kindergarten yet had the social-emotional level of someone who was in preschool; no verbal skills whatsoever. Kayden was so deep in her shell that even her mother couldn't beckon her out on most days. She would prefer to cry than answer to any adult.

Clearly there was something larger going on here and DD didn't deal well with it at all. DD saw her each and everyday and inside of their little room at her dad's house she was far more outgoing. This was who DD saw her as, an inquisitive, playful, and clever child. But to the rest of the world, she was completely inside herself. No one but DD could get her to open up and that wasn't with any consistency. So the first week was the roughest. She would arrive and just sit down in front of the TV and wouldn't even speak to Tony, or Angel, from the time she was picked up from the bus stop until DD picked her up. She never said hello or goodbye. It was uncomfortable for everyone involved. At first, Tony just figured it was going to take a little while, so he was patient and continued to speak and extend himself with invitations to do this or play that. Even when he helped with homework, it was more of a 'grunt and point' affair. Finally, Tony decided to force the situation and began to confront Kayden each day as she entered his car, home and presence of other adults.

"Aren't you going to speak Kayden?" He would ask. "Hello Kayden, how was your day love?" He would continue.

She would look at the ground or get bashful. Unlike before, he didn't let this body language deter him from pressing the issue. After he picked up Angel he would say to her,   "Aren't you going to say hi to Angel? He has been waiting all day just to see you. Say hi." He would say.

This is where she finally began to break. After about the second or third day, she started speaking to Angel, even began to play with his tiny little hand. And that amazing thing about children had begun. They were beginning to bond. As exciting as that was for him and Angel, it was equally as disappointing to see her still responding and reacting in the same way with Tony. She was super guarded with adults. Observing how harshly DD dealt with her, it was no wonder. She had absolutely no patience for anything outside of damn near perfection with Kayden. She snapped at her, or yelled at her for the slightest thing that annoyed her. Even worse, when Kayden finally did open up, although it wasn't done in the best way, DD would ignore her. This generally led to severe outbursts and tantrums where Kayden would throw herself on the floor or against a wall for attention, screaming at the top of her little lungs as she cried.

She was the most vocal at this time and she would often shout what was on her mind. Through learned behavior, she found it completely appropriate, once her dam of anger and frustration had burst to yell and scream what was on her mind. She could not otherwise communicate to those around her, even those who loved her. The very worst part of this entire little scenario was once she finally broke and started in on this route, DD would demand that she go off into another room, usually the bathroom, to throw her tantrum there, away from everyone else. She wouldn't ever allow her back until she had stopped crying. By then, there would be nothing left to discuss. Therefore, whatever it was that set her off would still be there waiting beneath the surface for the next time those feelings arrived. This was a very sad state of affairs.

Tony, being a teacher who worked with children for a good number of years, was going into his well of knowledge daily trying to figure a way to pull her out of this place. She, like her mom, was damaged goods. He knew things would be difficult but had no way of knowing that it would be this bad. He had considered that things might be bad but because Kayden spent so much time with her grandparents away from DD, Tony was certain it wouldn't be this bad. He was wrong. He started in on his parenting 101. Lead by example and this light, these truths would become evident as they bore fruit. This would reinforce this behavior with DD, either through shame, necessity, ease or a combination of them all. Either way, he figured what he would start and DD would have no choice but to continue because he knew they worked.

Phase 1

He started talking to Kayden more. Even at times when she wouldn't speak back, he continued anyway. He would talk about things he noticed that he thought was off; like not saying please or thank you, or not acknowledging an adult that spoke or entered the room. Then he would talk about things that she might be thinking but afraid to say in an effort to connect with her so she might start expressing these thoughts or ideas.

He began saying things like, "Sometimes being around new people can be scary. I too get nervous to speak around new people. There is nothing shameful about that so we must never lower our head, or eyes, when meeting people, because it says to people we are ashamed of who we are. You aren't ashamed of who you are, are you? I don't think you have anything to be ashamed of. You're a beautiful, bright, little lady. Remember to have courage isn't the absence of fear. It's the things we do in spite of it."

Although she didn't speak, he could tell she was listening. In fact, she followed him and hung on every word. Eventually the same little girl who would plop down on the couch and sit in her own little world would follow him into every room he entered waiting to hear his voice. At some point, she began to open up just a little bit at a time. One day when she got home off of the bus she entered into his car and spoke. Now it was time for

Phase 2

This consisted of bringing her around new people, taking her into public places, and trying to engage her the same way he had at home. When he first started to confront her behavior at home, she would go off into a corner and squat down and fold her arms over her face. She would often have her face towards the corner of the room with her back to him. It had the appearance of her crying. Often she was. Eventually she would just sit there and not speak at all. This is where he practiced what he called "given self talk." It was things he felt she could say to herself when she got afraid, or reason with herself, when she got upset.

When he first engaged her outside in a strange environment, was at the local supermarket and she did the SAME THING. She squatted down on the floor and folded her arms over her face and began to cry. He stopped talking to her as her cries got louder until they left the market, unable to finish their shopping. This was really disturbing behavior and he didn't feel it was something he could do in public.

He started going on walks with her in the park. He would go and walk with her around the soccer field and she would do this and he would just keep walking. Eventually she would stop crying so he could talk with her between the bugs nagging her and her not getting the attention she sought with that inappropriate behavior. She eventually learned to speak to him in that environment. Then he brought another long time friend of his from work on those walks and as Kayden reverted back to that behavior, the TWO of them partnered in speaking with her until eventually that too stopped. In just a few mere months, she had completely transformed herself from someone who didn't verbalize her feelings, threw tantrums, and yelled to a smiling talkative child.

As it turned out, she was a very bright kid and loved to learn new things, which most often took her no time at all. After a while, she, Tony and Angel had become very tight. This was about the same time that Tony had come to the end of his rope as far as DD treating him like the hired help. He had mentioned it to her before but the point didn't seem to be made. As it continued, they finally had a huge blow out about it and she started to stay awhile after she got home from work, although now she was the one annoyed.

Tony didn't even want to consider what all that meant in terms of their relationship so he pushed on. He chalked it up to DD's hatred for any idea that wasn't her own. She felt like following him under nearly any circumstances was her being "controlled." It was a twisted way of looking at things but he would be a liar if he said he didn't understand; knowing what he did about her past. He stayed right in there with her during those uncomfortable times with no arguments or fighting. He was determined to show her love without conditions, or control; a love of simply her and their life together. It was then that he noticed how things continued to be a struggle with Kayden, even after she had begun to make so much progress. Which is what lead them to

Phase 3

This is where they addressed the consistency of what he was trying to do with the kids. This is also known as getting on the same page as partners in parenting. DD would say things to Kayden like, "I don't care what you think," or "I don't care what you want to do. You're going to do it my way."

While he understood her point and where she was going with things, he talked to her about her need to express things differently, otherwise Kayden would continue to shut down. After about four or five tantrums and DD watching the rapport Tony had with Kayden, including his ability to bring her back very quickly and get her to do all the things she and Kayden fought over, she started to see the wisdom in what he was saying. Things changed after that and they all grew to that next level.

Things seemed to be moving along very well when DD lost her job and was again unemployed. She had a panic attack at work and was asked not to return. In fact, she was walked out by security as if she was a threat. Tony didn't understand that at all. He had never heard anything like it but as she had insisted that he never come to her place of employment, he had no idea of what was really going on up there. He had no choice but to accept what she said and let it go.

Another week had rolled by since DD had lost the only job she held since the time they had been in each another's lives. He was disappointed. With her being borderline depressed, he felt like they were losing ground on the progress they had made during her short span of work that had begun to bond them as a family. He decided that it was time to introduce DD to his family finally. Now he and his family used to be close but since he moved to Florida they had grown apart mainly due to the distance. He was growing as a man and, in a family full of women who were not used to being around real men, and didn't know how to deal with one, it was tough for him to move among them.

The women in his family were very strong-minded, opinionated women. On the surface this isn't necessarily a bad thing, unless they are stuck on the wrong opinion. Well then its hell. For the last few years they have been stuck on some bull shit. It made it extra difficult to be around them, therefore he wasn't exactly excited to bring his life or anyone in it around them. He had grown in the few years since he had moved from being around his family and they hadn't recognized it. This trip wasn't so much about them as it was about DD and him.

They needed some time away from all the things that made her so anxious. Whatever they were, it would be a break, at least. Although she had been to his home town of New York City, she had never spent any real time there and most definitely never had the world famous "Tony Tour," which of course included all things Brooklyn. He wanted her to feel like she was on vacation; like she was special. Most of all, he wanted her to feel the love he held for her in his heart. Although things were tight because funds were low, he pulled out all the stops he could on his budget.

First they headed to "C.I." or Coney Island. No trip to C.I. would be complete without a ride on the D train. They rode the D until they got to Brighton Beach and walked down because he wanted to take her to the aquarium. They then walked down to the piers and sat down by the boardwalk and watched the ocean come and go. Although it was cold out and no one was on the sand, it was nice to see the ocean again. They sat silently just soaking it all in before they got up and walked down to Nathan's.

"Now, if you never had a Nathan's frank from CONEY ISLAND, then you just haven't ever had a frank," Tony said, as he laughed. If there was one thing he could do, it was have fun. He knew how to make DD smile. With all the dark places in her past and throughout her life, he still knew how to make that woman smile. They laughed and smiled and joked that early afternoon away. One more quick stop at the Himalaya to listen to some music and take in another piece of classic nostalgic Brooklyn history for the two them.

They were standing there in the cold, among the crowd listening to the beats; he bobbing his head and she just taking in the moment. Funny thing about the Himalaya, it never mattered how chilly it got, people still come out and ride that damn ride and stand around watching. It's crazy. Then it happened. From nowhere he was back to 1989, standing there doing the exact same thing, heart pounding and just a damn boy in love. It was nuts. He looked at her as her face had begun to turn red from the cold. He loved that about her, and silently thanked her for that moment. He kissed her softly and they began walking back to the train station, smiling from ear to ear. They jumped back on the train and headed uptown.

They were headed to lower Manhattan but they weren't getting there by train. They stopped at Nevins Avenue, got off and walked through downtown Brooklyn. He showed her "Juniors," where his uncle was manager years ago before he died. And all the clothing and jewelry stores, mad dashes, hustle and bustle of BK baby. They headed down to his favorite landmark of all, the Brooklyn Bridge. He walked across it all the time when he was a kid and couldn't wait to share the experience with the love of his life. They walked slowly across as he pointed out land marks.

"There is Watchtower where they print off all the Jehovah Witness materials. There is the Empire State Building and there can you see the Statue of Liberty. That's where we're headed next. The Staten Island Ferry goes right past here. The poor man's Circle Line," he said, as he laughed. She, not being a native of New York, laughed although she didn't get it.

"What's a Circle Line?" She said.

"Never mind," he said, pulling her towards him. "Just kiss me lover." He planted a long, passionate kiss upon her lips.

They stopped for a wondrous moment they both got lost in only to be broken up by, "Ewwwww! Oh my god! Will you two get a room! Ha ha ha." Tony's cousin, Mika, yelled at them as they stood making out for all of NY to see.

They stopped kissing and shared a laugh as they continued on across the bridge, stopping every now and again to take in the sights. It was an awesome day so far. If it was up to him, it would only get better. He decided to save the statue for later on that evening since they lit her up at night and it made it a little more romantic. He figured it would be another good opportunity to smooch. So once they got on the other side of the bridge, they hailed a cab and headed for Greenwich Village. They walked through Washington Square Park and up and down the quaint streets of the Village. His cousin even took her into the Pink Pussycat.

"I can't believe this place is still here," he said.

"Yup, they moved it a little ways. But it's still here. Ha ha," she replied.

They got a good kick out of the place and walked down to Grey's Papaya and grabbed a drink, then over to BBQ's for supper. Then they headed back uptown to forty-second street and one last haul up to Harlem to check out the Apollo. They had gotten a full day in and could still manage to smile. They were tired and DD was already complaining about her feet from earlier in the day. Although he asked her several times if she wanted to stop and go home, she always said no. So they kept on. He was determined, however, to get on the ferry so he could share this romantic image he had in his head with her.

His cousin had gone on home hours ago so it was just the two of them. He had spent the entire day, wining and dining her, trying to make and KEEP her happy. It was such a difficult thing to do most days, but he was determined. So the fact that she wasn't smiling as big as she had been earlier didn't phase him, as this was her norm. As they got on the ferry, she seemed annoyed but they rode it anyway. Halfway across the water, he stood up and beckoned for her as they passed the Statue. It was the moment he had built up in his mind. She said no. No explanation. No give or even slight buckle. In fact, she got kind of loud with him in front of a boat full of people.

"I don't want to stand up to look at the statue. I've seen it before and it's not really all that," she snapped, as a crowded New York City Ferry full of people watched on.

He did the only thing he could do at that moment. He turned and soaked in the moment for himself. He did not, for a moment, dwell on the possibilities he had gone over in his head just about all day. He took full responsibility.

"She's just tired," he thought to himself, as he went back to the seat to sit beside her.

As he sat down, he went to hold her hand as he could still see the lighted statue and feeling romantic still. She pulled away and rejected his kiss even.

"I'm ready to go back to the house and lay down. I'm tired now. How much longer do we have to be on this boat?" She once again snapped.

All of those emotions and fond feelings were crushed and he sat them down right there at the bottom of the Hudson.

"They get off, then back on and we'll be back to the
house in about forty minutes," he said to her.

Those were the last words they shared for the rest of the night. That day that had started out with so much hope, so much grandeur and romance, ended with bad feelings, as they fell asleep holding bitter tongues and anxious torment. He never did understand these moments but refused to argue in his brother's house for all his family to see. That night, he was just trying to hold it down in hopes that this would pass and they could get on to something more pleasant before they met his grandmother. She was an opinionated woman whom Tony loved and respected dearly. The last thing he wanted was for her to see this "thing." Hell, any "thing" but bliss on his face and she could spot it a mile off.

*   *   *   *   *

They had one more day there in New York City with his family. They were to go to his mom's house so she could meet DD. Then they were off to his grandmother's house so he could introduce DD to her too. He had in his mind that this would be the woman he married. He loved her dearly and he really wanted them to love her too. She had her flaws and they had their problems but he wasn't perfect either and he was determined to see this relationship through. Either way, whether they liked her or not, he and DD only had another day here in New York City and then they were headed upstate to Rochester New York to visit with his eldest son and long lost friends since he moved away.

They were up early but still not really talking. They only shared minimal communication about who was going in the shower first, what to do about breakfast and things like that. He showered after she did, and once he came out, he could hear she was on the phone. She was on the phone with a man and the conversation was innocent enough but he could hear it wasn't her father or any other man in her family. There were these uncomfortable pauses and he could tell there were some things in between the lines that they weren't saying. As the conversation continued and they laughed and chuckled, Tony shot her the look of death and said to her whispering, "How could you be carrying on a conversation with some strange dude basically in front of my family? You're meeting them for the first time. What sort of impression do you think you're giving them?"

She told the man she had to go and got off of the phone. Now he was aggravated and embarrassed so he told his brother that he was going for breakfast, as he and DD left the house. They spoke about the call and she promised it was innocent and didn't see the harm in it. He disagreed but didn't want to make a huge thing of it although he felt like she was handing him a crock of shit because he knew he was headed to his mom's, and then grandma's house. He knew if ma didn't spot it, grandma would. So they grabbed breakfast and he did his best to put that mess behind him.

Once DD met Tony's mom, he could tell DD was doing her able best to subdue her normally loud personality. Tony knew this was a big mistake because his mom hated fake people or those who put on. People who tried to pretend were nothing more than liars to her and she, being a loud personality herself, could spot one when she saw one. He knew even if his mom didn't spot it that day, she would and she would always know what a capable liar she was. He had told her to just be herself but she must have figured herself wasn't good enough. So halfway through the visit he could see his mom putting on too and they both sat there having an all fake conversation.

"Wow," he thought to himself. "This is all bad," he chuckled to himself.

He wasn't too disturbed by it all because he had never really brought anyone home to meet his mom that she ACTUALLY liked beyond a sort of live and let live place. So later when he asked if she liked her and she said, "She's ok." He wasn't really surprised, but he was however surprised by what she said next.

"Be careful with this one. She is watching you like a hawk. She seems very insecure and controlling. She is sucking up to me which didn't surprise me; but how fake she is to YOU did surprise me. I don't think she is good for you. Feels like she sucks all of your spirit out of you and you have none left for yourself. Let alone any to share with those of us who LOVE YOU, the real, smiling, laughing and caring you that usually shows up here. Today you just look like you are on pins and needles. I hope it ain't about this girl, cause son she's already gone," his mom said with a serious face.

Now he never did understand what she meant by that but he sure wasn't about to invite himself to more misery than he already had to endure today by asking. He supposed he would just have to figure that one out when he came to it.

He of course denied her comments although he saw what she was saying about everything else and pretended not to know what she was telling him about all her insecurities and false presentations. He had already seen beneath that slip a long time ago and was amazed at how fast his mom picked up on it. She never had anything in detail to say about anyone, even April who she hated off top. She held that bitter piece of information for a long time. In fact, she was out of his life before she let it be known. She was far more likely to be critical of HIM than anyone he brought home.

They went over to his sister's house where they sat outside on the stoop talking and laughing while his ghetto ass family drank and blew trees. DD did her able best to look like she wasn't interested but they all saw it on her face as they offered her pass after pass and she refused. Even Tony who never smoked could see the deer in the headlights look in her face as she watched the blunt being passed from relative to relative. They finished up their small talk and as everyone around them began to feel the effects of their chosen high, DD and Tony bid them farewell as they once again jumped in a cab headed to "Big Mama's" house. The sun had not long set when they arrived and went directly into her building as it wasn't the kind of place you just hung out around at night. They went on upstairs and into her place, which was dimly lit, as she was already headed to bed.

"I didn't think you were going to make it today. You waited all day to come see your Big Mama, huh?" She greeted him with her big, smiling face.

Once Tony got into the doorway and she got a look at who he had brought with him, she immediately stopped smiling and that pleasant look she had on her face went from "so glad to see you" to "what the fuck is this?!" And he could spot it dead on. Before he could even get it out of his mouth to introduce DD to his grandmother, his grandmother interrupted him as he started to speak.

"Tony, I need to talk to you for a moment in my bedroom please. Go on into the living room young lady and make yourself comfortable. We'll be right back," his grandmother said.

As they entered into her bedroom, he was thinking to himself how odd this was for his grandmother. She was such a spiritual person, a true Christian, sweet as pie to everyone, whether she liked them or not. And there she was, being down right RUDE to his guest. She first sat on her bed, then propped up her pillows and went on and lain down. As she sat up in her bed, she asked him with just about the most disgusted look he had ever seen on her face, slow and softly, "Who is that girl you have brought into my home?"

"Well that's DD Mama. I was trying to introduce you to her. She is the love I had been trying to tell you about over the phone," Tony said, as he was cut off abruptly by his grandma.

"Her? This is who you brought to meet me? Tell me it isn't serious? Tell me you aren't thinking about marrying this woman?" She asked him with a mix of disgust and puzzled look on her face.

As he stood mouth open shocked at his grandmother's response, he was not prepared for her assault on him or the love of his life. It was like a bucket of ice cold water had been dumped on him. Like he was the clown in the booth and someone with a softball had just dunked him and his dreams right on in. Before he could mutter a word she went right in.

"Where are her people from? What does she do for a living? Does she even work? She doesn't look like the sort of girl who does honest work. Does she have children? How many? Does she have an education? What school did she attend?" She was shooting off question after question faster than he could answer when he could hear DD in the next room start walking into her bedroom door. She could clearly hear every word his grandma was saying in her small New York apartment.

"I'm sorry ma'am. I overheard you asking Tony about me, so I figured I'd take a little heat off of him and try to answer some of those questions for you," DD uttered, as she shot out a small laugh to break the tension.

His grandmother didn't laugh a bit and stared directly into her eyes, unmoved by her attempt at humor. As DD spoke, his grandmother sat there and watched her mouth move, never asking her a single question, just allowing her to speak. With each word, he could see his grandmother's eyebrows raise and her opinions going from bad to worse. As DD continued to speak, his 79 year old grandmother once again found her way to her feet and like a small child when they first learned to walk "cruised" from one side of the room, holding onto furniture placed about the room as she headed for the door.

Once she reached the doorway she turned and said, "Excuse me DD, I'd like to speak to my grandson a moment." And she walked into the kitchen.

She was sitting in the small kitchen in the little step ladder chair she used to grab things out of the cabinet but no one ever sat in. She was sitting there with the bible she keeps on top of the refrigerator that she reads as she cooks.

"Do you know what you have there in the next room? I mean do you know what you are getting yourself into? What you're truly dealing with? Ok, ok, I wont even go there, because it is clear to me you do not. No son, you know I am not the type to get into your affairs this way but you first have to know what it is YOU want in order to find it. Because a woman like that can never be pleased. Those who LIVE A LIFE OF COMPROMISE will only feel conviction and give you the worst parts of themselves in the presence of someone like you who has come to value purity. You have to be evenly yoked son. She has got to see and value you for who YOU ARE and more over, YOU HAVE TO FIRST. Can you see what I mean baby? Do you even know what it is you need? Forget what you want. Want gets us into trouble and all your good intentions count for nothing with someone like her.

"Just as the road to hell is paved with good intentions, so shall it be with her. I raised you the best way I knew how; taught you right from wrong and the Word promised me that if I showed you the path, you would never leave it. So I KNOW YOU KNOW. I know you have seen His face even in the cruel world, in this very house. If you have taken a stand in life for the path and the life you want, that person who does not HONOR or appreciate your standard is not the partner for you baby. But you have to know what you want."

Tony stood there motionless once again, mouth open for the second time that day.

"You have to get your mind in order. Know what you want, before you can be lead to how to have it. He will lead you but you have to allow him to," she pleaded with him.

"But mama you don't understand, I have prayed on this. I have spent a great deal of prayer and hours meditating on this and I know this is where I'm supposed to be. This is where I feel God has asked me to remain. I am not the same man I was. I no longer make

265

rash decisions and each and every move I make is done with the consultation of the Lord. 'Come, let us reason together and wash your sins as pure as the white snow.' I have reasoned with the Lord and this. I have failed at love, and failed at making a family many times because I know I didn't go about it the right way. This is the path he showed me and I have to see it through mama," he said, pleading his case.

"1 Timothy 3:5 *'If a man know not how to rule his own house, how shall he take care of the church of God?'* If you can't see you, how can you see her?" She said.

"Proverbs 20:6 *'Many a man claims to have unfailing love, but a faithful man who can find?'* Why can't you see I'm just trying to be faithful to God and what I feel he has asked me to do?" He shot back.

"Proverbs 27:7 *'The full soul loathes a honey comb; but to the hungry soul every bitter thing is sweet.'* There is no way you can fulfill his will for your life without being able to see yourself, the greatest of his lessons. Your walk in love begins with you," she said to him.

"Psalms 15:1-2 *'LOVE and FAITHFULNESS meet together; righteousness and peace kiss each other.'* You can't have one without the other mama. I just want to do His will. I'm not the boy I was. Why won't you listen to me? I know what I'm doing," he said, with tears in his eyes.

"Psalms 85:10 *'Truly when a man chooses the RIGHT thing, he finds the love and peace that his heart already possesses.'* It's already in you baby. Why are you lowering your standards? I can see how much pain you're in," she said back to him with tears in her eyes too.

"One of the most important components of one's integrity is the ability to follow through with a commitment no matter what the cost. Like in the book of Ruth, Boaz knew what it cost to make Ruth his wife and he was willing to pay it. I, too, am willing to follow

Him. NOT her. Him. She is the one for me mama," he said to her.

"Like Jacob said in Genesis 30 '*let your honesty testify for you.*' Can she do this? A man who walks in the light of God's words clears the path to a deeper love relationship. If you don't feel it, it's because it isn't there. It is within you son. Pray some more," she said, and closed her bible with bitter tears running down her face.

He turned, tears still hot, with a hot face and re-entered his grandmother's room to find DD shaking her leg as she often does when she is anxious and he beckoned her out. He silently kissed his grandmother's tear-filled face and headed for the door. DD looked back as though she wanted to go through the motions of saying goodbye but Tony waved her onwards. She turned and they left.

They grabbed a cab and he stopped at the nearest liquor store to grab a nip to calm DD down. She, too, was silently crying in the darkness of the taxi. He had stopped at this point because everyone who lives here knows you show no weakness in them hard ass streets. But he was certainly crying on the inside. He grabbed the Tequila 1800, his favorite drink, and they drank it on their way back to Jersey where his brother stayed. They stopped for dinner and finished the bottle before they got home; once again able to smile and feel no pain. They soothed one another after a weary day filled with a large spiritual and psychological battle and small victories. They had survived a huge test and were happy to still be in one another's arms.

$$* \quad * \quad * \quad * \quad *$$

As they got up the following day and prepared for their flight into Rochester, NY, they seldom spoke. So much had already been said the preceding day that the silence was welcomed. Up until that point, he thought this trip was about a vacation, even about visiting his eldest son in upstate New York. It wasn't until this very moment did he realize what this trip was really about. It was about approval; and him getting it from the women he loved. If their relationship had been contingent upon him getting it for her, the signs weren't looking good. Fortunately he didn't expect their approval but admittedly he didn't expect the reaction he got. Those who usually don't have much to say said a mouthful. i.e. his mother and grandmother. Those who usually have a lot to say, said nothing. (i.e. his sister, Tracy and cousin Mika.) If he had depended on them for clarity, he would be leaving more lost than he arrived. Even his brother, John, who damn near tolerated everyone didn't like her based on that phone conversation she had which she was sure no one would hear, or thought anything of.

They arrived that early afternoon and had a long visit with his son after they checked into the Hyatt downtown. He was happy he could return home and stay in a nice place with her and his son for the night. It meant a lot to him that he could do nice things for her since she had such a rough way to go before meeting him. Later that night, they went to dinner with one of his oldest and best friends, Larry, and she barely spoke. Halfway through the meal she got a call and picked it up. They could clearly hear a man yelling at her, asking her "Where was she? Who was she with?"

Larry and Tony both looked at one another like, "Whoa!" She excused herself after telling the person on the other end of the phone she would call him back momentarily. She told Tony she was going back to the room because she was done with dinner and he should stay behind and catch up with his friend. She didn't' seem to care for Larry. Or maybe she didn't care for the small town he had brought her to after such an elaborate and expensive trip right before it. Either way, she left looking aggravated and unappreciative. Larry and Tony finished the meal and headed to the bar and had a few.

"Listen man, every relationship takes work. I can see you really care for her and if you're all in I got your back. But don't let any woman steal from you what she can't take with her actions by way of giving her your heart. I don't know her but she seems shady. Just be careful man," Larry said.

He turned to the bartender and ordered them up their favorite drink, one they had created together. It was called "blockandfall" because once you have a few of those, and stand up, you have about a block before you fall. And that night boy did he need that drink.

Chapter 22
Requiem for Romance

Times were getting tougher as the economy tightened and the job market was shrinking all around them. DD having very little skills and no education wasn't fit at all for these times, or this harsh economy. His resume' and educational background pretty much made him damn near bullet proof. With his Masters degree in education and a nice start on his doctorate in the same field, he knew it would all fall on him. This was his role and he never set it aside or lost sight of it, ever. It was a great source of pride for him to know he could provide for his family. He had also begun law school right around the same time he started his doctoral pursuit and things were getting heavy on both sides of that fence. He could handle it academically but the pressures of his home life were really beginning to get in the way. Between the demands DD put on his time and the needy little games she played with her disappearing acts, club hopping and ultimatums, in addition to her inability to get a job, the pressure was high on the demands for his time.

He was going to have to find a way to increase his income. He either needed to find a niche, or go out and get another job. He knew he could find another job but he also knew it would handcuff him to a time clock, which he really couldn't afford with all he had going on. He decided to incorporate and start his own business. A paralegal business, between the paralegal work he was already doing for a local lawyer and his law school knowledge, he could most definitely create more income. The only problem was still finding the time for DD. He figured she would understand but of course, she didn't. As she faded away, deeper into her own depression and philandering ways, it wasn't long before he had to make a choice between the doctorate, or the law, degree. Law school demanded more of his time and energy, so he decided to sit that one on the side for now and focused on his new business and his doctorate in education. He was disappointed in having to give up one of his lifelong dreams, especially considering how long it took him to finally get back to it. But the writing was on the wall and he just couldn't see any other way to continue. When he broke his sad news to DD, she seemed happy that he had made this choice as it meant more income and more time for her.

*　　*　　*　　*　　*

"Tony, I just can't do this any longer. Living here is like being back in college. They are filthy here and never clean up after themselves. It's like living in a house full of grown children. And their inconsideration goes beyond housekeeping. They use drugs over here constantly. Since I've been here, I have already seen how this is contributing to the stability of the household. I can only imagine what sort of trouble may come here by way of either the wrong person one of these dizzy young chicks might bring home, us being evicted, or utilities out because they never have the bill money when these things are due. I'm getting too old for this shit man. I just can't do this any longer.

I know we moved out from one another because I was becoming too much for that small space emotionally but maybe we can revisit that. I really miss Angel. I hardly see him anymore because I refuse to bring him here to this rat hole. I would love to be there just to spend more time with him and both of us could use the help financially. Not trying to get in your personal life but does "she" even have a job yet? Last you told me she doesn't. I know you could use the help. All I'm saying is think about it Tony."

Sharon had spent the entire afternoon calling Tony trying to work out their schedule so that they could get together and have a play date with their son. This enthusiasm for a family day kicked off this conversation about her living situation and now for the last fifteen minutes he was listening to her make her case for why she should be able to move back into his apartment. He was completely closed to it up to thirteen minutes ago, still feeling angry about all they had gone through before and not wanting a repeat performance. Moreover, the last thing he wanted to do was confuse an already complicated situation and make it worse. But the longer he listened to her make this case, the more he thought about what was real about the situation.

He hadn't heard from DD in weeks. Although he figured at some point he would, he didn't know what their relationship might end up being once he did. Besides, Sharon was sounding more mature and settled than she ever had and was making plenty of sense. The bills were coming in and weren't very much different in costs while the income to pay those same bills were cut in half. So things were a little tight. He could at least be honest with himself about that. In fact, things were tight and doing it all alone was hard. The only reason he was trying so hard to maintain this separate household was because he knew how it would look to the world, and DD, if he continued to live with Sharon and continued to pursue DD. He would appear to be the same low down dirty dog that every woman already assumes every man is, especially one in that situation. As quick and easily as DD had laid out her needs of him in the past for his help, he knew she had no problems making demands on him. But when it came to what should have been her responsibilities in this thing, that was another story entirely. Tony had seen these shady women his whole life. Some of them were members of his own family, so he knew all too well, having had a front row seat many times, just how sneaky women could be when it came to getting their way. But DD wasn't the only person who needed help. Why shouldn't he be able to have the same relief that she was asking for? After all, he would have loved to have moved in with her and baby Kayden at this point but because she couldn't keep a job, he knew he could not afford to feed two more mouths without help. He knew he had no choice but to wait on her to get her act together.

"Why don't you come over and we can discuss it further. You might be right. It's time to reconsider but there has got to be some ground rules to keep our arguments and emotions in check."

"I agree," Sharon said. "When is a good time for you?" "I'm free right now if you have the time," he replied.

"I'll be over in fifteen minutes. I'm on my way."

They both said their goodbyes and hung up. Tony knew he had to set up some ground rules if this was ever going to work. Boundaries were going to be essential. His heart was still ripped open from the pain from all the things that DD simply refused to do that had things coming to this sad point. He knew within his heart of hearts just how difficult something like this was going to be for her. No woman, no matter how wrong they have been, or even are, would like these circumstances. But they were really going to have to be mature about this if it was going to work.

He knew from all the stories she had told him about past lovers and boyfriends how difficult it was going to be for her to trust him. In her past, if she ever showed her vulnerable side to these wicked men, they would twist her life in on itself and she would ultimately end up suffering in the worst way for showing the pathway to her heart and vulnerability. He wanted to empathize with her position as he always did but this came down to simple mathematics. It wasn't about hurting her or doing anything to spite her. No, this was about making a sound economic choice. He really didn't see how any of them were going to continue to make it without another income. So in his mind, it was simple. Either find a job or allow him to get the help they needed.

*   *   *   *   *

It was a brisk morning just before dawn as Tony helped Sharon with her things from the car into his place. After a long heartfelt talk, they had decided at this point it was the best thing to do. He had decided that even if DD couldn't stay with him under these conditions, he was just going to have to let her do what was best for herself. He was tired of struggling. They had attempted to talk about DD moving in with him before but he let her know under the current circumstances it just couldn't be done on his end. So to him, she already knew the time.

"How is it that women can be so demanding of men, making songs like 'You gotta have a J-O-B if you want to be with me' and yet feel like they should be supported like old school women if they aren't willing to do old school things?" He thought to himself. It made no sense to him at all.

It was with a heavy heart and a huge asterisk that he was allowing Sharon back into his home to live once again. But as doubtful as he was about this move on an emotional level, afraid of what this might bring up in him, and even the potential ruins of what was left of him and DD, he could not block out the fact that Angel was super excited to have his mother back in the house.

Funny enough, they had been spending so much more time together since she had moved out than when she lived there. So much so that Tony could only imagine how Angel's little head must have been spinning with how much things would change for him with her living there again. Her growth as a parent had increased dramatically and even Tony had to admit that she was now doing a good job.

For the most part they agreed on pretty much everything concerning 'little man.' Once they settled where the primary discipline would come from, they never deviated from it or any other plan they formulated concerning their child for that matter. They had become pretty solid parents. Of his three remaining children, he only had to deal with two of their mothers, as his daughter's mother had passed away due to complications during an asthma attack. This cut his potential four baby mama's down to two, with his first son's passing from sudden infant death syndrome. By far, Tony not only got along the best with Sharon but they also represented the best parental team.

It was no real wonder since they had planned this child and all the others were unplanned blessings. He loved all of his children but besides Sharon, he only really liked one of their mothers. It was a shame but a sad fact of life. For the most part, they didn't have any real difficulty living with one another either when they were together or when they had to live with one another as roommates previously. So he wasn't worried about how it would go down.

It didn't take very much time to get all of Sharon's things moved back in as she didn't really have that much. Her personal items and clothes were all she had brought, as that is all she had taken. She had always been adamant that all of the furniture and household items Tony had purchased, was a waste of money. He found that crazy, as he believed in quality of life and she didn't seem to think her money should be spent on such items as comfort and appearance. Even more, he knew her savings couldn't have been too substantial, since she was once again broke and needing to move back in with him for financial reasons. Oddly enough, this was one of the very first things she complained about living in her new place, how horrible and filthy it was and she never did have any problems showing off the nice place they shared to any of her friends. He was now figuring out she only had a problem paying for it. He just shook his head and shrugged his shoulders as she fell down onto the couch letting out a huge sigh.

"Ahh, the comforts of home. Feels good to have a real home to come back to. I can finally see what you were saying before. Being able to see what you're working for has become important to me," Sharon said, as she smiled.

Tony just smiled and nodded thinking to himself, "They say you never miss the water until the

275

well runs dry. Hmm, maybe now you'll take better care of the place, appreciate what it takes to have nice things."

Once he saw Sharon was getting comfortable with being home again, and Angel was too, he decided it was time to call DD for the follow up conversation concerning this major decision. HE was on pins and needles because when last they talked about it, she said it would be the end of them. So he was fully expecting to hear this break up on the phone as he went to place this call. He got up and excused himself, telling Sharon he was going for a walk and went down to the fountain in the front of his apartment complex. He took a seat on the benches out where he and DD had spent so many hours talking, laughing and getting to know one another. He took his cell phone out of his pocket and nervously called her number. As the phone rang, he was halfway expecting it to go right on to her voicemail as it did most early mornings. He was hoping for a momentary pass on having to breach this conversation with her again. Having already made what could be the final decision, brought extra tension in his voice. He was certain. He hadn't even taken the time to get nervous as he typically would have if he had been making this call with the expectation that she wouldn't be picking up. To his surprise she did.

"Hello baby," DD's voice sounded so pleasant and happy, as if she had never been touched by such things as those he was about to speak.

"Well hello lover," Tony answered back, now full of not only surprise, but full nervousness. He knew as he went into the conversation that his argument had holes in it. After all, she too was a single parent and he didn't give her that sort of help he not only needed, but wanted and expected. So why should she have to give him what he didn't? He realized the reality was that she didn't have a place of her own. So most of the things he hoped for, he simply couldn't do for her. However, he also knew this wouldn't stop her often smart mouth from saying, "You have never done those kinds of things for me nor have I asked you to." And as if on cue, there it was.

He never let his visions of their future and those things hoped for cause them more than a moment's argument. To him it was pointless because he was fully capable of cooking and cleaning and taking care of himself and Angel.

However, he never could understand that if this move really was what she wanted, why she never tried to make herself more useful in that way. It always seemed to him that she expected to simply have these things handed to her. She sat on this high horse as if it were a throne, or confidence, that she was so fine that she was beyond these sorts of things. All the while, boasting that she possessed those very wifely qualities he desired to see in her beyond speech. To her, it was no more than the natural course of events and she had a serious expectation that she would simply come into this life with him. But the last thing he and Angel needed was two more mouths to feed, shelter and clothe, while DD's grown ass self refused to pick up a finger to help her damn self. If she refused to help herself, how would she help him and his son.

With Sharon moving back, that conversation wouldn't come up again for as long as she was there. Although this was only a temporary situation, it would alleviate the pressure DD had been putting on him to move she and Kayden in with him. Because of the domestic, financial conversation, there was an even more difficult one looming. In his mind, it would be hard for him to see himself giving her the lift she wanted when he felt in his heart of hearts that she was doing him dirty.

The Atlanta thing just proved to him he wasn't so far off the mark. It would be a damn nightmare even thinking about her living with him under the current conditions. He would be going to work supporting their family, while she got high all day plus potentially having one or two of her "friends" by. He knew Kayden had been exposed to her drug use. There was no way she was going to bring that wickedness around his son. This would have to serve to ease the burden of those things he could do nothing about, if but for just a little awhile.

He had hopes that in due time he and DD would work out their differences on these matters and before long, they could move on and have the life they both dreamed of. Hopefully it would be by the time Sharon got back on her own two feet again and was ready to move back into her own place. This time they would be ready. He sincerely had every intention to commit as the good Word told him he should; but not from this willingly ignorant place that denial had already made a home for in their relationship.

Yes this conversation, or the reality that Sharon's move back in brought, was long overdue. With one decision and not a whole lot of arguing or fighting, he had managed to bring to the table a major issue and make a serious point without having to beat that same drum into the ground.

They spoke in great detail on this matter and DD wasn't happy to say the least. They disagreed about damn near everything, including his reasoning behind him not moving her and Kayden in, to his needing her help financially and otherwise. The one thing they did agree on was that from that point on they would be committed to speaking their minds on this and all other matters. They would speak the truth and shame the devil on all things so those crooked things may be laid straight. End result was that at a minimum, at least they both would know everything coming into and out of situations like this one. This way no one could ever say that they were caught off guard like this again.

"Hey, if we can't live in, and face, reality, and deal with shit head on, then we need to just go on ahead and leave each other alone. People who are ready of reality, can't truly be ready for love either," Tony said.

"I completely agree," DD followed.

He knew that all of these declarations of commitment and recommitment were going to have to be followed up with some action, preferably some romance. He, having been around the world, loved to travel, but he hadn't really done too much traveling with DD because their differences had been too steep. He just didn't have the faith in DD required to take her on such trips without fear of embarrassment. It wasn't so much her attitude. At times, it was like what happened on their last trip on the ferry ride in New York. She had some "tendencies" from her previous life that kept him worried about her possibly over stepping her boundaries in the company of other men.

He, however, was absolutely dying to take his dream girl around the world. He was just waiting for the opportunity. But he was discovering like just about everything else concerning their relationship, it was going to take a leap of faith on his behalf to make it happen. He was going to have to be the one to look THEIR fears in the face and conquer them in order to move where they wanted to be. He decided they needed a getaway in the midst of this new mess their life had just evolved into. So the time for pushing past these fears on faith was now.

Looking at it that way made it easy for him to be ashamed of himself for not having the foresight to have seen it this way sooner. He saw it now and was going do something about it, quick, fast, and in a hurry. That mattered more than self pity or shame. In the past, he had taken DD up to his sisters' place up in Jacksonville and it had gone all wrong. She had brought so much drama and disrespected him in front of his sister, arguing and fussing. It was these things that kept him blinded. But like anything else, there are always two sides to each coin and she could not argue nor fuss alone. So at a minimum, he was at least as culpable as she was. Tony would have to keep these thoughts close if she got anxious or stepped into that wheel house of emotion. It's so easy to get baited into that place if you aren't looking for it.

Her words always felt as though she just didn't have very much respect for men in general. Knowing what he knew about her gave him the grace to understand why but not the patience. In the past, he took it personal when she showed that nasty attitude. He felt she needed to address this and come at him differently before he would have taken her anywhere else. He didn't want to be disrespected that way by any woman. He could easily see things clearly through DD's eyes. He understood that it was completely possible that this attitude she put up now was something she more than likely built into her personality to protect her from all those who had treated her badly, and the rejection and disrespect was too much for her to endure. So this was her way to protect herself.

If she did it to him first, then when he got around to doing what she was sure would be coming any way, it wouldn't hurt as badly. Then, she would know she had done something to deserve it. She simply hadn't experienced anything else.

"Having this knowledge should account for something?" he thought to himself.

He was going to have to take what he knew and apply it towards building a better life for them. Otherwise, he was no more at work than DD and had no right to complain. But in order to put these theories into practice, he had to be there, doing it.

"No substitute for game time!" He laughed to himself. He was going to work on not taking this thing she did so personal with the full understanding of the TRUTH. Let go and let God change her spirit. His Word demanded this and he would be obedient to what he was asked to do. After all, the truth was, no matter what he did or did not do, no matter how many trips they skipped "waiting for DD" to get her act together, he could never guarantee she would ever do so. There was one fundamental truth he had solidly learned over the years and that is you can't change ANYONE. This meant he couldn't make her do anything, no matter how right he felt he was, or wrong that she may or may not be.

It was pointless to continue to try. All he did was put himself along with the kids into the same box as they waited for her to fix it. He could show her grace on this matter since he had a full understanding of the truth. So he covered her the way the Word said he should. He was certainly strong enough to do that. His favorite verse was, Romans 15:1, *"We then that are strong, ought to bare the infirmities of the weak."*

And there it was. As her would-be husband, his faith was going to take some work because everyone knows, "faith without work is dead." Besides, this was more than likely her greatest proof that he could never love her unconditionally. Since it was a shining example of the worst things about conditional love. It's like a contract. Most contracts are conditional. "I'll scratch your back, you scratch mine."

The unspoken part of that bargain is, "If you don't scratch my back or don't scratch it the way I think you should or within the time period I think it should be done, I don't have to scratch yours."

But he was seeking something far deeper with DD since he had done so many contractual loves and conditional half assed relationships. He was seeking a covenant and they work a little different. He understood that a covenant is not based on time frames or conditions. It operates on the principle of grace.

He had taken the time throughout this walk to pray, meditate and research these thoughts and it was time to put them on the field. There are many words used in the bible for this word grace. All in all, it is written in the old and new a total of 166 times. It has been defined as "someone who stood in kindness to an inferior," with the idea of inferior being someone who has more burdens than us. Also, someone who is "moved to favor by petition, be kind or show favor, be merciful, show mercy upon," or "the divine influence upon the heart and it's reflection in the life." He was a right brain kind of person, so in addition to this understanding brought to him by the Word, he had also looked it up in the dictionary and found more of the same.

"Unmerited, divine assistance given man or woman for his or her regeneration and sanctification. A virtue coming from God."

The one he came to that he liked the best was, "Grace is mercy given to someone, even when they don't deserve it." This was a really difficult thought for him at first, thinking back on his life and all the times he had needed mercy in this world and walked that lonely road without it. He had thought specifically when he was in DD's position having offended, lied and deceived the one person he loved the most in desperate need of mercy and some measure of grace and never getting it. The toughest thing about that time was watching her walk away and knowing that she did indeed love him but it was HIM and all that he had done and better yet ALL HE WAS NOT that pushed her to leave. But if he knew anything, he knew that this wasn't a lesson he had come upon in those younger, darker days and if you want something different you have to do something different. That meant in this particular circumstance, that as the Word says, if this is what you want, then he would have to become what it was he wanted.

Simple as that, "Do onto others as you would have them do onto you." Some say, "You get back, what you put out into the universe."

All in all, it was a comforting thought to think it would come back to him. Moreover, in order to be in, and follow God's will, he needed to do it. No matter what. Even if it never came back. He swore from that moment he would be a better man, so the next time God gave him that opportunity, he would be ready.

He had to let go of his thoughts of those darker days during which he prayed for God's grace and mercy from this beloved, to no avail. What he couldn't see was each time he prayed for mercy, he received in turn multiple opportunities to show mercy and grace, which he failed to do each time, feeling convicted, having lived that life of compromise his entire life to that point.

But he was here now with a much better understanding and outlook on this thing. The bible says in 2 Corinthians 9:8, "*And God is able to make ALL grace abound to you, so that in ALL things, at ALL*

282

times, having ALL that you need, and you will abound in ALL good."

When he first looked at that, he thought this was God's promise to us and that He would always have this grace for us. But upon closer examination, he realized that this meant that ALL grace came from him. This also meant that he, too, could have it in his heart and freedom would follow. Releasing him from the burden of sin as well as the inability to forgive. He had carried that unforgiveness for so much in his life, having been the victim of childhood abuse. He always felt he hadn't received justice for all those who stole from his life. His stolen childhood innocence caused him to hide himself away in darkness, as the original sin did Adam and Eve; he spent years in that darkness. He had not, until this point, been able to find this lesson in his heart truly. Until now, that is. It was in this scripture where it all came together crystal clear for him.

Romans 8:27, *"We don't know how to pray properly, so the HOLY SPIRIT intercedes for us (the measure that we are obedient) in accordance to God's will."*

This verse struck him the deepest, knowing all the dark places he was lead from. Knowing all the times he should have been dead on those streets. Knowing how many, many, many times he had sent him and his life to hell. It was clear. The life's blood of our relationship with God took grace to even begin. Why would this love be any different? It starts with our communication with Him. It is the budding of our life of prayer, meditation and the "getting of knowledge." Without it, we would only have "the law brought by Moses." As it is, among those we love too.

Tony now knew that this covenant was far deeper than any promise he had ever made to any person. This was a promise he was making to God to be obedient, in spite of what DD does or does not do. From this moment on, this agreement will stand in his heart, and his mind, but more importantly in her actions. He, being the one who made the covenant, would continue to walk in it. God designed the union between a man and woman to be bound by an unbreakable covenant, not a conditional contract. The fruit of that covenant was life, marriage, "the promise" he sought. And it was ALL operated from this principle of grace.

With these thoughts rushing through his head, he was in a daze. After one hell of a conversation and him taking the rest of the day to study and pray, he was exhausted. All he could think about was praising the Lord's name, then sleep. Bless God.

Chapter 23
Love Come Down

If there is one thing that life taught Tony, it was that time stood still for no one and either you adapt or die. Survival of the fittest was in full practice each and every day. With the few changes they had made in their lifestyles, they seemed to be surviving the worst of it; at least the financial end of things. It remained to be seen if the rest of their "would be" life could survive so many changes.

He had put up with so much from DD and in turn she too was now tolerating him having to live with Sharon again. Under the circumstances, he really didn't feel like there was much she could say. Put up or shut up time. Time to go to work man. He didn't want her back on the pole where she had been before they met but he damn sure wanted her to make a contribution towards their dream. But until that time, this would have to suffice. Trust came hard for him with her. She had so many shady dealings and had been caught in so many lies and mis-deeds that it made it ever more difficult for him to just put his trust in her and simply hand her money.

He already felt like she was sneaking behind his back with other men. She admitted to it at least once and he knew she was still indulging in occasional drug use, whether she was willing to admit it, or not. He would be damned if he was going to PAY FOR that filthy habit and she get to lounge around all day too. But admittedly, there were conflicts within him about his role in this matter. On the one hand, he was an old school brother who felt that it was his job to support the family. If there was a need to be filled, he was more than proud to fill it. To an extent, he didn't even mind so much doing it on his own, but in today's world and economy, it is a rarity that one income could do the trick. Even with a resume' such as his, it was tough to do it alone. Nevertheless, he wasn't beyond trying it.

The problem was he felt that sort of "life giving," life long commitment to someone should be reciprocated. It shouldn't just be him in this thing. His grandmother had a point about being evenly yoked, especially with concern to reciprocity. Not on a contractual basis, but in a helper as God intended you to be basis. Therefore, DD should be doing something to help the family if she was going to be a dedicated mother and family woman. In order for her to have that role, she should be dedicated to the family and helping at home, but she never helped him clean. She was angry about Sharon moving back in and refused to clean a house she still resided in. As much as he supported her, it made him angry to think she wouldn't help but he did his able best to understand her position and not demand too much.

His feelings were she expected his help why shouldn't he expect hers? In any event, what's left? Taking care of Kayden and Angel, right? Well she didn't have anything to do with Angel. No baths, no meals, not even laundry; she was strictly hands off. He picked Kayden up from school and bus stops, did home work, was on her emergency contact lists, paid for school clothes and provided her mom with a vehicle to pick up and drop her off daily. He prepared at least one meal a day for her and provided for another.

Ok well then, what's left on that list? How about loving? Well there again, she had been caught lying and sharing her loving with others a couple of times throughout the course of the relationship and her loyalties were completely screwed up. How on earth could he make such a hefty commitment to someone who couldn't even devote the minimum to their relationship in being faithful? I mean it all starts there right? If she couldn't be faithful, loyal or honor him, how could he love her in all the ways she needed to be loved, let alone support her and her daughter in all the ways they needed to be supported?

She didn't want to go back to school despite her lack of training, or education, to do anything beyond sales. Yet she had all those grand dreams. She was a total contradiction in terms, smart as a whip, but opinionated with all the wrong opinions. She knew as much but refused to change her outlook. Although, it kept her stuck in her predicament. He finally had to resign to the fact that he could only do what he could do. He would not extend himself into devoting beyond what he was able without a commitment back from her. He wasn't waiting on her to do it first before he did it. Hell, he was already doing it. He provided for her needs, even gave her a job to earn her own money. He just wanted it back. Some form of commitment, job, family, keeping her legs closed? Was that asking for too much? If you asked DD, yes. This, to her, was control.

The color of her thinking was completely twisted. In order to please her, to extend himself to show her this place of unconditional love, he had to enter into this place he called "upside down world." In this place, right is wrong and the things that are usually concrete in this world are only mere possibilities lined right up with all the things we call bullshit; here they too are possibilities. And to make it through a day, a week…hell, an hour in this place without the roof caving in and a hurricane of a fight, he had to dance the dance.

Sometimes he felt like she was the ultimate pimp and he had become the whore she put out on the track. All he wanted to do was love her but then all those poor lost souls ever wanted to do was help those abusive ass men too. He stayed focused on the Lord and His promise. He stayed focused on his mission - one he felt the Lord himself had given him. He had to show her the Goodness of the Lord in the land of the living. He was determined to show her a real man and what real love was. He wanted to show her a love with no boundaries, one that said you could have come from the walk of life she did and end up with a good, strong, loving man who loved the ground she walked on. And that her past sins could indeed be washed away clean, as pure as the driven snow, without hiding who she had been or lying about it either.

He had to stay focused on her and focused on God's word because every instinct in his body told him he was being played for a fool. Maybe he was, but in his mind, it didn't matter because it didn't change the debt, the mission or its intended outcome. It would still be had, as long as he remained obedient.

As it were, his efforts did bear fruit. Their family was growing and getting stronger with each passing week. Kayden and Tony were still very much bonded while Angel and Kayden got tighter with each passing day. Tony had watched their relationship go from budding friendship, to sibling rivalry, to Kayden's older sister protective instinct kicking in, and they were inseparable. In spite of all of the cheating, all of the lies, all of the uncertainty in their relationship, with doubt about commitment from DD, with Sharon moving back in and his obvious doubts about her, they were still moving forward in their mess. They were still being blessed as the business was doing well. He was keeping up with his studies and their family was still getting stronger. They were still moving forward even though DD's depression was crippling sometimes.

Recently, she had been going over her past and those decisions she made to compromise her life and virtue for others and had begun beating herself up about it horribly. Tony had led her back to prayer. He prayed with her and even tried to take her to his church. But since she wasn't Catholic, she got very little out of his services. One day, during the morning service he attended before work twice a week, a speaker got up before the priest and spoke during announcements about support groups going on as well as free or discounted counseling at the Crossing Church. This was a non denominational church and Tony felt good about leading DD there, since she would undoubtedly get more out of these services, not to mention possibly some professional help. This would take some pressure off of him and put it onto her where it belonged in the first place. It would hopefully get her strong enough to face some of these things so she could bear them. He went with her to the first few services and then even found his own men's support group. He wanted to show her support as she went each week. He knew from the beginning that this wouldn't be his cup of tea but he wanted to do everything he could to support her attendance, as he could see it benefited her to be around other women who could relate to some of the things and thoughts she was going through. She even started attending church each Sunday.

"Praise God!" He thought.

He even began to pay for her therapy sessions as they had no more free slots available and while she needed it, having no job couldn't afford it. They were indeed making it on down that road of life together.

*　　　*　　　*　　　*　　　*

Things were going as good as one could expect under such circumstances. DD was knee deep in therapy and going through some major changes in her life. For the first time in her life, she was facing so many things she had run away from. Believe it or not, they managed to have some good days without either one of them practicing the whole "willful ignorance" thing they both had perfected throughout their lives. DD was almost bi-polar when it came to good days and bad. She varied between smiling and laughter to balancing on the edge of life itself. Tony was still learning how to back off of her issues and deal with his own. This meant that he didn't get sucked deep down into her depressions with her.

After all, who would pull them out if he went too deeply in there with her? It was a delicate balance, learning to be empathetic, caring and understanding where she was without becoming too invested so that he wouldn't be overwhelmed by her sadness. He was still focused on his own healing and all the things he couldn't bring himself to either do, or not do, based on his own level of healing. Instead of being focused on DD's short comings, he was focused on his own. That way, as she healed, he would too so they would not only be in these trenches together but come out of them together as well.

Here is where he would find their even yoke. It was about this time he started seeking his own treatment. He knew he was no better than her and there had to be a reason why he always seemed to end up in these sorts of emotional relationships that left him in his current position. One of the things it lead him to was the need to spend more time with himself, developing his own interests and giving him the opportunity to find some of his own answers. He had always wanted to take up riding, as he owned a motorcycle when he lived back in New York but sold it as he moved to Florida. It was a smaller bike, a 600 series. He had always wanted a bigger one so he decided now was as good a time as any to take up this new hobby. It would afford him plenty of time alone, riding with his thoughts.

He bought a 900 series Kawasaki Ninja and got knee deep into his hobby. He bought it used and decided he would rehab it and learn to work on it himself. He had it painted and suped up the engine. He made it all black and chrome, having everything on the bike chromed out that he could. Pretty soon, he had a really nice customized bike which he rode often. He had managed to put in some serious hours of self talk on the seat of that bike and become a decent rider too. Eventually he and his neighbor became riding buddies. This allowed him to grow still, making new friends. Before anyone could blink, he was in a riding group. They were riding pretty regular by the time they began talking about attending bike week together. Tony really wanted to do it but he didn't want to do it without DD. Even though the guys never brought their girls or wives and it was a BIG no, no to do so and ride with the group, Tony went against the grain and snuck DD along with him on the trip. He did so by driving down behind the trucks everyone rode in and the trailer that pulled the bikes. He drove his own car, paid for his own gas and shared the cost of the trailer with the fellas, of course. Honestly, the fellas seemed a little ticked at him but he was a big dude who they knew could handle himself, so no one said anything; no matter who much attitude they put off. He had booked a hotel room although the fellas had already got a condo for the weekend. He didn't want to be anywhere near all that craziness they were talking about.

Tony's thought to himself, "Why would I want to be with some random chick I might link up with here? Who may or may not be any fun, or interesting? Where I may or may not get laid? When I can be with my best friend whom I always have a ball with and not only am I guaranteed to get laid, but I know the sex is awesome?!"

To him it was a no-brainer and he couldn't figure out why anyone would want to do anything else. One could imagine they were seeking some excitement in their "would be" boring lives; some adventure away from their wives and girlfriends. He just didn't get why the trip wasn't excitement enough; but then he wasn't with a boring girl so it would be odd for him. The entire trip down just reinforced his feelings about the entire thing as they talked the whole way there and fooled around off and on the long road to Myrtle Beach, South Carolina.

They arrived directly behind the 8 men who were riding in the two SUV's in front of them. He was certain he had already had more fun than they would probably have all that weekend. Outside of the rare occasions, these things always had a way of being more excitement and hype than any real fun that is typically had by the ordinary group of dudes. Once everyone was checked in and their bikes secured, he and DD went to the hotel they had their reservation with. On the way, they purchased a bottle of tequila and while the fellas were taking a nap, he and DD were having a few cocktails and exploring one another in ways that kept them up far past the small nap they were supposed to be taking before getting together with the fellas to ride. It was Thursday and they didn't care too much if they rode that day or not, at least on that bike. So they hunkered down in that room and got it in like two love drunk newlyweds and weren't heard from until late morning of the following day. He and DD turned off their cell phones and unplugged the hotel phone, hung the do not disturb sign on the door and it was a wrap.

Now Tony was in the moment, in the throws of love when the urge came over him to be intimate with DD in a way he hadn't previously been nor wanted to be. Tony had been molested as a child by a friend of his mothers and was coerced then forced to perform sex acts upon her, the primary one being head. He had been scarred for what he figured was life. When he got old enough to be doing the sort of things he had done at that young age, he had no interest in them. Anything beyond sexual contact initially-all those things that involved foreplay or even touching for that matter was not something he had any interest in whatsoever. He was finally facing all those demons in his own therapy and upon opening up that box, he realized that he had indeed done some good work within himself to have come that far. There he was in the throws of love, with the love of his life and for the first time since he was old enough to have sex, he was in the bedroom alone; no demons, no shadows of lovers past, or moreover past pains and abuses. He was there with DD and he wasn't over thinking things, or needing to go super slow to protect himself from the flashbacks that generally came out of that place. It was just him and her. This was as passionate and loving as he had ever been, unafraid to enter into that physical place as he longed for her touch, her words, her sweet body, lips and all those things that went along with that moment.

"I want to go down on you baby," he said, looking overly eager and smiling.

"Are you sure?" DD said to him looking shocked and nervous at the same time.

"I mean if you don't want me to . . ." he said to her, sensing her uneasiness and feeling her doubt.

"No, no that's not it at all? I just know why you have never done it and I have already told you if you never get to this part of our love, I'm ok with it baby. You don't have to do this for me, you know?" She said looking concerned, yet now curious about his answer and what it might bring.

In her head, she was thinking, "Could it be?" Honestly she wanted it. She had thought about it many, many times. Tony was a great kisser and loved to kiss her and he did it so passionately she could only imagine. Just his mere kiss always got her soaking wet and aroused. His mind began to race when he replied.

"Baby I want to do this, for me and for you. But honestly I really feel like I just want to do this with you. Can I?" He asked feeling closer to her than anyone he had ever been with at that very moment.

"I would be honored if I was the person you chose to come out of that place with, let alone for. I love you so much Tony," she said, smiling with tears in her eyes.

"Then lay back and let me try," he said, as he gently pushed her shoulder towards the bed.

That afternoon, he discovered her body and their love in ways he had only imagined before the moment he got free from those demons he carried into their bedroom. Suffice it to say that he not only did it and was successful at it but continued on doing it all that day, literally. So much so he more than made up for the time he had not and she had found her way to the first multiple orgasms in her life not only through foreplay but through the very act of intimacy itself. She had been through so much in her life. She was certain she was ruined in that way. "Over used and abused," she had always thought to herself.

But that afternoon came a healing for the two of them and she was brought to a place of acceptance of her past and embracing of her present and future with this man she loved so dearly. They passed out and slept like the dead until the next day came. This day had been filled with reassurances, healings and all of the grand reasons why Tony had chosen DD, and she, him. It was one of those days that affirmed sanity; all the hard work and the very life they were building. He rested easy and hard knowing that he had made an awesome choice to bring DD on this trip. All of the things that he thought were right and it would indeed serve to bring them even closer. In this he was confident and pleased.

* * * * *

The next day was a true testament to the roller coaster that Tony's life and their relationship was on. For as assuring and building as the previous day was, today was equally as confusing, frustrating and painful. The day started out with Tony being awakened because DD's cell phone was not only back on but was going off all morning. DD was a hard sleeper and it took a lot to wake her, especially when she had been drinking as they had been the night before. When Tony finally got the nerve, he needed to answer her phone, it was a hang up and when he checked the numbers and texts, they were from some guy who she had never told him about. He woke her to discuss this because it was unsettling to say the least. He really did want to trust her but their history said that there were definitely some things that needed to be cleared up. She assured him it was just business and someone calling for credit repair and everything he was seeing and feeling was a product of their past and there was nothing to worry about. And since he wanted to trust her and wanted to believe her, knowing full well this was a choice because no one could earn that sort of deficit, she was going to need some help, some mercy, some grace if you will. So he went within himself and although his memory was flooded with the pain of the misdeeds of her past with concern to this sort of thing, he let it go.

At the very least, he decided not to ruin the weekend with something he couldn't prove nor do anything about at the moment. She told him to stop calling and texting; she would handle what ever business they had during business hours and not to call outside of them again. It was a token effort at best but again he let it go. They had breakfast and finally took the dreaded phone call from the guys. Tony had figured at least he would be given a tough time, them breaking his balls for holding up the entire day they should have been riding for his girl. It was not a "man move." Ironically, to him, it was a "man move;" the only REAL man move any of them had made. But according to the backward ass programming most of them as men of color had received, he understood that he had lost some more cool points for his chosen way of time consumption.

Surprisingly, once he took the call, he found out that they weren't nearly as upset about it as he had thought they would have been. In fact, most of them were miserable having struck out the night before in the female department and his choice was starting to look like "the way to go next year," laughing as they said so. They finally got on the road and took that ride. It was awesome for him to be able to finally share this love of his with her. She enjoyed it greatly as well and they rode all day long, only stopping for food and to watch all the other bikers. Oh, and the guys did manage to pick up a few ladies and everyone was pretty much happy. Later on however, some of DD's tendencies re-emerged and she was behaving loosely and engaging in conversations that made Tony want to choke her like a common street thug.

Sex talk with the guy who was the perceived leader of the group that Tony had just become a part of which tested every tiny bit of Tony's new found walk with Christ. He wanted to check dude but he realized that there was nothing that he could say to him. It was DD who had engaged him in such talk. If she didn't respect their relationship, why should anyone else? Dude kept looking at Tony and waited for him to say something. He kept checking to see if there were any clear signs that Tony and DD were indeed a couple and not just homie-lover friends. Tony allowed it to continue, feeling like this was something he not only needed to know about DD but needed to see first hand. As this inappropriate line continued, Tony finally lost the stomach for it and walked away from the circle the group was in talking about unmentionable things. This was the pack of dawgs he had brought his lady into and he ought to have known better. In fact, he did, but he didn't think for a moment that she would be so disrespectful as to engage in such talk and behavior.

Tony crossed the parking lot they were standing in. He had walked off without a word and took a seat on a nearby bench. He just sat and watched as she continued smiling and flirting as he sat there trying to control his temper and keep his pride. Eventually she looked up and realized something was wrong. He would never be sure if it was because dude sent her back to him or if she actually caught herself but Tony knew right then and there that their weekend was over. He wasn't trying to handcuff her if this is who she wanted to be. He knew the code, "you have to let a ho be a ho." He knew it would go very badly if he tried to get in the middle of her desire to be that. He would just get his feelings hurt. He had all the answers he needed at that point. It was clear she was about to give dude some of her good-good that night. As if it wasn't bad enough, he approached Tony when DD went to the rest room a short while later.

"Hey dawg, not trying to step on your toes but is she your girl? I mean is she with you or do you mind if we slide off? She said she was down," Dude said with a straight face.

Tony just looked at him with rage in his eyes that said, "You're welcomed to try if you want but it ain't gonna really work out." What he actually said was, "Nah man, she's good. She's with me."

Dude looked shocked and said, "I'm sorry dawg. I didn't mean anything by it. I saw you just walk off so I figured she wasn't. And the way she was talking I figured . . . Well at least you know the truth now dawg.

She ain't shit. She was with it and she told me so big dawg. No disrespect big dawg. Now you know."

Tony just sat there in silence and never did mutter another word. He realized that she wreaked of a whore because she was. This is who she was used to being and anyone who paid attention to her was sure to get that from her. She didn't know how to interact with men in any other way, apparently. Once DD returned, he simply told her he was ready to go. Hungry and tired, he told her he wanted some alone time and they said their goodbyes and left. For the remainder of the weekend, they stayed to themselves, eating separately, even riding alone. He was pretty much able to block out the entire incident using that willful ignorance technique he had perfected over the years. They had found some healing the day before. He would focus on that and the rest would simply be time well spent. One more group of friends lost made no difference to him. He loved her and he wasn't going to lose her. She was the important thing, that's all, nothing else. True enough, the guys pretty much felt like he was a lame and never did call him after they returned. His embarrassment about the issue not only made him feel lame as well but gave him the fortitude to not give a damn that they never called either. All the while, he never made it an issue beyond letting her know that he knew that she was planning on sleeping with dude.

When she finally did ask why they weren't riding back with the fellas, he replied, "Dude asked if you were with me. He was under the impression you weren't and were free to be with whomever. I don't think it's a good idea we hang with them."

Totally embarrassed by the fact that dude had told her little secret to Tony, she turned red in the face and never brought it up again.

Chapter 24
Through the Fire

The return trip from South Carolina was spent exploring Tony's anxiety. Based on the phone calls and DD's actions, he had plenty of questions, creepy little whispers inside his head and fires to extinguish. Now, he knew if he addressed all of those fears, that ugly head that exists between them to argue, debate and even scream at one another with the vigor of presidential candidates would soon be out, full blown for like a ten plus hour ride. While no one in their right mind would ever want to subject themselves to something like that, most would find it at least as difficult to drive that distance with all the questions that burned in his mind. How he decided to handle it was through calm conversation in the form of hypothetical questions and "I know better" statements. Like,

"I know better than to even think you would do this or that BUT it looks like. . ." or "feels like . . ."

As long as he didn't go too deep or let the debate carry on too long, they could have a conversation without anyone getting too defensive. By the time they arrived back home, he was pretty well satisfied with all he had heard... well, at least what he could live with anyway. The humble truth was he knew he couldn't trust or believe her in his heart of hearts. He wanted to. In fact he needed to. Sadly he didn't know how and that was what this entire ordeal was about in his mind. Even though she presented as untrustworthy, and she probably was, there were enough circumstances where she proved she could be untrustworthy. But it mattered not, because it wasn't about her. It was about him and his inability to trust and let go. Go with God. Even if she had been perfectly trustworthy and never done anything against him or his honor, he would have still had a problem with this area. The better part of faith is not what you see, or think you know but a belief in something higher. He was not so much putting his heart in "HER" hands as much as his own. Sure people let us down everyday. Free will is a motha. But if we learn to lean on His grace and put our whole trust in Him, even when they let us down, we can find our own personal lesson in the matter.

But as the Words says, "With each temptation, leave a way to escape it, so we can bare it."

So he always knew that even if the pain did come, he would be able to find his way home and wouldn't get lost in the darkness of depression, regret or hopelessness. Even he knew there was a higher lesson in it for him. So he pushed on past that which CLEARLY smelled like bullshit and back onto that place he held himself in that said, "No matter what SHE does, I WILL DO THE RIGHT THING."

From here he would develop the discipline to know what it looked like as well as the ability to actually do it when he needed to. So even if she doesn't end up being the one as he hoped and prayed for, he would be equipped for her when she arrived. He wouldn't lose her because he didn't know how to have grace or accept imperfections. He would have plenty of patience for her and moreover, himself. So he wouldn't beat himself up too harshly, judging himself with perfectionist eyes. This single barrier kept him unable to seek or receive love out of a need to deserve it. This lesson here was teaching him through his love of her that you deserved love even when you haven't done ANYTHING to earn it.

This was huge in his psycho dichotomy growing up. He learned to love through deeds of perfection; anything short meant no love. Even against all those things taught to him in darkness where these demons lay, the second part of this tale untold; yet he learned it still. If he could learn to love her, and could see God loving her through him from a place she CLEARLY didn't deserve it, he could imagine God loving HIM. And if God could indeed love him that way, then no matter what his childhood said, the abandonment by his father, the abandonment by his mother, being an only child with no real connection to anyone beyond his trust which was damn well pretty hard to attain. Beyond all the years of perfectionist, doubt, fear, anger, denial and never, ever truly seeing what love looked like, he knew if God could send her love through him, the kind of unconditional love he knew he held in his heart for her, one that only God could send, HE KNEW TONY TOO COULD FINALLY LEARN TO LOVE HIMSELF, TRULY.

This sounds so simple, far simpler than it is unfortunately. He had always loved his good looks, his body and keeping in shape. The way he looked, his intelligence and speech, he had always loved his ability to do things; sports and all other accomplishments. But deep down, it was never real to him; he had always secretly hated himself for allowing himself to be abused, learned hatred of himself at the hands of others. A hatred that said no matter how well he did something, no matter what he was able to accomplish, he was never truly good enough. So he never celebrated any accomplishment. Even more sad, he never celebrated HIMSELF. His love for her, him learning to love her unconditionally through his love for God, lead him to a much needed, much deeper place of love for himself. He knew that no matter what, this was something he could never quit, never give up on. Giving up on DD meant giving up on himself.

So by the time they pulled into the driveway to meet the guys to unload his bike, he was as much in love with DD as he had ever been and she was all ears, still baffled by the love she could see all over him for her. For the first time in her life, she had someone to love her without strings, without motive or desire to have, keep or control her life. Someone who loved her beyond her flaws and mis-deeds. While she didn't fully understand it, she could not only see the blessing in it for her and Kayden, but the God too; and it reinforced her faith in God.

That weekend had been like a test for them both and they needed it more than either one of them could see at the time. Past the need to be alone or romance.

Past the get away from the kids and the need to have fun. They really did need to reconnect on a more intimate level in order to move to the next level and that is what this weekend felt like it did for them. They had leaped another hurdle towards their finish line of marriage and happily ever after.

It was amazing that through all the murk and the day to day confusion, they still dared to dream. They had visions of grandeur, past all of the practical things that most folk look at and consider. All the ordinary make or break lines people put in place to tell if they are compatible. Hell, most of those lines had already been broken, let alone crossed, but they were moving on faith and full was this love that neither one of them had held on to another human being long enough in that way to feel.

At its best, it was absolutely the most amazing thing either one of them had ever experienced. At its worst, it was the gut wrenching fear filled place of old men on steroids. All of those negative emotions and fears multiplied because your best friend could also very easily be your worst enemy when they held all your secrets. Holding the key to one another's heart was a magnificent miracle to see, until you feel it held over the flames of fear and destruction. Then it makes for the absolute worst feelings and days of your life because of the simple fact that you end up caring far more than you have at any other time in your life. That in itself makes you more invested, which drags out far more than even you know you had to protect inside, what you had only assumed was a shell of a heart, those things left behind by all the loves past.

But once you open it up, you find out that inside there was waiting this entire wondrous world that wound up being far more worth protecting than you ever imagined at this point of your wounded life. So it becomes a steady as you go, one step at a time process. Never leaving the shadow of your fears too far. Honestly, up until that very moment, good or bad, you had never been there before. After all, who are you without those fears? It was a scary thought indeed for the both of them. No matter how much they loved one another, it was never a simple task putting down those irrational fears even after identified.

They were crossing brides when they came upon them but after this weekend they found themselves a bit more directed and willing to take a hard look - well at least a semi-hard look - at some of those factual things that they knew had to be addressed and overcome in order to go where they both dreamed of going.

Tony had always liked DD's family, even though they never really seemed to like him. This fact always did bother him. What bothered him more is he felt helpless to do anything about it. He had tried to go around them and even tried to make a good impression but nothing ever worked and his efforts only ended up being misjudged as fake or somehow always misunderstood. Maybe it was fake since he "made" an effort. So he thought to himself, he would go back into this wheel house but this time merely be himself and either they would see his authentic love for DD and like him for who he was, or not.

"It couldn't get any worse," he thought. "They already hate me," he snickered, even though he didn't truly find anything funny about the situation.

This was one of those areas between them that he knew was a deal breaker for DD. Although she did her best not to emphasize it or speak on it too much, she had before and he was well aware of it. He knew at some point he was going to have to find a way to make these people like him as much as he already liked them. DD had told him plenty of stories about her sister's husband and all the petty crap he had to endure for the marriage he now shared with her sister. The disrespect of her mother and brother. The disloyalty her sister had shown him at points in their relationship. Tony couldn't see it. All he had ever witnessed from those two was loyalty to one another.

DD's sister and her husband chose each other and their family over everyone and everything, even when the decision didn't make much sense. Yet, Tony decided that he needed to believe that, despite what he thought he knew. Besides, he had witnessed damn near everyone bad mouth the poor guy behind his back, so how far off could the truth really be? Tony decided he would subject himself to this world and "pay his dues" now so he could have their DD for his. He didn't want to "steal" her away from their family. He wanted her to choose him and walk into this new life together WITH their blessing. It would start this weekend. They spoke about it briefly on the ride home and they both agreed it was time.

*   *   *   *   *

"Well this idea was a bust" Tony thought to himself sitting on DD's sisters' couch.

There he was knee deep in drinks and laughter. It should have been a great time as the four of them sat there socializing. But the undertone and even the overtone was one of dislike. It was clear to Tony, if he never knew it before, that they not only didn't like him but didn't respect him at all. The dislike he could stand but the disrespect was something he was having trouble swallowing. He had been holding back from breaking homies' face all night. DD's brother-in-law, Del, short for Delroy, was a pussy ass gum bumper who had far more mouth than he had action. Maybe another time in his life he was hard but today his wife wore the pants and was far harder than he was. HE talked and she backed him up like a cheerleader, and a good number two, should. He knew if he said what he wanted to, their relationship would be over. He also knew if he did what he really had in his heart to do - bust this dude's grill wide open - that DD would probably stop messing with him all together. But, moreover, his entire goal was to get her family to like him and this would not only secure that DD's sister and Del didn't but everyone else in her family who wasn't there would never forgive such a transgression and disrespect of their home and family.

He had to show restraint. After all this is the very thing DD kept telling Tony that Del himself went through. Maybe now he felt like it was Tony's turn to feel the heat that he had to endure in order to have one of Big Grady's little girls. And since DD's mother and brother, the ones who hazed him, weren't there, it was his duty to ensure he went through no less. Tony couldn't figure this entire situation out. More importantly, he was trying to hold his pride in check so he didn't let his anger get the best of him. Once the night was over, he and DD fell asleep with him still trying to figure out how on earth he was going to find his way through to the other side of this thing under these circumstances. The horrible part of it all was that DD and her sister had such a sibling rivalry that her sister treated her just as badly. DD didn't seem to care so much. She constantly did foul or embarrassing things to her and DD often made excuses for her and let things slide. Tony often wondered what DD felt she owed her baby sister to endure such maltreatment. He remembered many times DD recalled childhood stories and her feelings that she had abandoned her younger siblings when she left home. He also recalled the horrible treatment she knew she left them to endure at the hands of her ultra controlling mother. This was the primary belief DD held as to why her relationship between her siblings and her was so bad.

She felt like this was her time to pay her dues in order to re-enter their family too. Her mom didn't speak to her. She had written her off and her brother didn't even acknowledge her existence unless their mother brought it up. Her sister was the only one who even dealt with her. So DD was holding on to the only family she had left. Tony couldn't really blame her but on the same token couldn't say he really understood it. At some point, in his mind, she would have to rise up and be her own woman.

"Why was she holding on to them and their ideas of who they believe her to be? Why does she

304

subject herself to that, especially considering how negative it is most times?" He thought.

Her family needed a fall guy for all the pain that existed between them. Currently she was that black sheep. She was the scapegoat they leaned on instead of candidly dealing with all of the real pains that ailed them. They talked about this the following week before DD could finally let go of her false guilt long enough to admit that the way they dealt with her was not only unfair, but she didn't deserve it. After all, hadn't she punished herself enough? Hadn't she been through enough? She hid from them, enduring so many things in the streets at the hands of those who claimed to love her but used and abused her every which way but loose. During that entire time she dragged poor Kayden through it with her.

"Didn't she at least deserve better? Didn't she deserve to see something better through you?"

She knew in her heart of hearts the discouragement she was building and teaching her daughter to become later on in her young life. She could see it in the way she lacked confidence in her own young life, barely able to look anyone in the eyes, the speech of a mouse.

It was time for something else. It was time for a change and she knew it was going to have to be her example that made for this change. She had stood up to them before and lost. Now she was more afraid to leave that realm than ever. But what did she have to lose? She was already the lowest of the low. She would have to go out and gain their respect and she certainly wasn't going to be able to do it by groveling. She was emboldened by Tony's talk and encouraged through the shift in Kayden's mannerisms. Therefore, she decided to stop chasing behind her family's approval.

She and Tony set out to make their own way and had taken one more step towards that brass ring. She stopped setting every Friday night aside for her sister and brother-in-law. She stopped running to watch their children at the drop of a hat without respect for her time.

She even stopped allowing her friends to lead her around by the nose out of the same sick need for approval. There would be back lash. Everyone had not only begun to hate Tony worse than they had ever before but they lashed out at DD and everything that was wrong in her life suddenly became his doing. He knew this wasn't true, although it did bother him. As long as DD knew the truth and could see how much he loved her, and sacrificed for their life together, he was ok.

He worked so hard in their relationship that it was almost cruel and inhumane treatment for them to heap so much shit on him when he had brought so much light and love to her and Kayden's life. Unfair did not begin to touch the situation. He was resigned to the fact that until they were ready, they would never see it. If they hadn't learned to unconditionally love and accept DD, one of their own, there was no way they were ever just going to accept him, no matter what he did or how great it was. He knew that it was something going on with them, not him. There was never going to be anything he was going to be able to do to please them. And he certainly wasn't going down that road of approval addiction to disprove the theory.

He had already gone through his very own battle with his family with concern to this very same subject. No, he would have to be the man he knew he was and stand his ground. The problem was that it was wearing on DD and she was getting weak and falling deeper and deeper into depressed states. She put so much of her own opinion of herself in what others said and thought about her when they didn't approve of her. She couldn't approve of her, so he was who she leaned on. And foolishly he thought he could hold her up until she could learn to stand. Until one day he got an email from her would be "best friend" Tonya. It read:

Hi~

I hope that this finds you in good spirits and health. My name is Tonya. I am DD's friend. I found your email address on an email that DD sent to me quite a while back. I would like to stress that DD has no clue that I am sending you this, although, I know by the time you finish this, you may be contacting her in regards to the points I am going to touch on.

You see, I haven't talked to DD much since she is currently back talking to you. The problem with that is prior to last week, I saw and spoke with DD regularly because you were currently out of the picture. This pattern that she uses when you are around is beginning to cause me concern as her friend. Because in my eyesight the relationship she carries on with you is not healthy to her. I know that DD is a grown woman and capable of handling her own relationships with people but being one of the people who has loved DD for WHO SHE IS, I feel I have the right to stand up for her when she won't stand up for herself.

YOU ARE NOT HEALTHY FOR DD! However, for whatever reasons beyond me and a few others, she loves you unconditionally. She loves you so much that she doesn't even take the time or make the time for her friends and family because she is constantly stressed, worried or following after your well being.

DD is a great person. She has her faults as everyone else does but when you read the fine print, she is an exceptional woman, friend and mother.

Until you came around. You make her second guess who she is, how she should feel, if she even should feel what she does and how to handle it. In my opinion and I stress MY OPINION...YOU DON'T DESERVE THE GUM OFF HER SHOES!

If you could possibly sit back and place the pros and cons of your relationship with DD on paper, you would see that you are not up to standards to even have DD in your life, yet, she constantly battles with you to keep you around. For what...I HAVEN'T A CLUE! She is steadily asking for your time and attention, she constantly is in arguments with you over what you feel and how you feel and what you want. But I ask when can she argue for what she wants, feels, needs, expects and should have. For nearly the past two years of this relationship that you and DD have had, I have thought to myself as one of

*her best friends "Why have I not spoken with this man,
seen this man, hung around him or know anything past
the fact that DD loves him?" The answer is simple to me
but it bothers my friend because for whatever reason,
she has convinced herself of the fact that it is her and it
is her friends and family that pose the problem. But let
me set the record straight because WE are not the
problem, YOU ARE! Every time I have a function or
something that I want to involve my friend in, I invite her
to invite you in, attempting to get to know you as a friend
of my best friend. But you always turn her down or
present this disillusional idea that it is because of
something that had NOTHING to do with you.*

*For the record, it was, it isn't and it is no concern to you
about what happened between me and her in Atlanta.
For whatever reasons or statements made to you about
the trip, me and DD solved on our own. The trip to
Atlanta was a trip for me to visit a friend and DD was
set up to visit with her family but things didn't happen
that way. It resulted in DD speaking with a friend of hers
and for whatever reason you feel I coached her into that.
I had nothing to do with it or had any idea of it until
after the fact because I, as a grown woman was doing
my thing like originally planned and was not aware that
DD was in the situation she was in. But even in the end
of all of that...it had NOTHING to do with you! It's one
thing to say that you want to hold that against me, but it
is another thing for you to step up and be a man about
why you really don't want to meet or hang with DD's
friends and family. You don't know anything about me
yet you judge something that happened between me and
DD and you convince her that she is the one that doesn't
want you to be around us.*

*Now when DD announced her engagement to me I was
excited, even though I haven't a clue on who you are. I
wasn't clear when your relationship had reached a point
of marriage, seeing that you all don't share a common
household together, you are constantly battling with*

each other about your issues, you stand firm by your misconceptions of who she is, was and is going to be, as well as how your relationship with your future daughter was...and you two are getting married? WHAT!??? But all in all I was excited because my friend felt that she was going to be with the man she loves. Well since the engagement DD has changed but you didn't! I was completely appalled to the fact that she had accepted under the circumstances that she did, but for whatever her reasons she was willing to say "Yes" to being your wife and "Yes:" to pleasing you as her man. Even now I sit and say what the hell is going on....

Bottom line, I don't know you, you don't know me and frankly if it weren't for DD I would care less to know anything about you! But as a real person who loves DD and wants her healthy and happy, I know that it is not my decision who she chooses to be with. So with that I listen when she cries when she stresses, when she is happy, when she is facing things that she should leave in God's hands, when she just wants to vent or maybe even praise things about you and I go in stride. ..because her happiness is ultimately what counts as far as our friendship goes. I know she wants the same for me.
As hard as it is to know that she will be furious with me about this email, I prayed to God and asked him to give me strength to do this because DD is someone that I care about in both aspects of a friend and family. So if it is in God's Will then DD and I will remain friends after this. I don't want this email to pose as hate or dislike towards you but to show you that there is a problem and in my eyes, heart and mind it's YOU! How that will affect you, I don't know and at this point could really care less! My main concern is that YOU stop stringing DD along and be a man and say what it is that you really want from her, expect of her and ultimately what your plans are for you and her. Even if that means NOT BEING WITH HER!

Until then be good, be safe, and above all be BLESSED!

PEACE GOD 2104!!!

Kind Regards,
Tonya~

Tony's response was well thought out and came quickly, it read:

Tonya,

I have never judged you nor have I ever thought ill of your friendship with DD. I have never disliked you or anyone in her family. I have never discouraged her from calling you, her family or tried to influence the time she has spent with any of you. Which is why it floors me when any of you would think that I do. I am going to do the best that I can in explaining things from my prospective, fully aware that you couldn't give a hoot. But I love DD too and want to set the record straight because it sounds like you were mis-informed. I understand how this happened; she is your friend and so you are only going to get it from her point of view. Why would you care about mine? Right? Well, if you truly cared about DD as you say you do, you might want to know if it is truly me or if there is something that is inside of her that is keeping her from being happy. That way as her friend, if it is your desire to help her, you will know how best to do this.

Let me start out with your second point because to me being her friend it would seem most obvious having known her longer than myself that NO ONE stops DD from being DD. DD has her own mind, mouth and heart and no one big, small or in between has ever stopped her from speaking up for herself, regardless if she was right or wrong. She has defended herself to me with just as much vigor

310

knowing and admitting she was wrong as when she was right. All in the name of voicing her opinion. She WILL be heard, even if it is to her detriment. She is not the type of person that is EVER going to allow you to pee on her head and convince her it's raining.

This leads me to point two, accepting her for who she is. The above stated reason is exactly why I fell in love with her and continue to love her to this second. She is a strong woman with strong opinions and ideas. I will be honest and say that recently I have had to come to terms with who DD is and have let many things go in order to continue to be in any type of relationship with her but I realized that was my junk, not hers.

Pros and Cons, I recently did this and didn't like what it looked like. And for the record her pros did not outnumber her cons. And to the contrary, I think if you knew DD not just as a friend but in an entirely different light, the light she is in with me, you might understand. I know through talking to DD that you have had some problems in your relationship and am glad you have worked them out with Chris. I say that to you to say as I begin to explain to you what my light looks like that you will understand having been through some things yourself. One of the cons in our relationship until about maybe a couple of months ago was that DD used to always feel the need to talk about her ex's. Not just regular talk but about them and their relationship and even their sex. I ask you as a woman, if your partner was doing this for the last, I don't know year and a half, would that bother you? Well, this wasn't a major thing like I made it some cross to bear. I eventually told her how much it hurt me and she got down on herself about it. I loved her through it although I felt wronged. I got over it because I realized it wasn't something she did purposely to hurt me. Now you may still be confused because what I said onto and by itself may

311

seem like nothing and I can see that but let me add to that picture another from the list which in my opinion falls in together making for a much worse picture. Imagine if you will, your partner having multiple female "friends" that he took calls from at whatever hour. You could be sitting with him and having a conversation and the phone would ring and he will pick it up and not only carry on an entire conversation with this other woman, his "friend", as though you weren't there but you would hear this woman asking him where he was? And who he was with? And why? And you watched your partner's mouth move snapping to answer as if they were the ones in the relationship. Would you be comfortable with that? How about if you found out that he was still giving out his number romantically, or that he had been out with someone he met by giving that number out? Would you feel as though you could accept him for who he is and continue to love and stay with him regardless if he went on dates with other women while you were in a relationship with him? Listen I'm not trying to air out DD's dirty laundry, simply put, you only know what you know from her perspective and you don't care to know or look at things from where I sit. I, like you, have found DD in compromising positions with others, as you have with Chris, and chose to forgive and try to forget. But the funny thing is this isn't what we have most of our arguments about, if you can call them that. I will also get to that in a moment. I want to address the rest of your points first.

You said that each time you have had a get together or event that you have invited me through her. I have never until now received that invite. But I can say that honestly if I had, I probably wouldn't have gone any way. You say that not going around her friends and family is my fault. And you are correct, I have never made any bones about that. I have chosen not to put myself in that position. And although once again I know you don't care but in an effort to clear the air I am going to explain it any how. It is difficult for me to go around those I KNOW don't like me and have said so either through DD or to me directly. Why would I want to do that? Put myself in a place where I walk among people who don't like me and have already formed their opinion about me based on their view of what their loved one has said or at a time felt about me. And as you have already said don't care a thing about me. Should I be doing this for the comfort or happiness of DD? No, I don't think so. Not for DD or anyone else. I don't know what DD has or hasn't told you about me but I am nearly ten years her senior and have a daughter just four years younger than her and was married previously for ten plus years. I say that to say this, I have had plenty of experiences in my life and I have never seen that situation be fruitful for anyone, EVER.

How did it become what it is? Well, DD and I will go through something, whatever it is and she will either be upset or depressed. She may or may not have anything negative to say about me but based on her being upset there is an "opinion" formed. Eventually that opinion leads to a belief and not even knowing the entire story the belief is, "she was happier without him," therefore she is better off without him, she shouldn't be with him. I can see that and completely understand that from where it sits. I have three sisters myself. I have run to defend them, fought for them, shot for them and get myself involved in all sorts of things back home in Brooklyn defending those women in my life that I love. I too have had my "opinions" and beliefs about their relationships. But ultimately I had to realize that I didn't know the first thing about what was going on and let it go as something that they had to work through, not me.

313

So back to my point, if you knew that these folks had this negative "opinion" or belief about you, would you go? I choose to spend my time and days where I'm wanted and respected. If she wants to be with her friends, I have never, EVER but once tried to stop her. The one time being your last event, which leads me to my next point.

You talked about what happened with you and DD in ATL and it not being any of my concern. Somehow I am getting the impression that you think I hold you responsible for what happened there or that I am upset with you for what might look like you perceived wrong. All that stranded in the street business and not being able to get a hold of you. If this is what you are referring to or your thoughts, you are so wrong. I am not, nor have I, been involved with you on any level, let alone in a way I could ever call myself being upset with you for any reason. DD made a choice that weekend, of which once again I never tried to stop her from doing. She chose to go with you to ATL because she wanted to, she chose to link up with and old "friend" who later tried to sleep with her and she ended up in the street. See here is where I have a problem. It's not that she chose to go to one of her friends and put herself in that situation. It is that she had to lie to me to do it. She lied to me on why she went to ATL in the first place. She lied to me on where she ended up staying and she maintained that lie until she had told so many lies, she could no longer hold them all. Once again, if your partner lied to you on a regular, would you have a problem with that? You see DD could have called me and I would have made sure she didn't have to even put herself in that position. Staying with another man? Why? She has me to fall back on? But her pride has been and remains a huge issue and it refused to allow her to do what she knew was right on that and many other issues. So yes, I was upset about her lies and what I perceived as her making a fool out of me. If your

314

partner and I were friends and he lied to you all the time and I knew about it, how comfortable would you be coming around me, especially considering the fact that I don't even like you anyway? I felt disrespected and rightfully so and all I asked is that if I was going to ever go around her friend, because lets face it, we keep using the word in its plural form but you are it. There is only one other person she even talks about and from what I understand you two don't get along, so don't hang around each other much. I don't know, only what I've been told. So there is no group of people I'm keeping her from being around. I have had her drunken, alcoholic, stepmother call me up and we have had at least two or three similar conversations. It has also been expressed that Lana has very similar views about our relationship. I for awhile, until it was obvious, continued to visit and do things with them and their family, so it's JUST YOU. Back to the point all I asked is that she fixed the situation, make it one that I don't have to go around and feel like I did. Ashamed and made a fool of because this shouldn't be my burden to bear. I asked her to make a better choice, one that would build instead of continue to cause pain, conflict-evident in your message still today and confusion also evident today. I wanted her to clear this mess up with some real talk before either one of us moved in any direction. I have NEVER put my foot down in that way in this relationship before. But it had gotten to the point where I felt like I HAD TO STAND UP FOR ME because she wasn't and still hasn't done it. So she went and I chose to leave. But that was based on the totality of the circumstances, not you or your party. You or your relationship with DD will never be that important to me and our life to base that type of decision on. This leads me to one of my two final points.

There is something inside of DD that won't allow her to be happy. That won't allow her to be

315

loved or fully accepted. YOU don't know this and you NEVER will because WE have a completely different sort of relationship than you and her have. This is evident in the fact that while DD has readily admitted numerous times that she has been emotionally and physically abused to damn near anyone, she has not once come out to you until she met me, that she was sexually abused too. Why didn't she make that discovery with you? How come you guys as friends haven't discussed or dealt with that? THIS THING, the sexual abuse, is far more harmful than anything I could EVER do or have done to her, yet you were not the one to pull that healing and extract poison from her. WHY? Because we have a completely different relationship than you and she have, so you will never see or know the DD that I KNOW. There is something inside her that is broken that won't allow her to be happy. It comes from a place that says she doesn't deserve to have it. Years of those around her who SAID THEY LOVED HER, sold her in her head that she wasn't anything to be valued, treasured or to be made someone's wife. Those who loved her but beat her and talked to her in a way that was beneath them. I can go down the line and point fingers at all of you who love her, who stood by and watched her make bad decisions or better yet didn't stand up or by her when she needed you the most. See you didn't fail DD when you weren't available to take her call when she found herself in that situation. A better person or friend would have honestly questioned her friend about the relationship she was in and wondered why, maybe even taken the time to ask, why she didn't call the man she says she loves for the help that she so obviously needed? Isn't that what this whole man and woman partnership is supposed to be about anyway? You get yourself in a bad situation and you can't call your partner? Isn't that what friends do-keep their friends from making mistakes uninformed? Surely you had to think that? Or maybe you were to busy being "grown" and "doing your thing" to be a true friend at that moment? I don't know, not judging you, hadn't even given that thought a second of my time or energy until just now. All I'm saying is you know she was abused on multiple levels, how do you think that plays itself out in an intimate relationship? I'll tell you how. Every time I have found myself in the position that DD has said she wanted to be in, one that she said would make her the most happy, she has found a way to sabotage it and make it unhappy.

Example: damn near every time I've taken her out of town or went anywhere with her that way, she sabotages it. I remember us coming home from watching a Winky Wright fight at the forum and feeling so good and full of love. And in the middle of sharing that moment of happiness with DD, she freaked out and became someone else and started fighting and arguing with me all coming from a place of dysfunction within her sexually, stemming from her abuse. A night we had enjoyed and laughed, hugged and kissed, ended up in tears and arguing. Ultimately we needed a time out and she ended up dating someone else behind my back. All from a moment of happiness. Can you imagine being with someone like that? I have taken her to my sisters, she embarrassed and disrespected me. My brother and then best friend, she disrespected me all at times when I was showing her the love and acceptance she claimed to desire so much. It doesn't take a degree in counseling to know that these are some deeper lining problems when this type of thing happens. I have accepted her and forgiven her and it has been her who has gone into herself and found these things lacking and not wanted. Who wouldn't? This is all coming up for her now because she sees these things clearly at

317

this moment in her life. She always knew these things, her junk, her baggage was there but for everyone else's benefit, she packed them away to play like she was the happy girl, life of the party, all the while hating who she was inside. Did you hear me say, HATING WHO SHE WAS INSIDE? Now that might not matter to you, as long as she is smiling but it matters to her and it also matters to me. I cannot tell you why she hasn't come to this point in any one of her other relationships? Maybe she didn't care enough about them to go any deeper. Maybe she was just playing and enjoying her life. Maybe she thought that she could pretend that these things just didn't happen to her for the rest of her life. But I want a real relationship so when these things came up, I didn't just leave like every other man in her life, including her father and brother. I stayed and loved her through it and for that, all I have received is judgment and hatred for my love, "for my love you are my adversaries" Psalms 109.

No matter, I am not in a relationship with you or her family, although I hoped it would be different. I decided that to stand by HER and SHOW HER LOVE was more important than if you all hate me or not. So when she pushed me away, I didn't just leave, I asked why? When she lied and cheated and even stabbed me in the back, I didn't leave, I stayed and loved her through it because I saw her for who she was and it was greater than her actions would lead anyone to believe. So when she disrespected, embarrassed and tried to make me leave so she could go down her hole of depression, one she had long before she met me, one she got from her mom, that told her suicide was a viable answer and she spoke about it often, I stayed and dragged her out of that place and to a true place of God and understanding of his love. Today you don't even hear her talk about killing herself or that being something she would ever do.

318

Did you know she talked about ending her life? What did you do? None of you recognize that she had another face she lived with everyday, and behind that mask she hated herself so much, she often thought about leaving Kayden motherless. She walked around smiling her big smile just like her mother taught her, laughing her big laugh just like Randy taught her. But no one, NOT A FLIPPIN ONE OF YOU taught her how to LOVE HERSELF or cared enough to spend the time to love her enough to bring her to this place.

I loved DD from the minute I laid my eyes on her, she is my "dream girl" and I say it all the time. It has nothing to do with her obvious good looks, although they do matter. I love her strong voice, her strong will and her determination to be heard and dealt with. She will never go quietly into that good night. And while all of that is in her and even more of the most wonderful qualities I've ever known exist there too, they all lead way to my falling deeper in love with her and I found out that most of it was just a show, a front. I didn't make her confused or have her questioning who she is. She always did, but she hid that from you, her closest friend out of love, so that you didn't have to see her hurting or deal with her pain. She has always felt like it was too much and would swallow up anything good left in her life, including Kayden. She just wanted everyone to be able to go on in their lives and be happy. But she had become a product of her mother's voice, her father's absence and her abuse, where she didn't even feel worthy of a real friend that she could share all this stuff with and not feel judged or that she deserved the kind of love that would help her through this. She just thought it was too much to ask and I see why now. There has been many a day that her venom and the voice of her mother has cut me to the bone and had me hiding from the pain but I never left.

319

But despite all of this, during her time in sharing our lives, know that she has lead to reading the bible for the first time probably ever, and to her mother, to a place where they not only are talking, before she found out she was sick, but now that she knows, can actually be of some use in supporting her. Not having to dig back into all those unresolved feelings between the two of them, wasting valuable time over a past that will never, can never change. No, she dealt with it ahead of time so God could use her at this time to help her mother. She put on her big girl britches and dealt with it, her and I together. We cried our way through it, loved our way through it and talked until the cow jumped over the moon. Did you bring her to that place? Did you show her love and how to love and be loved? Were you the one who fostered that forgiveness in her heart and lead her to that perfect place with God so she could be in that perfect place for her mother at her most critical time of need? Have you ever? How could that ever be unhealthy? See, as you sit back and judge me, understand that you will be judged the length and the measure. I am here for her, love her, and if it is up to me, won't ever leave her. But I only have my side of the equation, on her side is whether or not she will stay and fight those things within her to continue to grow and become the woman God intended her to be and allow herself to be happy. I don't control any of that nor have I ever tried.

I have never strung DD along. I asked her to be my wife with the understanding that neither one of us are perfect people. We both have our own prospective issues and things to deal with that we both bring to the table. At times mine greater than hers and she helps lead me to a better place. And yes she brought Kayden and I brought my four children and none of those "things" were resolved. But as I said, we are not perfect people and we gave ourselves about two years worth of engagement to work out the details. During that time, as if I need to explain this, we intended on living with one another and taking the natural progressive steps in order to reach its natural and intended conclusion. But in the meantime, how do you move forward to this place with all this junk in the way? I am not in the habit of ignoring the huge pink elephant in the room and would never consider moving forward in a life, a marriage with someone I knew was so broken without helping mend her heart. Because hurt people, hurt people. I have always known that I can't do it, only she and Jesus can, I can just lead her to HIM. And pray that throughout her journey, we stay or become of like mind and stay yoked so we can make it. I am powerless in the process but that.

I have no ill feeling towards you other than your judgment of me. And let me state the obvious although it may not be necessary. But it makes perfect sense that you would hear from her more or even everyday if we had broken up. First, she would have more time, which it takes plenty of to build a relationship, besides all the problems I have discussed, let alone moving towards marriage. I don't know but it seems like those things might require more time and commitment? Second, if you are the friend that you say you are to her then it stands to reason that you would be the one she leans on in her times of heartache. And that wouldn't change if she decided to let you know that she was hurting or not. That is what friends do. I know you miss your hang out buddy and everyday convo as her friend but YOU NEED TO GROW in you guys' relationship and understand that IT HAS CHANGED and may NEVER be the same and that has not so much to do with me as you think. I could be Joe Doe and who she is today wouldn't have her in the same position she was in before with you and I know she would be dealing with her life and love differently, me or no me. This change in DD is not about me! It is a shift in her and what she sees in herself, her worth and values. Why would she value your friendship, no matter how great it is, over one with her husband or potential husband? And for you to expect that of her is unreasonable. If that wasn't your point then I don't understand your opening paragraph about your communication or lack thereof. If considering nothing more than the fact that we just broke up and are trying to reconcile, you as an adult should understand that this takes time, so talking to her everyday under this circumstance is completely unreasonable. A real friend who was truly interested in knowing their friend was happy would understand that. Time is precious; you can either invest it in YOUR OWN LIFE and happiness or making your friends' happy. You cannot serve two masters.

In closing, without sounding too defensive or that I took your message too personal, considering you don't know a thing about this relationship or me, I'm going to say this. I do love DD for who she is, was, and will be, which is more than I can say about you at this point. You seem more upset that you are missing time with her and more concerned with her "instant smile" than the REAL ROOT of her problems and path to her happiness, both of which she had far before she ever spoke my name. I am healthy for DD. She isn't talking about killing herself, or abandoning her life. She isn't hating her mother (remember the poem she wrote about her mother? That vision was heartbreaking) or family. She is loving herself more, has gone to God completely. She is attending church, a support group and counseling. Did you suggest that to her? Did you help her find her therapist? Or her support group? How about church? Did you stop her from killing herself with the drugs and booze to numb the pain and quiet all the voices that told her she was no good? Considering you have spoken out of your butt, you are the one who doesn't deserve the gum off of her shoes because you have left her, abandoned her, as a friend for far less than I have stood by her through. And since you don't know me, how can you judge, if I have changed or not? Now you saying THAT was just strange? And finally, the only stringing along I have done as far as DD is concerned is I have strung out all of her good qualities that she possesses so that I could only see the good in her heart. I had fainted, unless I had believed to see "the goodness of the lord in the land of the living" and stood with her through the tough times when she could only show me the bad.

I respectfully ask you to stick to your life, what you know and can speak intelligently about for peace sake. I am not your enemy, nor do I wish to be. Please have the same respect I have shown you and leave me alone. If you have any further feelings on the matter, please take it up with your friend, if you still have one. For the record, I haven't spoken ill of you to her or shared any feelings either way, as far as her decision to continue to be your friend or not. So how ever she feels about what you two have or do not have has nothing to do with me, as you have said. I love you Tonya, go in peace. That isn't a witty come back, sarcasm or some words I'm using to hurt but words I sincerely mean in the best way for someone I have never met.

I have always found it funny when people behave selfishly with a narrow mind coming out of their bag with speech and the words they use against God's wishes, "Let no corrupt communication proceed out of your mouth, but that which is good to the use of EDIFYING, that it may minister GRACE unto the hearers." Ephesians 4:29 and then talk of God's will ("So if it is in God's Will then DD and I will remain friends after this email.") without even knowing it in the first place.

"Wherefore my beloved brethren, let every man be swift to hear, slow to speak, slow to wrath. For

the wrath of man worketh not the righteousness of God." James 1:19-20

EVOLENO,
Tony

Chapter 25
Vertigo

The email that Tony had written to Tonya went around her family like wild fire. It was suddenly an indictment of not only Tonya but DD's entire family. They were outraged to say the least. Who was this guy who knew absolutely nothing about them or all the struggles they had been through with DD to open his uninformed mouth about them or their family?

"How dare he?!" This was the consensus among the group. The heat that Tonya should have felt for writing the message in the first place, or DD for spreading all those half truths, was now squarely laid upon the wide shoulders of Tony. The person who had already sacrificed so much of his heart to the pain and inequity of this harsh situation was once again thrown under the bus and given the very same scapegoat status DD wore. He became the bad guy for speaking on the things DD had told him and all the foul and backwards things he had witnessed in their company, as he was silently sat outside the group.

There didn't appear to be any recovering from those words. He had stirred up the hornets nest and they were fiercely searching for someone to sting and all those years of guilt, hate and anger built up around all those things they never spoke of was spewed upon him. He didn't mind taking the heat. He felt like he had finally stood up for someone who was literally afraid to speak up for herself, and all those backwards things surrounding her and her family. She had tried so many times to speak on how she felt but she was too close to it. Because these were the people she cared so much about, there was so much on the line for her, she was still so very devastated by all those very things and they carried so much emotion for her, she could never verbalize them in a way that made sense past her anger. And because these people were so close to her and they were in that very same place too, seeking to avoid those very same hurts, they knew exactly what to say to push her buttons so she never could get past those emotions. He had become her mouth piece in a world that, although filled with all these ripping emotions, lacked the words to deliver her. Now there he was in the pit of her worst heat - the thing that kept her from evolving out of this place she had been held in all these years with the perfect advocate, someone who had nothing to lose, nothing invested, insightful and well spoken too. She expressed those thoughts to him. She thanked him for having the word and the strength to use them properly.

For the first time in her life past her early childhood, before she was molested and betrayed, she felt like she had an ally in this thing she had been in alone for so long. Not that there was some award in beating her family over the head with all those demons of the past. Not that there had to be some reckoning and all those who were wrong had to be brought to bear. No, it was about being victorious over those demons that still ruled that part of her life and that still ruled her world with regard to them. That little girl inside her that was molested and never acknowledged was told she was worthless when no one protected her, came to rescue her, or stood up and said, I SEE YOUR PAIN by way of acknowledging the existence of it or that it happened at all.

And after some time, it got so bad that it became her shame, when it never belonged to her in the first place. Instead of those who had failed to protect her - those who saw and said nothing, those who knew or maybe figured it out along the way - being there to support her, or talk her through it, they too carried around all that false guilt that kept them bound in the enemy's web of lies and deceit. The longer they refused to speak the truth, the more entangled they became until they were all tied to their own demons that they lashed out at one another whenever that painful place was even hinted of.

This is why they couldn't bear to look at DD when she was struggling to look like nothing was the matter and she couldn't hide all those things she bore, in an effort to protect them - protect those who preyed on her when she thought she was hiding. So when she spoke, all they could hear was that THEY were somehow the prey. If they would have set their own pain down long enough to stop being defensive, they could have heard her pain and suffering, which is all she needed - all she wanted. He had given her that opportunity, that voice, that moment of clarity where everyone was forced to consider it. Now, at first they lashed out at him, with threats and anger. But at some point, they did have to go within themselves and consider those things he had said. The stone wall of silence began to crack and that crack was all that was needed to start the fall of the liar.

DD's stepmom called Tony up in a drunken rage, angry, cursing, yelling and slurring her hateful words. But as she called him names, he hit her where it hurt, with the ironclad truth. She told him he was controlling and insecure and he needed to stop accusing DD of misdeeds and grow up, be a man and stop laying all his insecurities on her. He was tolerant with her at first but eventually she began to threaten him and told him she had plans to have DD's uncle and her son to come over his place and hurt him. Now this didn't make him afraid but made him take the gloves off and deliver the cold and hard truth of the matter.

"So you want to send someone to hurt me? Why? Because I am unwilling to hide behind the bullshit and lies DD throws me and accept defeat? Just because you quit on your life doesn't mean everyone else has resigned too," Tony said to her.

"I don't know what you are talking about. I haven't quit on anything. You are just an insecure little boy who keeps accusing DD of cheating and she hasn't done any such thing to you," she said, defending DD in her slurred speech.

"Well, in fact, you honestly don't know what you're talking about. When the last guy she cheated on me with called in my presence, I confronted her about it and kept confronting her with all the other inconsistencies until she finally got honest with me. She admitted to me she had cheated; she told me the entire twisted story. Ask her. She will tell you. We settled that a long time ago. You see tears and assume it's me. I am the problem. I am the one making her miserable. Never considering that maybe it's her and her own choices that are making her unhappy. She is crying because she is unhappy with herself for the choice she made and having someone that gives a damn enough about her to confront her and her behavior. This is probably the first time in her life she was with someone who didn't just leave but stayed and dealt with it. Therefore she has to deal with it. It ain't no easy road. YOU SHOULD KNOW. Look at your marriage. You know full well your husband has a mistress on the side and yet you stay and do nothing. He calls her right in front of you and you are resigned to defeat, living in a bottle, instead of confronting yourself about the truth and the fears that keep you feeling like you can't. I applaud DD for coming out of that place and moving towards healing and pray the same for you. Please stop calling my phone and threatening me, when you need to get your own home, marriage and life in order. If you want to talk to me about DD or any thing else under the sun that doesn't include cursing or disrespecting me, I will talk with you. But this can't happen again. Don't call my home this way. You don't know me or my life, so how can you judge me?" And then he sat silent, waiting for her response.

For a long time he heard nothing but the silence of her breathing. Each second that ticked was like an eternity and her breathing got heavier and longer. He could hear her sighs and breath getting hotter and more broken.

"Well you don't know what it is you're talking about. And I don't know why DD would admit to you she was doing something she wasn't. I am going to talk to her about this and get back to you on it. But you have no idea what you are talking about," she said, now sounding as if she had begun to cry.

"I may not. You're right. There is that possibility but who admits to something like that who isn't doing it? And one thing I absolutely do know is that if you called your AA sponsor instead of me, or making that daily trek to the liquor store, you would most definitely be in a better mindset to find out the answers to these questions. I don't want to judge your life, but I think this is what he meant when he said judge not lest ye be judged. When you throw stones living in a glass house, you had better believe there will be shattered glass," Tony said.

This was abruptly followed by what sounded like DD's stepmom whaling as she slammed the phone down. As hard as that conversation was, it was necessary and eventually fruitful. As it happened, DD walked into their house at that exact moment and was taken back by seeing her stepmother in such a state. She had never seen her that way. She was a tough cookie, former military woman who prided herself on being stronger than the average person. They talked, and DD admitted to her what she had already admitted to Tony and they both cried and talked about those things that her stepmom had misjudged, which at first brought up her stepmom's anger and defensiveness.

She spouted things like, "What the hell is wrong with you!? You shouldn't be a parent! Your dad and I are going to take custody of Kayden. We have already discussed it and we don't think you should have this responsibility anyway," DD's stepmom shouted, as she gritted her teeth.

DD stood there stunned and enraged all at once. Instead of shouting and yelling as she may have in the past, she was so hurt she honestly went into those feelings with very little fight left in her and began to cry at the betrayal she felt subjected to.

"I don't know why you needed to hurt me this way? I am already at the lowest point of my life and each time I reach for the rug above me, someone I love is there to step on my hands and push me back downward. Why do we love like this man! I can't do this with you Shonna! I love you but you are a different person when you're drinking and I can't do this any more!" DD shouted, crying her eyes out as she stormed out of the room.

This immediately brought about even more water works from Shonna, as she stayed behind in the kitchen sobbing. Then a light went off. Something TONY had said to her, "If you called your AA sponsor at these times instead of me . . . .," she remembered.

"Or lashing out," she murmured to herself, as she reached for her cell phone.

She turned her kitchen light off and reached for her bottle for one last swig as she dialed her sponsor. When she picked up, she began to pour out the remainder of the bottle, continuing to sob into the phone.

Shonna hadn't taken another drink since that night. Tony knew from that, first hand that although painful, these conversations could be fruitful if all the right circumstances conspired at that one moment that person was ready for a change. And it seemed like their family was. After DD's mom had that cancer scare and DD walked with her through it, praying together and bringing her back to God, Tony prayed for her, as he knew that their healing and their families' blessings was not done. DD's siblings needed to heal too and this letter seemed like it just might be the catalyst.

At the moment however, it was still raw and not much common useful dialogue was taking place beyond bashing Tony. At least it was being talked about. Moreover they were finally communicating with DD about it; they had finally sought her voice. So he would take the heat, stand on the outside and allow her to handle things with them and find some healing. He knew it would more than likely get worse before it got better but he also knew that the only way to heal was through confrontation. All her life she sought to keep the peace by avoiding this but this confrontation was the only way to truly find that tranquility she sought. At a minimum however, it had served to bind Tony and DD tighter than they had ever been before. They spent time having happier days, living, loving, agreeing to live and love for damn near the only time in their existence.

It was a wonderful place and they talked about these things openly. It was great, like they had started all over again. The next few months were wonderful and after all this time, just what the doctor ordered. They had finally become what he had dreamed they could be from the beginning. It was time to press on and push forward.

*   *   *   *   *

It was mid afternoon as Tony rushed across town in a cab headed for the Port of Tampa. He was running extremely late because he had so many things to do that afternoon. He knew it would be a struggle but being the type of person he was, he was determined to get it all done. As the car pulled up to the port and Tony rushed to grab his bags out of the trunk, DD had already checked in and was waiting for him to get up to the boarding deck where they had to check in before the ship departed. Tony had booked them on a five day cruise to the Caribbean, to include stops in the Cayman Islands and Cozumel, Mexico. DD had never been on a cruise before. In fact, she had never been on a vacation outside of the childhood road trips her mom and their family used to take across country visiting relatives during their summer vacations from school each year.

She was as excited as a child during their first Christmas, smiling and giggling for no reason. He loved to see her that happy. It was always amazing through all that pain and those things they went through how truly compatible they were beyond that mess. He loved her deeply and at times like these, he never wanted to be

331

apart from her. He was indeed the happiest he had ever been in his life. As he rushed for the gangway, he sent DD ahead and ran back for the suitcase he had left at the counter.

"Hold on a sec, I think I forgot my wallet. I'll just be a sec," Tony said to DD.

"I'll come with you baby," she said, smiling not wanting to be away from him for a moment.

"No, it's ok boo. I got it. I'll only be a second," he told her.

The truth was he had forgotten the ring in the suit case and wasn't really sure if he wanted to leave $9,000 worth of diamond stone to the chance of luggage inspector. The luggage handlers seemed almost offended by him retrieving the jewelry but he cared not. He laughed to himself.

"Really? Like things don't come up missing? Whatever," he said to himself, as he stuffed the ring into his pocket and ran back to catch up to DD.

Once he got there, she was sitting on the main deck just staring up to the center of the ship, marveling at all the shops, piano bars and places to dance on board. It was like a little city and she couldn't believe how much fun it looked like she was about to have. She was smiling from ear to ear. He was pleased that such a simple thing could please her. She had been complaining that her brother, a big time NFL player who had plenty of money, had just taken her sister, her husband, their three children and their mother on a cruise to Cozumel and how much it hurt that she was the only family member left behind. Following the letter he had written and her backing him, she knew it was intentional. It had made Tony feel like crap to know how much something so simple could hurt DD so badly, so he went ahead and booked their cruise shortly thereafter.

He wanted to show her that she didn't need her brother or any other family member for that matter to have the life she wanted; he was perfectly able to provide for her and Kayden for the rest of their lives if she would just trust him. This was a step towards showing her that and she couldn't have been more pleased in his efforts. He needed her to know how far he would go to merely please her. He had been her fool, her whipping boy and her pleasure principle, all in one being. He wanted her to look at him like he looked at her and Kayden - his future, his love, his wife, the last and only love he would have for the rest of his life. He was so deeply in love with her at that moment that his heart could hardly contain it. He was bursting at the seams with joy, high spirits and laughter. He loved those moments they shared within the solitude of one another, where nothing and no one could touch them. It was ironic that they would be out to sea when he popped the question. It was totally symbolic of their love on a ship only they could, and were destined, to sail off into this amazing love together where nothing and no one could touch them in that place, not a phone call nor a text, just her, him, God and the sea.

They hurried back to the room to wait on the luggage. Tony was certain it was going to take half the night with all the bags he saw still being loaded as he was one of the last to arrive. He had tipped the baggage handler heavily when he arrived but he was thinking that not even that mattered after he offended him when he went back to get the ring. But to their surprise, the bags were already there waiting for them. Tony had been on other cruises so he knew they only had a few minutes in their room before the announcer on the ship would be calling for the safety drill. Everyone would be grabbing their life vests and headed to their muster station shortly so he pushed her inside for an alone moment. Once inside, they looked around the room and DD smiled at the little elephant the cabin steward had made out of a towel.

"This is so cute!" She said, smiling ear to ear.

They were high enough to have a really nice view with a window so large it took center stage for the entire room and displayed a fabulous view of the calm waters they were about to set sail upon. As DD leaned over the window still admiring the awesome view, Tony

333

had quietly snuck up behind her and began nibbling on her neck and gently kissing her ear lobes. She knew where it was going and the stiff poke in her back let her know she was right on target. He continued kissing her neck and back, pulling the pretty delicate blouse she had worn off her back passionately and licked her spine from the top of the back of her neck to the base of her spine as he worked on her Capri pants. She was so weak. Her knees began to give out as he pushed her onto the bed and before you know it they were lost in time. Loving one another in that wondrous place only they two shared, where only they two could hear the sounds of their moans and reverberation of their breathing as it quickened with each, and every, loving, moment. They were completely lost in one another's eyes and love when the ships director finally began calling for the safety briefing and they were still there when the director made his final call.

"All passengers to their muster stations please. This is the final call for the safety briefing," the announcement said.

They never even attempted to stop. When they made love, it was like no one else in the world existed and they were so into one another. Their senses were only tuned into, and for, one another. In fact, the cabin steward had knocked on the door checking for them several times and walked in to deliver a bucket of ice to their stateroom and found them there. He knew they should have been upstairs on deck at the safety briefing; not even his entry stopped them. The cabin steward quickly apologized and darted out but they barely noticed him as the door slammed shut. An hour later, they lay still panting and sweating, having spent every ounce of that afternoon's desire on each other, still holding hands and staring into one another's face.

"Would you have it any other way?" she asked him.

"Never, you are my dream girl and I couldn't imagine anything more at this point," he said, still full of emotion, looking deep into her big warm brown eyes.

They laid there for a moment until they could clearly hear the guests milling about and another announcement came of their departure in fifteen minutes. They both wanted to see the departure and had solid plans to sit on deck and watch the sun go down together over cocktails. They got themselves together and whisked on deck and found a great spot to just chill and watch the mainland get smaller and smaller. They talked about everything freely. They mostly talked about just how much in love they were with one another at that very moment. They sat there professing their love for one another over Rum runners until the great big fire ball in the sky was a small orange dot descending into the deep blue sea. They then went inside and sat down to a wonderful rib eye dinner, DD's favorite, with a few more cocktails and a nice desert; it was the perfect day. They laughed. They smiled. They held hands for the entire day but it wasn't over, not by a long shot.

Tony said, "Hey lets go to the lido deck. It's time I taught you how to salsa," he said, smiling.

"I don't' know how. I don't know. Maybe I'll just watch you," she said, nervously.

They got there and the air was filled with the live music of an awesome salsa band playing while the sea moved east as their back drop. There were so many Latin couples there and everyone was dressed so nicely, smiling and laughing. It was a beautiful sight. Tony was excited to get DD out there on the floor.

"Listen, all you have to do is follow me. Here, let me show you the basic step and then all you have to do is allow me to turn you. Follow and I'll lead," he said to her, smiling.

DD followed him to the dance floor and he pulled her close, his hand on her right hip and her hand on his shoulder and they were ready to dance. He showed her the basic step. Although she was nervous, she seemed to get it. She was grinning once again ear to ear. The next song began to play.

"You ready mami?" He asked, smiling.

They began the basic step and it was looking really good until it came time for Tony to lead. As DD pulled, he pushed and as he giggled it off and pushed, she pulled. He relaxed his grip and allowed her to find her way into the turns so she could get her bearing. Then he pulled her close and whispered in her ear:

"Ok, now that you have it, it's my turn to lead. If we're going to do it, let's do it right."

He took the lead and once again, they were all over the place and she once again pulled as he pushed and continued turning herself as they danced. He stopped again and pulled her close.

"What are you doing baby? Just relax my love. Let me show you how to do this," he said, whispering softly into her ear.

Once again they tried and still having the same difficulty she just walked off the dance floor and left him standing there. He laughed it off but no matter how much he tried to coax her, he could not get her to return to the dance floor. He continued dancing for awhile alone until he noticed that she was no longer smiling and realized she was becoming annoyed. He stopped and sat beside her and had another drink as she sat there smiling awkwardly trying to pretend she wasn't annoyed. As he sat there, he clutched the ring in his pocket as he reached for the straight shot of tequila he had ordered.

"Cocktail hour is over and I'm going to need a stiffer drink," he thought to himself.

He figured he wanted to stay clear headed because this was the moment and place he had planned to propose to her, in front of a full dancehall of people where everyone could see their love. But after their little dance number, he was sure he didn't want to start out their marriage that way.

"Besides, after that whole mess she might have said no," he laughed to himself. They sat for a few more minutes and went back outside to enjoy some more of the night air. He didn't bring up the Salsa dancing again as they once again began in with pleasant conversation. It took a minute to get DD back but eventually he was able to get her back to that pleasant mood they had entered into the lido deck with. He could be quite charming when he wanted to.

After another hour and a few more drinks, they were feeling great and DD suggested they go back to the room. They did and found themselves for the second time in those few hours aboard the ship back in the throws of love. About an hour later, they laid there naked, the window curtain drawn wide open and the full moon shone in on them and their naked bodies as they once again talked lover's talk. He was looking DD in her eyes so deeply; she looked as if she wanted to cry. He leaned over the bed and reached into his pants and pulled out the box. He was stark naked and got down on his knee.

"I have been trying to find the perfect moment to tell you. One that was public, one that would show the entire world how much I loved you but I just realized that here we were in the perfection of our very own love and that was perfect enough. I love you DD and I want to spend the rest of my life with you. WILL YOU MARRY ME?" He said, with tear drawn eyes.

As the tears from her eyes fell, she leaned in and hugged him and said, "Yes Tony, I'll marry you."

They held one another tightly crying and kissing. She tried on the ring and it fit perfectly and they continued crying and kissing until they for the third time since they boarded that ship found them selves back in the throws of love.

For the rest of that trip they floated on a cloud, swam in the oceans of Mexico and the Cayman Islands. They ate great food and enjoyed wonderful scenery and most of all one another. It was a wonderful time. It was great and neither one of them wanted those moments to be over. They wanted to stay there for the rest of their lives. But they knew reality and the return of their real worlds was approaching as surely as the hour and the shore line. Even still, DD was excited about their engagement and couldn't wait to get home and spread the news. She was certain this would change things and how her family viewed Tony and even their relationship. So there was budding excitement as they pulled into the harbor port, home once again.

* * * * *

It had been four days since their return home and DD was still waiting for her first congratulation from someone in her life that mattered, but it was worse than she feared. No one in her family was happy for her. No one congratulated her. In fact, everyone was angry at her for accepting Tony's proposal under such circumstances. After all, he still had to live with Sharon because DD still didn't have a job. So all they could see was him still living with his son's mother. They felt like it was shameful and somehow he was just stringing her along as the other woman while he lived with his real family. Nothing could have been further from the truth but there wasn't any possible way to make any of them take a real look at that reality.

Even if they were willing to look at DD's life, what she truly was and wasn't, it would never matter greater than what he was and wasn't. What he wasn't to them was single or available to fulfill the promise of that ring he had just given her. Unfortunately, his stock actually went down with his declaration of his commitment to her and there would be more pressure brought upon her to end her relationship with Tony. Her brother outright denounced her.

"When you are ready to stop messing with this guy who is obviously taking your life no where, come on and move down here to Miami and I'll help you get your life together. Until you stop fucking with him though, you can't get anything from me," he said.

Upon hearing this, Tony was devastated because he too had held out hope that things would change if they made the step towards that final commitment towards one another. But although it hurt him greatly, he had to admit he wasn't completely surprised, as he knew her family prided themselves on holding grudges. They literally NEVER let things go. So he already knew his chances were slim to none for a better outcome than had befallen them as recently as that email to Tonya.

This was no help to DD and her fragile state around the desire to please her family and gain their approval. Big Ron, DD's father, was the only person in their family who had given Tony's proposal their blessing. Her entire family not only disapproved but decided to give DD the silent treatment as their way of protesting her decision to accept Tony's proposal. Tony had strong feelings about not STEALING DD away from her family and starting things off right, so he was sure to go and talk to Ron man to man and ask for his daughter's hand in marriage, even though she had already been married once and had already had a child outside of that marriage. Tony believed in doing things traditionally. More than that, he wanted her family and her father to know especially that DD would be safe with him, and that Kayden would be safe with him.

He would never leave her stranded or alone. He would never cheat on her. He would never ask her to sell her virtue or put her in danger or compromising positions. He was hoping that her father would be able to see his heart and know his intentions were pure. Hopefully through Big Ron, everyone else would get to know and see that too. But Big Ron was the strong silent type and unless asked, rarely gave advice or random conversation. Whatever he was thinking, or feeling, he kept to himself. Outside of him saying yes to Tony, he gave his approval, but no one would ever know what was on his mind.

He wasn't the expressive type at all. He was closed and after many years of being alone with his thoughts, he was used to not sharing. It came as no surprise or help to DD during this time as her silent ally stood by as she once again began to slip back into her previous pattern of depression.

She began drinking heavily again and fell back into heavy drug use. She once again went back to keeping late hours with "friends" and stopped showing up for Tony and their relationship. She had told him she just needed time to get her head around this thing. He knew she was falling back into her hole but she wouldn't come to him for help. She wouldn't come to him for love and she even stopped going to the support group, counseling and church. All the things she should have been going to for support, all of the healthy things. But she was out of strength, out of time and out of the ability to hold up this facade together any longer.

The pressure was too high, too much, dragging herself to her counselor, then to group and then still manage to have something to share with Tony was exhausting. She just needed some time to figure things out in a way that made sense to her. And nothing felt better than the CHRONIC rolled up in a Swisher Sweets and pint she had stashed in her purse as she headed for the darkness of her room. She spent weeks in this stupor, high and drunk, living in this place of avoidance and denial. It was a place she lived in for most of her life, her chosen method of coping.

She came out of it long enough to show up for Tony's birthday, although she was a fraction of herself. In her guilt about her absence and all that she knew had transpired during that time, she went overboard with the gifts for his birthday. It did not go unnoticed. Tony was well liked at his job and so many people showed up for his luncheon to wish him well and bring him gifts. More than a few of his female friends commented to him secretly that it seemed a bit odd the measure his intended was going to in order to appear to be the good wife. After which, Tony took notice and with each passing moment could see the cracks in DD's armor. As the afternoon pressed on and his guests found their way back to work, Tony being concerned, tried to address DD and what he recognized was her obvious depression. He tried to, once again, be there for her during this time. But at this point, she had begun to blame him in her mind for the separation she was again suffering with her family. She had not had a sufficient relationship with her family beyond her father and sister for quite some time and she had learned to live with that reality. She thought that one day she may be able to reconcile with them. But to have had them finally start to see her and acknowledge her the way they had begun to, only to have them push away even further than before opened up old wounds. Wounds that ran deep - deeper than even she let on.

Tony knew and she was having a very difficult time dealing with them alone. She had been spending her time keeping company with other men, men she had slept with to ease her pain and it was all over her like the smell of onions on a burger to a hungry person. The scent was distinctive and hard to miss and even in his wanting place of willful denial, he couldn't ignore it if he wanted to. He confronted her about all her missing time and the pattern she had fallen back into. After some time talking, she admitted she had not been honest with him. They sat in his car as she gave him this tearful admission, as he asked her for the time and space he needed to make up his mind if he could pursue their relationship any further. She seemed surprised at the possibility that they wouldn't make it after her admission.

As she left his car, he sat there stunned and after some time cried like a baby amidst another broken heart. His world was dark. Even though it was his birthday, he could no longer see any good in it. He could no longer do this. He could not longer be her fool. He couldn't marry her the way she was. He thought he could carry her to Jesus. He thought he could carry her and Kayden out of that hell they lived in, but he realized now he was only a man and there was nothing he could do beyond DD's wanting and she clearly couldn't want anything past her pain and learned coping ability.

It was time to decide if he could finally salvage himself from this muck and leave this pain behind him. He was tired of crying. He was tired of hurting, and he questioned if all the happiness he felt when he was with her during those great moments they shared was worth it at times like these. Even thinking about DD with another

341

man made his heart explode with rage, like a pain he had never considered in his world of blissful ignorance. The pain was too deep. It was too much for any one man to bear. He had taken off his cape. He didn't want to be superman no mo.

As he was lost in his emotions for the next few days, at some point DD decided she wouldn't wait any longer and took the only decision left for Tony away from him. One day as he returned from work, the Mercedes Benz he had given her was parked in front of his place with the key beneath the drivers side mat. And just like that, it was over. No talk, no ring, no more tears or difficult fears to face. It was over and all that was left was to unburden himself from the five hundred dollar car note that put a monentary amount on his love each month.

Chapter 26
Some Love to Keep

It was late on Friday night and Tony was at work, focused in on all the day to day tasks that his work required. It had only been a couple of days since Tony had last heard from DD. She still hadn't returned his calls or made any attempts to contact him but to him it felt more like a month. Work is how he kept himself from missing her, doubling and tripling up on the mundane employment tasks would ensure he didn't have the time to even think about things. It was especially easy in this field, where the ordinary is usually full of the sort of drama that is usually only on television or movies. Sounds strange but focusing on someone else's drama kept him from his own dramatic thoughts that usually kept him from being effective in any other part of his life during times like these.

He had taken a job as a social worker for the child bureau of welfare about a year ago now and saw the value in what he did. Although he didn't always like it. There were two sides to this bureau, the side that removed children from the homes of abusive, neglectful parents and the other side of which he participated in, which worked with the parents of children that have been removed to help them comply with all the court orders so that they could get their children back. He had started out in this job feeling good about the work he imagined he would be able to do. He thought to himself that he would be able to bring some good into the world if he could put some of these broken families back together again and heal some of the wounds that the cold hard foster care system brought to these already torn families.

These pains, he had seen long ago in his life, way before he ever decided to take on this job.

Unfortunately, it didn't take him long to see that this bureaucratic system was far more concerned with stats and numbers than it ever was concerned with the actual good work it required, or the good that would come from doing that work, if they actually did what they were supposedly there to do. Nevertheless, he had chosen to put in the time and work rather than to go home to the loneliness and despair. He didn't want to face thinking about the recent break up with DD yet again. He was shaken to his core with her cold mention of the possibility of other men or even women in her life. She didn't ever come out and say it directly but she had told him that he wasn't the only man in her life and he was devastated. She later tried to clean up what she had said but it was clear to him what she meant and it was far too late to go back into that place of willful denial. Naïve denial is what the psychologists call it. From where he sat, there was nothing naïve in it. He knew exactly what it was and he didn't want any part of it, at this point.

　　He once again had to face the truth about his situation no matter how much he didn't want to. His work day had ended a long time ago. Yet he was there going over case loads and details that fall just short of obsession. He was just dialing into one of the more thick family files stacked up on his desk as he searched his mind for family interventions when his cell phone rang. It was DD. He was hesitant to answer the call but honestly, he was in no way prepared to be apart from her.

　　Actually he had just, once again, opened himself up to the very real possibility that she could really love him the way she said that she did. The way she showed up for him during his birthday really left him feeling it was more true than not. His heart longed for her and that kind of love. So, as much as he was there to block out all the things he didn't want to think about concerning her and their relationship, he knew he was going to take this call by the second ring.

　　"Hello?"

"Tony, I just can't take this anymore!" DD started in sounding tense.

"This house. It's just too much. All the filth was bad enough. Now my father's septic tank is backing up back into the house and no one seems to care or be too bothered by it. I need your help. I have to get out of here." Tony could hear the fury in her voice that he recognized all too well. It wasn't quite the anger that comes with hate but more like the anger that comes with being helpless. He could sense that she was on the verge of tears. His mind began to race once more into her world and all the things she had told him about her needs and how many people had let her down in her life. He always knew he never wanted to be even a portion of who those guys were to her. The last thing he wanted to do was remind her of any one of those fucking bastards. So he already knew, whether they were speaking or not, at this point, this was an opportunity to come through for her and to maybe even gain favor with her.

All he wanted was for her to see him as the love of her life as he did her. To recognize the good man he had always wanted to be and knew he was for her whether she acknowledged it or not. But somehow it never meant as much to him, no matter who else could see it, if she did not.

"Tony, there is SHIT backing up into the damn tubs in this house and no one can even take a shower. Not to mention the smell. I just can't live like this anymore. Are you going to help me or what? I have been living in my father's house for so long and you haven't lifted a finger to help me and my daughter out of this situation. Now it's worse than it has ever been. Are you going to help us?"

Tony sat there in his tiny cubical stunned. He had never really heard DD quite so emotional. She was always cool and collected and never let anyone see this type of raw emotion. But more importantly, he had to quickly get over the fact that she was now on the phone with what not only sounded like demands of him but an ultimatum. This, only a few days after she had just alluded that she was indeed seeing other people was not only a huge question mark but a serious blow to his ego. As much as he wanted to take her call as a vote of confidence that he was indeed the man that he knew he was and that she was beginning to see it, he couldn't see past the big ole buster sign she had painted on his forehead. Instead of feeling complimented, he could only feel the shame and humiliation of even considering helping her out after what she was putting him through. After all, coming from where he came from, anyone doing the type of shit that he was still doing and considering to do now was certainly a chump in that world. And although he had worked so hard to remove himself from that mindset and place, there was still so much more left of that type of thinking left inside of him from when he was raised.

After all, this type of thing only happened to lames that had no game, no money or were ugly as the hump on a toad's back. He was none of those things; in fact he was quite the opposite, very handsome with striking features, great personality, and a ton of fun. He had mass appeal having dated across all boundaries and boarders. Being from New York City, he had seen his share of women, also dated top shelf women exclusively for a time in his life before he figured out it simply wasn't and couldn't be about what someone looked like. He could only assume that is what had brought him here, full circle dating someone like DD who was still marginal at best considering her way of life. Her inner beauty still dimmed by her outward behavior of arrogance and betrayal. In his mind, no matter how good she may have looked beyond this vision of her as a liar and cheater, she could never be truly beautiful. She would need to take the part of her that made those flaws down, way down to hit the standard of beauty that included mind, body and soul, that he had always dreamed about. He believed in his soul she was capable of it. He just questioned if she would ever believe it beyond her own naive denial. She had so much potential, possessing so much inner beauty if only she could see it.

346

He had literally spent years trying to get her to look up and see it and frankly he was getting tired and had begun to think he was never going to make any progress.

"Listen DD, I don't know if we're in the right place to be talking about moving in together at this point. I mean seriously, you just finished breaking my heart, pretty much telling me you were seeing other people. I don't know if I can live with you after that conversation because I have been seriously questioning if we could even stay together." He just put it out there. It was done with feeling but more than that, it was also done with fear. He knew he was afraid because in his heart of hearts he knew he didn't want to lose her. She represented his hopes. She represented his dreams and all that was good in this world outside of his children and he had spent so much time investing in their relationship and her. So much of his life was connected to her and Kayden and he knew it was going to be a lot more difficult to walk away from her than mere saying those words. He paused to allow what he said to permeate because he needed a real response. He deserved a real response other than the silence he got from her the last conversation they had, the current cause of his heavy heart. Then she broke the silence.

"Listen I understand where you are. I did the other day and I never meant to hurt you. I never wanted to hurt you. I cannot take what I did back. I can't rewind time. I never actually cheated on you by way of sleeping with another only spent time and talked to people I knew I shouldn't have. It was a sick and twisted time in my life when I was really confused. You still living there with her kept me a lot angrier than I ever talked about. And sometimes the only way I could deal was to have those conversations I knew were wrong but made me feel better about myself. Because frankly, although I knew we were the couple and we were together, you being there and living with her made me feel like a mistress, like I was the other woman. This made me feel cheap, like a slut and a home wrecker and I didn't have anywhere to go with these feelings. I couldn't tell my

347

family about them. When I did, it only made things worse between you and them. They ended up hurting you because they saw me hurting and assumed the worst. They figured you were like all the other no good guys out here. And because I needed the support, I never corrected them. I couldn't talk to you about it because you have had good cause to do what you have done and I knew it. And each time I tried to talk to you about it, you reminded me of it and all those feelings of guilt came close behind.

"Combine those nasty feelings and the ones I was already carrying around about being a home wrecker, I dare not bring it up to you. Not to mention we went through hell through those conversations, arguments about trust, arguments about my mistakes and all the problems. It was just easier to do what I did. I was really wrong for that. I wish I would have never done it. I wish I was strong enough to have done the right thing by you and us. But I'm weak and flawed, which has me and my child still here in this situation all fucked up. You always say I don't submit to you. You always say that you need to see my softer side and that you are needed and wanted in my life this way because I don't ask and never say so. And you're right.

"I have hidden behind a mask of false strength and it has cost me, us and unfortunately you. And again for that I'm so sorry. But I'm here now and I'm coming to you as the man in OUR lives and telling you that I need you. I need you right now. We can't keep living this way. I need your help Tony. Are you going to be the man I know you are? Or are you going to tell me that this is too much and let us go out of your life because this is what we need? If it never had before, our entire relationship has begun today. So you tell me, what's it going to be?"

She had totally put his feelings into a perspective he had not considered to this point. Although he was still raw from thinking about her betrayal, he had to admit she made a pretty solid case. He did have some responsibility in it. She was absolutely right. Once again, his eyes were opened to his sin, his part in his own pain and he knew his house was not in order. So although he was hurt, he had more than enough real evidence to step through his pride and do what was right by those ladies. Still hurt and holding onto his bit of pride, he slowly answered.

"I don't know DD. I just don't know. Let me think about it. Honestly I have reservations. Give me a minute to think it over."

Again the phone went silent. You could hear DD breathing and she didn't sound pleased. Tony was confused. What did she expect him to be at that moment; he was still picking up his heart from the ground?

"Fine Tony, you figure out what you want to do and Kayden and I will wait on the sidelines of your life as we always have," DD said, sounding more cold and upset than before when she genuinely sounded open. Again, Tony was confused by her tone and the entire way she was dealing. She was talking to him as if it was he who had done the transgressing. After all, it was she who cheated. She said she didn't sleep with anyone but how did he know? He had always felt like she did but could never prove it. He did indeed have a lot to consider.

"Fine I'll call you back in about an hour or so," he said to her, equally as cold.

He got off the phone and instantly knew it was time to put his fears, pride and all those raw emotions in check. He recognized right off that this was not just what was going on with them at that moment but more than likely a cumulative hurt that reached all the way back to his former relationships; maybe even his childhood. It included some of those nightmares - the ones that kept him up those sleepless nights. He knew he had to get a second opinion. He took out his sword and set about a journey but first he stopped a moment to ask God for guidance and discernment. He prayed right there at his desk. There was no one in his department at the time. But if there had been, he knew he would have done that anyway.

He took a moment to open the bible and he began to read. As he continued to read and meditate, he realized he wasn't looking to be convinced. He had already made up his mind. He decided he would continue his reading in a moment. He wanted to make a few calls while he could catch the place he thought would be ideal before they closed. So he called the apartment place and spoke with the agent and set up a time to look at the place. He had a half an hour to get there. He grabbed his bible and his laptop and headed for the door. He got into his car and sped over towards the apartment complex. He pushed the number two button on his cell to call DD back and let her know what he was doing and that he had come to his senses. The phone just rang and rang until the voice mail picked up. He tried five more times with no success at reaching her and finally decided to leave a message.

"Hey love, it's me. Call me back, it's important." He was upset but sounded pleasant as he was feeling better about his decision, with each passing mile. He reached the apartment place and took a look at a two bedroom apartment on the first level. It was spacious and clean in a beautiful complex, it had tennis courts, a b-ball court, new appliances, a large pool and game room complete with ping pong tables among other recreational games. It had a nice hot tub, and even a racquetball court. It was plush with full lawns and manicured landscaping. He knew she had never stayed in a place so nice and was super excited at being able to even offer her and Kayden this type of apartment. He loved it and told the lady he wanted to have a lease drawn up. A year was standard. After the credit check, he was approved for the apartment and his lease would be ready the following day with a move in date of the coming Monday, just three days away from now. He had just gotten paid so the move in wouldn't be a problem, besides she didn't have much anyhow.

He was already plotting in his mind getting them new furniture and stepping up as the man she had just for the first time expressed she needed him to be. He couldn't help but to be excited about his new role and the possibilities it presented him with. He would finally get to be the head of their little family and there would be no denying it. He would be the head as the Word said; not the tail. He tried to call DD again and she still didn't pick up. Over and over again he called leaving message after message trying to get her to hear his good news but she never did. He left her all about twenty messages regarding their new apartment and she never did call back. Saturday came and went with no call from DD and Tony not signing the lease because he didn't know what she had planned to do and didn't want to be on the hook for another rent while he was unsure if she would be moving in at this point.

Sunday, then Monday, came and went the same way and finally Tuesday he finally informed the office that he was no longer certain if they were going to be taking this apartment. He would have to lose the four hundred dollar non-refundable, move in fee he had already put down. He was more hurt that DD was doing him this way. Hours turned into days and days then turned to weeks until it had been a full three weeks since he had heard from her at all. So the decision he was pondering on before he got that call ended up being the deal. She took the decision out of his hands and set out into the world and left HIM behind.

He was confused to say the least. Her disappearance was timely, as he really needed to figure a few things out. Maybe he would finally have the time alone he needed to completely figure this thing through. He had been feeling like that since he found out about her stepping out on him this last time. But each time it seemed like this was the order of things and he would have that time. She either reappeared or things took a turn, this was one of the evidences he reasoned that said maybe this relationship was destined to be more than it seemed it would be. Because each time it was headed for failure, each time it was headed for what looked like a final break, it always turned around. He could never truly tell if it was his doing and all that he had learned in

351

following what he believed was God's word, or if it was indeed divine intervention.

He had always known that places like this were the poorest place for reason and logic, so he was always looking into things deeper. Like this entire mess with DD and what she revealed to him lately. He fully understood her short comings and what drove her to it. He could deal with the fact that maybe it wasn't personal, maybe it was just what she presented, just what God had been revealing to him that she was weakened in character, in nature, in her resolve to have the life she wanted by all those things that went bump in the night. She was crippled by all those demons of her past life and the horrible choices thrust upon her in the form of abuses and absentee parents, at times she may have needed them most. But adding that to all the horrible decisions she made following that made it almost impossible to have any better outcome.

She was damaged goods. Although he knew in his heart of hearts that he too was damaged goods, he wasn't out here ripping her heart out of her chest every time an old demon raised it's head in his life. He was really going to have to consider if this was something he could continue to do. Did he have the heart left in him to give? Did he have the resolve to see it through without the fear that would ultimately screw things up anyway? Would he have any patience or grace left later in life with her when they as a family may need it? Would he have spent it all in places like this? Would it be wasted in these matters of emotion with none left for future more meaningful tests? He needed to pray. He needed to asked God for vision, for the ability to discern where he was going from here if only he could quiet his longing heart but for the time he needed. If he was being honest, he would be a liar if he didn't admit that even now he missed her, wanted her still, hurt and all.

After a few more days of silence, he decided he would no longer leave the decision to communicate up to DD, and if, or when, she would choose to communicate back with him. He was going to finally take the time he needed to seek out God's face undistracted. He had been thinking about getting away for quite some time and it didn't appear to be any better time than the present. He asked and was granted a leave of absence from his work, which had such high turn over rates in his position. They were happy to do it, in order to retain him after. The job was such a high stress and emotional job that few people could bear to stay, so much heartache. He promised to return, renewed and refreshed and was granted a leave. He went into his retirement fund and booked a trip around the world. He would leave and be gone for about two months, with stops in Australia, Hong Kong, Tokyo and Mainland China. He had always been fascinated with the Asian culture. Japan, China and Southeast Asia were calling. He had always wanted to see the outback as well. A visit to the land down under was a wonderful addition, since it was likely to be the closest he would ever get to there. Again, he decided to do it all. He would spend two weeks in Aussie, two weeks in Mainland China, a week in Hong Kong and a week in Japan. No phone calls, no texts, no email, no visits. Just him and God in the world. Bon voyage.

Chapter 27
Hammered

When he first arrived, he really didn't do too much. He explored the area a bit but was too tired to do too much of anything. The flight was super long from Tampa then ATL then LA. Both flights had layovers for a couple of hours each. Once he got on the flight overseas he told himself, "It wasn't too bad. Only 14 hours, I could do that without too much of a problem."

The seats were pretty spacious and the little TV they had on the back of the seat was really awesome, far better than Jet Blue. It had games, a huge movie selection to choose from, as well as a large audio selection to choose from, including one of his favorites, Evolver which he noticed, if you look at it the title actual says, over love.

"Wow Johnny, you got some love issues huh? Who hurt you Johnny? Who hurt you?" He laughed to himself on a crowded flight full of sleeping people.

The television had about 30 different channels to choose from. It turned out he didn't need any of those million and one things he had brought to keep him entertained for the plane. Although it did come in handy in LA where he watched some Katt Williams, along with half of the airport over his shoulder.

Once he finally arrived on day one, he spent the entire day walking around, looking at shops, as they have a ton of malls. Since he was staying in China town, he ate about three or four small meals - Chinese food mostly. That evening, he walked down to the local Pub for dinner where he had a good old fashioned burger and fries, ironically prepared by a Thai couple. The burger was awesome, thick and juicy. He could really tell it was hand made; just the way mama used to make, using ground beef and a lot of love. He then sat and drank until he got a little buzz, and kicked up a little conversation with the locals. It was so cool for him to be talking to local folk about all things Aussie. That was pretty much day one.

Day two was a blast, as he walked down to the one harbor closest to the hotel and caught the local cruise line. It was called Captain Cook's Cruise line. He boarded the cruise right in front of the Sydney aquarium. "I have to get back here. I think I'll come on Sunday. No, no, there is no time like the present. I'm going as soon as we get back," he thought to himself.

The cruise was pretty cool. They took about thirty passengers out on the harbor and trolled through the bay, stopping and giving them a little history about Sydney and the sites. He took plenty of photos and managed to squeeze himself in a few too. It was really cool for him because he got to take all the pictures of the opera house and the bridge in the day time; this was on his list of things to do. These landmarks looked totally different than they had the night before. He got off the cruise in Circa Quay, which is the harbor port right by the opera house and the bridge. After he left the aquarium, he went walking around the area, which really reminded him of New York City's South Street Seaport. He got adventurous and took the hike from the pier to the bridge. As if he were home at the Brooklyn bridge, he then walked over it to the next town and back.

Many hills, stairs, uneven walk ways and paths and he enjoyed every bump and puddle without a single thought of DD. This was more sightseeing than he had done in a while, so it was a major challenge in the first few days but he endured. By the time he was done, he was beat down, but he figured between these hikes in addition to the way they ate over there, which was far healthier, he should return better off than he left. All the fresh air and meeting new people just added to his already huge pile of Awesome!

"God bless and thank you Lord. I feel like I'm seeing the entire world brand new."

He was seeing an entire place that didn't look or smell like misery. It was filled with happy people, within the hustle and bustle of a big city and yet there were so many opportunities to enjoy nature. No time to sit and sulk, yet plenty of time to stop and think. All the walking created plenty of time with himself, while doing something new, fun and interesting. It created different scenery, even though a lot of what he was considering was old things and thoughts. He was admiring God's beauty and mans ability to duplicate it on a small level to live with one another in peace with good will. There were plenty of people but it didn't feel over crowded, even amongst crowds of people, and in huge shopping malls. Most people were nice and happy to talk to you.

The thing he loved about it the most was there were no places he had little flashbacks and memories of DD or anything related to their life back home. There was nothing about all the things he was doing that brought her to mind, so he actually got to choose when he thought about her. When he was ready to stop, go back to enjoying his new experiences, then call her back, he could when he was ready. With so many things around him to do, the only real time she popped up was at night. But he made sure he returned to the room each night so tired that all but one of the nights he fell straight to sleep, a rarity even when he was home.

Forasmuch as he was beat and complained in his mind of how bad the trek was across the bridge, it ended up being a blessing in disguise. On day four, he booked a tour through the outback. The folks over there call it a WALKABOUT and by God you had better be ready! Because when they say walk about, they are not fooling around. Evan was their tour guide and he was getting it in. He wasted no time, experience, nor air. These moments were to remember for certain. He had Tony doing things he had not done since he left the Army.

He was using muscles he forgot he had. Seriously, it was sincerely cleansing to the soul. "If I didn't know God, I think I would have found him in the BUSH," he laughed to himself.

This place was amazing, one part rain forest, one part desert, one part caves and all of it awesome. They called the desert "the never, never."

"It's because you're never, never supposed to go there," he laughed with Evan. They never made it there but Evan told them enough stories about the very vast desolate place it was. Hell, they just did survive out there where they were, so to get an eye ball on it was good enough for him. They walked a FRESH mountain trail, which involved rock face climbing about 75% of the way, either up or down and the rest was some beaten trails.

Now these trails were nothing like what we call trails back in the U.S. No, the word trail there only means that someone had barely cut the bush before we got there. It was a serious physical challenge. Not like the leisurely strolls he was used to taking on the scenic trails back home. Of course everyone there was SUPER skinny, fit and prepared for what was to come. He had no idea. He booked the tour at the hotel thinking how interesting it sounded. So needless to say while the group struggled, he was damn near dying inside but wouldn't give them, or the world, the satisfaction to know that "big man" was feeling those extra pounds that all his misery had helped him pack on.

Eight hours later, he emerged from the OUTBACK, THE BUSH, scathed, but alive, without major incident. With all the heavy breathing, he managed to gather plenty of pictures and even more stories.

The group smiled and hugged, congratulating each other for making it out of BUSH, just happy to be alive. Everyone seemed pretty impressed at Tony's mental and physical stamina to make it through something most wouldn't attempt. It had never dawned on him how amazing his mind was in that way. Once he set his mind to do something, he never quit until he succeeded. All of his tour participants kept talking about it because they were all, avid hikers who did so every week and Evan had managed to wear them down.

Everyone who had come brought a partner to help push them and help them in case something happened, they felt like they couldn't keep up, or make it, because they had heard about the break neck speed you had to come through the bush in order to make it back out within the eight hour time frame.

And here was Tony, out of shape, not having hiked seriously in years alone. Just on a whim, he had decided back at the hotel to take an eight hour hike through some of the roughest parts of the country. It had honestly never really crossed his mind that way. It NEVER even occurred to him that he wouldn't make it? But one thing was clear. Once they got in the BUSH, with only one way in and one way out, you had better be ready to walk out. It was serious business. That much he did know.

Evan told them before they departed the meeting point that many had called it a life changing experience. Upon entering, Tony didn't doubt that but he never imagined it would change him. In fact, it had. It reminded him of who he was on an immediate and almost primal level. It tapped into a strength, courage and mindset he had not used in years and he was grateful to have rediscovered it. Not only the fortitude but the belief in himself to remember he could make it and he could make it alone with the help of God if he needed to; something he had learned but forgotten a long time ago.

IMPOSSIBLE IS NOTHING. It took him back to something he heard one of his childhood heroes Muhammad Ali say. "Impossible is just a big word thrown around by small men who find it easier to live in the world they've been given than to explore the power they have to change it. Impossible is not a fact. It's an opinion. Impossible is not a declaration. It's a dare. Impossible is potential. Impossible is temporary. Impossible is nothing."

He had countless stories in his memory bank where he should have been defeated long ago. He wasn't supposed to graduate high school. He wasn't college material. He wasn't graduate school, or law school, material. And he wasn't able to do doctorate level work. Time after time, he had proven them all wrong. He was living proof that you are what you believe. Today he realized he had been listening to all the wrong opinions about himself. All the nay sayers, all those who didn't truly know his character anyway, including DD's family, who had weighed heavily on his mind. He hadn't realized how much stock he had put into their opinion of him. Even his family and their shying away from him during his times of trouble, plus all the years he had spent with DD outside of their approval. He had started to lose sight of what made him great and the things that carried him over at those times. All of the great gifts God himself had bestowed upon him. He had taken a literal trip through his fears and found it laying in wait within the dangers of the outback, all the way in Australia and he didn't even blink.

No, he was far stronger than he remembered. He had chosen Australia because it was an English speaking country. He did have some fear about going off to these countries where English was not their first language. What if he got lost? Could he get stranded somewhere? All the fears he hadn't given any real thought to, let alone allow out of his mouth, were at once realized. He could now see clearly, how things like this he considered small, could stop him from having the life he wanted. It was a valuable lesson.

He had been moving forward to the best of his ability but he had some pretty major blind spots. As it turned out, he wasn't moving as far, or as fast, as he thought he was. He wasn't quite as fearless as he saw himself. In fact, he had succumbed to what others set out for him to be, yet again, in this area, and he could see it so clearly now. He had not been moving as strongly in his faith as he saw himself and he needed to continue to seek that "bold as a lion" spirit he knew God had set inside of him.

From this second on, he wasn't going to allow fear to slow him down any longer. He had faith to take this trip, and faith that God would bring him through and home safely. Now he was going to delve into the faith, trust and belief in his Lord that he could go deeper into those places to enjoy and truly live throughout this trip. He was aiming for fearless faith from this point on, on this trip, onto the other three countries he was headed to. He was also prepared for when he headed home to whatever waited for him as far as he and DD was concerned. Most importantly, he was looking forward to him living a more fearless faith throughout the rest of his life.

The rest of his time spent in Australia was spent in that peace and place. Now he was headed for the terrible dog leg to Hong Kong. He did so, embedded with the spirit of Christ and all His love around him. No worries about DD, who she was with or what she might be doing. He knew that no matter what it was, it could not be as wonderful as this. So often in his life he would come upon some blessing God had shared with him and he wouldn't truly be able to enjoy it. He would always be thinking to himself, "Things like this were meant to be shared and are only as wonderful as the company you keep."

But today he was overjoyed, filled with peace and happiness because he traveled with all the solitude the Lord had given him and today his traveling companion was God. And it was good.

*   *   *   *   *

He arrived in Hong Kong with the same spirit amplified by the echo of his, so far, positive experiences. It really seemed that he needed this far more than he realized. His subconscious must have had a very real agenda because all of the activities he had booked for himself, even the ones before he left were all physical challenges. It was almost as if he had forgotten he had put on the extra weight over the course of his relationship with DD. And each place, each challenge was a miniature reminder of the lesson he learned in the Outback.

In Hong Kong, he went to Lantau Island where there was a large Budda where you had to climb hundreds of stairs in order to get there. And the city reminded him of what he imagined, having never been there, San Francisco must have been like, with all the steep hills and sidewalks. He walked everywhere he went and it was wonderful. The food there was spicy and very different. They used fresh ingredients and they cooked with much more fruit for sweetness, much more than he was used to. It was very good and he never felt weighed down by anything he ate, which was also good.

When he arrived in Japan, there was more hiking and walking through the city. He hiked up Mount Fuji and surrounding bays. They possessed such awesome views and scenery. Standing on top of the highest point they went to was like standing in heaven. He was actually standing among the clouds. He was looking down on the valley below and taking pictures through the clouds when he saw through his lens, a young Asian couple, standing closer to the edge hugging, cuddling, then kissing. They looked so very much in love. For a split second, he caught himself feeling like he was lonely.

Ironically enough, he didn't feel the faint heart of missing DD as he usually would have. He actually realized that he just missed love and what that looked and felt like. A place where there was little fighting and ugly disagreements. A place where they could embrace and know it was for more than just the moment and there was more where that came from. He admired the couple and their fondness for one another and actually took a picture of them while they held one another looking down on the valley. He smiled and continued on his way. He came to a little red house way up in those mountains that sat totally alone.

"Wow, this place is so beautiful. What a view!" He thought to himself. "What a waste, such beauty put up here, where no one could see it but those who traveled this far. No one to share it with but those willing to take the hike," he said to himself, as he walked the long stairway down from the home he had come across.

Then it dawned on him, "Maybe that's what love and a life as beautiful as this is supposed to be? This beautiful mountain. The awesome view and the solitude of this little house I came across. It's been here for a very long time but until I got past my fears, I never did see it. I never even knew it existed. Until I got past all of that and got off my ass and hiked up here, I never even knew it existed. I never knew how wonderful this place was and how life in a place like this could be," he thought to himself again.

He was going to have to expand his possibilities, past those that said he could only go as far as he could see or think. He was beginning to understand that if he couldn't, if she couldn't, then neither one of them would, could or even deserved to have this beauty. He knew he was going to have to be the first one to leap if this was where they were going to go. Although he hadn't spoken to her since before he left, he was there in his mind preparing himself for their return upon his return. And at the same time, getting his mind right if it was God's will he take another path. All these lessons were valuable ones either way.

Once he got to China, he was to set out upon his final journey and lesson. He had spent some time in Shang Hi which ironically reminded him of some hood parts of Brooklyn. They say all around the world the same song and he was starting to believe it. "Same crap, different day."

They were speaking a different language and he could hardly make out anything past his little book of translation but he could see the hustle a mile off and boy did they try. Most of the time, the assumption came in the form of their belief that he couldn't do the mathematical conversion of money in his head. It was pretty sad and funny. So they were constantly trying to over charge him, double and sometimes triple charge him, even for a cup of coffee, which was terrible by the way. By the time he arrived in Beijing, although they did have an over-priced Starbucks, he was done even trying and went in with the natives and drank hot, unsweetened tea, which came complimentary before and upon request after every meal.

Beijing was his final destination before returning home and it would be a place where he would receive another life affirming message. No one there outside of the appointed person from the state the government assigned to you spoke any English, nor did they even attempt to. So he was completely alone, more so than Australia, Hong Kong and Tokyo combined. He had spent hours walking through the city through Food Street and beyond without speaking to a single person. There were people the government assigned to him that pretty much followed him but they were supposed to be invisible so they didn't talk to him.

The great wall of China was amazing and was another physical challenge. He went on the wall to a place called Victory Mountain where the stairs were so steep, they practically went straight up in the air almost like a step ladder. In order to get to the very top of Victory Mountain, you had to climb past three landings. About halfway up as he started to get tired, he realized he hadn't really taken any pictures. He hadn't taken in any of the scenery and with all the hard work, he wasn't even enjoying the climb or the experience. So he decided to slow down and look at the marvel he was climbing. It was amazing. He only made it to the second level. It wasn't the top of the mountain but it was further than most made it and he still felt victorious. He took a ton of pictures and actually got to slide off alone onto one of the many little nooks and corners and had a private moment of prayer thanking God once again for such an amazing experience.

During his time on the wall, he became aware of himself in a way that when he was home he had been numbed to. He was a large man in China; not just tall, as he was about six foot tall, but he was also far larger than the ordinarily tiny people. When he left the U.S. he was about three hundred and fifty pounds. He knew he had lost some weight. He could tell by the way his clothes fit him day to day. Although he wasn't aware of how much he had lost. He was ashamed of himself for having allowed himself to get as large as he was through his emotional eating. When he first met DD he was only two hundred and thirty five pounds, he was fit and worked out five to six days a week.

While he didn't blame her for his problem, he knew he had made the choice to go down this road. He had never done it before and was down right angry at himself for allowing himself to do as he did. But here, the locals not only stared but pointed at him and talked about him openly and even though he didn't speak the language, he understood the gist of it. He had read in the little book about tourism in China that staring was customary and not considered rude in their culture, as was passing wind in public which no one there shied away from either.

This, however, wasn't so funny, as he was quite sensitive about his struggle with his weight. At some point throughout his time there, he had become desensitized to the staring, the pointing and even the people who wanted to take photos with the giant man; some even touching his stomach in the pictures for luck. He had also read in the book that a big stomach meant good luck and some considered it almost Godly. He knew in his walk with God, it was his weakness and literally considered it a deadly sin he was struggling with as he was struggling with his emotions in and around this and life overall.

His final lesson overseas in China came when he reached the Forbidden City. It was as vast as it was beautiful and there was once again a great deal of walking. The crowds there were twice the crowds at the Great Wall and the people were far more condensed. Here you could see that billion plus people China was supposed to have. And it was here that he was greeted and treated like somewhat of either a super star, or a side show attraction, depending on how one chose to view it. He chose the previous rather than the latter. At first he was just trying to enjoy the exhibits and walked along with the groups' tour guide, listening and doing his able best to learn about this culture that had fascinated him so much. He followed the brick path that lead him through the middle of each building until the tour guide explained that the brick everyone was walking on was new. It had just been laid down recently as Beijing had recently hosted the Olympics and so many tourists had come to see the Forbidden City and they wanted to refurbish the place.

They had put up fresh paint and cleaned all the areas they could that were dirty and the rest were replaced. He had come to see history. So when he found out that the bricks on the outside of the walk ways were over ten thousand years old, this was where he chose to walk for the rest of the tour. Most times it was way further as far as distance and out of ear shot of the tour guide but he didn't care. It drew more attention to him as he was always off by himself away from a crowd. The crowd that might conceal his shame but he cared not. He wanted to walk along with those who had walked those stones all those years ago and it didn't matter what anyone else thought or how much they pointed and stared. At some point, after he realized he had made his own decision for himself and didn't allow anyone to pursue him, it became a sense of pride and he walked that way. It wasn't long before others followed by the time he reached the point in which they called the center of the earth. He had taken a great deal of photos and many had taken the photo of him standing on top of that point. Lessons he had breezed through so fast as a youngster, overcoming tall buildings with single bounds on the wings of angels never even stopping to figure out how he did it. Hell, he never did have the time. He was just happy to have made it out of his own personal hell. So when it came time to duplicate this effort more slowly, and more deliberately, it was not only difficult but at some points impossible without understanding. And for him that is what this journey was about, not only knowledge of self and God but understanding, and a closer look at his will.

At trip's end, reflecting on all that he came home knowing, he had achieved that in aces. He was emboldened, encouraged and replenished for what he knew was going to be a difficult, radical and very different look at his life. He was ready to stand up to the scrutiny he knew he was going to have to endure in order to bring his desired family to the next level. He was going to have to forgive DD and let all of what had happened go and walk in faith like he did in the Outback and he would have to do it in the light of day amidst all those who watched, laughed and ridiculed like those in China.

He felt like he was ready. He was feeling especially confident and good about himself. He had lost thirty pounds since he last set foot on U.S. soil. He had done a great deal of soul searching and came out ahead. He was standing on the threshold of a renewed life. All he had to do was grab it. Now was the time to reach out and find out. As he headed to the baggage claim and waited for his bags to come around that belt, he powered up his phone and waited for the dings that would surely come of new and unheard messages he was sure to come after being gone for a month and a half.

Bing. And there it was.

*   *   *   *   *

He was doing his able best to drag his healing heart towards the light of day. In spite of all the messages of glory he got while he was away, at this moment he was trying to recall why it was he had decided to come back to DD, besides remembering all of the reasons God had lead him to. It was trying at best. He was remembering that sticking in this relationship was equivalent to not quitting on himself and what love truly was. Moreover, how to do it was just as important as doing it. He needed to find that heart full of grace he had stashed away for days like today. He was still hurting. After all, he was only human and the way she had left him was painful. So there was no shame in falling short on all the things that he could ever remember loving about DD in this world filled with so many contradictions.

Against every bone in his body, every whim, every single thing he had ever been told or taught about human relationships, he was going against ever word, every bit, ever inkling of a thought. He was walking headlong into that fearless faith he had learned about. It felt like he had just barely dragged himself off of the floor from a devastating departure that DD had left him holding that still stung like it happened yesterday.

This was partially because she never apologized or made a single excuse for her behavior and partially because it was like yesterday. She hardly seemed sorry for the transgression. It was as if she didn't even view it as such and he was the lucky one to even be in her presence. He had done so much to really empathize with her position that he had managed to block out all of the pain to walk into her position and what it might feel like, look like, smell like to have been loved so incomplete her entire life. She had had so many in her life walk in and simply take from her all she had to offer, strip her of her dignity, her worth, her pride, her virtue, not to mention her money or any worldly goods. She and Kayden had suffered enough from the hands of wicked men like that enough. He could see that she was afraid and this was the reason she needed to behave the way she had. She was expecting him to run off as the others did her entire life. She had no real expectation that he would stick around as he had always promised, let alone protect her as he had sworn to himself and God to do from the moment he realized that she would be the one to bear his name.

He had learned a long time ago that when DD was afraid, and her anxiety got the best of her, she pushed, and ran towards the drama head on. She had always claimed it was in an effort "to get it out of the way." Her expectation wasn't IF he would leave but

367

WHEN and she was doing all that she could with her negative attitude and clear mistrust of him and anything he would say to her as her way of running him off. The truth be told, if it were not for his calling to do something else, his fear would have long ago had him with this year's fastest track shoe on his feet. Elbows and asshole is all she would have seen of him in years past. The bible talks about walking out "your own salvation with fear and trembling" and this he certainly was.

He was going to stand up, no matter what she had said, or done. He was going to do all of the things he had spoken to her about and more. This was who he was and she needed to see that. He needed to be able to do that, be himself, the kind, giving, loving self that could do this in his sleep when he thought he could trust someone. He needed to walk on faith with this one. Believe in something his eyes could not see. He needed to love someone completely without assurances, without a checklist, without all the little things he required that said she was trustworthy and thereby deserving of all his love. He himself wasn't always deserving of a best friend, let alone that sort of love. But this never stopped him from wanting, or desiring, it. After all, it is at your worst when you need those who say they love you to settle you as the Lord has done, and we pray for. Such a woman would be a blessing, a God send for sure. Well he was finally understanding that if he wanted that woman, then there was no way around the fact that he was going to have to grow the hell up and be that man. There was no other woman in the world he could imagine that he would want to be THAT woman than DD. So he would make his stand here, NO MATTER WHAT IT LOOKED LIKE.

He had talked to DD just nights before about her brave new move into her new place. She was afraid and still building up the courage it would take to stay rooted in this decision she had made to take herself and Kayden out of that environment that she knew she could no longer live in. She had NOTHING but she knew she had to go. Her time had come. She had endured as much as she could stuck there in that place. She had high hopes that she would be moving into a place with Tony but considering the circumstances, she didn't know if that would ever be possible considering all she knew and he did not. She was willing to concede but only on her terms. She had to be able to hide her true self from so many. With others, she never had to bother to try because they simply didn't care and those that did she never stuck around to show them anything beyond what she wanted to. Here she was in the most meaningful relationship of her life and she couldn't move this man past her crap and she knew it was going to take her, and them, a lot longer than she was willing to wait. She didn't blame him because she knew who she had been. When it came to this, how they would live, it didn't even matter. All that mattered was, if it was or wasn't, because Kayden couldn't sleep on a wish OR A DREAM. So she needed it to be real.

He could see that about her and her position all too clearly. He knew that the time for talking was over and it was time to step into his manhood in this relationship. He could only pin his HOPES on this being the thing that would show her the truth about his heart and intentions within him. He needed to be so much more if he was ever going to overcome himself, let alone all the things she brought to the table. It was time to take this love out of fantasy and into the realm of reality for the both of them but most importantly so that these two families they had kept at bay, kept holding on for all this time would finally be taken out of the limbo that they had been frozen in for so long.

It was definitely time to come on with the come on and he had put his proverbial foot down and this weekend was the start of it all. DD and Kayden were going out of town to Orlando with her extended family; her mother, sister, brother, niece and nephews. They were going to Disney for a fun-filled weekend complete with amusement rides, Donald and Goofy too. The adults enjoyed it just as much as the children did. This

369

was more about them staying connected as an adult family of siblings than it really was about the kids. Although everyone was certain this would be a trip the children wouldn't forget. Tony was conflicted about DD and Kayden going. On the one hand he knew that they both deserved it, especially Kayden who worked so hard in school, becoming classified as a gifted student last year, having worked her way to the honor roll for the entire year.

All he and DD had to offer her was praise and glee for her ability and desire to turn that potential into practice. This he recognized as the key concept of success that so many with brilliant minds fall from grace from while missing the point entirely, leaning so hard on their loins instead of putting some hustle behind that muscle. She had indeed made strives all for the love of education and simple praise that those who loved her shined upon her when she met and, in this case, exceeded their expectations.

But the other half of the equation was that they were going with her extended family and not him. He wished he had been better suited financially so he could have afforded to do something so nice for them. But he was up to his ears with bills, savings, trying to provide for the children he was responsible for, in addition to helping DD and Kayden, as best he could. But more than that, Tony knew that her extended family hated him in a big way. On many occasions they had talked against him, told her to leave him and even forbade her to leave their presence if she was talking to him. He was a black sheep to say the least and at this point he was a secret in DD's life. As she had told them that she and Tony had broken up, so she didn't have to constantly be reminded that he was a bad choice for her and the long talks and lectures that accompanied his name stopped when they thought he was gone. So as far as they knew, he was gone. He hated feeling like that and with so much going on with them this week with her being with them this weekend and out of contact with him it was definitely going to be a real test of his will.

370

He never did understand why they hated him so much. He had always meant the best for DD and Kayden. He thought he had always done the best by them as well but they had given her ultimatums concerning their relationship far too many times for him to fool himself to believing that any of that meant a damn thing to them. He had no idea the extent of which DD had poisoned their mind against him but he did recognize the flavor, having been in that particular seat before. She had told him that they knew he still lived with Sharon and needless to say, they did not approve, no matter what the circumstances. He couldn't understand how ANYONE in their right mind could see it any other way than he did. It was devastating to him to know that it didn't matter what good he did, it would never be good enough to gain their favor. And no matter what she did, no matter how dastardly, it would never be enough for them to ever acknowledge him as a good man, let alone taking his side on any of the would-be arguments he and DD had throughout the years they had been together. It always made him feel like quitting. The idea that he would never be good enough for her in their minds and seemingly hers from time to time made him feel hopeless. But again, he was up against many thoughts like these; some real and others perceived. All these thoughts challenged his will to follow God's will for his life and the full lesson in that idea for himself.

So this was going to be a challenge on multiple levels and it started that morning as they left without a word. He had been given a key to their new place and free reign to go in and do all the things he had discussed with D. His list of items was as long as her needs in that apartment. It was in a lower economic area so it had plenty of those holes in the walls, horrible paint and lights that either didn't work or looked like they were straight out of the 1970's. There was no way she was going to be able to dress that up no matter how nice the things she put into her place were.

After talking it over with DD and hearing her fears and concerns, the idea he had come up with to go

371

and get her some furniture on consignment as he had done for himself on a few occasions would no longer fly. He had intended to do this as a surprise, with the idea that he would be paying for these items which he thought would take away her worry about keeping or maintaining the furniture. But he realized now that this wouldn't work; she would worry still and if they fell out completely, he couldn't say with certainty that he would even want to continue paying for items that would certainly be used in her next relationship. He had decided to take the leap for her and give them all of the items in his home and replace all of his things with items on consignment. The things in his home were practically new. He had purchased them but a mere two years ago and taken great care of them, so they definitely looked close to new. He knew she would be pleased with those things, as she really seemed to like them in his place. More importantly, they were free. But before he could bring any of the those things into her new place, there were a ton of things he needed to do to get that place ready for a real move in.

First, he had to sand and prime all the walls as they were painted with a high gloss finish with many imperfections, like lines of paint running down each wall or several places on each wall, almost as if a child had done it. All of these "drip lines" had to be sanded down as it was so thick merely painting over them would never cover them up. He went and purchased the items he needed and went over there first thing Friday morning and began to work on those walls. He first had to clear out the mountain of trash and old furniture the last tenants had left behind. It was more of a mess than he thought he remembered and it took half the morning just to do that but he was finally done and began to run the sand paper across the walls and was starting to lay on the primer somewhere mid afternoon. He told himself if he could just get the place primed by noon, then he could break for lunch. Since he had a light breakfast, he was starving by ten thirty. It was now three forty-five and he was still working with the primer.

It was a half hour later before he had the opportunity to put the primer down and grab something to eat. Since there was no furniture at the house, he went to the pizza spot around the corner and grabbed a slice and sat down at the tiny, shabby looking table. As he replenished his energy, his mind couldn't help but fade to thoughts of DD and Kayden and what they might be doing, if they missed him or would like the work he was doing on their place. He decided it couldn't hurt to try and give them a call since all this work in their new place had them so much on his mind that he actually missed them to the point that he wanted to have a phone conversation with them. And for him this was a big deal since he was most definitely not a phone person. He took his cell phone out of his pocket and pushed DD's photo on his main screen as she was in his "fav five" and it dialed.

He put the phone to his ear and listened as it rang. It rang and rang until it rang out and went into voice mail. Once he heard her voicemail come on, his stomach went into knots as he knew it would have if she didn't pick up. He told himself then and there that this was a bad idea to have called her at all. He hung up the phone and decided to leave it alone. There was very little room for him or this phone call to have a happy conclusion. In fact, there was far more opportunity to be hurt or disappointed than there ever was for anything good to come out of it. What was he expecting anyway? Best case scenario, she would be hurried or rushed so they didn't hear her on the phone with him.

Worst is they heard and asked her to hang up and she would. No, he decided to just leave it alone because there was just too much pain there. Even as he looked at the upside, the enemy was creeping into his head with lies, telling him she hadn't picked up because DD was there with another man and would be the one to inherit the family he had worked so hard to build. He resisted the temptation to immediately dial her number back and found a magazine that was at the front of the store and began reading that to distract himself from what would only take him out of the mindset he needed to be in to complete all the many things he set out to achieve while DD and Kayden were out of town. His plan worked and he was done with what should have been lunch for him and headed back to DD's apartment to begin painting in the rooms. The primer was already done drying when he pulled into the driveway of their place and his cell phone rang in his pocket. He reached inside his pocket as he put the car in park. He turned it over to see DD's picture and smiled with just as much nervousness as happiness to see she had called.

"Hello sweet stuff," Tony said, trying to sound pleasant and sweet.

"Hey, you called?" DD replied, coldly.

There were two ways DD answered the phone when she was around her family that hurt like hell. The first was when she answered the phone as if she was having the time of her life with the most awesome group of people and she was mildly annoyed that he had called and disturbed that time with them but she veiled that beneath a layer of sarcasm and fake pleasantries, as he found out most southerners do when they don't want to be bothered with your butt. This stung to his core because he was accustomed to being wanted and well liked, so this not only threw him off but threw him into auto pilot where he felt like he had to be ultra amenable to correct the problem. Well at least at first that is how he approached it until he hit the hopeless level and a real understanding of the next level and realizing that this was the NICER of the two. He learned to appreciate this tone, knowing it was the lesser of the two crappy responses. Then there was level two, the current forum in which she had answered the phone, in that "What the hell do you want" tone of voice.

"I was just calling to check in on you and see how you guys were doing." Still trying to sound pleasant, hoping to avoid yet another scene in front of her family who he felt hated him enough. He was just trying to get off of the phone without incident at this point.

He was thinking to himself, "They hate me enough, let me just get off of this damn phone. I already know ain't nothing good in this conversation."

"Oh, well we're fine," she said. Then in a whispered voice she said, "I have to call you back later. Were all standing in line and they are talking but trying to figure out who I'm on the phone with. I'll call you when I get back to the room, ok?"

"Ok," he replied.

And just like that DD hung up. No I love you, see you soon, I miss you, nothing. He couldn't help but feel at times like this that he had done something wrong and deserved this sort of treatment. Ironically, he had done so many things wrong in relationships throughout his life that this should have been a position he should have known all too well. But when it was actually time for him to pay the piper for whatever it was that he had done most times, he never took responsibility for it. And the times that he did, he did so too little, too late and lost whatever potential relationship he had intended to have. Not to give anyone the wrong idea, he had with the major relationships, stuck them out all the way to their bitter end but no matter how much work he put in, ultimately it was too little, too late. He had learned those lessons too late.

So while this should have felt familiar, he rarely exposed himself to such subjugation. Truthfully, by all rights, he shouldn't have. But the irony was it all felt so familiar to him that he didn't even protest for fear of losing the opportunity that God himself had laid in front of him to heal. There was something far too recognizable about this feeling of defeat and worthlessness. He had been thinking about it for a very long time and knew it was a sick link to his twisted past and some equally twisted feeling that he needed to pay for things he had done in his past. This pain he likened to that of which he himself had given to others so cavalierly just years earlier, with no regard to how it affected them, only to how it served him. He had been all too familiar with that old saying his mom used to say when he was younger,

"Boy, you better be careful. Because one thing you ought to know, what goes around, comes around."

He could hear his mother saying it now as if it were yesterday. Back in his unenlightened days, he thought it was something he could avoid with slick talk and simply dipping out the back way when the bill came due. But he knew that this thing, this balance in the universe was unavoidable. If he was ever going to find true happiness, he was going to have to face not only what he had done, but most importantly HIMSELF. The church calls it doing penance; he had heard others call it getting their due. He just knew one thing, he owed and the bill was damn due.

"It's time to pay up man. So man up, grow up and do what you should have done a million years ago and do right, LEFT!" He said to himself.

He had thought he was through punishing himself when he walked away from his last relationship. Just as he thought he had been done when he was fired from his marriage and entered into that one. Clearly he must have been done punishing himself but the universe wasn't done with him. But more importantly, whatever lesson he was supposed to learn from those difficult and bitter times had not been learned otherwise and if he knew anything at all, he knew he wouldn't still be here, looking at DD and this barrel full of pain.

So as he put his phone back into his pocket with that familiar same old "why me" feeling filling his chest, he sighed loudly, already answering the question before it ever had the chance to leave his mouth. He jumped out of his car and headed back into the house for a night of painting and thinking. Secretly, although he did miss DD and had called her, he hoped she didn't call back. The silence and hard work was therapeutic for his mindset and all he wanted to do was work so hard he couldn't think, and stopped feeling. He entered the doorway with the empty brain required to finish his task. He found the nearest dry wall and paint can then got to work. As he methodically wet the roller and emptied it onto the wall carefully to make certain that each stroke was even, his only thoughts were of the lines he was trying to avoid, the evenness of each fresh coat and how much better the room looked from one coat to the next.

He was on auto pilot and his mind was numbed out by the sights, the sounds and the smells of good labor. On many a day THIS IS man's best friend. Hard work is like baptism, by fire sometimes. It cleanses the soul and the mind if done right. He was seriously appreciative for the chore. Eventually he found his Ipod in his pocket and popped the buds in his ears. With ears now filled with the sounds of John Coltrane and other jazz greats, he was swept away until his muscles could only remember the pain of labor and not the one that lingered on his heart.

This went on for hours. DD did eventually call him back that night but he was so busy with his work and his music was so loud he failed to even notice the phone ringing. Small wonders never ceased, as it wasn't a call he was really looking forward to. When he finally did get around to listening to the voice message she left, it was her once again whispering in the bathroom this time, confirming yet again his status as an unwanted secret. He deleted it with no intentions at all of returning the call. Hell, she didn't even ask him to. At daybreak, he finally stumbled out to his car early Saturday morning for a few hours rest, only to be back again to finish what he had started.

By the time he got back over to DD's house, he had forgotten all about the phone call and the tone that accompanied it when he had spoken to DD yesterday. He was happy once again to be focused on the small things that lay in front of him. Once he finally finished the painting, which took all afternoon because he decided to reface the countertops to go with the fresh coat of paint, he put on the cabinets and headed down to Home Depot to pick up the light fixtures he needed. He decided to buy a ceiling fan for the living room, brown to match the furniture, two ceiling lights with the same Tiffany finish and style, the large one for the dining room and the other for the hallway. He purchased two stand up lights for DD's bedroom and another for her little office nook. He was feeling like a real design show and getting into the fun of creating something new. He loved doing home repairs, but taking something broken and fixing it, this was even better to him. The idea of taking a space from nothing to stylish or nice put a smile on his face. People had always liked his design style and DD loved his place and said many times she always wanted a space just like it.

"Neat, comfortable and stylish" were her exact words. It gave him a decent start and the rest was in his imagination. She too had a keen sense of style. After all, they were very much alike. With this in mind, he decided to be sure to leave her with plenty of finishing touches for her to handle. He would just handle all the larger items and jobs.

"Man's work" is what he told himself. He went from aisle to aisle picking up little things from light switches and bulbs to towel racks and pot holders. All in all, his vision was to furnish her entire place with every detail covered. He got her a microwave oven, curtains and blinds for each room, since the large open living space was tiled, he purchased a large area rug for the living room and a smaller one for the hallway and another of a totally different style for the bedroom. DD's backyard was huge with an open space that was at least four times the square footage of the home she was renting. It was going to need some serious yard work. He had visions of grilling spare ribs and chicken breasts on the weekends. He had to get a grill, which turned into some lawn chairs and tiki torches. Before you knew it, he was WAY over budget. He put the budget out of his mind as he threw the charcoal and lighter fluid in the cart. He really was trying to cover every detail.

When he was finally finished, he ended up in the parking lot of Home Depot playing musical items, trying to get everything he had purchased into his Mercedes as even he thought he looked silly doing. He had not considered the possibility that everything wouldn't fit and where his lack of consideration had left him. He laughed as he finally did it.

"Mission accomplished!" He said out loud.

He jumped in the car and hurried back to DD's place because he knew he had another full days work fooling with all of these electrical outlets and racks. Little did he know it would be more challenging than he thought as the wiring was "set to stun" as Captain Kirk of the USS Enterprise used to say.

Most of the wires were crossed, so even when you turned off outlets marked on the panel in the circuit box, the electricity still flowed. It was a mess. He just took out the rawhide gloves and pushed on, laughing to himself.

"Ok Lord, only you and I know we're here. Keep me safe God." As he laughed now, "That prayer was oh so serious."

Another late night and he was done with what was phase two of his move in surprise special. Day three. Sunday morning started out with him picking up a U Haul truck to load his furniture and headed for DD's place. With no friends that approved of DD to speak of and therefore no one he would or could tell about this thing he was doing, he was alone on this one too. He lifted everything from the couches, tables and chairs to the large entertainment center with only the help of a dolly and hand truck. It took some serious muscle and far more time than he ever thought it would be, but he managed to get it done without breaking a single thing. A major accomplishment, considering all the stairs and ramps.

He was gloating inside, knowing he was doing such a great thing for someone he loved so dearly. So seldom in life do we get the opportunity to really show someone what you really think of them or give them their true worth. It often seems that those that are in this position are only there because they don't realize it and are thereby bound to screw it up. Many times anger or petty grievances keep us from showing our true heart. It would have been easy for him to turn his back to so much work. It would have been far easier to stay in bed this morning or allow his wounded feelings from DD's phone call the other day to work as the enemy intended and just quit.

This was his test and he was honored to attend to it. This was not only an opportunity to show DD her worth by way of the love he had for her but also an opportunity to follow God's law, his word and will for his life. Thereby he would finally pass this test he had failed so miserably time after time throughout his life. As each hour crept by and his body became more and more weary, he was urged on by just one happy thought, how pleased he imagined DD and Kayden would be with him and his choices for the décor of their new home.

As he was rolling the long couch down the ramp that was placed directly into the back sliding door with the dolly as a stand in for the partner he should have had walking this bulky and awkward piece of furniture, he lost his footing and missed the ramp altogether and although there was another ledge right beneath the edge of the truck that he could have caught himself on if he had been lucky, he missed that too. Straight to the concrete ground with one leg to support his entire body weight. Over two hundred and fifty pounds with the heavy couch in tow, he landed hard, still holding the couch shoulder height. As his foot hit the ground, he was not for an instant worried or concerned. His knee, which was damaged playing college football, a sore subject, he thought about his lost NFL dreams, never even buckled.

He stood there, having never even lost his balance and pulled the couch to his right and maneuvered his left leg beneath himself and backed into the door angry he had made such a mistake. It wasn't until he threw the couch against the wall did he realize he should be on the ground crawling for his cell phone in pain begging for an ambulance. By all accounts, his knee and maybe his entire left side should be in traction. He knew immediately that only God could hold his surgically repaired knee up to such standards. He knew it had to be a miracle as he was exhausted and could barely hold himself up off the couch at this point. He sat down for a moment to rest and reflect on what had just happened. He couldn't allow such a thing to just pass as if he didn't know the severity of this thing.

As he went back to work, he was far more deliberate than he was hurried to be done. He was tired but focused. He only had another day to get everything into the apartment, get things set up and finish all the last little touches that would make this apartment a true home. He was working himself like a rented mule and he knew neither his body nor his mind, could sustain much more. He sat there for a few moments trying to gather up the strength to continue unloading the truck. He was dog tired and the last two days were finally catching up to him in a major way. He went into the kitchen to look into the refrigerator to find something cold to drink, hoping this would give him a second wind. He was going to need a second, a third and maybe a forth considering all of what he knew was in front of him to do but he thought one moment at a time as he laughed inside his head. He reached into the refrigerator and grabbed the juice and without even attempting to look for a glass, opened it and took it to the head. He figured he would kill it so it really didn't matter. "No one but me will be drinking out of this carton," he thought.

As he headed for the dining room chair that he had already placed in the small little area that was to be their dining room, he just sat there, still searching for his wind and trying to get over the brain freeze he had just given himself. As he rose his head up from holding it in his hands trying to soothe his temples, he noticed the book shelves in the little closet area DD was to use as a desk and office area. There were a number of bound leather books with no titles and some spiral notebooks too that caught his curiosity. He had a few moments to burn since he was still trying to get caught up on some rest. So he stood up and reached for the shelf and pulled down the thick black, leather bound book without a title and opened it. Looking through the papers, he discovered pages and pages of hand written notes. It was then he realized that he was looking at DD's private journal. His face went flush as he began to choke on the very words he had hung on this entire relationship. Even now as he pushed through one of the most difficult moments in his life, he hung on the truths he had come to believe despite his better judgment. Page after page, it was like a train wreck, a horrible car accident that he knew he should be looking away from but just couldn't pull himself away from. Entry after entry he read and not only found many of the very stories she had told him but almost all of the events since they had met. His heart pounded and he could feel himself light headed in disbelief as he read on. Even those he read that brought him hope at first tore at him with the savageness of a demon hell bent.

"Journal entry: I miss Tony so much today. I can't wait to give myself to him completely. I dream about him all day and what it might be like to finally be in his arms. Today I finally gave in to this dude who has been trying desperately to kick it to me, I haven't been giving the time of day. I miss Tony so much I decided to give dude some time so I don't have to think about Tony so much. I'm always wet now thinking about him. I decided to give old boy some to take the edge off for when I meet up with Tony later tonight. I won't seem so needy. But I missed him so much I had to sneak off into another room in the middle of fucking with this dude to call Tony. I was honestly second guessing my choice to come. But I got his voicemail and I knew he was at work. So I left him a message. I told him I loved him for the first time, it was over the phone and by voice but I couldn't hold it any longer."

On the edges this could have been some twisted compliment, except she was cheating and lying. It was a poor misery and torment to swallow. The very first time your love uttered the words she loved you was directly out of the throws of another man's bed. And it went on. Rod, the guy she told the long story about from Atlanta. She swore she hadn't slept with him, but she had, several times in fact. The truth was, he put her out because he wanted to screw her anally and she refused, so he threw her away like a used piece of tissue and put her out of his house. She had a lesbian relationship with her best friend where they dredged the night clubs for a man to take home and share sexually. This relationship she and her friend carried on for years, with and without men, which is why she was trying to get her to move to Miami without him, which is also why her friend hated Tony so much. This is why he could never meet her or talk to her. She knew he would be able to spot it but for the obvious role that DD played in that relationship. She was the "stud" man in the relationship. According to her journal she gathered much joy and pleasure from her dominant role. It was everything he had always feared about DD, things he spotted way off from the very beginning but just simply refused to believe.

She had cheated on him more times than he would admit to himself or really had a clue about. Even the phone calls from the guy while they were in South Carolina, from this guy named Cash. She had been in an on going sexual relationship with him too. She wrote about a time he accused her of cheating and he remembered back to the time when he was in the middle of laying with her and felt like she was off. She didn't feel the same. She didn't even smell the same and he told her so in the midst of their moment. She jumped up half as if she expected him to snap or get violent but he wanted to give her the benefit of the doubt. As she swore he was wrong and denied it completely, he accepted her lie. She not only had slept with someone else but as it turns out she had slept with some random stranger after meeting him in a Wal-Mart parking lot and proceeded to follow him to an abandoned apartment where she not only screwed him but sucked him off too, a mere two blocks from his home just the night before. In fact, it was after she had left Tony's home. It was then that Tony smelled that day and it turned his stomach to finally know the truth.

Past all the sex and cheating as if that wasn't enough betrayal beyond the honeymoon period of their relationship, every single entry she wrote in her journal she wrote about Tony was miserable and unhappy. He pushed too much, asked for too much, and she had not only grown to resent him but it read like she hated him most entries. Conversely, all the entries she wrote about her pimps were like love letters. How much she missed them, their sex and their life. He even found out that she was a street walker which she had denied when he asked her. She had spent some time in Texas transporting drugs and guns back and forth from Texas to Atlanta and her pimp left her there as collateral for some consignment and she had to subject herself to multiple, what amounted to be, gang bangs in these little dance parties they had where she was the only woman.

It was supposed to be a strip tease but it was all about the sex for these monsters. He could see where she had omitted so many portions of her life but left just enough truth for it to be believable. The whole truth beyond the lies was impossible to take on all at once. All he could see, all he could feel, all he could touch and speak on were the mountain of lies he found himself beneath. Month after month he was reading a detailed log of all the times she lied to him, all the times she had cheated on him, all the people she made him a fool in front of. It was more than he could bear; there simply wasn't enough God in him to sustain him. So first he sat down as he had been standing over the shelf paralyzed, shaking in his shallow breath. Once he sat there, he let out a scream as he burst into tears. These tears weren't tears of pain, more than tears of rage and anger for having been such a fool.

"Where THE HELL are you taking me God! My GOD, how the fuck can I take this, WHAT THE FUCK!" He screamed aloud.

Chapter 28
Push
(Coming Together to Make the Tip of the Blade)

Tony had prayed long and hard for the answer to this one. He had been reflecting on the lessons learned overseas for days on end and yet his heart could not find it's way back to the forgiveness he needed in order to go back over to DD's house to finish what he had started. She would be home in a few days and her house was in shambles. The walls were half done, all the furniture was still scattered about the house and nothing in place. It looked like he just went over and dropped things off half- heartedly; there was no love in it. If she returned with things that way, she would know immediately that his heart wasn't in it. She already had serious doubts if Tony could forgive her for her leaving in the first place. She was on the line with her heart like him, with trusting him not to hold all he had been hurt by in his heart and against her as they moved forward into this new phase of their life.

As it was, he knew if he indeed intended to be the leader of this family, he was going to have to LEAD. That meant no matter how difficult it was. In all actuality BECAUSE of how tough it was, he was going to lead this one from the FRONT, by example. He was going to have to walk out of this shit smelling like roses if he had any hopes of ever having anything that resembled a relationship, let alone a family. He was going to need every ounce of that fearless faith he was working on while he was in Aussie and every bit again of that boldness he learned by walking the 10,000 year old brick in the Forbidden City in Beijing, China. He knew this was going to be the most difficult thing he would ever approach knowingly, with his eyes wide open, mainly because he knew what he had to do. The first thing he had to reason with past his hurt ego, his hurt pride was the truth of the matter.

Yes, she had lied to him. There was no doubt about that. She had omitted much but the truth was that much of what he read, she had alluded to but never said. And the things she didn't say were things full of her sin and shame. After all the grilling he had done thinking about it, it could not have been easy for her to admit those things in her past. Especially considering his level of forgiveness in the beginning of their relationship. He had a hard time truly letting go. He would talk with her for hours and convince her she was safe to tell him her secrets and then when she finally did, he would not only be incapable of controlling his hurt feelings but he actually held it against her on some level. The mere fact that he couldn't let it go, and forget it completely said that he held it against her.

He wished he had been able to do that for her, especially in the beginning of their relationship but his healing was not nearly where it needed to be in order to do that. He was much better today and here was the opportunity to prove it. He was going to have to suck it up and admit to himself that we all sin and if she had an honest and unimpeded look into his former life, there were plenty of things for her or anyone else for that matter to judge and deem wanting. He had not always been the man he was today; he had a lot of forgiveness to seek himself. Her girlfriend and all she had done during those times, had to be forgotten. She said she was done with women. He had no choice but to accept that, at this point, if he intended to honor his promise and move forward.

Her street walking past, her selling herself, her dancing in the strip bars, had to be behind them and spoken of no more. It was shameful for sure but not his to carry. And if God could forgive her, if he could let it go and leave it in her past, "clean it as white as snow" then he can give her the grace he sought himself from the father on high. Besides, he had already had that conversation with himself about Jesus and the prostitute.

He was certainly no better than God, so if he was to follow his example then this was nothing.

Now all that was left was the lies and betrayal during their time together. Would he be able to let those transgressions go? It was a bitter pill to swallow but he had made up his mind that he needed to see this thing through. For Kayden, for DD, and moreover, for himself, and all the reasons he already knew of. He had to know if she was indeed the woman of his dreams. Things were so very awesome and then so very horrible and so often he wondered what it would take to stay in this place of awesome. Anyone with ears could hear DD as she claimed it was this or that, and Tony had his own gripes. If she would just get a job, so on and so forth. He was fed up with all the excuses. He was fed up with not having the fortitude it took either of them to push past their fears to be able to commit to the relationship both of them said they wanted. He had been hurt in his life.

He had been betrayed but nothing on the level that she had compromised her life to being, so her bags were far heavier. Besides, if anyone was going to LEAD, it was supposed to be him. Not to mention, he was the one who saw this lesson. He was the one God lead to this place of enlightenment. If there is one thing he knew, God didn't anoint people to do nothing. He had been anointed. He had been blessed, so he knew it was for a purpose and this had to be it. Oftentimes in the Word of God, people who had been blessed didn't see or feel like it but it was a lesson in it if they could just push past what they could see or what they thought they knew. "Lean not on your own understanding."

If one could just be obedient then one could overcome the lesson with success, and have victory. He knew there was a part in it for him, one that said he was to cover her, keep being supportive, move out of that place he was in and do all the things he knew he was responsible to do, even if she did not. Because only he was responsible to answer for them before God as to why he had not. More importantly, only he was responsible when he didn't receive them in return. It would be because he had not done them, "the measure and length."

The toughest part of this gamble in his mind was, in all of her writings he had become her teacher, her beacon of light onto the path she had long departed from. In fact, she had even begun to compare him to her mother, called him by her name on some occasions. He had traded places from her lover and confidant to her teacher/parental figure. So while he was leading her down the righteous path, one they needed to find as a couple, he was also sacrificing that very thing by opening up her paths to learning those very lessons. She had come to despise his teachings, even though they weren't his, but God's. No she did not hate God. In her mind, He had no judgment, only Tony because he was the only one who spoke on it, not God. His voice was silent, therefore she got to interpret it how she saw fit, and forget all the obvious truths.

If he continued this way, he could lose her altogether, becoming the enemy in her mind even more than he already was. He would never receive the labor of hidden fruit; she would leave him angry and making him out to be this parent she would defy, and walk into the next relationship, where some other man would receive his harvest. He would do all of the work and receive none of the fruit. He would be damned if he would let that happen.

In her writings, he saw that he had given her room to re-establish a good relationship with her mother. He learned that had she been right about so much through all the conversations with him while he pointed it out. But as it turned out, she was a lot easier to deal with now having been exposed to Tony and all that he believed. If he kept going down this path, he knew there was more than a real chance he would lose her.

So at the end of the day, this was going to be tough but if he was going to be obedient to his work, God's will for his life, he was going to have to submit completely. He was going to have to admit that he didn't have all the answers, nor did he need to in order to follow God into belief, with full faith that God "would never lead him into a place that he didn't make a way to escape, so that he could bear it."

To walk along with Jesus in these matters was no small charge. They are essential and the very essences of which we are made. They are what charges us as individuals and our very souls. The bible says "pick up your cross and follow me." It also says, "If you can't pick up your cross, you don't deserve my love." It's pretty clear for most of us. These areas are our crosses, and when we can't pick them up, do we deserve God's love? If we can't deal with our own personal issues, aren't we sitting that cross down, and if so, where does that leave us? These seemingly small battles are literally the gateways, or barriers, to our kingdoms and salvation and they all lay within our reach. Not unlike Kings, we control our own destinies through free will and our decision to follow in faith, or not, and how we do it. Through the school of knowledge, banging that head over and over, or obedience, where we will never have to learn this lesson again.

So often he had heard so many talk about the will of God and following it and submitting to it. It was so easy to talk about and even to do as long as it was the things we wanted. But how about now? Here he was, faced with the most difficult thing he ever had to do outside of putting his infant son in the ground years earlier. That was the one other thing he could think of in a life filled with disappointment that could compare to how hard this was to do. And here he was the enemy, the thing that stood between his happily ever after, with or without DD. Because truth be told, whether or not they made it, whether DD was indeed his dream girl or a figment of his imagination, this was a lesson they both needed to learn, with or without one another. So to the world it might look like his submission to a horrible cause but he knew that horrible cause they saw was really himself. If he couldn't love her from right where she was, if he couldn't accept her, NO EXCUSES and step out of his fear and into the life he wanted, then he didn't deserve to have it.

He was going to have to finish what he started. Moving her in, furnishing her place, replenishing his faith. He was going to have to move forward and help her find a job, pay her bills, completely commit to Kayden as her dad, finally move out from Sharon, and even more, in with DD. Surrender his life. If he expected DD to follow, he had to give her something to follow. He was going to have to LIVE by example; that fearless faith he talked about. Full and complete submission to God and his promise.

The first thing he was going to have to do was confront her, her words, those she used to describe him in her journal, her actions, were these acts of malice, or mere weakness? To most, the details didn't matter. But to him, they were the key to everything at the moment. For "he that knoweth to do good yet doeth it not, onto him it becomes sin." And they say in order to do better you have to know better and he was banking on the fact that while she may have known better in the way we know sperm whales exist but most of us haven't actually seen one but we believe they do, it's not the same as seeing the power of that magnificent creature. He was going to show her the genuine article and not only will she know but moreover she would "knoweth."

But on some level, it was more about her knowing he knew and that he could let it all go and love her no matter what may come. He was going to stay; he was going to love her and all the great things about her, outside of the things that hurt until she took her last breath. He was completely committed to her and Kayden in a renewed way and his heart that should have been trampled was full of faith, full of God's love and forgiveness and full of grace for his life, wife and family.

So he would confront her but not wait to judge if what she said was true or not true, he would go and get tested for HIV to be sure he wasn't secretly dying due to her hidden sin. Since they had extended their stay, he had a few days to finish his work there at the house and get things in order and decide how he was going to tell her he knew her truths and how he planned on moving forward with things. And the most important thing was he was going to finally, after years of being with her, move their family out of the darkness.

He would no longer wait for her to earn it by way of doing the things he considered correct by him and their ensuing family. He would give it up front, on credit so to speak, in faith. They would spend holidays together as a family. Halloween and Thanksgiving were coming up and then Christmas. Everything was going to change. He was doubling up and going ALL IN. Nothing would be in reserve from this moment on. What was his was hers. What was Angel's, was now Kayden's. No holding back. Fully letting go.

It would be months before he would know for sure he was in the clear by way of HIV but all the tests he took came up clean, of all STDs and viruses. God was truly with him, and DD had been safe. He went back to DD's place and finished what he started and when the girls returned home, they were happy as they could be. They had a huge back yard, he purchased a grill and some lawn chairs, back yard wind chimes and some tiki lamps and even charcoal; they were set for a move in bbq. He purchased a washer and dryer outright and for the first time since she was on her own, she owned one. Full apartment of furniture from bathroom to kitchen, new light fixtures, bedding, table and chairs. It was like that show, While You Were Out, Home Make Over Edition. When they left it was an empty hole in the wall and when they returned, it was home.

They began going to her church together every other Sunday and Tony attended the support group each week along with DD. He went to the men's group and dealt with his stuff and she went to her group and dealt with hers, while the kids went to the Christian day care and did bible study. He got over himself and opened up his wallet to their life and began to help her with the bills as he should have before. He could see that now. He had

391

given her the opportunity to earn income by giving her a job but that wasn't true commitment, especially for someone who had been burnt as many times as DD had been. So he paid the bills when she didn't have it and considering she had moved in with her tax return, she had no idea where the money for that place was going to come from.

He sat down and had the dreaded confrontation conversation with DD about her journal and cheating. It was tough to say the least on the both of them but in the end, DD was amazed at Tony's ability to stay and love her when even at that moment, she was ashamed of herself for what she had done and the lies she had told. He did his able best not to throw it in her face or hold it against her. Although, he was human and still hurt so there were rough spots and probably would be for a while to come. But for the most part, they worked through it and he continued on in faith. Eventually once she got past the disbelief and made it to a place of her own faith, she was able to join him there and they both walked hand in hand in this place. There were more good days than bad in that place. But as usual, when it was bad it was awful, while good was equally as awesome.

Neither of them had ever had nor even seen anything like the good, so they held on tight to those days letting them outweigh the bad no matter how they were predisposed by way of their negative wiring to be drawn to, and respond to, all the negative in their lives before they ever even tried the good.

Trials and tests did come as DD reached her milestone in her support group and was asked to give a testimony in front of the entire group on stage consisting of maybe 90-110 people. She jumped up there and thanked all her group partners, buddies and friends for her success and all the good places she had been taken in her life. It stung like a knife in the back knowing full well she was standing on his shoulders in more ways than one and to not receive the credit he felt he was due at that moment. The grace, the mercy, the patience. After all, he had lead her to the counselors for her and Kayden, to that very group, to the last two jobs she finally took and was now holding, the groceries she ate each day and the lights she switched on, down to the key she turned, he was paying the rent. The only thing he wasn't providing for was the car she drove - a hand me down p.o.s. her sister had given her. Yes it hurt like hell and he even tried to express it to her as he stood in the crowded room standing there listening to her thank all of those people and leaving him out. But he sucked it up, and got past it. It was not for the credit or recognition, he did these things. So as that P.O.S. kicked the bucket shortly thereafter and he gave her his Mercedes Benz to drive, he knew that it was God's way of reminding him that he not only had a job to do but that HE could see his good work even if DD didn't.

They had come together and formed the point of that sword, the point in which they refused to settle, the point in which he put on the full armor of God and Tony thanked God for bringing him to this place. He knew without Him he could have never seen this home in the mountains, nor would he had ever even known it existed. The full armor of God sounded good to him and the more he thought of it, the more it sounded like his life and an awesome prayer. At this point in his life, he was prone to writing what he called text sermons, as he often sent his bible studies out to his close friends. This time, what he researched, he intended to take it a little further. This is what he found:

*Ephesians 6:17 The **sword of the spirit** which is the word of God.*
*Psalms 110:11 Thy word have **I** hid in mine heart that I might not sin against thee.*
*Psalms 27:1 The Lord is my light and my salvation whom shall I fear? The Lord is the strength of my life of whom **shall** I be afraid?*
*Psalms 109:4 For my love they are my adversaries but I give myself unto **pray**er and they have rewarded me evil for good, hatred for love set thou a*

*wicked man over him and let **Satan** be at his right hand when he is judged let him be condemned. **And** let his prayers become **sin**. Let his days be few.*

*Psalms 101:3 For I hate the work of them that turn aside. It **shall not cleave to me.***

*Romans 15:1 **We then that are strong** ought to bear the infirmities of the weak. And not to please ourselves, for even Christ pleased not himself but as **it is written,** the reproaches of them that reproach thee fell on me.*

There were two messages in this list of scriptures. One was the obvious and written straight forward in the line of scriptures he chose. The other was outlined in red and this was his silent prayer to be read separately. When he was done with this, he was so inspired. Although it may have been contradictory, he had it tattooed down the entire length of his right arm to remind him of the power of God and the power Tony himself possessed to wield it. Alone with a small sword aside it, he drew strength from it that very moment with no one ever knowing why he did it or it's purpose. His younger cousin who had spent so many years in the streets of Brooklyn wreaking havoc saw it and was so inspired by him and God's work in him that he had the exact same tattoo on the entire of length of his back and ended up completely changing his life.

God is good. It was his time to find a new path too. He married, had a son and walked into a life long commitment to labor and love. Not that he had done anything that he could take credit for in anyone's life; least of all his cousin's. He had to be ready to make that change and he was the one who was responsible and had to do all the work to get there. Tony was just grateful for the very small part in it that the Lord our Father allowed him to play. The part he played in all of it, in his and in their lives. His existence had changed all of their lives in a profound way because God had touched and changed him, which changed DD's stepmom, DD and her mother's relationship, Kayden, and even DD's sister.

He could see God working through him and his gifts of strength and ability to be obedient. From that moment on, Romans 15:1 was his favorite scripture, to be used by God was a wonderful and blessed thing. Bless God.

Chapter 29
Normalizing
(Rise of the Phoenix)

There he was doing his able best to render his version of a man for their new and aspiring family. This came complete with all the daddy drop off and pick ups, engaging with BOTH children now to find out how they two, as parents, could make them more successful people. So in addition to getting Kayden the therapy she needed, he found her an arts and crafts program at the YMCA because she loved it so much. But before that, he brought it to DD and they decided to pull Kayden out of public school and he would pay for her to go to the same private school that Tony's son, Angel, attended. He purchased her uniforms and filled the house with the same types of food and sort of amenities that his son had, which sounds small but goes a long way towards feeling equally considered as a daughter.

He covered all the bills that DD couldn't cover. They managed to have date night each week where DD got to choose the place and arrange it and he would trust her to just go for the ride. This was difficult for him because he hated surprises, while she really loved them. It made sense considering he had such a difficult time trusting coming from his childhood history and her desire to be trusted blindly. He could see that so he agreed to it, knowing full well the potential for double healing if he could step outside of his fears. Thinking it was so small, it had the least potential to hurt him but the up side was far greater. They discussed and decided that he wouldn't move in with her and Kayden right off, as it would be too much too fast, not so much for the two adults in the equation but more so for the children with special regard to Kayden who was attached to DD at the hip. They had slept in the same room and the same bed for the first six years of her life. In essence, a part of her counseling was for DD and Kayden to sever their unhealthy relationship. Kayden had become more like an adult, where she and DD had more of a friendship and interpersonal relationship than a true parental relationship.

She had to "break up" with her daughter and make room for DD and Tony's relationship. At first this put an obvious strain on the family dynamic. Kayden was constantly jockeying for position with Tony in DD's life. After some time in individual counseling, couples counseling and group counseling, they were finally able to work this thing out. By now, DD was on her second counselor and still going to her group. Therefore everyone in the freaking house was in counseling except little Angel. Tony sought out, obtained and paid for all of these things to keep his family together, thriving and growing. On the outside, it would have seemed strange but as messed up as some of the personalities were, it was really needed and actually very effective.

So instead of moving right in, they decided he would stay over three nights a week in the transitional stage. He would stay four nights at the other place and three nights at their place with the idea that eventually they would all, DD, Kayden, Tony and Angel end up under the same roof. Each year Angel and Tony went out and picked out costumes for Halloween and they went trick or treating together. Angel loved it and on a real child-like level, so did Kayden. This year, they would include DD and Kayden who did the same each year on their own. So they went and chose costumes and happily hit the street collecting candy and those good childhood and family memories that we all need and want building up our life's memory banks. Their first holiday together was pretty awesome and a real family building experience and their confidence was high going into their next one. They had already decided that they were going to do their first Thanksgiving together but they were going to do it at their new place. They would both cook a dish or two and spend that evening together.

Now the funny thing about this idea was that each of them had very specific ideas on how things should go and be but they never discussed any details, which was a poor start to begin with. So they entered into the holiday season riding high off of Halloween and with that success came the high expectations for the following holiday. Without any communication anyone could see how this was bound to fail. DD and Tony, unknown to both of them, had had some pretty bad experiences around holidays that neither one of them had expressed. So neither one of them had any ideas of all the things that could go wrong or all the ways they could let one another down.

DD had, in her mind, that every holiday was perfect and was the time that her family came together and enjoyed one another's company and celebrated the seasons. But deep down, she was burying the holiday that her parents pretty much announced their divorce to the children. It was not a formal sit down, "Hey kids, this is what's going on." It was more like a huge fight that the usual family dinner didn't consist of and the fighting was so horrible that they never came to the table. The children ended up eating alone for the most part. By the time their mother finally joined them, there was so much tension at the table as their parents yelled back and forth that no one really ate, let alone enjoyed that holiday.

Tony's experience was different from that because he couldn't even recall a "good" holiday from his childhood. So the upside was huge if they could pull it off. The truth was, the expectation was grand so the chances were slim and even slimmer without communication. They started out with the greatest intentions but by the time the day came upon them, they hadn't talked about their plans from timeline, what time they would eat, or even get together down to what each was going to prepare. Both of their anxieties were high to begin with. As the day went on and each met their expected disappointment in one another while completely missing their unexpressed desire, things were quickly moving towards disaster.

The day was filled with disappointment spent mostly apart, cooking and bickering about petty things that on the grand scheme of things didn't really matter. The awesome thing about all that therapy and all the time they had taken to think of one another's perceptions had given each of them the ability to consider each other and the empathy needed to see one another from the other person's eyes. This may have saved the would-be catastrophe this day would have ordinarily been in their life. By the end of the evening, they were able to lower their defenses and talk to the point where they could agree to let some of these personal things and gripes go. By the time they actually sat down to the table for dinner, it was about 8:30 pm. Both adults sat down full of anxiety still and nervously went into the Lord's prayer as they said grace over dinner. The kids nervously watched the adults to decide how to feel. Once they began to eat and the children began to talk to one another and jump into silly little conversations, that kept the adults not only interested but playfully laughing and all the tension quietly left the dinner table. By the time dinner was over they were sitting there laughing and chatting and they looked and sounded like a real family enjoying one another's company at a holiday dinner. It was an awesome testament to the power of prayer and an equally awesome moment for their family. They had made it through an emotionally tough day.

After dinner, they retired to DD's bedroom where they all huddled up on the king sized bed to watch a family movie and enjoy one another's company. They were watching the movie laying all over one another, Kayden's feet on Tony and her head in her mothers lap and little Angel's head in Kayden's lap. It was a wonderful scene and an even more wonderful one considering how their day began and what it took to get there.

Halfway through the movie DD's cell phone rang and she hit ignore. Tony saw it and his antennae went up because of their bad history around cell phones and forwarded calls. He fought himself not to say anything and to give her the benefit of the doubt; she should be able to forward calls. He needed to develop more trust and less suspicion, so he was going to hold his tongue and enjoy their holiday moment. After all, it was well deserved as hard as they had worked that day. Then the phone rang again and she forwarded it, then a few minutes later again. Finally he asked,

"Who keeps calling you on a holiday evening like that? Is it family? Why wouldn't you just talk to them?" He asked.

"It's Sheldon," she responded.

"Your ex-boyfriend?" Tony asked.

"Yes," she answered.

"Why would he be calling on Thanksgiving? Isn't he married?" Tony asked her.

"I'm not sure why he is calling. I haven't spoken to him in some time," she replied.

"I know he is married but does he know that you have a family now too? I mean I can't see why he would be calling you at this time under the most innocent of circumstances? I'm truly confused," Tony said.

Just then the phone rang again and Tony looked at the caller ID and it was Sheldon again.

"Why don't you answer it and you can find out what it is he wants," Tony said.

Tony and DD hardly noticed the kids getting nervous around hearing the conversation and the evening quickly turning into something other than they had managed to work themselves into.

"Hello?" DD answered the phone, sounding annoyed.

Tony could hear a man's voice on the other end of the phone responding. "Put the phone on speaker please so I can hear this innocent conversation," Tony demanded now, seeing in DD's nervousness that there was something going on deeper than she was letting on.

"Listen Sheldon, I have decided to leave the past in the past and I'm moving forward in my life and family. They are sitting here with me now listening so I don't think there is any reason for us to continue to speak any longer," DD said to the silent phone.

"I understand, cool. I won't call you again," A man's voice said from the other side of the line. And then the line clicked.

"So I'm confused? If you guys haven't talked in a while and you don't even know why he is calling, why did your conversation just sound like a break up?" Tony asked with his suspicion on high.

"I don't know Tony. You're paranoid and you are a master at making things more than they are," DD replied.

The truth was that Tony wasn't a master at making things greater than they were but exactly opposite in fact. He was a master at sniffing out bullshit and lies. Having formally been a master of lies himself, he had plenty of opportunities to get familiar with the techniques, having used them himself so often. The problem for him was that after he sniffed out the lies and the bullshit, he usually minimized them so he could stay in his relationship with DD. Not this time however.

"That sounds like a lie DD and I am so not up for another round of you cheating and lying. Listen, the past is the past and if you did anything before now that you want to come clean about please just do. Don't drag us through this. If there is anything you want to tell me, tell me now before this lie, this thing gets too big," Tony pleaded with DD.

"There is nothing Tony, neither in the past nor present that I have lied about or you need to know," she said.

Tony let the conversation go, although he was very uneasy. He was going to drop the conversation with special concern for the kids who were watching intently. He had plans most definitely in coming back to this subject. But more than that, he was going to look into this thing deeper. DD had a great history of lying and deceit between them, so it was not a thing he could just let go.

After he and Angel left to return home, he was already searching his brain on how he could figure out what he was sure was the truth about this situation. He remembered half way home that he had been given DD's email access awhile ago and he never did check it but always wanted to. He had fought that fight within himself and his weakness to do so many times and won because he never did check it. He got home and, after putting Angel to bed, he immediately went to his computer and began to search DD's email. She must have been thinking along the same lines because as he searched her emails, Tony found all the correspondence between DD and Sheldon in the deleted bin. She not only lied to him about when she had spoken to him last but the nature of their contact. She had been seeing him romantically even though he was indeed married with two children.

She talked about her feelings for him and them dating. They even spoke about having spent time making out. There was no sex talk but Tony was convinced that this is where their talk was going if it hadn't already. They had been seeing each other for months now. They had started seeing each other before he left for over seas and since his return. Once again, Tony had felt the difference in DD during that time and felt like she was seeing someone else. He even confronted her about it and she admitted she was seeing someone else. It was him as well as a few others he found in her diary she was getting high with regularly. Those Tony knew about but he hadn't had a clue about Sheldon. It crushed him to learn this truth after all they had been through, after all he had persevered through and what it had taken to go inside himself in order to do so.

When Tony left that evening, DD was complaining about abdominal pain. He wasn't too much concerned about that. He figured it was nerves because they both knew she was lying. But just as he was dealing with the reality that she had indeed cheated on him again, DD was calling Tony to tell him she was probably going to be headed to the emergency room for the pains in her abdominal section. She mentioned that she hadn't had her cycle and the possibility that she could be pregnant. The timing couldn't have been worse, because he knew he was holding information that made it entirely possible that if she was indeed pregnant, it could be Sheldon's. She said she was going to give it a little longer and if things got worse, she would be headed to the emergency room. He was really in a bad place because he could hardly muster up the care in his voice to sound concerned.

An hour past and he was indeed on his way to the emergency room because the pains had not subsided. After spending hours there, DD did pass what appeared to be a pregnancy at the hospital that night. The horrible part about this for Tony was that he really didn't know how to feel. So while DD expressed her sadness for the loss of what should have been their unborn child, Tony could not express the same sentiment. He was still holding down the bitter pill he was choking on about Sheldon and he knew it was the total and complete wrong time to even try to bring that up. He would wait until a time when they could talk about this thing in private. In the meantime, he did his best to support her through the tough time she was experiencing, having lost what could have been their child.

He knew in his heart, he would never feel that way, no matter what was said between them. Minus DNA proof, which would be indisputable, he would never change his mind. And since that was never going to happen, probably wasn't even possible, he was most definitely holding what amounted to a bomb shell within his head and heart. For now, he was as cool as still water, minus the attitude he was trying so hard to hold down.

They finally got released from the emergency room and went home and he managed to hold it down until she spoke about it and even then he didn't come right out and smash her with it.

"Tony, are you ok? You seem so disconnected by the whole thing. Didn't you want this child? I know you always said you wanted to have children with me," DD said, still sounding drained by what she had just endured.

Tony took a long pause and just sat there and considered his answer. He didn't just want to blurt out what was on his heart unfiltered. No matter what she had done, having been through something as traumatic as she had just gone through, if he loved her as he said he did, no matter what the details of this thing, he as a man should and could do better. So he was just thinking and staring off into space when she interrupted his thought again.

"Tony? Are you not talking to me? Are you upset with me?" DD said sounding upset now seeing that Tony was ignoring her.

Tony sighed, not really even wanting to truly breach the topic at this point. But he also knew there was no way he was going to be able to hold this kind of thing in. This is the kind of thing brothas have heart attacks silently in bed thinking about. Not him. No. He might give her ass one but he wasn't going to let her secret kill him, hell she had too damn many of them.

"I just lost our child and you won't even talk to me? Is my worth really weighed by my ability to hold your children? As a woman on some level, we learn that unspoken lesson. So I'm sitting here feeling bad enough and now you won't even talk to me? Imagine how that is making me feel? That's so unfair," DD said, sounding as if she wanted to cry.

And right on cue, as if he needed any more egging on, she had given him the little push he needed as she always did to go on in and get it off his chest.

"You know what's not fair? It's that I want to empathize with where you are. I want to be able to tell you I am saddened by what all just happened in there. But I honestly can't say that because what's unfair to me is I don't even know if that's my child you just lost," he said, with a stone cold serious face.

"What? How could you say that?" DD said, sounding genuinely surprised by his words.

404

"Did you think you could carry on a relationship with Sheldon for the time frame you came up pregnant, with him just calling you as recent as this evening and I not question who this child belonged to?" Tony said, now sounding more hurt than angry.

"I swear on my life, on my child and on everything I love I did not sleep with him. This child I just lost was yours Tony. I swear," DD said.

Now keeping it completely real, he believed her. There was no hesitation in her voice whatsoever. She said it with such conviction, like there was no doubt in her mind at all. There was truly only one way she could feel that way outside of being a stone cold liar and that was if she was telling the truth. She had been a liar but more often than not, she wasn't that great at it. She had always done enough to be convincing but for the most part there were always cracks. Tony was always the one too afraid to pull at the loose threads he always spotted, afraid of the unraveling. He wasn't afraid anymore. At this point, he couldn't see any to pull, so it seems like for the first time in a long time, she was telling the truth. But of course he would never tell her that. And furthermore, he had decided that since there was no way for him to know that, he would not believe anything she couldn't prove when she was under suspicion in these types of matters. Truth be told, he really wasn't ready to deal with the thoughts of losing another child, so it was probably easier to believe it wasn't his than face the fact that the opportunity had been taken away from him.

He expressed the fact that he would take her word for it and hold it down for arguments sake. This meant he wouldn't make a thing of this, especially considering the fact that she was just released from the hospital mere moments ago. He also made it clear he still didn't believe there was no way that the possibility didn't exist that this child wasn't his. She, too, didn't want to argue or fight any longer. They both were pretty well battle wary and sought higher ground. He put it out there and there was nothing she could do to convince him otherwise. He dropped the subject and let it go as far as discussing it and now it was her turn to carry around that bitter pill because he wasn't about it. When you lay down with dogs, you come up with fleas. And her fleas were the fleas of mistrust that come with deception. One plus one equals two in his world and it was what it was. They rode home that evening in silence after that and he dropped her off at her place after they picked up Kayden from her dad's place, still not speaking a word. He helped her inside, made sure she had everything she needed and departed for his place. There was no way he was going to nurse her to health under the circumstances; that was simply too much for him to do. He went home and life for him went on.

*   *   *   *   *

With each passing day, you could feel DD hold her bitter pill a little tighter and tighter to her chest. She was emanating a little more and more each day the venom she was holding inside of her about what the truth was concerning this child she had just lost. Only she and Sheldon knew the truth of the matter. As far as Tony was concerned, she could hold on to that pill for as long as she needed to in order to figure out she shouldn't have been toying with his heart in the first place. If she hadn't lied and been going behind his back then there would be no reason to be suspected of anything and that was his point. He didn't want to torture her but it felt nice to him for once to actually hold her feet to the fire about something that she would take responsibility for. Because even though she denied it, she did admit that if she had not done what she did by deceiving him, there would be no question. But it was eating away at her pride and insides to have to play low when she was so accustomed to playing high with concern to him. But he was genuinely hurt so he had cause to be where he was.

At some point she stopped caring about right and wrong and the reasons why she did what she did mattered more. That was the exact moment "why" stopped mattering to him. Why had always mattered to him. Whenever something happened between them, he would always seek out why to explain what had happened between them in order to find the grace and mercy for her and their relationship. But after the attitude she showed, he no longer cared and he told her so.

"Why, no longer matters to me. I am less concerned with why than the fact that you continue to do these kinds of things. At some point even God counts these things as sin and I have to look at that as the example. Hell, you know better yet you continue to do. So when you say sorry for something you knew better than to do, are you really sorry? Or was it a calculated risk? Did you measure the outcome and decide you could get away with it? How many times is too many?" He said.

He was starting to sound like a man who could clearly see her fading against the will of God and he had questions. "If you are the Christian you say you are, carrying yourself to that church three sometimes four times a week yet you continue to do the same stuff, are you that person?" He asked.

"I'm trying. I'm only human and doing the best that I can do," she replied.

"Do or not do. There really is no try. Everything else is an excuse, which are tools of the incompetent that build bridges to nowhere and monuments of nothing. Those who specialize in them seldom accomplish anything," he answered.

They went on like this for weeks as November rolled into December and they still had their differences. One day they returned home after coming from picking Kayden up from the YMCA and there was a note on the door from the landlord. It was a demand for payment or eviction would be forthcoming. Tony asked her about it. He assumed DD had paid the rent as it was already the second week of the month and she hadn't even mentioned it to him. That's how it worked between them. When she couldn't cover a bill she would let him know and he would cover her. Unbeknownst to Tony, DD had lost yet another job. While he went off to work each day, she still hadn't replaced the income necessary to provide for her and Kayden's monthly bills, nor had she informed him that these bills were once again delinquent.

So the first whiff of this mess Tony caught was the notice on the door about the rent. He tried to talk to her about it but she was so in her emotions about it she refused his help. He knew it was because she was in her pride about him not letting go of this thing with Sheldon but who could blame him. Now typically he would hear her say she didn't need him or want his help and he would do it anyway but he was determined to abide by her wishes. If she said she didn't want his help then he would not give it to her. If she didn't want it and until she asked him for the help she just turned away. He made up his mind to let her live out her wish.

He always did Christmas for the kids but this year, he had made up his mind that he would truly treat Kayden as his own as he had with everything else. The same amount of money he spent on Angel is the same amount he spent on her. He went shopping and purchased more toys than any two little ones needed on Christmas morning. It was awesome. He had recently opened his heart up to Christmas since the arrival of Angel and now he was a Christmas junkie. He was looking forward to sharing a little more love of the holiday spirit with his new daughter. All of his attention to her and the details around her was paying off. By years end, she was already making decisions to hang out with Tony and Angel more and even told him she loved him. He was floored, this coming from a little girl who barely spoke to him for years.

He took it with a grain of salt because he thought it might possibly be a bit of manipulation around the season of giving. It was innocent enough; all kids are little con artists when it comes to toys and sweets, he thought. By the time the season was upon them, DD had finally reconciled her emotions with her logic and spoke to Tony like the man he was and gave him the respect he deserved as the sole provider for their family. Most days she acted like it was nothing, a small thing. She even told him once that he had done the least for her than any man had. Adding that dudes that didn't even like her had done more. "Wow," he thought to himself.

He knew it was all game, as from the time he met her, she was on her ass and never got on her feet until he put her there. He didn't sit her up on a pedestal. In fact, he just helped her open the door so she could see the life she wanted and see the good in it, and see the God in it. She walked through it the rest of the way. He couldn't take full credit for it. She was beginning to change and more often than not wanted to change and truly put forth the effort to do the things she had always talked about. It made him want to try harder, pushed even him to be a better man and show up in ways he had always wanted to but had held on to that last bit of fear that kept him from it. She was growing as he had and they were finally growing together. He had taken the lead, stepped out of the shadows of fear into full blown manhood within their relationship and his example was paying off.

When he contacted the landlord, he told Tony he no longer wanted the money, he wanted the place back. At first DD was worried and he was feeling the heat of her worry having to move quickly if this guy wasn't going to take the rent money. But prayer changes things and Tony was able to secure a condo closer to his place, larger with an additional bedroom and all the amenities he was trying to give Kayden and DD in the first place, with only an additional $50 in rent.

They had weathered another storm and he managed to pull their family's feet out of the fire and it was beginning to look more and more like they were making their way down that road. Things were hard. Nothing seemed to come easy except fighting and hard times. As a child, he could recall many childhood days growing up in a home just like this one, where they fought hard, lived hard and, at times, loved hard too. Although, the loving and anything good, never seemed to stay too long.

Even though he swore that he would have something different for his adult life and he absolutely wanted something different for his children, as he made his way in the world, the further down that winding road he got, the smaller the possibility of anything became. Each failed love and relationship presented him with the same opportunities to have the dream at first, only to find the same old thing at the end. What he wasn't seeing was that it wasn't there. No, that wasn't it at all. The possibilities lay all around him for something else but could he see it? And if he couldn't, would he be able to create it? Well he didn't know a thing about that. All he knew was heartache and misery.

This thing that started to feel more like life and just as familiar as the things he had always known, he knew not only had to change, would change, but had already begun to. Things were getting softer. She was getting softer. He was getting softer. They were getting softer. The bible says, "Submit ye to one another." And it's not that she thought that she should be leading their family. Hell she most definitely didn't know any better than he. She, too, came from a broken home. In his eyes, it wasn't how you started but how you finished. So yes, she was no better prepared than he. But he knew he was going to have to submit himself to her ideas of life and him as well, at some point.

He was going to have to show her he respected her. He loved her from where she was with his actions and that he trusted her in that there was more than one way to do things, his way. With each step, he reached out to her to give her something that showed his strength in manhood like the new place and more new things to fill it up. He would try harder to do things her way, to show her he valued her and her opinions. Even more so, to show her that he could submit to her in trust and believe in her ability to be a good mate, a good wife. He knew his ideals about life, love and marriage were still a bit warped and had some growing to do but he believed in her and their ability to grow together.

Chapter 30
Hardening
Always and Forever

It had been far past time since he made this move. He was finally ready, and strong enough to do what had to be done. Angel was old enough, and Sharon's and Tony's relationship as parents were solid enough and there was no better time than the present. DD and his relationship was still rocky at best. She tried to break up with him for like the ten millionth time this year. He would have none of it and talked her down off of that ledge of anxiety and they managed to stay together to see another day. No matter what their relationship status, there could not be a deterrent at this point or he would never make another move in his life, sort of how they had been living for the last six years. Funny how he could see that now so clearly but missed how much of a hold up his hang ups and fears had played into their current position. Looking back, if he would have been strong enough to submit to this thing and allow DD to be who she was years ago and still have the strength, the bold and fearless faith to move forward, the answers to all these questions could have been clear then. But no use crying over spilt milk, he was here now and there was no backing up or slowing down.

He had always told DD he could love her for her and unconditional love was where his heart was. Recently she had been putting all that to the test as she clearly stated that she had not been being true to herself or him. She was going to make no effort to hide who she was from him and they would either deal or not. She too had grown tired of all the why's in either one of their equations and it was time to shit or get off of the pot as the old people used to say. This was one of the main reasons she had tried to break up with him recently. She had given him this long speech about how he would never be able to accept her for who she was and she needed to be more true to herself, and so forth and so on.

The truth was her mother, sister and brother-in-law were coming to town to visit with her for the coming weekend and she wanted to have the time to hang out with them. But when they all got together they usually got high and she wanted to be able to get high with impunity, knowing how he felt about drugs and her smoking weed. He had grown up in a family of drug users and weed was the primary drug of choice. He was more than familiar with the drug, although he himself had never smoked it.

It was hard to believe by most that he had been from Brooklyn and been amongst so many weed smokers and never smoked any himself. It just never had any fascination for him. He had seen weed lead to many other more addictive drugs. Frankly, it scared him, being from a family of addicts. He was always afraid that the first time he ever tried anything, he would be headed down the downward spiral of drug addiction himself.

It is said that there is a gene that determines these things. He wasn't certain about that. The one thing he was certain of was that in his family, most all had addictive personalities. Therefore, there was a good chance that the blood running through his veins had a pretty high chance to have the same addictive properties. Either way, fact or fiction, in his mind, it simply wasn't worth the chance. Therefore, from the first day he was offered his first joint, the answer was no and it had been that ever since.

What was even more striking to him was not just the addiction to harder drugs. DD always made her case for weed and why Tony was over-reacting by saying how she had never gone any further than weed and neither had anyone else in her family. She always said you weren't bound to be a drug abuser or graduate to anything else just because you smoked weed. He agreed and this wasn't even his major gripe with weed.

His gripe was that it bred apathy; the more often you smoked, the less likely it was you were doing much with your life. All of the hard core weed smokers he knew were pot heads and didn't do much with their lives. And those that had managed to do anything could have done leaps and bounds more if they didn't spend so much time chasing behind dealers, wraps for their weed, rolling up, smoking and baking. It takes a lot of time and the mere fact that it is illegal means you have to spend a good deal of time obtaining it correctly otherwise get locked up.

He felt that ANYTHING, drugs, porn, cheating on your wife or husband, ANYTHING that had to be done in the dark was done in the enemy's dominion, the devils domain. The darkness was where the enemy lived and when you leave those portals to his world open in your life, he can enter through them at any time without an invite and snatch something or someone you love without warning.

You had to purchase it in dark corners, or secret meetings, always worrying about being caught, arrested, shot, robbed, or worse. A dirty urine test on a job or weed seed falling out of your child's nap sack could literally ruin your life. He had seen it first hand. You could be on the block copping something and someone get shot up the street and you or someone close to you get hit, or they lock down the block and you get busted. Anything was possible was his reasoning. It wasn't that this was an ordinary occurrence. In his opinion, it just wasn't worth the chance.

The most unattractive thing to Tony was a woman smoking cigarettes. There was only one thing worse, a woman smoking weed. Now this ill feeling may be tied to his mother and her bout with addiction which played prime time during his childhood and development. After years spent dealing with those thoughts and having forgiven his mother so long ago, he would have liked to think that wasn't the case. But the sociologists all say these types of issues run deep and almost always run back to your parents. So if that was the case, he was willing to face that and accept his part in it. But he had visions of seeing women high, looking and being loose, lowered inhibitions and whorish behavior.

So often he had seen people do things they wouldn't ordinarily do under the influence of drugs and he just wanted a lady and DD already had some serious tendencies. He just felt weed only worsened her chances of keeping her legs closed. It didn't help matters that she always got high in secret, hiding it from him with people he didn't know and doing God knows what. The more he thought about it, the more he needed to learn how to accept her for who she was. His main concern however, was how this thing affected her. If this thing was as he thought it was, why would he want her out there in the world in that state? If she was clear, this was something she wanted to do for the rest of her life. If she was, he had better figure out if it was something he could honestly deal with. Because like it or not, it was better she did it around him than if she didn't.

So after a super long talk, he not only convinced her that he could accept her for who she was and would not buckle under the pressure if this was indeed what she needed and wanted to do. Also he would support and love her no matter what. She was excited that he had finally come around to seeing things her way and would accept her for who she was. After all, it wasn't like she was going to be a pot head. She didn't need to smoke every day. Hearing her say she wasn't going to become a pot head was a relief, although he didn't honestly think she would be.

Although he was glad she had brought up boundaries. Since she was the one who had brought them up, he went in further. They discussed it fully, striking an agreement that she would only smoke on weekends and not every weekend but every other weekend unless her family was in town or she there and then she could smoke that weekend no matter when that fell.

He felt good about that agreement and felt he could support her in that place and so did she, as she sincerely felt she could honor such an agreement. In fact, she took it a step further and told him that family or not, she only needed to smoke one day during the weekend. So if she smoked Friday then she didn't need to, and wouldn't, smoke Saturday, or vice versa. He was encouraged by her willingness to consider how he felt about it and her putting up the extra boundaries made him feel like she had really considered how he felt and the ground he had given to make room for the real her in his world.

So there he was in her neighborhood looking at a town home but a stone's throw away from the condo he had moved DD and Kayden into. He was finally moving out and while he wasn't moving in with DD and Kayden, he was doing the next best thing and moving right up the street from them. It was very exciting to see how far they had come, since he got back from his trip and walked into that fearless faith. It was even more exciting to finally feel like things were moving towards the dream he had for them years ago.

He got the place and went to the consignment store once again and found an entire house full of furniture, three bedrooms worth. There was a bedroom for each of the kids, a nice sized living room and a huge master bedroom. There was even another nice sized room off of the living room where he went and got a full sized billiard table and his place was furnished, neat, modern and stylish, well, as far as the furniture went anyway. The walls were white. The standard when you move in most places these days. He immediately went and purchased paint because he couldn't stand all white walls throughout the place. It drove him crazy. It reminded him of a hospital or more like an insane asylum.

DD and Kayden were excited that Tony was moving so close and although Tony could tell DD's anxiety was high, he down played it and happily accepted her offer to help him paint his place. Tony wanted to have his place painted and ready for company by the time DD's family arrived this weekend. A few months ago, DD's sister and her family had moved to Miami where their brother and mother lived. This was their first time back since they left and Tony wanted to show them all the strides he and his family were making. It was superficial, sure but it was all he had. To him, it represented all the work he could manage in the few months he got home as compared to all those years spent spinning their wheels while they watched.

For the rest of the week, things were pretty good as everyone was just buzzing with all the work that needed to be done. Tony had not long ago just finished all the painting at DD's place and moved all those things in alone and now there he was doing it all over again for himself. Kayden seemed more excited than everyone. It was as if she was getting a dad and a brother. Even though they weren't moving in together, she got right into the spirit of things. She quickly picked out some furniture and wall paint for her room and filled it up with her personal things. Tony had bought her a thirty inch television for DD's place and she made it known to Tony that she expected a thirty two inch flat screen in her "new" room, giggling as she said it.

She had become such a little lady and he was falling in love with her all over again as he had watched Kayden come out of her shell and blossom into a very pleasant young lady. She had such a bright smile and awesome personality, nothing like the reclusive little girl who wouldn't speak to anyone. Between the counselor, the bible study, church and new school, she was a new young lady indeed. He had bought her guinea pigs for getting all A's and she wanted to bring them over to Tony's place to keep him company on nights they stayed at their place.

It was a really cute gesture and Tony could see what she meant. Kayden had just turned eleven and was five feet tall now. He could hardly see the four year old, knee high to a Johnny pump, little thing he had met all those years ago. She was definitely coming into her own.

All the changes these past two years, with particular concern to this week, had really affected her. She had told him she loved him more this week than all of last month. She was so happy and this made him happy.

By the time DD's family arrived, the place looked like he had been living there for months. They had even managed to get the fresh paint smell out of the place, thanks to some scented candles. The first night they arrived it was just her mother, sister and her husband. They didn't bring their kids and DD's brother and girlfriend were coming the following day. They had spent the entire day at DD's place admiring her new place and furniture. They had never seen the place, since she had recently moved in and everything in the place was new. They had plenty to talk about as women usually do when it comes to décor and such. Tony and Del, DD's brother-in-law, pretty much just sat there making small talk allowing them women to catch up on all things family and beyond. At some point they made their way around the corner to Tony's place to play a few games of pool. They had managed to go the entire day and night without smoking any weed.

They had been having cocktails throughout so Tony thought to himself maybe they weren't going to do it. But once they got to his place, DD went upstairs saying she had to go to the bathroom and once upstairs called for him. When he got upstairs, DD told him that they were going to smoke just to prepare him and make sure he was still ok with it. If there was going to be a scene or any discussion about it she figured it would be best handled upstairs in private. Tony didn't blink and said it was cool, although his stomach was all over the place. The very first time he was going to witness it, "It had to go down at his place?" He was thinking.

Well, he said he could handle it. This would be the true test. He went back downstairs and continued on playing. As the night went on and the girls got high, he was cool and managed to hold it down, although Del was getting more and more drunk and getting on Tony's nerves. Tony had just got back into good graces with

417

DD's family, so he was feeling like he really didn't need the drama that would surely come if he put Del in his place. As it was, he was already pretty much a peon in Miami as DD's brother treated him like the bitch everyone recognized him to be.

Things would only get worse if Tony exposed that truth too. So he played the back as dude ran his mouth for the rest of the night until everyone went home. DD stayed at Tony's place, while her family went back to her place. DD was high and horny which is exactly what Tony always feared with her getting high. But he found he could handle it and deal because all of her attention and affection was on him. She wasn't anxious; she wasn't argumentative or even edgy. She was calm, submissive and playful. Wow, who was this girl? Tony was figuring out he kinda liked high DD. They fooled around that night and outside of him demanding she brush her weed breath which made for a good laugh, they were good. They had passed yet another pretty major test and things were even better than they had been. It felt good to wonder in this sense what tomorrow would bring.

*   *   *   *   *

Tony had passed the test and at a minimum, DD's mother seemed to warm to him more so than she ever had before. Whereas, he was certain she couldn't stand him, she told him he was full of shit the first time they met, she was dealing with him completely different now. After DD and he were dating, and even being engaged for so long now, it seemed as if the entire family had finally come around. They wanted to like him and even more, they wanted DD to finally be happy, to finally have a life and family. DD's sister had a husband and three kids, even her younger brother, the baby of the family was engaged and talking about getting married next year. DD was the eldest child and was never able to find someone she could be happy with and Tony had represented the closest thing she could find to that.

So even though they had been up and down, the family having had a better, longer look at Tony, was rooting for him, her and them. Her brother arrived the following day and the family went to lunch and spent the day out and about. Tony, who was teaching college level courses had to work and couldn't hang with them but caught up to them later that evening. TONY could see clearly the shift in DD's mom, as she was subtly guiding this first meeting between Tony and Martin towards a positive outcome, as any good mother would. She wanted to see a good outcome for her two children, DD and Martin.

She knew it was important that Tony and Martin put this silly beef behind them. She made sure that by the time Tony got out of work, they were already at Tony's house waiting on Martin to arrive there instead of DD's place. This would make Tony feel more comfortable in the sincerity of the get together for its intended purpose. Not to mention, it should humble the two men. If Tony was sincere, he would want Martin to feel comfortable in his place; and if Martin was sincere he wouldn't have a problem going to Tony's place. Besides, Martin was not the kind of person who was afraid to tear someone's place up whipping ass if things weren't right, neither was Tony for that matter. So these men who were finally behaving like men were gently guided to a good place all by a mother who Tony could see had shifted her perception of him and wanted him in their family. This was the first time Tony and DD's brother, Martin had seen one another since all the bad blood had gone on between them with concern to DD. It wasn't necessarily that he didn't like Tony. He just didn't want to see his sister unhappy and by all accounts it appeared that Tony made her miserable.

Like any other brother you have ever heard of, or seen, he wanted better for his sister than the dude who made her miserable and still lived with his baby's mother. Tony knew how bad he looked and how they may have never seen past those things to understand his position. There is a process we all go through when we face those things in our lives that make it difficult to be happy or more forward in a positive light. Most often we realize those things aren't about someone else, they are ours and ours alone. During these times, most often we get down, some of us way down and there are tears o' plenty depending on how deep that thing runs. For DD it ran pretty deep.

So she cried a lot and seeing her that way and him being the quote unquote problem in her life, he could see how things could get twisted. Besides, there was more than enough reason to hate him with just by him living with Sharon alone. But today he was letting go of all those hang ups. He was letting it all go and so were they. They had actually sat down the night before and said so. Therefore, Tony knew where he stood with them all outside of Martin.

Martin had a history of holding on to things as did their entire family. They weren't big on forgiveness and as it was, it seemed like he was the worst of the bunch, holding onto things the longest. But of all the things he had been hearing about Martin, these last few years it really sounded as if he had done a great deal of growing as did he and DD. So Tony was hopeful. Tony and Martin talked, small talk mostly and played pool. They had a few beers as they both were fans of Miller High Life. They shared a few laughs and things seemed pretty good. Tony offered his place to Martin and his lady and let him know he was going to be staying at DD's place, so he was welcomed to stay at his place. Martin surprisingly accepted the invitation and although he was a millionaire, slept at Tony's place, showing he had finally accepted him as family. The night ended once again with the ladies getting high. Even though it was against DD's no smoking two days consecutively, Tony wasn't upset at all. The day had gone too well to hold petty grievances. Once again they retired to the bedroom with the same very amenable, even sweet DD.

"Who the hell is this chick?" He thought inside his head. Confirmed, he liked high DD. That morning Martin got up early to hit the road. Apparently, he had only come to Tampa to bury the axe between he and Tony, so they all could feel free to move forward in their perspective lives together as family. Tony had no idea that this was the deal but seeing his early departure he figured this had to be. It was the only thing that made sense. Martin went out to pack his truck and found he had a flat and called Tony for help. Tony came by and helped him run his truck up to the tire place he usually did business with. Once the tire was fixed, he went back to Tony's place to catch a shower before they left.

During this time, Tony and Martin had a candid conversation about life, Kayden and even DD and his relationship in a roundabout way. Well at least Tony did. He just spoke on it. Martin was a pretty big guy himself, pro athlete and full of machismo, so that kind of talk was sort of foreign to him and Tony saw that but he wanted to put it out there. More than that, he could tell how Kayden was responding to Tony and that things had changed. She had come with Tony to help Martin and never left his side, from the lifting and lowering of the truck, the removal of the tire and drive to and from the shop. She was stuck to Tony's right leg like an appendage. It was almost like Kayden was trying to send a clear message. "I know you have been my 'father figure' but this is my daddy now."

Martin looked a little disappointed but happy too, more like relieved. He had always worried about DD but moreover he was always worried about Kayden. She was so precious and he, too, had noticed the growth and who she had grown into. Seeing those two together this weekend, there was no doubt where this new found growth had come from and he was relieved. He also knew that he would be starting his own family soon and because he had been Kayden's only father figure, he was worried how she might take it. Now he could see with his own eyes she was well adjusted. Tony returned to DD's house to catch a shower and headed out to church with DD and her mom. Once he returned home that evening, there was a refrigerator full of Miller High Life

421

and a note left on the countertop for Tony from Martin which read:

> *"What up bruh,*
> *We appreciate the hospitality and I had to get you some beer to show you so. It's the least I could do. They told you that I ain't no reader and shit so I didn't read the letter you wrote moms but I just had to squash all the bullshit. The past was the past bruh. We were both in the wrong at some time or another. Let's let that shit go and move on with life. My concern is for my sister and not knowing you made me worry. I was going off word of mouth and things can get easily misconstrued with the he said, she said shit. If DD and Kayden are taken care of and as far as what I can see they are, so we are good. We all had fucked up childhoods and affected our actions as grown up but let's change the process. Let's give the next generation of Kayden and Lita's crew, your and my future kids a loving, caring black family that so many of us never had. I'll be honest nigga, we are family now so let's make the family a happy and tight one. Come down to Miami when you can and fuck with me nigga. Ideally this could have started years ago but let's go from here.*
> *P.S. I ain't no author either so sorry about the handwriting.*
>
>

Martin"

It was like a small miracle to see God having worked on so many hearts. It was amazing and as if that wasn't amazing enough, after church when they were leaving the car, Kayden called Tony Daddy for the first time in their history. DD's mother's face turned ghost white as she and Tony were the only ones to have heard it and that made for some extra praise in church that morning. Weeks later, she, having the chance to go to Miami with her mom for the weekend, which she loved, she turned down to stay home with Tony and Angel. She had really grown to love him. God had truly blessed him and he was amazed at his journey. He did his best to hold it down but he shed a few tears praising God's name on these great matters of the heart. And at that very moment reading Martin's letter, he felt similarly and a few did fall for the glory of God.

*   *   *   *   *

Hey baby! I wanted to write you a little love letter. Lately I have felt more love and more in love than ever before. I feel accepted by you, mind, body and soul, flaws and all. Your love with the absence of judgment and the desire to share everything with me is amazing! Finally, I have found and KNOW love without restraint. After years of tearful prayer, I now share with you a love relationship that I feel totally FREE! I do not feel afraid of showing you who I am at any time of any day. I am not terrified of losing you because I know I have flaws I cannot ever begin to fix. I BELIEVE that you are not disappointed in my lack of perfection. You are not considering me a mistake every time I mess up. We are working together to be better people and a better couple overall. We have a family Tony. We have a family. Not just you and yours, and me and mine. We have a family that is OURS baby! The joy that brings my heart is inexplicable! You are so amazing to me! I am so impressed by you Tony! This last month or so, since you decided to make me happy, you've done just that! In spite of your fears, in spite of our past, in spite of my hard words and stance, you have stayed in and not fallen to the way side. I am totally taken, like a Gone With The Wind take my breath away moment, every time I see you now. I am more excited about being in love with you now than I have EVER felt before!! It's almost impossible to explain!

"I have never felt as excited about a single solitary relationship in my entire life. The manifestation of God's presence, love, grace, mercy and forgiveness between us gives me and my heart permission to finally let go and experience JOY! Not happiness, not enjoyment, FAR MORE than contentment. BECAUSE OF YOU, I know joy. An essence, an outpouring of

delight that is rooted deep within my heart. It's the kind of feeling that cannot be taken away by the tedium of everyday life or the futile fumblings of the devil against me. It is a sense of peace about my very existence. You bring me joy. You brought me to it and your face, your smile, your eyes and your lips (thank ya Jesus for them) are all through my joy. It smells of you, it looks like you, it sounds like you, it feels like you, my joy. I am so grateful to you. I am so thankful to us for fighting through the deserts so we could make it to the promised land.

"A constant evolution into more and more of our greatness within the glory of our Father keeps me encouraged. I get frustrated but no longer get discouraged. I get sad but no more depression. I get upset but not overwhelmed by those old demons that used to saturate every aspect of my life. I never really understood that old saying "love conquers all." But now, I know first hand that a love like this can beat anything! Skeletons, devils, ex's, baby mamas, baby daddies, finances, fears, history and ourselves!! Our love has overcome all of these things!

Love DD

Tony found this letter in his lunch bag that Monday morning and once again could not stop himself from feeling emotional about so much wonderfulness in his life. God had led him to the very real understanding that He loved him and therefore everything was possible. And each step Tony had taken, each difficult movement, there God was taking the other nine, "He is such an awesome God!" Tony said, as he refolded the letter and put it in his pocket.

DD's family left that weekend and things felt brand new for everyone. He finally felt affirmed and wanted. For the first time, DD was lifted from black sheep and could join the part of her family she seemed to desire and love the most. And with that, Tony was also lifted. Day after day and week after week, they moved in the family way and things were awesome. It had been the best it had been all the years they had been together.

They hadn't yet made the decision to live with one another but DD and Kayden stayed with Tony almost every night. They had evolved into a regular routine. DD would drop Angel and Kayden off to school in the mornings and go off to work and either Tony or Sharon would pick them up, depending on if Tony had a meeting after work or not. Tony never did return to the social work job at CPS.

He took another teaching job, two counties over, because it was one of the best in the state to work for, not to mention it had the best union in the state. He was being paid better than he ever had to teach in the state of Florida and he was doing the exact same job under much better circumstances and he could see his life forming before him. One of the things he knew he was responsible for was to always be sure he could support this family financially. Each time he made a move, he made better money. He felt really good about that. Even still, in order to do his job effectively, especially splitting the incomes between two households, it would still take coordination. This meant that there had to be cooperation between the two working adults to ensure all the bills that needed to be paid were paid, and paid on time.

So they didn't incur unnecessary late fees or run into any other trouble that comes from not taking care of bills when you are supposed to. This meant the sharing of information, how much each bill was and how much money each of them made. For Tony, this wasn't a problem because he had been doing this for almost as long as he was an adult, having lived with Sharon for most of his adult life. But DD was leery to share this information as she had become accustomed to handling her things herself without having to share these types of details with anyone and it had to feel good to her to know that she had someone to take her back if she fell short.

She must have felt like if he knew everything, then there would be no need for that support as Tony would ensure he took care of those things directly. As the information was shared, there were inconsistencies in the money she made and money available for bills. Now Tony knew that women need to feel secure, they need cushions and also something extra to spend on themselves. Sometimes that just wasn't available, especially when there were two households to support and the financial responsibility was so lopsided.

In his mind, this frugal attitude wasn't forever but just until either of them combined expenses when they moved in or at least until they got their bills under control. This meant accounting for every dime between them until all the bills that were behind were caught up and they started a little savings. In his mind, it was the smart way to do things because you never knew what would come up and living paycheck to paycheck was dangerous. If any emergency ever came up, they wouldn't be prepared. This was a constant source of anxiety for DD and this also made for a weekly, if not daily, fight.

Tony knew it was her anxiety but he needed to make her understand that this is how things had to be if they were going to make it. They had to share and they had to trust. DD was having a very difficult time letting go and so struggled with this in a major way. She was nervous most nights, all the packing lunches and getting school clothes and work clothes ready each night, preparing dinners and playing her role as mom and wife under what felt to her like, Tony's watchful eye, was a lot of tension to her. Her nerves were so bad most days that she found herself taking a Xanex, which she had been prescribed previously but had never used but a few times.

She was taking one each evening to get by as her anxiety seemed to rise more and more each day, as did the arguments about damn near everything. Finally she needed to either have a drink or a smoke in addition to the Xanex and that's when Tony knew there was a problem. They talked about it and DD explained she needed both because she only had a few clips of weed

426

left and probably needed like a half an L in order to get straight without the Xanex.

Tony hated to see her this way so he agreed to go along with it so she could ease her tension around the house. She had planned on getting the weed from her dad who usually copped an ounce every other week who would break her off a little piece so she wouldn't have to go out into the streets to buy. For the moment, this was the decided upon solution to their anxiety/arguing problem. After the first couple of weeks, her pop didn't say it but he cut her off and DD needed to find her own way. She was in the midst of running through all her ideas of contacting all her old connects for drugs when TONY decided it was all a bad idea. He did not want her out in the streets and linking up with all her old homies. She was out of that world and he didn't want her back there ever again. He decided he would stand in the gap for her and get what she needed so she didn't have to put herself in that position.

His brother smoked weed regularly. He was a pot head, and he knew that he was a good place to start to get what she needed. Between his brother and his brother's friends, after some weeks Tony had sorted out who the best connect was as far as prices and product through what he brought back to DD and her grading it and telling him what was worth the cost and what wasn't. It came down to him copping an ounce every two weeks of some high grade smoke from a guy across town but that wasn't it.

He had to develop a back up in case this guy got low or got knocked. So there he was with three connects and copping weed every two weeks an ounce at a time and he didn't even smoke. It was like he was in the twilight zone or something. All the things he hated about drugs there he was enduring them all and more for the love of DD. It kept her mellow and sweet and even easier to get along with but it was starting to bother him that she was getting high each and every day now in order to cope. They talked less and less, dealt with one another less and less as she smoked more and more. It had seemed like a good idea at first but now it was a barrier.

Whereas before each Friday they would have a drink, play pool, maybe go to the movies or rent one from the red box and laugh and joke. Now she just got high and sat there baking. There were no more conversations because she was high, so having a conversation with a high person sober was always loopy at best. He stopped drinking because he was drinking alone. Once she smoked she didn't want to drink because it was too much for her, so it was as if he was drinking alone. It felt odd to be drinking solely to catch up to her high. It felt more like alcohol abuse than socializing. So he stopped drinking but she continued getting high and before long it was about supplying her habit while he sat there bored and alone. She got high, she baked, they screwed around and went to sleep.

That was the routine - work, kids, weed, sex, sleep and up the next day to do it all over again. They had eventually grown apart completely. No talking, no hanging out, no friendship. This is what he traded for no arguments or anxiety - a drugged up absentee relationship and some sex. And even the sex lost its luster when he realized that he could have been anyone. As soon as it was over, she fell asleep like a rock and hardly remembered what happened the night before. He was more miserable now than when they fought. At least they had a relationship then.

Even though things were starting to get rocky, they finally moved in together and combined the bills. Things were bad but they had endured worse so he was moving forward in what he still believed was God's will for his life. He hoped this would take DD's anxiety down but it did not and her continuing to smoke drugs each and every night not only didn't stop but she was smoking more in quantity. At first she was smoking a clip, then a half a joint, now she was smoking an entire blunt. He had become responsible for buying her blunts and wrappings, her weed and even the lighters. He was back to feeling like the ho in this pimp- ho equation that he was starting to see was the perception DD lived out her life.

They were even starting to disagree with regard to the children and that was major. She was back in her fears and everything was once again becoming a power struggle. One day, upon confronting Kayden about not doing her homework, DD checked him and not only undermined his authority with her but pretty much took it away as he confronted her in the lie she had told him. DD supported her and Kayden's lie of omission and affirmed her behavior by allowing her to live the double standard that although omitting lies was no good for Tony, the father and supposed leader of the family, if it came up with DD, it would be okay as long as she didn't do it to DD.

This was a major problem and when Tony tried to talk about it to DD, once Kayden returned to her room, she wanted no part of the conversation and placated him until there was nothing left to discuss. Things were going down hill fast. And although after almost seven years, they finally lived together. This was hardly the vision he had in mind for their family. He was starting to think he had gone too far with his compromise. His submission had only served to turn over leadership of their family to DD, who had turned over her mind to the dark places the enemy dwelled. Therefore, this is where his family currently resided. Although he didn't want the fight, he knew would come, it was time to confront these things. It was time to put a stop to this and it was time to finally set this family straight. He had waited too long to have this life to live this low and he knew he was outside the will of God in a major way and that alone he wasn't good with. Something had to change.

Chapter 31
Sharpening the Sword
The First Cut is the Deepest
Matthew 7:6

Things were getting progressively worse at home. DD and Tony hardly spoke unless she was high and then the conversation was usually laughing at something silly or some other meaningless conversation. DD was most often so angry that Tony tried his best not to ask her for anything, or speak to her until she was ready to be spoken to. Unfortunately, that was only once a day after she was already high. The kids weren't even the same. They spoke freely, laughed and played with Tony and one another until she came home. By that time, there was so much tension the kids stopped speaking too. It was the same when Tony wasn't home and it was just DD the kids.

When DD and Tony were together, there was so much tension the kids just went into their own rooms and shut themselves off. This was affecting how much time Angel wanted to spend at his dad's house and also how much time Tony wanted him around this type of environment. It was clear they missed and wanted to be around each other but at that time there was nothing more Tony wanted than to get to the bottom of this question between DD and himself. Not even the love he had for Angel trumped this love of God and his obedience to the answer of this ever burning question. It sounded senseless.

He knew until he followed this thing through, he would only eventually end up right back here at some point in his life. And he was so tired of being tired. He had heard that expression before and previously thought he understood its meaning. Today he could truly say, with a sincere heart, he really did know now and he was so very tired. DD was so angry all the time now and she couldn't hide it any longer. Each time Tony tried to confront it, DD herself never could fully explain it outside of her anxiety. She was coming face to face with all those same demons she had been dealing with in her past. All the compromising of her virtue that she had done for those men flashed in her head now that she was where she wanted to be.

Now the tenderness, love and compassion she should have had for Tony was gone, replaced by fear, anxiety and this gut wrenching anger for deeds, not yet done, but anticipated. She was angry at all those men, all those things, all those times and having no outlet but the loving home they had built. It was Tony who would be the bearer of this burden yet again. He was running out of grace. He was short on mercy and even shorter on patience. His feeling was that he had been paying for these fellows all along. Each time she had to lie, run off, and hide her life and true self from him. Each time she couldn't trust and he had to play the role of the bad guy, it was one of their sins he was paying for. He had been dragged through hell for the sins of those who came before him as he was sure she too had to pay for someone that came before her but the cost was getting to be too high.

One of the greatest messages he had in his head was that she was worth it. In fact, it was one he discussed with her often in the beginning of their love and relationship. He knew full well when many of these things came up what they were and where they came from. He told her in words. Moreover, when he didn't hit the bricks it said that his love for her was ironclad. It was because she was precious to him, she was loved by him and most of all, she was worth it. Worth every bit of suffering. Worth every bit of shame, torment and time he had spent finding the patience, grace and mercy. Funny how she had just used those words in her letter declaring her full blown love for him. How far she had come from that moment?

Today she was so filled with anxiety and anger she just looked like pure evil. One day after working a fourteen hour day, teaching at the elementary school and going directly to the college where he taught night classes, he got home exhausted and asked DD to help him take off his shoes. She was so angry that she looked as if he had asked her for a kidney as she walked over to him screaming and snarling.

"What do I fucking look like? Your fucking maid?" She snapped, as she reached for his hurting and swollen foot. She yanked his foot off the floor as he protested seeing how awful things were going. But she twisted his ankle as if she were trying to rip his foot off. He pulled his foot out of his shoe and her hand. Through the pain, he wanted to snap but he could all but see the horns coming from her forehead. He watched as he could see the enemy coursing through her veins. She reached for his other foot and he pulled it back asking her kindly not to even bother. She snapped again and walked off.

The hours he worked were long and tedious and she had stopped helping him with his work clothes and things around the house. She also stopped preparing meals. Often, by the time he got home she and Kayden would have already have eaten and been in bed. He was being worn down at both ends. Between the long hours and the stress he had to endure at home, his immune system was suffering and he could feel himself becoming ill with something that was threatening to keep him bedridden for a few days.

He knew that would leave him at her mercy, but he wanted to believe he could trust her to do the right thing beyond the rotten emotions she seemed to be stuck in. As the germs and stress finally overtook him the following weekend, he was indeed bedridden as he feared he might be. Not only was DD not there for him as he feared she may not but she wouldn't even fix him a meal, a cup of tea, or anything. In fact, she stayed busy and out of the home for the entire weekend and he ended up needing to take a few days off to nurse himself back

432

to health. They had only been living together for nearly a month now and everything that he could have ever feared was real, and in the flesh. He was living it out and walking through it every day. It was a nightmare to say the least and something had to change. The petty fights and arguments about everything under the sun. The evil and nasty attitude. All of it.

In addition to tearing apart, and undermining the family it took them six years to build, she was physically trying to hurt him. She had informed him of her plans to take Kayden to Miami for Thanksgiving. He was really upset by this as it was going to truly be their first holiday together since they moved in. They had last year but it was ruined by Sheldon and her miscarriage shrouded in mystery and deceit, not to mention all the anxiety they had endured throughout the day. They were finally going to have a real family holiday in the same house that they shared and it upset him to no end that she didn't see it that way. She told him she was giving Thanksgiving to her family and he could have Christmas. It figured to him that she would want him to do Christmas considering how much he spent on the holidays. Why couldn't they get Christmas?

It was silly because he didn't think they should be getting either at this point. They should be spending that quality family time and building up their memories. Later, if her family wanted to share them then they would be equipped to go off to extended family holidays having spent at least one together as a family first. There is so much pressure around the holidays that they themselves buckled under them just last year. There was no way their new family was ready for an extended family get- together at her brother's house. He was tired of being the only one to see things this way and most definitely didn't feel like fighting her to see his vision of family and what these things should be. So when she told him what she intended he didn't say anything; he just nodded and let it go. He was still sick and didn't have the strength to even start a conversation he was sure would end up in a fight.

But more than that, he had so much on his mind he needed to think this entire thing over. It was time to go back to God for discernment; he was at his road's end. He had followed God's will and done everything he was asked to do and this is where it ended. He knew this could not be the will of God. This could not be where God was taking him and his family. He needed to pray, meditate and find his path once again. He needed to check back in with his Father God and find out if indeed this is where the Lord would have him to be. He decided he would take eight days to pray and meditate on these things before he made any decision. He needed time apart to do this and to nurse himself back to health so he could return to work. He gathered up some of his things and packed his truck up and headed for Sharon's.

The home they used to share was comfortable and easy to be comfortable in. It had all of the things he had bought and left there for her and Angel. She had left the altar he made to pray, and he would need it. The significance of eight days in the bible is renewed life and this is exactly what Tony expected at the end of his eight day fast, meditation and prayer.

*　　*　　*　　*　　*

The first day was spent in bed sipping soup, blowing his nose a lot and sleeping. He dropped off into some of the most comfortable sleep he had gotten in about a month. He prayed to God for discernment about his love and aching heart. He was starting to be able to detach himself from the emotional part of himself that was so intertwined in the emotionally crippling relationship that had taken the bulk of his life over the last six- plus years. He knew this was God weaning him from this emotional sickness so he could have a clear look at what the truth of this situation must be.

When he awoke the following day, he took his sword of Ephesians out and began in with the tough questions and what he found were even tougher answers. The burning question was, "What now Lord?" Should he be buckling in for yet another round of submission or should he be asserting himself as the man he was? Was it time to take his rightful place in their family? He knew what his place should be. In her heart, DD did too as they had discussed it many times. Where she was unable to submit, he went within himself to do it for her. It was his intent to show her how to do it while believing she could be trusted. He wanted her to see that he should, and could be as well. But none of this had worked beyond his sacrifice, so it was time for a change. Before he would go to God and seek out DD's heart and his answer from that perspective, he would first search his own and be sure he had indeed been the man he saw himself as. These were the answers he came to in his bible study.

A Faithful Man

(I got you covered, walking you through, letter by letter, follow me. **Hebrews 13:17)** (**Psalms 128:1-4)**

They say a good man is hard to come by,
"But a faithful man, who could find?"
(Proverbs 20:6-7)
I'm longing to feel her **silent** quiver
In a world filled with **thunder.**
I'm looking for destiny
That which requires far more than fancy
BUT will,
The one you must follow in order to receive the promise   **(Hebrews 10:36)**
And the other you will NEED to get you there.
This throne, shall be given by a woman
(Isaiah 16:5)
In faithfulness
and I shall sit upon it.
Like the pollination of many flowers
By millions of bees,
With her this journey shall be of everlasting.
(Jeremiah 31:3)
One that shall bear no ill consequence,
Just honey, Sweet honey,

435

Honey comb,
Honey cut, nuts and honey,
Mo' honey,
My sweet, sweet, **<u>sweet</u>** honey.
(Matthew 7:16)
This world will be filled with romance and my imagination,
Where we'll be holding each other tight
Beneath countless crossed stars
And a moon lit sky,
Wrenched tight to this thing called belief.
(1Corinthians 10:13)
Where fire breathes passion under water.
(Mathew 14:29-30)
A place where ice cream kisses aren't just a dream
You have never known and pretend not to think about.
I'll show you mine, if you show me yours.
(Ecclesiastes 4:9-10)
For this life was meant to be shared
Because "two is better than one"
The question is, and shall always be,
Can you handle it? Can you stand it?
The rain, the pain that coming out of your position to meet me in this place of love requires?
For "A man must discern if she is ready for love."
(Ezekiel 16:8)
So I ask again.
What if my love,
This thing we have waited for all our lives,
felt like "manna" tasted?
(Numbers 11:8)
Would you run?
Think about it, and get back to me
See I'm not here to play games **or** with your emotions. **(Proverbs 28:1)**
I'm here to discover the sonnet of her soul
And all the secrets it posses,
Explore it INCH by ever loving INCH,

For as many YEARS at it may take.
I'm here to figure out this question of you!
(1 Corinthians 2:14)

So let me know. . .
Until then I'll be waiting to write my name upon
those sugar walls
Making love, with only words
Pondering still,
The question of you.

*(***2 Samuel 23:3-5***)*

These words were his hearts desire which he had indeed walked and lived. Having searched himself, he found that there was still quite a bit of romance within him in spite of all those things that said he would never have them, at least from where he was today. It was surprising that he wasn't more negative or even depressed, considering where he was emotionally. It was a true testament to God that he was still so hopeful, still so steeped in faith. Although he was where he was at the moment, this wasn't his life. This wasn't his promise. He wanted these things. He had given these things and therefore deserved to be given them in return. This was the natural order of things and after day two, he was brought this point. So as the bible says about Christ "upon searching himself and finding nothing," he went into day three with the same questions. It was time to consider the other half of this equation and this is where he was lead to. He had written it out as he always did. It was eye opening, frightening and jaw-dropping all at once. This is what he found:

"This is very personal to me. One I never learned. A message I was completely unaware of. This message, however, I have felt in my spirit many a day but never had the spiritual backing nor the clear understanding that comes with the word of God. Knowing this now, something that may seem so simple to so many who have heard these verses before, brings a certain peace over me. I finally understand not only my mistakes, but their products, in a way that I have always

sought but never found until now. I now possess a peace that comes with true understanding, finally making the transformation over to the realm of wisdom that resonates with me in a way that I am filled with courage and renewed faith in God's promise."

This was written by King Solomon, the very man who wrote Songs of Solomon, the greatest love songs and stories known to man. So beautiful, it tells a tale of almost perfect love. Steeped in the hem of God's garment, it is righteous, pure, full of love, fulfillment and true romance which so many of us are searching for in the natural realm. Stuff they make movies and write books about. But King Solomon didn't leave it there. He knew that if he had then we as men would have thought the message and RESPONSIBILITY stopped there, completely ON US! He knew there should be an equal part. We know it takes two; and we also know to expect this relationship to be a partnership. But how many of us have fallen so deep into our faith that we can't look past our duty to forgive, show mercy and give grace to admit that we just might be with a woman that God WANTS US TO QUIT ON. It's hard to hear, especially if you have poured your heart, soul, years, time, love and passion into a relationship for any amount of time. The bible had taught Tony strength and exactly the opposite. Consider these God's words delivered by King Solomon himself.

Proverbs 21:19 It is better to dwell in the wilderness (the desert), than with a contentious and angry woman.

Men get fooled by these women who also know how to cater to their ego at times. They hide their true mal content behind their rights to opinion and for the sake of argument. Argument? Think about it. Do you really want to spend the rest of your life married to a woman you have got to fight until you go home to glory? A woman who may have not reckoned herself with God, her past life, or sins; and will torment you for

438

the rest of your life because you didn't have the wisdom to see her for who and what she is. Now I'm not talking about egotistical, chauvinistic, cave man definitions of women's roles.

Tony wanted a blessed, spiritual, intelligent woman of strength. But one smart enough to know the enemy is out there. A woman who knows the wars, battles and fights can be saved for him and all those he sends against us. He wanted a team, a partnership that doesn't have to fight, but can reason. And when that doesn't work, they can pray and spend time working on the issues within themselves so they don't have to dump them emotionally on each other. He wanted someone who would listen and learn along with him as he gathered up this wisdom that God left for him and his family. But he never did see fighting as a part of that equation. However, some men get fooled into believing that they can fix this. They are strong enough to hold this together. If not them, then certainly their faith would lead them to victory. But what if it is outside of God's will? Then what? The bible says, again through King Solomon,

Proverbs 30:23 for an odious woman when she is married: and a handmaid that is heir to her mistress.

The bible describes the first part of this text as: *An ill-natured, cross-grained woman, when she gets a husband, one who, having made herself odious by her pride and sourness, so that one would not have thought anybody would ever love her, yet, if at last she be married, that honorable estate makes her more intolerably scornful and spiteful than ever. It is a pity that that which should sweeten the disposition should have a contrary effect. A gracious woman, when she is married, will be yet more obliging.*

Tony processed all this information thinking, "So will you fool yourself into thinking your grace, your

439

mercy, your love will be enough to overcome her past hurts, her past injustices, and allow her to see the goodness of the Lord in the land of the living? God's promise of a good man and husband when she didn't believe someone like you existed? Instead of the love and honor that should come when blessed, she is even angrier, which explains much for me. I believe all this is set up by design so that she will seek HIS FACE FIRST. And me as the priest of the home should be dropping her off there, to God, first and foremost."

If he still didn't see it, and compound his folly by taking it a step further, even more awaits. Once again, in Proverbs the bible says:

Proverbs 19:13 A foolish son is the calamity of his father: and the contentions of a wife are continual dropping.

The product of a contentious wife is a foolish son, fathered by and unwise man. And she like that perpetual dripping of a faucet will drive him mad. So says God's word.

This was scary stuff and not what he ever thought he would find. In the past he had found patience, grace and mercy. Why had he not found these verses before now? Most days he read the bible and scoured its pages dogmatically as if he were in the seminary. Why had it taken him all these years to have found these passages and this discernment? It was clear that this was his time to have found them. He was either coming to the end of this lesson and possibly this relationship with DD, or about to have the break through victory he had been praying for all these years. He wasn't certain which. What he was certain of was that at the end of this time, things would be changed forever.

The writing was on the wall. This season was over and he was being moved into the next. He prayed until his knees were sore because as frustrated as he was with DD and the situation, he knew it could be good. He had experienced that much at least. He had loved her from the moment he laid eyes on her. He couldn't say why or how, but he knew it within himself. He missed the way they were and hoped against hope and prayed to the Lord that they could save what it was they had started. The last thing he wanted to do was go back out into the world to seek out yet another love.

He was hopeful that God ultimately had his promise, whether it be with DD, or not. But he was sure hoping to save himself the heartache and time it would take to build that sort of love. After all it had taken more than six years for him to come as far as he had with DD. If they didn't make it, he could only imagine how much longer it would take for him to form the relationship that would blossom into the future, and life, he wanted. It was enough to send someone who wasn't as strong in faith as he was into a slump of depression; but he was still hopeful. In his mind, some time apart and this discovery the Lord had walked him to, would be enough to carry them through; to take them to their next level. It never really did sink in to him that this message he was receiving was not for the two of them but for him alone. Heading into the following day, he and DD had not spoken. Although the messages he found were all about a contentious woman, which should have given him a clue, he was still holding fast to the promise he had received the vision for earlier in his life, and that vision was DD.

For the next two days, however, as he stayed obedient to his call to pray, fast and meditate, he opened himself up to words from others and their interpretations of the word. His favorite inspirational speakers of the word were T.D. Jakes, Creflo Dollar, and Joyce Meyers. He started off with T.D. Jakes who had just released a new series lecture on Submission for the Thanksgiving season. It was touching, to say the least, as it hit on everything he was going through and spoke about letting go and submitting to God even as the things we don't want to do are put upon us. The message was starting to become more clear and he was feeling like these messages were meant for him specifically, and the tears for Christ did flow.

T.D. Jakes talked about the submission it takes to one another in order for marriages to work. He spoke in depth and even went so far as to talk about families who could not and where that took them. It also addressed how to submit yourself onto God when this happened. He spoke of accepting God's will for your life, submitting yourself to his chastening. It was all too much for Tony and he was doing his able best not to break down. Honestly, for as much as he knew, he would accept whatever the answer. It was brought to him through his prayer to the Lord, but he had not truly considered this outcome. He listened to that series for two days before finally he finished it and felt ready to hear something else, something more encouraging.

Truth be told, he was looking to rig the deck and search out a positive message, one he knew would encourage him to persevere once more; a message that would give him the resolve needed to go back into the covenant he had created with DD. He was looking for some word - any word - that would give him permission in God's name. For it was God that had brought him here, and given him the resolve, all these years, to stand here in love. He couldn't see past this place onto that negative resolution. He wasn't really ready.

He decided to listen to the minister he had never heard of before. His name was Jamal Bryant and the message he chose was "Why do people stay?" He was certain this message was one of hope and how to hold on to the word of God to come through your toughest times. Unfortunately, he was right about that much - the holding on part. But it wasn't nearly as hopeful in the direction he was looking for. Mr. Bryant went on to talk about how many people hold on in hopeless situations because they don't truly believe in the word of God. Or, they couldn't exhibit their full faith until they let go during those moments we are tempted to hold on to - those crumbs life throws us out of desperation.

"Crumbs," he thought to himself. Weren't they crumbs? She treated him like a second class citizen. She dishonored him constantly in almost all her ways during their entire existence. Once again he was questioning how he never received this message before now. How had he wasted so much time if this was indeed the message? He was immediately brought to that lesson of "The cross" and how Jesus said if you didn't pick up your cross you weren't "worthy of my love." He was a direct line to God's love for DD. He believed himself her husband and even covered her as such, although they had never gotten far enough to take the leap. In this place, what he was discovering made sense and he was beginning to see the logic, the word and the spirit in this word. He decided to go on and submit himself to this line. After all, if he could not, where was this going? Where was he going?

He decided to stay right with Pastor Jamal Bryant as he was a new minister in his life and he hadn't heard any but one of his messages. He felt lead to him for this moment in his life. Odd that Pastor Bryant had been here this entire time but he had never listened to one of his sermons. There were only ten messages that existed on I-tunes. The message was called "Quit while you're ahead," and it was everything he had hoped and feared. Most messages he was used to hearing from ministers were ones that spoke out against quitting and the temptation to quit on something when it got too hard. But Mr. Bryant questioned that saying, "What if it's God that wants you to quit?"

Tony had never heard that concept preached before and it stunned him to tears once again. He was at work sitting in his portable which was in the very back of the school. There were no other classrooms attached to his so there was no possible way anyone could see him in the snot-nosed, heart-wrenching cry he was passing through at the moment unless they walked up the metal ramp to his door. This would have given him plenty of time to dart into the bathroom and get himself together if they had a key to his room. And since only a

443

select few did, this time he was given to deal with his emotions, he knew could only come from Him who sat on high. He looked at it from the vantage point that all things happen for a reason, in that place where nothing was coincidence. Even the location of his room was purposeful. He allowed himself to delve deep into the word, and Jamal's understanding. He leaned on God's words as he allowed himself to experience those things he had not considered. He allowed himself to face, for the first time, the reality that she was probably not going to stay and he was going to have to face the other side of this outcome he had hoped for.

Just then pastor shouted, "God told me to tell you to let go! You have done all you can do for her. You have taken her as far as you can go with her! And until you let her go, I can't do what I need to for her! God told me to tell you that he has got it from here and it's time to take care of you!"

Oh my God! As he buckled under those words and stood on his feet, he began to pace the room crying uncontrollably. He could not stop himself from crying. He could not pull it together for even the smallest of moments and he was oblivious to all the things around him but Jamal's words. He finally stopped pacing and stumbled towards one of his students' small desks, doubled over it and cried until his tear ducts were dry.

Luke 23:44 And it was about the sixth hour (his sixth year) *and there was a darkness over all the earth* (his world) *until the ninth hour* (It indeed was nine a.m.) *45 And the sun was darkened, and the veil of the temple was rent in the midst 46 And when Jesus had CRIED with a loud voice, he said, Father, into thy hands I commend my spirit: and having said thus, he gave up the ghost.*

Jesus was in the dark? HE QUIT? To hear he quit anything was ground breaking. The Jesus of heaven and earth, who walked on water, who commanded demons out of folk, who took a single loaf of bread and one fish and made a feast? Jesus QUIT?

"Lord speak to me my father. Unto thy hands I commend my spirit," Tony cried.

Jamal shouted, "You have come to the _crucible_ of your life of a CROSS making decision. It is always difficult to quit but there is a WORD WITH YOUR NAME ON IT.

"You cannot quit just because the situation is painful because there is pain in the purpose. Because the race is not given to the swift nor to the outwardly strong, but to those that endure to the end! You have to ask yourself, HAVE YOU COME TO YOUR END? HAVE YOU ASKED FATHER GOD? MAYBE HE HAS LED YOU RIGHT HERE, RIGHT NOW TO HEAR THIS MESSAGE. THAT YOU ARE FREED FROM THIS BURDEN. FREED FROM THIS TORMENT, THIS PAIN. PRAISE GOD! HE, WHO BELIEVETH IN THE SON, IS FREE INDEED. AND THIS YEAR, THE REASON THE LORD HAS GOT TO BLESS YOU IS THAT THIS YEAR YOU LEARNED TO FIGHT THROUGH THE PAIN. EVEN WHEN THE PAIN WAS IN YOU, YOU REFUSED TO QUIT AND YOU REFUSED TO THROW IN THE TOWEL. HEAR ME. FAILING IS NOT THE SAME AS QUITTING. AND BECAUSE I QUIT, IT DOESN'T MEAN I FAILED. FAILING MEANS YOU WILL NOT ATTAIN THE DREAM, THAT THE GOAL WILL NOT BE MET. FAILING MEANS YOU HAVE NO OTHER OPTIONS. FAILING MEANS IT IS NOT IN YOU. CONVERSLY QUITTING MEANS I REALIZE I HAVE ANOTHER OPTION. THIS IS NOT THE END OF ME. I AM GREATER THAN THE SITUATION I'M IN. QUITTING MEANS I'M TOO GOOD FOR THIS AND THEY DON'T KNOW YOUR VALUE. QUITTING MEANS I CAN GO SOMEWHERE ELSE BECAUSE I'M TOO ANOINTED TO BE TOLERATED. I'M SUPPOSED TO BE CELEBRATED!"

Tony could hardly breathe in between sobs and could not believe this man was not speaking to him directly. It was as if God had sent this word to him for this moment.

"Sometimes God will make the situations in your life so unbearable so you WILL QUIT just so he can open up another door to bless you. You are 'more than a conqueror' because you walked away from a situation and not carried away.

"Coping is a bad alternative to quitting. You're fasting and they are eating. They have taken your kindness for weakness. They always think you are going to be their rescue agent. And when you can't show up they are mad at you? What is it you have to quit right now that you can't fix? Trying to be the SUPER GLUE! When is the right time to quit? When sticking to it is killing me? Jesus teaches us that it's ok to quit. There Jesus was with all the responsibility of the world and all its sin. Before Calvary when he wanted to quit and he said, 'Father, let they will be done.'

"You see, when Jesus said in *John 19:30 ITS FINISHED*, it was done. Sometimes it needs to be finished in your spirit as it is in the tangible. When there are no more conversations or agreements, no more reasoning and apologizing. Don't send me no more cards or chocolate. I'm finished. You don't need to call to see if I'm ok. I'm alright. I'm finished with you! While JESUS WAS IN THE *CRUCIBLE* OF HIS LIFE, ALL THE TORMENTS AND SUFFERING he endured upon his way to the cross, it wasn't until he endured that he was allowed to quit. And the bible said in *John 19:30 and then he hung his head and GAVE UP the ghost.*

"It wasn't until he said, 'Now Father, I commend into thy hands' could God go to work. The entire time he was on the cross, God did nothing. But as soon as he put it in God's hands, it was then that God said, 'now take him off the cross, bind him and put him in the tomb.' And three days from then, he was risen in the very spot! God has been waiting for you to quit so he

446

can start working on your behalf. As soon as you take your hands and worry off of it, he can deliver you onto your blessing and not a moment sooner. That's when GOD can show up! While you're trying to figure it out, the Lord has already WORKED IT OUT! TAKE YOUR HANDS OFF OF IT! You cannot fix this. But what you can't do, I can do if you trust and believe in me. There is nothing too high for my God."

And like that Tony got a release in his spirit like the first time he had ever gotten the good news that HE IS RISEN! PRAISE AND BLESS GOD. And he wept. He cried tears like a NEWLY BORN, FRESHLY BORN, REBORN BABY. His faith was renewed and a peace came over him. All at once, he let it go with God. All his worries about tomorrow, all his pain and suffering, all the things DD had done to him, all the things he didn't believe would ever come to pass, all the things the liar had sold him about who he was and what he didn't deserve, who he had been, who he was today, all the lies, all the crutches, all the footholds the enemy had over his mind, were at once broken. And he made up his mind with a renewed spirit, with a truly RENEWED MIND, he was going with GOD.

*   *   *   *   *

Tony had spent the rest of day five praying and reading the bible. He knew he had been brought to the right and correct place. Had he not been exposed to the possibility of this reality he would have gone into the meeting he had called with DD for that evening ill-prepared. He felt a peace over himself that he hadn't had for awhile now. He was certain that everything he had learned the day before was true within him. It was time to turn this thing over to God and stop pushing this boulder uphill on his own. He knew he had done everything humanly possible. Now it was in His hands and he had walked DD to God. If it was his will that they make it, then they would.

That night, he went back home to sit down with DD. To his surprise, as they sat down, DD's eyes weren't red and she didn't appear high. She appeared sober, but anxious. He had a calmness about him that made DD more and more nervous as their conversation went on. He walked her through all the word he had been led to and his desire to be placed in the position of man and leader in their family. He wanted her to allow him to lead. He wanted her to consider where she had left him in her desire to be high every night. He wanted her to see how her choices were undermining their family and his ability to lead. He needed her to address her anger and deal with those things that made her want to twist his foot off or snap at him; all those things that said when he was sick, she couldn't bring him a cup or soup or care for him. He was tired of being a second class citizen and he said so. He finally had the courage to say what he was feeling about his submission and where it had taken them in the world and the eyes of God.

He expressed his desire to have a full family holiday together and what it would mean to him and their family. When he was done, she expressed how horrible she felt that she had put him through so much, and Kayden too. Kayden hadn't slept since Tony left. Each night she went into DD and Tony's room looking for him and when he wasn't there got in their bed and cried herself to sleep. On the other hand, she expressed her opposition to spending the holiday anywhere but with her extended family saying that he was trying to keep her from her family. Tony calmly went over the fact that he never tried to keep her from them. In fact, if she searched herself, she would remember that he had accepted them and they him. He had always supported her going there, even when he didn't want her to. She acknowledged that and started to go into her thoughts about her decision and what she may, or may not, want to do. Tony stopped her and told her he had prayed for an answer and was expecting it the EIGHTH day and that day was tomorrow.

"I want you to pray on it. Ask God for discernment and sleep on it. We will talk tomorrow," Tony said, as he stood up.

DD seemed shocked and couldn't believe he was still leaving after all they had come to. She was visibly upset and he could see the tears in her eyes. He touched her faced to comfort her and said, "It's ok my love. We are going to be fine baby," as he smiled.

Tony drove off that evening with high hopes that this conversation and how he handled it - maybe even his courage -had been enough. The dead end fate he saw was not set in stone. He was encouraged by DD's reception of all their shared words and he fell asleep with love on his heart yet again.

The following day however was another story. As the hours walked by painstakingly, he was dying inside as he waited for DD's answer. He called but she did not pick up. He texted with no response. Finally, at the end of his work day she texted him back and told him that after almost seven years, it was over. She had already been home and removed her things. She had been to the school and gotten Kayden's records and withdrew her. She was leaving for Miami tonight and he would never see her or Kayden again. And so it was. After six plus years, all he had endured, and so many tears, years and hours spent on his knees praying, she was gone with but a mere text message without regard to his or Angel's feeling. She was just gone.

Chapter 32
Sheath the Sword
Ghost Dog

The following days were hard and went by like a blur. It was so difficult to believe that only a mere few weeks ago, he and his would-be family had shared this same home that felt so empty now. He refused to give in to the sorrow and depression that lurked in all the shadows of his mind amongst all the would-have, should-have possibilities that still lingered. He was letting go. This meant moving on in the very same fearless faith he had pushed into this entire ordeal in the first place. He had not called nor texted DD since her text about it being over. He was shocked as to how she communicated it to him. If she was going for devastation, she had attained it. He couldn't believe someone could be so cold-hearted; not just to him. He could possibly understand that but to Angel and Kayden too? Wow! That was a blow. She treated him as if he was some sort of domestic case she was fleeing from. But that, too, he had to let go.

Undoubtedly, she had learned that move from someone who had done something similar to her and devastated her as much. She was truly living out the predatory portion of her predator/prey mentality. He wasn't going to dwell on it once he got past the shock of the whole matter because he was certain that what went around came back around so nothing good would come of it. He had to decide what to do with the last of her things. He didn't want to call or text and he didn't want to see her again; not ever after an ending like that. So he decided to email her and keep his distance. He wrote:

"DD, I respect your decision; truly I do. I am just concerned with Kayden and how she is, or will, take this whole thing. I really do love her and am going to

miss her dearly. So is Angel. He is going to be so hurt when he truly finds out he lost his sister. Anyway, as I said, I respect your decision but out of love for Kayden, I am reaching out again. I have not made a move so as to give you another day to make up your mind completely. Today is that day. I figured maybe you, like Haggar and Abraham, might have made an emotional decision and God, or one of his angels, might call you back before you walk away from this blessing we call our life and family. I have taken my hands off of you and this so God can intervene on my behalf. I am not seeking to influence your decision one way or the other. I am not asking you to come home. I am not trying to beg you back or bring you to your senses. I am just giving you this day to have some more time to figure this thing out so you can make a decision based in your reason, wisdom and possibly spiritual discernment. But I don't know. You could very well feel like you already have.

For the record, I will say once again, if I need to, I am not unhappy with you or our life. I just need it to grow because the season in our life has obviously changed. I know you aren't ready and that is okay; seldom are we ready. I did not kick you out. I did not ask you to leave or leave me. To the contrary, I wanted you to stay; just not in the same way you, or we, have been. But I completely understand if that is too much. I'm not the same man I was last year, six months ago, three months ago, or even a month and a half ago. Hard to believe but when you are ready, you can move mountains if you can just get out of His way and allow him to. Submission; to God and this journey. Anyway, I am talking far too much. If I don't hear from you, if you never get this message until next week or whenever you decide it's time to check your messages and even then decide to never respond, its cool too. I got my answer. And if that is the case, I will do my absolute best to only write you one more time, more than likely tomorrow or the day after. But if you don't get this message, and I don't hear from you at all today then I will assume you have made your final decision; and it and I are no

451

longer on your radar or agenda. I will act accordingly. I love you DD and am very sorry that you have decided to do this. But please stop putting it on me. You are not leaving because you can't please me. As with everything else you have struggled through, this isn't about me. Please let Kayden know I love her very much. In my heart, although I could never be her father, I will always be her DADDY. I will continue to pray for you.

Tony

       Two days later, after no response he sent this email to DD:

"Ok well I didn't want to call you or text. I don't want to push in on your time with your family or take anymore from your life than you already feel I have. Therefore, I am writing you this e mail. I wanted to let you know I moved all your things out into the garage. Everything you left in every closet and room, even the garage here is there. There are a few exceptions; those being the art on the walls. I decided to keep it. I know you don't care and probably didn't want it anyway. But they mean something to me and I don't mind looking at it at all so I kept them. The code over there is 1236. I'm sure you probably remember. All you have to do is punch in 1236 then the "Enter," or bottom button and this will open the garage. It's the same to close it. Anyway, that is everything. I have NOTHING else of yours left here. I am DEEPLY saddened by your decision and wish things were different but there is absolutely NOTHING I can do to change it. I will respect your decision completely. I can't promise this will be my last word but I can promise that I'll do my best not to ever bother you again. I know in your past you have completely disappeared from the lives of those you left behind. I pray that this won't be the case with me, but again I have no choice. I wish you and baby Kayden the absolute best. If I, or you, forget anything, I will be right here for you to contact by email and I will contact you as

well. Take care, I love you and Kayden.
Tony"

Two weeks later Tony finally got this message in return from DD:

Hello! I have been scared to say anything and scared of opening my emails. I picked up my things today. The only thing that I do not see is the things I wrote on your other computer that is behind the orange chair in the bedroom. I am heart-broken right now as well. I asked God to tell me what to do and I was told to let go. I don't know why and can't begin to imagine what life will be without the future I imagined with you. I don't mind keeping in touch via email. I am just very anxious and fearful of anything more right now. Not because you are dangerous or anything, but because it's just a part of me. I am very sorry. I know I am hurting you very deeply. One thing you said did stand out to me though. You were on an eight day renewal with God at the time I was asking for my answer. You took your time while I was getting my message. God's will is to be done in our lives and it appears that while both of us hoped for something different that this was the answer we got. I will always love you Tony. You are beautiful and I wish you nothing but the best. God's promise will be fulfilled in your life and it will be greater than any dream you ever possessed. I am so sorry you had to hurt to get there. I love you.

I love you,
DD

Tony was true to his word and his last message was his last message truly that. He walked firmly in the path that the Lord had laid straight for him. He prayed that dear God would lay one just as straight for her. Two months later, Tony got this message:

Hello Tony,
I hope you and Angel are doing well. I am contacting you now to make a humble request. <u>Please</u>

453

may I have a copy of the story I began in your computer and the first short story I wrote with you. I lost my job, and while looking for other employment I am trying to enter some poetry contests. I hope that you can return those works to me. If you want to email them, feel free. I pray for you and your family and hope that you have found peace, love, understanding and support. If you find this email upsetting, I apologize. I tried everything else I could think of before I reached out to you again. I am sorry to have to interrupt your world again. I know you understand creation and how important my work is.
DD

Tony recognized the potential for no good and smelled a rat in the fact that she had to mention she lost her job. No doubt she was fishing for his superman, but "that nigga dead," he laughed to himself. He never responded to her nor contacted her again. He was on to better things. He had a date with destiny and needed to get himself together to get out there. He immediately got back into working out and started running distance races as his new found hobby. It had only been two months and he was back down to about the weight he was when he had met DD; a svelte 245lbs. Once again he was back on the market, looking good and headed for better. He was so ready to get to the good and all that he KNEW God had in store for him.

*   *   *   *   *   *
*   *

"And a woman spoke, saying, tell us of
Pain.
And he said;
Your pain is the breaking of the shell
That encloses your understanding.
Even as the stone of the fruit must break,
That its heart may stand in the sun, so must
You know pain.
And could you keep your heart in wonder
at the daily miracles of your life, your pain

454

would not seem less wondrous than your
joy;
And you would accept the seasons of your
heart, even as you have always accepted
the seasons that pass over your fields.
And you would watch with serenity
Through the winters of your grief.

Much of your pain is self-chosen.
'It is the BITTER POTION by which the physician
within you HEALS YOUR SICK SELF.
Therefore trust the physician, and DRINK
HIS REMEDY in silence and tranquility:
For his hand, though HEAVY AND HARD, is
guided by the tender hand of the Unseen,
And the cup he brings, though it burn
your lips, has been fashioned of the Martin
which the Potter has moistened with His
own sacred tears.

KAHLIL GIBRAN-
The Prophet

THE BITTER POTION – *After a time, once one has
done some measure of healing. Having dealt with
enough truth to get in the back of that closet, he may
reach for the largest and most heavy stone. One he may
have previously considered too heavy to levy against
one's own rational reality in those moments we were the
most out of our minds. When we can take the veil off and
look at things as they really were and deal with them
honestly. It does not mean that they are necessarily
accurate or that they be completely full of infallible
truths but only that we face them. Move that stone out of
your closet and drink that bitter potion for it holds the
key to your healing. Rarely can any one person be called
completely bad but during the time of removing these
shadows, these doubts you have to get out your biggest
broom, your BULL (shit) Dozer and block out what may
be under normal circumstances good, in order to
maintain your resolve to heal yourself. Tony had finally*

455

reached that point. A point of just as much pulling as pushing, pushing the bull out, while allowing himself to pull life in. It was tough, as were his thoughts and even judgment at this time; but he was only human.

*   *   *

She stood five feet eight inches tall, 135 lbs of curvaceous sexiness. She had hazel eyes so intense they burned right through you. She was a dance instructor so she stayed fit; with an ass and abs so tight you could bounce a quarter off of them. Her name was Shawna and she was the perfect picture of southern beauty. She had lived in Georgia her entire life. She was a therapist with a thriving practice in the Atlanta area which kept her tremendously busy, so her time was valuable.

Tony knew how important he must be to her for her to fly back into town purely for a date with him. She had a master's degree as well as a doctorate in her field and was super bright. The amazing part about it for him was that neither her accomplishments nor intelligence frightened him at all. She was so down to earth and easy to talk to. Her sense of humor was so laid back and they would literally talk and laugh for hours. She was an easy-going person with a personality to match.

DD had the most amazing legs he had ever had the pleasure of being with and when she left, she took those legs with her. He swore since it took so long to find them in the first place that he would never see another set so fly. He couldn't have been more wrong. In fact, Shawna's legs were more toned and longer as she was taller than DD and he really liked long legs. Additionally, she actually had an ass to go with those thighs, a fact he over looked with DD in his daze of love. He was now able to see the flaws in DD which he overlooked. DD's abs were non-existent. She walked around with a stomach that almost always looked like she was in the early part of pregnancy. Shawna had no such concerns; she was everything DD was not. Since meeting Shawna, he hadn't even thought of DD except to compare her deficiencies.

Shawna was refined, classy, educated and always carried herself like a lady. She didn't swear, not even when she joked. She never got loud, neither when she joked nor was upset. This was absolutely the most pleasant part of being with a real lady. She was intelligent and not afraid to speak as such. She was a lady and not afraid to present herself as one everyday. She had low-cut hair that she had recently allowed to grow out. It was wonderfully curly and she kept it immaculate. She was quite unlike DD, who wore her hair in a bun so tight it only looked like a bald guy with a knot on the back of his head. She refused to look like a lady or even remotely attractive. In fact his family referred to her as "his man" behind their backs because she looked and, most of the time, behaved like a man. She was loud and vulgar and because she had spent time courting women, she did have some bull-dagger tendencies. This always made him uncomfortable because he never knew who was going to show up. Either she was going to behave like a slut and hit on his male friends or she was going to flirt with the women she either brought around or they came in contact with. Consequently, he kept no friends and they hardly went anywhere to keep them from the fights that were sure to come. She walked like a butch as well, very heavy footed and always slouched whether sitting or standing.

All of these things he overlooked in his state of love. It was truly a God thing because he saw all of these things but refused to see her as simply those things. He thought of all the stories she told him about guys who accused her of being a man, when she was out trying to prostitute herself. All of the grotesque stories she had told him about the abuse and ridicule she endured by those who said they loved her but never treated her that way, he knew she didn't know what beauty was. Although, for a time when she was young, she was certainly attractive. He knew that even if she didn't know that beauty was skin deep, the way she walked, talked, behaved, took care of herself, or lack thereof, all said she was tragically ugly. Despite it all, he had mined her out of the darkness and soot, and led her to the beauty of God the father and all His love. Even though she was treated like a lady and loved greater than she had ever experienced previously, she was never a reflection of that light and love of him or the Father. Sometimes you can grow and become a swan but still act like a mud duck. Although she had a closet filled with dresses she only put anything nice on when she was headed to work or Miami to party with her sister, brother and mother.

In that regard she came by it honestly, as they all got high daily, sat around drinking, talking and laughing loudly. It was ironic that somewhere along the line their mother learned how to be a lady and was soft spoken, intelligent and always looked nice. Neither DD nor her sister ever respected that. In their rebellion, they worked extra hard to appear vulgar. He never did understand why they didn't see the example their mother tried to present for them, until he finally saw their mother getting high and then drink with them. She even ran to the same club with them night after night, party after party. She was a fifty-something woman still running to the club behind her twenty-something children. She was drinking the same drinks and doing the same drugs. Why would they respect her or her way?

She hadn't learned any more than they had. In fact, they viewed themselves above her because they were doing the very same things she was, only earlier in their lives. She was the sad old broad they got to laugh at, who was worse off than them. It was really sad how they isolated her and treated her like she was completely insignificant whenever they felt like making themselves feel bigger. For the most part, from the time he knew her, she turned out to be a really decent person with a lot of wisdom to impart once she stopped with the open hypocritical judgment of others. She was sensitive and kind and always seemed to be considerate where her children weren't. Once she got high or drunk she would sink to the gutter with her children. This is who they came to view her as. In their eyes, this was truly who she had become.

The ultimate lesson she had taught them was judgment of others and they were the best at it. They could pick apart anyone or anything; find the negative in a spiritual. They were not only negative towards others but, secretly, back bitters of each other. Unless you maintained your distance, nothing good in their realm could survive. It was honestly sad because individually they were okay but together they were like crabs in a bucket; never allowing each other to get too far from the group. With the exception of the youngest child, DD's brother, he escaped that persecution because he was rich and provided them a meal ticket. But if he didn't do what they thought he should do with his time or money, he was back in the bucket just like everyone else. He didn't mind paying for his position. In fact, he flaunted his position, choosing when or if he would decide to help his equally co-dependent siblings and mother.

Tony watched as he allowed his second oldest sister and her three children to lose their home, vehicles and file for bankruptcy while he was sitting on millions. Ironically, during that same time Del had lost his job as the economy went bad, and Martin visited with them in their home, drinking, smoking and partying in the very living room they were on their way to losing. They sat there hoping against hope that if they entertained him, he might show kindness and save the life they had built for themselves there in Tampa. He didn't. As they suffered and moved from state to state trying to figure out what they were going to do, he laughed, partied and dropped thousands in the strip and night clubs, night after night. He literally partied with their monthly bill money, blowing more than that amount nightly. He often joked about it with them to add insult to injury.

He told his sister point blank, "When you are ready to top fucking up your life following that dummy there, you can come by me and I'll look out for you. But until you leave from there I ain't really trying to help you."

And it wasn't until they agreed to move down to Miami from Atlanta, where they were living since they lost their home, did he give them any substantial help. Once they moved there, he helped his sister Linda get a job, a new car and a new home, while he allowed Del to remain ignorant and unable to provide for his family. Del was in a position to never be a man for his family. Her brother, the children's Uncle was the man of their family, simply due to his money and his manipulation to keep them subservient to it. Because of a training that said that this sort of thing was the thing to do, everyone remained fearful of leaving the circle for fear of failing in their family's eyes.

Their oldest son was on his second retention and still couldn't read, while his father, feeling ostracized and emasculated as a father and man, wouldn't lift a finger to do anything about it. He simply developed an apathetic attitude. This completed his submission to castration in the form of their lust for money, party, drugs and wine. This served two purposes. Firstly, it kept his sister in control of that relationship. Because as long as her husband submitted unto the brother, he would, by proxy have to submit to the sister and the mother depending on what her status was in the family circle at the time. Therefore, the sister ran the relationship. She had the only job to support the family through the brother. And when the husband finally decided to try to do something himself, they allowed him to pursue some ridiculous dream of customizing and detailing cars in an economy where most people were struggling to keep their vehicles.

Encouraged by his wife and financially supported by the brother, once he failed, it was one more reason why he couldn't be a man, bread winner or supporter of his family. It would serve as one more reason why the decisions and leadership needed to be left to Linda. The second purpose was to keep Linda dependent upon Martin. By breaking Del, this left Linda vulnerable to the world and in search for cover. As the bible tells many tales of vulnerable women who were covered by family, this woman had a husband and should rightfully have been covered by him. But she would be covered by her brother who in essence took her husband's place and ran their family. Her husband was then reduced to Martin's errand boy, doing things that even Martin felt was beneath him.

Linda talked to him terribly, even in front of his children; what a sad thing to witness. They all sat around, including his wife and privately ridiculed him. As was the family's way, Linda was also mocked when she wasn't present. Tony was certain they had ridiculed him and his relationship with DD too; but he kept his distance. Tony knew if he intended to grow and become the man he intended to be, he could not do it hanging out with people who were not trying to do the same. He needed to be around positive people, who were on his level or higher. He didn't get high, nor did like, or go to clubs. He was not a party guy. He was a grown-assed man who was about accomplishing something with his life other than trying to corner off a portion of someone else's millions. He was not going to get his kingdom, his throne, his million dollar blessing watching, spending and counting someone else's money. If he never got to be a millionaire, his kingdom would be fruitful. And from what he saw, there was no fruit in that. Del's willingness to leave his wife and children to the whim of her family out of fear ain't no man as far as Tony was concerned. Del sold his soul for a system and tradition that equaled nothing more than death. The worst part about it all was that they were killing each other with their enmeshed codependent relationships. The hooks were in so deep they didn't know what life was without them.

Out of all the great things they could be doing with that money and the all the time these people had on their hands everything was self-serving or completely carnal. If even one of these people would have set their sights on doing God's work at one of the thousands of schools or neighborhoods, it would have created such a spark, a flame, or passion. He never doubted that the riches they all sought behind Martin's money could have all been had ten fold. Sadly, they all lived for today. Whatever they couldn't obtain in a microwave moment wasn't worth the time spent to have it. Therefore, ALL of their relationships were corrupted beyond what that person brought to the table to serve them. Anyone of substance with any sort of light couldn't stand. They would be chewed up and spit out without a moment's thought. This sort of manipulation and treachery was rampant among them and par for the course.

DD's brother had told her the very same thing he had told Linda, "When you get tired of fucking with old boy, you can
come down here and I'll help you. Until then I'm not helping you do much of shit."

This was the golden parachute, the back door offer that was always looming over Tony's head when he wouldn't do what he was "supposed to do" by her, according to her of course. She had threatened him with it many times, directly and indirectly. At some point, it had absolutely become a major influence in their relationship. He realized that he had to face this barrier, just as he had to face all of the pressure for him to join the group and the ranks of the dead. This was one of the things he prayed on when he made the decision to give her the ultimatum. This was one of the factors he knew kept him from being the man of that family completely. And ultimately it ended up being the very thing it was intended to be, the influence for lust of money, the choice in sin, rather than choosing herself, God, her life and family. She pulled that rip cord and away she flew as if he and the last six years never existed. He could see it all. Yet he was still amazed at the precision and magnitude of the process. At the same time, after being confronted with so much truth, light and success, it was staggering to watch her walk right back into the same fears, insecurities, bad influences and relationships; the hell she just escaped from. If it was one thing Tony understood, it was the power of fear. It, too, had ruled his life for a very long time as the enemy was a powerful liar. Attended to by the renewing of your mind, backed by faith and solid work, you have a chance. But it is only a chance, not a certainty. But in order to have any of it, you have to choose it.

She chose to walk back into the same old dead friends, including the girlfriend who secretly didn't want to see her do better than she was. This woman laid traps, minefields and stumbling stones in her path towards anything good, but was quick to take her out to do sin. She would run to the club when she had a good man. This friend led and left her in the arms or better yet, the bed of another man who intended to have nothing to do with her but sin and sex, usury and self degradation, all the while claiming that she loved her. This however, was the sort of relationship she was used to. This is what she recognized as love; all she knew of love and loyalty. It was a place where good intentions and a good heart outweighed someone's contrary actions overall. It is what her birth family taught her and sadly was still passing on this same family curse to them.

"The seeds of the father shall be revisited upon the son."

But DD was her screwed up friend, the one who had all the problems, all the drama, who she could hang out with and feel better than. She was the friend she could typically call on at any time in her life to ask to do something foolish, like run to the club, hang out, spend that time doing nothing and she would always be there, always be down. She used to say that Tonya was there for her so many times and in so many ways she would always be eternally grateful. As long as she was doing horrible, they were tight, but when she dug herself out of that hole with Tony, Tonya was gone, blaming Tony for her departure. Does that sound like friendship? To judge you for your choices? He wasn't beating her, emotionally, physically or mentally abusing her. He was asking her to question herself and her choices for herself and her daughter. And as her life started improving, as

463

she found God and life, this is when you leave? Doesn't sound like friendship at all. In fact, it sounded like the same back biting manipulation her family used by holding their love and money for ransom. She either did what they thought she should do or she would be cut off.

Tony's family, at some point, tried to do that same thing to him but he rebelled, understanding even then that victory had to be gained by confrontation and not retreat. He had to move all the way to Florida to wean himself off of sick relationships and deeply buried hooks that were anchored in black holes filled with pain. When he finally came back, he was far less codependent and was beyond their manipulation.

On the other hand, she returned to the same old friends, those who used her, watched her stumble and fall, and belly crawl during her worst of days and stood by and did nothing. They heard her crying out for help and did nothing. They didn't have the ability to pull her from that death because they themselves lived among it. Therefore, even if they did have the ability to do so, they wouldn't anyway because everyone knows misery loves company. She sought out her old boyfriend Myqual and a host of others, including Kayden's corrupt father who prostituted her in the streets and strip clubs, beat her while she was pregnant and raped her afterwards when she refused him sex. She befriended all the ex lovers, ex boyfriends and old cut buddies she and Tony fought over the last time he caught her cheating on him. She was right back in the same old place, FACEBOOK.

"I swear the creator of FB has got to have a special place in hell," Tony thought, as he shared a little chuckle to himself.

She went back to the same drug users that lead her down that same path of depression and suicidal tendencies and feelings. She went back to the same casual sex that stole her light and killed her soul before they had ever met. But worst of all she went back to the same codependent and manipulative relationships that never gave her any real support for her life, love or the healthy rearing of her daughter. It was indeed sad that she couldn't see any of those things or how down right ugly they all made an otherwise beautiful girl.

One afternoon past the NFL lockout, Tony awoke to find DD's brother, the same brother who told DD she would never have to worry for a thing and how she should leave Tony, had been cut and lost his job at the meat end of his contract. Tony was hurt to have heard such horrible news. Martin and Tony had buried that beef years ago but it did ring in his head those hurtful words nonetheless. He searched the net to find out more and found that DD had lost her job, yet again and was once again totally reliant upon her brother who had just gotten married months ago, and was now unemployed. Tony found it so sad to find this young man who had worked so very hard his entire young life, who was responsible for so many people around him, had refused to put in a fraction of his effort towards anything meaningful in their lives. If any of them would have put forth a piece of the effort that they spent on all the hair-brained, half- baked ideas that they wasted his money on, they may have made something of themselves.

It's funny because if anything, considering the situation, one would think that he would have felt more compassion for a single mother who was once again unemployed in this cold hard economy. It would seem like under any circumstances that this person deserved more compassion than any millionaire that the NFL had created. However, Martin was a hard worker and although in his younger, more brash days he said some things uncalled for, Tony recognized that today he was caught in no better of a position than he was just a mere few months ago. He was stuck helping someone whom he loved dearly out of a hole in life that not even money could fill. Money is a powerful resource, one the Lord put here to serve us as much as any other resource. Used wisely, the blessing could take you and your family into untold places of freedom and joy. It requires wisdom and humility as a fool and his money are shortly parted and you know what the word says, "It is easier to squeeze a camel into the eye of a needle than it is for a rich man to go to heaven."

For the second takes much humility, which generally isn't associated with monetary wealth. He had to come to this difficult place on his own and undoubtedly at this stage of their relationship, although Tony doubted seriously that Martin would ever give up, he knew that Martin was at a minimum seeing things a bit differently. This is a woman who would rather lay on her back and sell her body, dance naked on a pole somewhere while men groped and fondled her body than to go forth and truly better herself. After all, this took work, hard, committed work; the very same things she ran from in him. It had made sense to Tony months ago; if she wasn't willing to commit herself to God and his teachings, commit herself to her very own struggle, who was Tony in the grand scheme of things? She used to tell him that he motivated her, that he could get her to do things that she would not otherwise do for herself. He always took that with a grain of salt but he knew by the end that this was far truer than he had ever given credence. You see, for their entire relationship, Tony had made huge misjudgments in calculations. He had bought DD's lines and con games that they were of like mind, that they were headed in the same direction, that she was actually going to be a contributor in a meaningful way in their life. These things he took for granted, like she wanted to work and earn an honest day's pay for an honest day's work. He assumed that they would work together, play together, buy their home and make a life together, equally, as partners. She would go in as he did and they would eventually have more children, teach and raise them into the path of that very same salvation and they, too, would never leave it. Not a lot of wiggle room for bullshit or excuses in that world. The mortgage doesn't get paid, and the bank usually doesn't really care why, only that it didn't' get paid. You are living a hypocrite's life, smoking drugs, squandering your God-given gifts as your children grow older and recognize this behavior. You may tell them not to follow you down this same path but it won't really jive, nor make real sense to them as they have watched you their entire life live this way.

It doesn't matter the "reason" why you are stuck there, only that you are stuck there. And if it was "good enough" for mama, why isn't it "good enough" for me? He had heard DD say in his mind hundreds of times how she always wanted to date someone like him, someone responsible and upstanding. It took him a very long time to realize the hidden agenda behind that statement, a much darker place than even he was willing to acknowledge. For their entire relationship, he was always trying to pull her closer to God and His teachings. So when she would say things like "if it is God's will" she would actually understand what that will was so she herself could move within it. He worked to pull her into the light, to show her how to work and become self-sufficient, strong enough to stand on her own two feet without fear. She would always have God even if they didn't make it, and she would in the process be showing little Kayden how to stay on that path and NEVER get lost down those same roads mommy got trapped in.

DD had told him one sad story after another of how she was "forced" into situations where all she had was her body as currency. Her ex had sent her to Texas to be the direct pipeline of guns and drugs back to Atlanta and literally left her there for a month without cash or any means. True pimp issh, and she hit that track, and all his boys who she ran in between for business ventures. Nasty little perverts, the very same people who invented the donkey show, who hired her to dance and have sex with entire rooms of people. He later smiled in her face and shorted her on drugs which she later had to find a way to "fix" once again with her body. She sold herself up and down that same pipeline running illegal contraband from state to state. This sounded like the saddest heart-wrenching tale until you get through the crap. Each time she went there, each and every time she made it back to Atlanta, she went back. This and every situation like it she entered into of her own free will, choosing to desecrate herself completely than face that very same light. With each and every act it made the black hole within her deeper and deeper until it was endless. No amount of money would ever fill that. This was a willing salvation she had to choose. The very same choice it took to walk in, SHE HAD TO BE THE ONE TO WALK OUT.

As the old saying goes, "You can lead a horse to water but you can't make him drink it."

You can pray until your knees are bloody. You can meditate until you are damn near mad and only hear your own voice. You can enter into the monastery and become a holy man or woman, but the bottom line is your salvation and victory comes not merely through your beliefs, not merely through your faith but WORK. We have all heard, "Faith without work is dead."

They had talked about the blind man that sought Jesus out to be healed. He didn't just heal him, he sent him out to WORK, and be a real partner in his own healing. So Tony completely believed that DD had prayed for a man like him - maybe even him. He could see God all over their mess. But what he could never understand was how she could be given this opportunity, the very thing she prayed for and not put forth every dying effort. How could she walk so readily into those dark places, filled with sin and horrors and fight him every inch towards the light? Those demons that had attached themselves to her soul had sliced so deeply into her psyche that she couldn't recognize her sin nature from her own salvation. She had fallen into a victim's mentality, not in the sense that she always wanted to be a victim tread upon. She was only willing to go but so far before she had an expectation to be carried the rest of the way. In fact, this was built into her definition of manhood by way of her parental relationship and what she witnessed. She had told him years ago how angry her mother was about her father losing his way and income and the pressure it put on her mother to work. She went from enjoying a good life with her dad to having to become a major contributor in their family equation. Their relationship never survived this set back. He was certain there was more to this story but this was all DD harped on when she told it. How she never wanted to grow up and be that sort of burden, or harbor that sort of bitterness about having to work for her family. And yet there she was; an apple that hadn't fallen any distance away from the tree. She wanted to contribute little but control much. They had fought incessantly about this predicament.

He had given to her, bent to her in almost every way imaginable. Yet she was always angry about having to work especially after he had helped her get her own place and all the nice and wonderful things he helped her fill it with. Kayden had come to love it and changed immediately. DD was filled with pride for a life she always wanted and never had. All of her family gathered around her and rallied to her cry for something more. It was far too much for her to quit and simply turn back on now. She was tired of working. She was tired of bearing so much responsibility. It was too much pressure, and it brought on far too much anxiety for the things she would have to save. She was leaving him and back into the loving support of a brother who had seen with his own eyes her change her ways. A credit DD never really had with Martin but she had earned by way of Tony's pushing her onto this new and better place.

This entire trip of torment, Tony kept trying to figure out how she could be so happy with this move and how things worked out. Had he truly made her THAT miserable? Was he as horrible as she made him out to be? Sure he was demanding, no more demanding of anyone than he was of himself. He was his own harshest critic. He never had any expectation that ANYONE would live up to the expectations he set for himself. As he literally sat for days upon days, which turned into months, pondering what he was missing and what he couldn't see about maybe himself, he couldn't see the forest for the trees. It truly was a simple matter; they were simply not in the same place. To her, he was a sucker, having spent all that time and money on an education, only having properly equipped himself to work himself into a grave created by the debt of obtaining such degrees in the first place.

"A job ain't nothing but work," she used to say.

Pretty much calling him a fool right to his face as he never stopped pursuing a higher education nor a more lucrative employ. The very things she said she loved about him were the very things that made him a fool in her eyes. To her, those of us who use our gift and bust our asses trying to make this world a better place, for our families and for those who love or come in contact with us, WE WERE THE FOOLS. We were just suckers who hadn't figured out a hustle so we didn't have to work as hard. And she was the mastermind who figured out a way to make it through life without ever having to work. That was the game. Who can come up with more by doing less? What a pity! What a waste of talent and time. Tony loved to labor and was by no means lazy, as he often worked physical labor jobs just to stay in shape. Providing for his family was his ultimate and most proud position given to him as a man and he LOVED his job, just as FATHER JOSEPH loved his job and spent his life in labor. This is how he could be so happy in having found this place on high and she could be so outside of this place, so outside of this will and still be happy. For as many times as Tony had read Proverbs 31, it never made more sense to him than the moments leading up to his decision to allow her departure, uncontested.

Proverbs 31:31 *Give her the fruit of her own hands; and let her own works praise her in the gates.*

To a selfish, lazy woman, the scripture brings no comfort, nor peace, only condemnation, judgment, and images of perfection. To a woman who had not had her virtue stolen, lost and then sold, this is an invitation to work her way into her kingdom upon equal share, given on the foundation of the Lord's words. What could be more solid?

This is why on a day that should have been completely filled with sadness and worry for her brother's future, her Twitter status said this, "I cheated on my fear, broke up with my doubts, got engaged to my faith and now I'm marrying my dreams."

Only someone so lost could be "Marrying a dream" without means on someone else's labor without care for a way of their own. Only someone so lost could be so deeply immersed in "faith" that they couldn't see STILL that it is dead without WORK. A dream? A dream? Really? Only when everyone and everything is a meal ticket. What a shame she had not shaken those same demons off of her. But there she was "marrying her dream" on her brother's worst day. This was the problem. They were two people not yoked and headed in apparently two different directions. She viewed labor as a burden to be endured through life's torment and he viewed labor as the blessing that allowed room for your gift, which the bible says makes room for you at the table of kings. He viewed his gift as something to be honed, shared and made a blessing to others THROUGH YOUR WORK. She only used her gift for flash showings and moments of pride. Each and every time she, or someone in her immediate cipher, came into money, it was something to be flaunted, bragged on, full of pride, full of a boastful tongue which brings us always back to that eye of the needle. This for her was all ego stroking and game playing to stay in good graces. At least he felt that way looking at it. There was no way a woman who couldn't afford to buy herself new under garments from year to year could afford to be that full of pride. But this is the public face, the mask they all seemed to wear around one another. He tried with all that was in him to stop such an arrogant act to no avail and alas this is where her intentions lay despite whatever her actual heart might feel.

Pity Martin had to learn the hard way as did Tony that DD, although arriving late, was the primary person who seemed to benefit from his success. Her Johnny-come-lately appearance in his life gave her the appearance of self-sufficiency and pride in herself and work but it was false; there was none. Her true desires were only to party, get high and work as little as possible. She was only in Miami a mere month and already was known via the World Wide Web as a party person. She took a job as a club promoter and even that job didn't work out. Apparently partying also required too much work. Yet she snatched Kayden away from her life, and the only father she ever knew, the only man she called dad, back into her fucked up world of clubs, partying and drug use. From what he saw, with all the parties she attended and helped promote, all the jobs she ran through and what he read about her on Twitter, she was still up to her old tricks as far as men, attached men and married ones alike were her men of choice. These men didn't require her commitment and allowed her to live the careless, drug-filled life she wanted. Such a shame what these women were teaching that young girl. Damn, just sad.

He closed his laptop and bent his knees for Martin and his young wife. He really liked Martin and his new wife, who he had met only once, seemed cool too. He prayed for a good outcome for Tony and his family. He prayed for DD and all she must be thinking and enduring. Most of all, he prayed for Kayden and all the confused thoughts she must be having being dragged from place to place her entire life. They had done a lot of healing together, Tony and DD. In many ways, she would always be a mighty love if not the love of his life. The mountains that they tackled together created a special place that only they two would EVER understand. It brought a lot of healing for him, them, Kayden, and even her family, to an extent. But it also left a huge gaping hole filled with pain. She would always be that same amazing woman to him in that dark place and beyond. But today, it was sincerely sad to see DD in no better place after all these years, all these life lessons and all time spent learning and loving. Even worse, she appeared to be headed right back for the same hole he had found her in all those years ago.

"Jesus help them," he prayed. "Amen."

Matthew 5:43-48 "You have heard that it was said, 'You shall love your neighbor and hate your enemy.' But I say to you, Love your enemies and pray for those who persecute you, so that you may be sons of your Father who is in heaven. For he makes his sun rise on the evil and on the good, and sends rain on the just and on the unjust. For if you love those who love you, what reward do you have? Do not even the tax collectors do the same? And if you greet only your brothers, what more are you doing than others? Do not even the Gentiles do the same? You therefore must be perfect, as your heavenly Father is perfect.

*   *   *

Shawna, however, was cut from a different cloth altogether. As sad as DD made him when she left, he was now equally as overjoyed. He found himself coming back from this thing like the conquering lion he was, roaring and asserting his dominance once again with pride in himself. In fact, he felt like he had more than when in started. It was an incredible feeling.

His eyes were full of this caramel dream that glazed his very soul. On the way to the airport, he was listening to Jahiem's new album, which he had listened to many times. Well it was as if he was listening with new ears to a brand new album when "Her" came on. It was like they had crafted that song for Shawna. He was feeling every lyric in the song almost as much as he was feeling her especially since they were playing the same heart strings. He was doing his able best to hold down that shit-eating grin that was busting at the seams to come out as she walked slowly towards him in her black pumps with the stainless steel heels. She was looking so ATL fly and he could hear the words to that song.

Her hair was a bleached blonde which spoke volumes about her style and personality. Since she was a light skinned black beauty, she called herself a "pseudo blonde" which he found crazy cute. She was confident on a level that said she was greater than the false bravado we sometimes resort to when the world has beat us down and left us with no other alternative. When all we can utter is, "I don't' give a f*$% what anyone thinks," when the truth is, that is the only thought that keeps us up off the ground. Bravo for those who can pull it off.

Tony wore his heart on his sleeve. Sadly this kept him far too honest for most. Most were intimidated by his honesty and ability to be vulnerable and remain in that place in the face of all his fears. Shawna was the first person he had met since DD that wasn't afraid on a very real level to go there with him. She was amazing on so many levels. She had so much swag from this authentic place that, just being around her made him feel the force to take it on by proxy. As their eyes met and locked, she smiled and removed her shades to show off those big, baby-doll, hazel eyes that melted his heart like wax to a flame.

She threw herself into his arms like an old flame. It felt so good and right. He immediately was taken by the way she looked at him, like she had known him forever. He couldn't help that it made him feel at home. They held one another so tight that it would have made that long embrace in *Gone with the Wind* look like puppy love. He was at the precipice of what he knew was the start of his new life. With all the grit he could muster from the recesses of his mind, he put on his tough guy exterior and ushered her to his truck, opening the door for her. As she sat, he hurried around to the other side to drive them to dinner and a whole new world from where he lived now.

*   *   *   *   *   *

The weekend had been filled with little moments of awesome coincidences and smiles along with anxiety-filled nervous moments. She was so much of what he wanted; he couldn't help to become afraid at some point. After all, it is human nature to pray for something so long that we just don't believe that it will actually arrive. Once it does, not only do we question it but we either run, push it away or find something wrong with it so we don't have to face it. If this experience with DD had taught him anything, it had indeed shown him that, up close and personal.

In that, he didn't find what he was feeling at all strange. It was frustrating for sure that he still had those feelings packed deep inside his subconscious, since he thought he had pulled that out of his closet some time ago. He had, but as they say, with every level comes a new devil and this was no different. She certainly was vastly different, and this was the problem. She was seemingly perfect. It forced him to take a deeper look at himself. He knew he was a bundle of nerves and raw emotion, even if she had managed not to see it. He was still reeling from all of the pain he had suffered at the hands of DD. Although he had managed to do a damn good job propping himself up and working through all this mess, there was no way he was truly ready to face himself in that state - in that place.

He thought she would be able to see right through him and pull all the half torn pieces of his soul right out of his mouth, or better yet, through the windows of his soul. Each time she looked him deeply in his eyes, he did his best not to allow those emotions to pour out of him - unlike the way he spent most nights since DD left his life. He had poured his mortal soul upon the very pillow cases she had purchased and left him to lay on. He thought he was doing a good job holding it all down. They were finally hitting it off when she reached for him in the middle of a sentence within a deep conversation and placed her head on his chest, pressing her left ear to his heart.

"I just needed to hear your heart Tony," she said.

As if on cue, his heart rate increased immediately and he began to quiver slightly as she reached to put her arms around him.

"I can see so much pain in your eyes, Tony. Your eyes look as if you're crying, even when you're smiling. You truly do wear your heart on your sleeve."

She slowly pulled his head towards her and reached up to gently kiss his neck as she took her right hand from behind his back and began to run her fingers through his curly locks. The music on his Ipod was still playing. He had put on some Coltrane, his favorite Jazz musician. It was a safe choice for him as it had no words, except the ones he created within their conversation. But just as she took her left hand from behind his back and reached up to touch his face the music changed to the next play list. As he heard the beginning of the song he knew instantly he was in trouble. As "Far Away" by Marsha Ambrosius began to play, she had begun to run her soft hands up his jaw line and into his hair. He could feel the tears welling up in his eyes and she brought her face up to his and as she looked deeply into his eyes. She had done just as he predicted. She had managed to pull his pain from behind the smoke and mirrors through the windows of his soul.

And as those hot tears streamed down his face, just as he tried to speak she said, "Shhhhhh baby. No, please baby, let me love you."

She began to kiss him gently on his face until she worked her way to his lips. Her lips were soft, gentle and tasted of the strawberries she wore in her lip gloss. She was an excellent kisser but more than that, she was calling out to his soul to join her. It was a familiar feeling, and one Tony hadn't felt in a long time as it woke him up from the inside out.

He began to kiss her passionately as his emotions began to flow from him freely now. He had lost sight of the fact that he was weeping and that she was seeing him in his weakest state. He began to throw all the love he had been storing inside of himself onto her. He barely knew her but he kissed her and began to love her as if he had missed her so badly, for so long. He rose from the couch and took Shawna's tiny dance frame from off of the couch and carried her up the stairs to his bedroom as the soft music filled the candle lit home, where they remained until the following day.

*   *   *   *   *   *

Upon the bright morning sunrise, he could feel all his life's hope upon her sleeping shoulders as he was still holding her now curled up body close to his. She was a heavy sleeper and to his delight, she didn't snore or make a peep.

"Damn she even sleeps like a lady," he thought to himself.

She was asleep with a sort of smile on her face which fed his hopeful feelings. He showered her neck and back with gentle kisses. She was so soft and felt so great. He wanted to do something special for her. He wanted to make her breakfast in bed but at the very moment remembered he didn't have any groceries. He slid out of bed as quietly as he could and threw some clothes on. He went up the street and picked up some breakfast foods. Through the weeks they had been talking, he thought he had come to know her pretty well and his selection of food would be the test of whether or not he knew her as well as he thought he did.

On the way to the register, he was going through the floral section and he thought to himself, "What a lovely purple arrangement! I think she would really like those. I think purple is her favorite flower color."

He finished the purchase and went on home and began working on his little surprise. French toast, eggs, mint tea, fresh black berries and black berry yogurt he made into a parfait. He broke the flowers into two arrangements, one for her breakfast tray and another for her trip to the airport which would be in a few short hours. They ate, talked, and laughed their way through breakfast. Once it was over, he cleared away the table and laid beside her as they watched a little T.V. and continued talking. In the middle of one of her big laughs, Tony reached for Shawna and ran his hands up the back of her neck and through her hair. In the midst of her laugh, her eyes left their gaze at the ceiling where they were fixed in their big laugh position and searched his eyes out to find him there waiting on them as he pulled her towards him quickly. She let out a sigh as they kissed one another passionately.

"I'm going to really miss you love. Are you sure you have to leave today?" Tony said.

Shawna once again let out an audible sigh.

"I really don't want to but I have appointments and people expecting me tomorrow," she said, looking completely miserable in her decision. But she also looked pretty certain that this was what she needed, and intended, to do.

It was his turn to sigh as he expressed his hearts disappointment in that decision. They once again fell into one another's arms kissing in a tight embrace not knowing the next time they would share such moments together. They spent the rest of those precious moments engaged in similar fashion with plenty of sharing of dreams and wishes until the reality that only time can bring set in and they made the inevitable mad dash for the airport. The ride there was quiet and somber, despite their efforts to minimize the sadness with small talk. As they reached the airport, you could cut the silence with a knife. As they pulled up to the terminal, they held each other longingly. He exited the truck and grabbed her bag from the trunk. Upon meeting her at the door, she leapt into his chiseled arms, as he wrapped her up tightly. She wrapped her legs around him and they kissed shamelessly like long lost lovers should.

He picked up her bag and walked her inside as they continued kissing and holding one another. When they finally stopped, they parted slow and speechless. For two people with so much on their hearts and minds, neither of them could find the words. Tony got back into his truck and drove home in silence. He was imagining what it would be like to have Shawna, full-time, as his lady. He had always felt that being in a relationship was like looking in the mirror and when he looked at Shawna, he liked the reflection he saw very much. He was doing his best not to allow the sadness he was feeling by her departure to pull him into more tears. After all, he should be happy having met her.

He had found an awesome woman and this trip just confirmed that she was all that he thought she was and he now had someone he could give his heart to. It should, by all means, feel full of the love she had just given him. Then why did it feel so empty? The moment her face left his presence, his world went instantly grey and he wanted nothing else but to keep her there. She was so comfortable, so soft and so much of what he wanted. Why couldn't she live here? Why couldn't he have lived there? Why? Why? Why? As he drove, he could feel his eyes getting heavy - a familiar feeling. It was one not of being genuinely tired but a tired born of depression and the heavy reality that he had no answers, again. It was easy to just lie down and allow himself to sleep away those moments. It was better than crying or pulling out his hair, trying to pretend that moment wasn't real. It was far easier to "just be tired."

No one would question being tired. He had two jobs and went to school. He had every reason to be sleepy. All he had to do was make it to that bed. As he parked his truck in the driveway on that bright and sunny Sunday morning, one full of life and plenty to do, he could hear his neighbors milling around, getting ready to do all the things he should be doing at this very moment instead of feeding into this "tired." It mattered not to him. All he wanted to do was make it to that bedroom and let his head hit that pillow. He knew he would sleep soundly. Once inside his door, he kicked off his shoes and slid into his slippers and walked up the stairs toward his bedroom. As he entered, he looked upon the bed and saw the little arrangement of flowers he had made for Shawna resting on her pillow, on what he told her was "her side of the bed" and he could no longer hold it.

He fell to his knees as he reached for the flowers and burst into tears. With his face buried deep into the pillow, he wailed as he cried, asking God why? He gathered himself up and reached for his cell. He had to let her know what she had done to him. He had fallen in love with her and there was no stronger evidence than how he was feeling at this very moment. He had to let her know before she got on that plane. As the phone rang out, he was once again disappointed as he figured she had already departed. He wasn't sure if he would have the confidence or strength to tell her what he had come to later once he woke up from what he was sure would be a long nap. He fell face first into the pillows, once again, as the tears returned quickly. He allowed them to wash over his body, full of emotions he had been holding in for far too long.

In between sobs, he could hear his phone ring. He intended to ignore it but his curiosity got the best of him and he reached to answer it. It stopped ringing but he checked the call log. It was her! He quickly tried to call her back but his phone rang again as he pushed the button and he answered the call to hear Shawna on the other end of the line crying just as hard as he was. They both began speaking at the same but lost their words. They could each hear the sincerity of the moment in each other's tears. They both marveled at how emotional this meeting was and how much love they had found in such a short amount of time.

"This isn't the end of it. Not for me. I can promise you that. Shawna I . . . I …,"Tony said with words full of love, then hesitation.

"Shawna I . . ." Tony started again.

"I know," Shawna said. "I know. I have to go now Tony, but I want you to know I love you too."

"Oh my God, is this possible? I love you Shawna," he replied.

They sat there weeping for another moment when Shawna spoke up again. "I have to go baby. I'll talk to you soon." Shawna sounded as if she was ready to burst at the seams.

"Ok boo talk to you soon," he responded. And they hung up.

Tony immediately lay back down on the bed and got beneath the covers. Without another thought or word, he slept the entire day away. Later that evening, Shawna called to let him know she had reached home safely and what a wonderful time she had there with him. She told him how much she wished she didn't have to leave and how much she felt for him. They talked about his choice of flowers and how it had floored her that he had served her blackberries, which were her favorite. She, too, confessed her need to sleep and had already set aside her sleeping pill to ensure it happened in a timely manner. They hung up that night and things would never again be the same.

"Good night fair lady, I miss you."

*   *   *   *   *   *
*

The days drifted in and out as they turned into weeks. As the sun fades into dusk, so did the budding relationship and love Shawna and Tony had begun. She had told him upon entering his life that she was a master of self-sabotage as he confessed that he was the same. She also confessed that she was a runner.

"I will admit that I usually run when things seem perfect which makes no sense but it has been my history. I promise to do my best to keep my feet on the ground and not run from you." This was her confession to him.

He knew as she spoke those words to him that this was not a real promise she could keep any more than he could promise her that he didn't still love DD; or that if she walked through that door right now he would happily take her back. He was just as confused and messed up. He accepted her and this chance to come through this place with her together, conquering their fears and weaknesses together. But alas, it was not meant to be. She made good on her prediction to run when things seemed perfect. Maybe it was her fear. Maybe it was an inability to block out that she knew he wasn't really ready for the love he was calling for and was indeed still in love with DD. She wasn't up for the potential heartbreak that this sort of love and situation could hold for her knowing he may still love another. Either way, he couldn't blame her. All he could do was push forward, pray and work on his healing. Each week he did just that, healing and challenging himself more and more towards his path of liberation. It wasn't that far off now but sadly he knew when he reached there, no matter how much he wished for it, Shawna wouldn't be there.

And so his fairytale was ended and he was again immersed into the cold, hard reality of a dream deferred. He could get off into his emotions and cry a bucket of tears, telling the world how he had loved. Yes, he had loved to the very best of his ability, to the bottom of his soul, to the essence of everything he believed he was and beyond. All for the love he wanted, desired, prayed and begged for. One he worked so hard for, only to have it walk right out of his life. Oh yes, he could cry for days telling about his disappointment and how love leaves, even when you stay. He could do all of those things. But he knew deep down in his soul he really hadn't known love until that moment before it left - until *she* left. It was when he finally and truly found God and God's love for him. And it didn't look anything like the love he had previously desired to give to another. What he did find was a love he wanted to give to himself, amazingly for the first time. Which is why he was still able to stand today, still smiling, still happy and most of all still hopeful. STILL BELIEVING IN LOVE.

For the very first time in his life he could say with absolute certainty that he knew what it looked like, what it felt like, what IT SMELLED LIKE. And it didn't smell like the trash from whence he came. Also, for the first time, he knew just where it lay and how to access it. The Lord had brought him through thirty-nine years of life when he finally realized, through all his trials and tribulations, that if he could only stay obedient this greatest lesson, LOVE, would be given to him. HE that sat on high will bring him all that he had prayed for in a wife. Shawna was the proof. So no, he didn't cry nor did his heart break. She had given him proof, and assurance, that it was indeed out there without fear, or pain of lack, as he had always experienced it. When he finally realized their dream was over, he felt confident about life and love. Therefore, on that day, no tears fell for sorrow's sake. He could only pray that Shawna hadn't shed any either because he knew that as sure as the Lord could bring it to a wretch like him, he could bring it to a fine lady like her.

Chapter 33
Chosen Way of Life
Ephesians 6:17

Deuteronomy 8:2

Remember how the LORD your God led you all the way in the desert these forty years, to humble you and to test you in order to know what was in your heart, whether or not you would keep his commands.

The Beginning of Rapture

It had been six months and Tony had been steeped in routine and a mountain of work. He had begun a journey to pursue yet another of his life long dreams. He would enter into the fraternity he dreamt of during his undergrad years. Long story short, the guys he went into it with to his amazement quit. He played football with these guys. He partied, and even lived with these guys. He was more than shocked that they would quit on something like this but they did and he lost his opportunity.

In the midst of his coming out of the latest curve ball life had thrown him, he was introduced to a brother who helped to bring his name before a graduate chapter of that very same fraternity. They say that God doesn't make any mistakes and in everything there is a purpose. He could see how God loved him so much that he saved something so special for a time in his life he needed it the most. At a time so far away from family and childhood friends, he met and became brothers with men of like mind who held him up in times of trouble just like they said they would. "Friendship truly is essential to the soul." And there was no greater truth from where he was sitting. In mere months, he went from lonely and alone to a house full of BROTHERS. Men, real men who understood life, love, and the daily struggle to put one foot in front of another on days you'd rather phone it in.

> Proverbs 17:17 A friend loves
> at all times, and a brother
> is born from adversity.

If ever he could clearly see God's grace, "the goodness of the Lord in the land of the living," it was now. He was fishing, bowling, golfing, and putting that pool table in his living room to plenty of use. He was even going out socially without fear or hesitation for the first time in more years than he could remember. He had real friends - people he could talk too. As he started coming out of this bad place he had been for so many years with DD, he could see God moving in his life. His obedience had given him space, room and the opportunity to bask in the greatness of the gifts of the Lord - his anointing. He was still working that great job that he loved more than any job he had ever had. He worked at a school which exemplified the very reasons he became a teacher in the first place.

Each day, he was reminded why he wanted to teach the moment he arrived on campus as those students who loved him called his name. It was indeed an awesome opportunity to use his gifts. He could see his daily impact and knew he was needed. It was completely life affirming. There is nothing better than doing what you love while being paid well to do it. He was happy there and for the first time in his life he had true allies, and friends on the job; something he NEVER had in his life. He had three friends at work with Meg being his closest, then Faith and Hope. He never stopped laughing at the irony in the names but God always did have jokes. One day he looked up what the name Megan meant and found it meant someone who possessed strength and boldness; *a pearl*. It described her perfectly. She was the best teacher he had ever worked with. She made him better at his job and he was grateful for her.

He had support at work, real friends, a great job, his son and he was in his last two semesters finishing up his doctoral degree. Things were awesome and he was actually happy. Six months ago, he couldn't see this day, but he was here. Life wasn't perfect, however. He still didn't have the love of his life. The woman currently in that position was just as unstable as DD and came with almost all of all her issues. He knew she was not good for him. She was needy and constantly brought drama, but she was a love he was familiar with and he felt "something" which was better to him than walking through life feeling nothing.

He had dated so many in such a short amount of time. He was shocked at how much interest he had drawn, and how many gorgeous women wanted the opportunity to be in his life. There were actually "good women" out there in the world, willing to work for the love and life they said they wanted and he had come across many; some that even professed love for him. But the timing was never right. He had finally reached a point in his journey where he was ambivalent to it all. He had stopped caring about finding that love. In fact, he had stopped feeling those feelings altogether and had begun to even wonder if he ever would again. He found pleasures in simply spending time with someone he liked and made him laugh.

Gabrielle was five-foot-seven inches tall with a thick built frame and a very voluptuous body. If she were a car, you would say she was "fully loaded." She had huge, light-brown doe eyes that begged you to love her. She had lips right off of a magazine cover, long hair and a clear complexion. She had fair skin and a sultry voice, and was far prettier than DD. Everyone who saw her said so. This was a point that made him proud. They vibed physically and had great conversations. They laughed a great deal, but she was ultimately afraid of her own shadow which prevented them from taking it to the next level. In fact, each time they had any type of disagreement she would break up with him. For awhile, he dealt with it the same way he had dealt with DD when she did the same - remained loyal and waited upon her return, as he was sure she was going to return at some point. Unlike DD, he did not chase after her. He told her from the beginning that he wouldn't do that. This meant that it would be weeks before she would get back from her fearful track meet. At some point, within those three months of off-and-on, she would be gone far longer than she was there and this is when he decided that he could no longer wait.

Upon his decision to take her back this last time he told her point blank, "Listen Gabrielle, the next time you walk out of my life, I won't be waiting for you to return. I need more at this point. I need you to make up your mind what you want to do and if you really want me. I can't keep doing this back and forth thing. I did this for six years with my ex and I won't do this for another month with you. So if you are back let this be it and stay. If not, I will be moving on. I just want you to know that this is it."

She replied, "I understand and I already told you it's just my fear that keeps me doing this and I promise I won't ever do this to you, to me, to us again."

It was enough for him that he told her how he felt because if he was certain of anything, it was that she had made a promise he knew she would never be able to keep. When your fear runs your life, in small part or all of it, at some point, it doesn't matter. It is difficult, at best, to resist it. This was something his college football coach told him when he first made the conscious decision to stop quitting on things in his life.

"Once you quit the first time it becomes easier and easier to quit each time. After awhile the reasoning is just an excuse to give in to your anxiety, seeking relief from your fear and losing your life in the process."

Truer words about quitting could not be spoken and he knew she had no idea what she was up against or how deeply the fear ran through her life. He could see it all over her from the very start but once again it was a situation and feeling he was accustomed to and frankly what he could handle at the moment. The funny thing

487

was that he didn't think he could, at first, but falling back into that old habit was as easy as putting on an old tee or pair of shoes; it was painless. But he was now at a point where that old and tattered thing needed to find the trash. Shortly after he and Gabrielle had broken up again, he met a woman named Meagan (not to be confused with his friend Meg from school). He decided he wasn't going back this time and he was going to move on and meeting Meagan was just the thing he needed to pull himself out of his very own human booby trap. This was his test for this ultimate happiness he pursued.

The first time they went out, they went to the park and walked together for hours, just talking, laughing and sharing. Tony loved to laugh and make others laugh so having a sense of humor was a huge deal and Meagan was easy to talk to. They walked until the sun went down and parted feeling like they made a good connection. She was perfect but Tony was almost numb to it because she seemed "too perfect." He had been with DD who had told him so much of what he wanted to hear and it all turned out to be a lie at some point. While he wasn't jaded to the point where he didn't believe anything anyone said, he did feel like he needed to take what others said to him with a grain of salt until he could at least see for himself if indeed they walked it like they talked it. He hadn't been brave enough to do this with DD. But today, he was a new creature and was ready to see the world for what it was. More importantly, he was ready to see Meagan for who she was instead of who he wanted her to be. He was still deeply devoted to his love walk with the Lord. He meditated daily and attended church each week, as he could have NEVER come this far without Him.

She also claimed to be on a similar walk, so he decided to call her truth to the mat. She seemed by all accounts to be a lady but he wanted to see it further. So the following week he invited her to church, and to his surprise she accepted! She actually seemed genuinely sincere about her desire to attend. They attended church, walked in hand in hand, and moreover, she walked with her head up, unafraid, proud to be with him, and proud to hold his hand for the world to see. She was a true beauty. Her hands were perfectly manicured, so tiny and soft. He was pleased just to be holding her hand; it was wonderful. They listened to the message and agreed with the word, and left higher than they arrived and just as proud as they walked in.

Their following date was another meeting in the park to walk and talk. This the very same park he had met DD years ago, but it felt completely different. No drinks. No sexy nature or talk. No middle of the night rendezvous. They met in the middle of the afternoon each time. They left at nightfall but that was under far different circumstances. Everything about it was wonderfully different. She was only twenty-nine but she, like when he met DD, seemed mature beyond her years so he was willing to entertain the notion that they could be a couple. As their walks continued and the days turned into weeks, she was indeed turning out to be what she appeared to be. He had gotten so much advice with this new dating thing. Someone had told him don't take any date out to a place where you have to spend money. The thought was that if they were truly interested in you then it wouldn't matter where they went. Besides, taking a woman somewhere you have to spend money would be a waste of your resources and it kept her from really knowing you anyway. One of his oldest and best friends T, told him don't rush to allow someone to know where you live or into your life, so he had waited weeks before he finally invited her back to his place for a meal and a movie. It had all been good advice and things were progressing well.

The first time she came into his home, she was washing dishes and cleaning up after their meal. He was more than impressed. Gabrielle had been in his home several times and NEVER lifted a finger to do anything except for herself. In fact, she had him running around waiting on her. Now there is nothing to say that he shouldn't be a gentleman and help with things she wanted in his home, but he felt at some point she should have asserted herself into the woman position in his life, if she wanted it anyway. It never did feel like she did, as she never even tried. Suffice it to say, it was enough to invite Meagan back and each time she came she was equally as impressive. The following time she arrived, she came with arms filled of little things she saw he needed. She prepared meals and purchased small items she saw he needed, including a tube of toothpaste as she saw he was running low. Hands down she was the most thoughtful girl he had ever dated thus far. Things he had to fight for in his previous relationship, she was showing up with in hand without being asked. It was amazing and he couldn't lie, he wanted her. Somewhere around week four he decided he had seen enough and made the decision to date her exclusively. They spent a few nights together and each time she stayed she made meals, ironed clothes and was a true help to him and his life. He was amazed and overcome by the presence of the strangest thing - FEAR!

He couldn't believe he was actually afraid that she was too perfect. Would he measure up? For so long, in his past relationship he had been told how small he was, how unattractive he was, and at some point he believed it and bought into the bull that he didn't deserve any better. He could feel himself fading away from this good woman and for the first time started to see a piece of what Shawna must have felt like.

"Is she for real? Is this just an act and she is going to bust my heart in a million pieces once I give it to her? I don't even know how to approach this thing. I thought I was ready but I don't think I'm as ready as she is." All these thoughts crossed his mind a billion miles per hour and at some point they began to be all he could hear.

Now Gabrielle hadn't stopped calling him although he no longer answered her calls. She was writing him emails and text messages trying desperately to get him back but he never did respond to her. He eventually deemed himself unworthy of someone as good as Meagan was and convinced himself that he didn't "feel" anything with her. In his mind, it was true because for so long he had separated his sex from his love and real love usually felt like nothing to him, while sex was an emotional experience. They had not shared such an experience. But Gabrielle and he had. This is the experience he reached back for when he searched his mind for something to feel and it broke him down.

He responded to Gabrielle's messages. They spoke and eventually agreed to meet at his place on a Friday evening. He had lied to Meagan and told her he was unavailable as he met with Gabrielle so they could talk about their potential relationship. At some point, he had convinced himself he couldn't trust Meagan because she hadn't shared her life with him. She was so closed and seemed so perfect. There was no way she would be able to love someone like him, someone who was so scared and carried around so much baggage; she was too perfect. But Gabrielle had so much baggage herself, he felt like he could trust her to protect him from the world when it came down to it. Although she was crazy, she was a crazy he knew, so he felt safer with her. That night, he decided that he would go back to Gabrielle so he didn't have to face his fears or the possible rejection he was certain would come with Meagan and her perfect love. He would settle for the safety in the lunacy he knew instead of the fear he did not. That night Meagan called his phone, but he didn't pick up. When Gabrielle asked who was calling his phone and why he was avoiding the call, he told her who it was. After some time Meagan had called his cell and his home phone and after he didn't pick it up she came to his door! She knocked and rang the bell and Gabrielle was more than uncomfortable.

"Why don't you just go down there and tell her what you have decided? Why not just tell her now? If you intended to do it, you can do it in front of me so I will know you are being honest," she said.

Tony knew it was her fear kicking up but refused to give into that. It didn't matter how much Gabrielle made it sound like the thing to do, he refused.

"Listen I just made this decision to go back to you and she has no idea. She deserves honesty, no doubt, but not like this! Not me telling her with some other woman already in my home, in my life in the background watching or listening to her pain, rejection or embarrassment. It's not right and she doesn't deserve that. She has never hurt me nor did a thing against me. Why should I hurt her like that? It is bad enough I have made this decision, do I have to add insult to injury by doing it this way? I can just wait until you are not here and sit her down and explain it isn't working and not subject her to that sort of embarrassment. I know you don't agree but I REFUSE TO DO IT ANY OTHER WAY. SHE DESERVES MORE THAN WHAT YOU ARE SUGGESTING." And for him the conversation was closed. So no matter how many times Gabrielle tried to bring it up, he didn't respond.

Eventually they went to bed and the conversation faded behind them. All that was left to do after Gabrielle left was call Meagan back up to come over so they could discuss this thing. She didn't deserve to be left hanging in that place. He would handle his business like the man he was, like the man he should have handled it like from the beginning. He could completely see the cracks in his armor but he didn't have the time or energy to figure it all out. Firstly, the shame was beginning to weigh on him and he didn't want Gabrielle to see the doubt in his face as he was making a selfish decision; one that was based in his fear and running and not so much his true desire to be with her and all her crazy crap. Secondly, in order to face the "why" in this equation, he KNEW he was going to need more time than he would be allowed to have, especially since Meagan had already knocked on his door, called and texted his phone. She wanted, needed and deserved answers. Besides, it is situations like these where dudes get caught up all the time, "trying to figure their mess out" then get busted and labeled, rightfully so, as a cheating, lying, no good motha f*%ker. He wasn't that and he wouldn't allow his fear to let him walk down THAT road ever again.

So he made this decision and although it was hasty and he was certain it wasn't any good; a step backwards never is. He was going to have to live with it because today he was going to let Meagan know the truth. Well somewhat. He had no way of telling her the entire truth because he himself hadn't figured it out completely. He was instantly brought back to Shawna and how fearful she was, running from him and her admission to him that she, too, was a self-saboteur of the good and worthwhile things in her life. He was finally getting what Shawna must have seen, and felt like upon meeting him. Meagan was saying the sweetest things and most perfect things. She was so beautiful and was always considerate. When he thought about himself, he was not unlike that type of person, who was thoughtful and said kind and perfect things; at least he thought so.

He had never considered how frightening someone like him could appear. He thought that what he brought to the table looked and sounded like a good catch but then he had never been confronted with anything remotely resembling himself in that way. Now he was face to face with himself and something that more looked like a fear than a good catch and could finally relate to her running and hiding from him. It made him reconsider his entire approach, his entire picture, what he looked like and presented to those he would hope to love. He just didn't have the strength, time or emotional wherewithal at the moment to delve into it properly. These thoughts and those of more doubt stayed on his mind all night. Had he made the right decision? But he had already made it. There could be no turning back now. He convinced himself that she was too pretty, body too perfect, and had too much going for herself, to be real. She had to have a motive. It seemed like everyone in this world today had a motive. Most of his life that motive was to manipulate him for one reason or another. Gabrielle had a motive and Tony could see it clearly and this made it easier to choose her over Meagan. So Gabrielle was safe and he could trust her bullshit but Meagan would not stop until Tony loved her. She said so several times.

"I'm going to make you love me, and then I'm going to turn your entire vision of what you think love is upside down. I'm going to treat you better than any woman has ever even tried. I know I can make you happy for the rest of your life," Meagan had said to him.

To the common ear that sounded awesome but to him he could only hear the bullshit that lay in wait. Sure she was going to continue to be perfect and he knew he could love her. She was everything he could hope for but then what? What would she do with that power? Would she honestly use it to love him beyond his wildest dreams? Not likely in his mind. Most used it to get what they wanted and that usually required more of him than he could afford to give away. DD had taught him that in a major way. He knew he could not afford another such lesson. So this time, he would not be swayed by beautiful words or futures told. He would not be pulled into a fantasy bought and paid for by all the thoughts HE WOULD put on it within his mind, stirred up by all those things she would promise and say. No, this time he would choose with his eyes wide open and walk into what he figured he knew. She probably would never understand, nor would anyone watching this thing from the outside either but he knew he had to protect his heart. So that morning when Gabrielle left, he was just about ready to do what he had to do with regards to Meagan when she texted him.

"Listen we really have to talk about your time and not being around so much. I had no way of knowing once we got together that I wouldn't see you this much."

He replied, "Yes you're right. At some point we need to get together so we can talk about things. If you are available this afternoon we can sit down and talk. If not, I understand. After waiting on me all night with nothing to show for it. I understand if you don't feel like clearing your schedule for me. But we should talk."

He wasn't telling her the entire story but he thought it would be far more difficult to get her to come to his place if she knew he was going to break it off with her. He just needed to sit her down and talk to her face to face and maybe he could see the reality and accept it for himself as well. It was going to be difficult for him but it was the right thing to do if he was going to do it. He was just about to step into the shower to get himself cleaned up for his afternoon meeting with Meagan when the door bell rang. He was surprised, as he wasn't expecting anyone at that moment, so he went to his office window and looked outside. He saw Gabrielle's SUV in the driveway and went back into his room to throw on the sweat pants he had just taken off and went down stairs. He opened the door up smiling.

"What? Did you forget something?" He said still smiling and holding the door open.

She walked in without a smile or a word. As she crossed the threshold she turned around and said, "Who is this?" as she pointed out the door.

Just then Meagan popped from the side of the door. "What the hell is going on here Tony?" Meagan said.

Tony was floored as he knew that Gabrielle knew full well who this was. They had spoken about it just the night before, watched her walk back to her car and the whole nine.

"This is the woman I told you about Gabrielle. This is Meagan. We talked about her last night," Tony said trying to stay humble and not come off angry or with an attitude.

He felt he was, clearly, wrong for having made this decision the way he had so he didn't want to add fuel to the fire nor, more importantly, did he want to add insult to injury for Meagan. Although, he was pretty confused and pissed at Gabrielle. Why did she feel the need to drag Meagan through this? He had told Gabrielle about Meagan. Why couldn't she just stay out of this? Or did she really just need to hurt her?

"This is crazy," he mumbled out loud.

"You damn right it is Tony! You're a fucking liar!" Gabrielle shot out.

Tony looked at her in confusion.

"What? What are you talking about?" He said to Gabrielle looking confused.

"You lied to this woman and you lied to me. You were seeing both of us at the same time! Are you going to deny that?" Gabrielle shouted.

"Huh? But you knew this. We talked about it! I am confused right now. If anyone should be pissed it's Meagan. I lied to her, NOT YOU. I told her I was somewhere else last night and I was with you and I explained all that to you last night. I don't get what you are doing here?" Tony said, still confused.

"He told me he loved me last night. This nigga was in his room with tears in his eyes telling me how much he loved me last night while you were outside calling him. Did you know that Meagan? This nigga is full of shit. Don't trust him or believe a thing he has to say," Gabrielle shouted.

Tony just stood there in amazement. He couldn't believe she was saying all this stuff to Meagan. It was clear she was trying to hurt her, but why?

"He laid up with me in that bed last night after you left and fucked me twice. I bet you didn't know that either? He ain't no good. A fucking dog is all he is," Gabrielle continued.

Tony stood there with his mouth opened as Meagan stood there crying, "Why, did you do this to me Tony? I was nothing but good to you? I did nothing but respect and treat you well, how could you hurt me like this? I love you," Meagan said, as she started to cry even harder now.

He could see in Gabrielle's face she was getting some sick, twisted pleasure out of twisting the knife he had stuck into Meagan's back and he was getting more and more pissed by the second. He felt like he had to stand up to Gabrielle, not for himself so much but because Gabrielle was doing the very thing he said he didn't want to do, which was hurt Meagan unnecessarily.

"Now hold on a minute. I'm no fucking DOG. I lied sure but one lie doesn't make me a liar. I made a mistake. CLEARLY I DID. But that doesn't make me a fucking DOG and I refuse to allow you to continue to talk to me like this," Tony began to shout now.

"So tell me why you did this to me Tony. I just need you to explain this to me," Meagan said, still sobbing.

For the first time, he could feel the deep pain he had caused Meagan. He never even thought in a million years that she actually cared for him the way she was now showing him that she did with her tears. She hadn't budged. She hadn't even asked for the things she had left in his home as of yet. She still had feelings for him at this very moment of great betrayal. At that very moment, one of the dirtiest and wrong moments of his life, a moment he was absolutely wrong. He could see his mistake clearly now. He took a step back and looked at both these women. One on his right, crying, still looking at him with love in her eyes, admitting with her own words that she still loved him, though he had just fallen down flat on his face with arguably one of the biggest mistakes he had recently made with his love life. The kicker was that this mistake was the knife in HER back; the betrayal of HER. He looked at his left to see Gabrielle, who was still shouting and cursing, still angry and being completely nasty; not once showing, admitting or acknowledging any love for him.

Just then Tony had a revelation, like an epiphany from the sky, from He that sits on high. Almost like a voice in his head:

"Pay attention to what you learn about each other during trials in your relationship before marriage: chances are, those revelations will hold true after you say your vows."

Not often is a man who is split between two women ever in a position to look at those two women, side by side, face to face and compare them physically and otherwise. Outside of the horrible circumstances under which he was standing before these two women, he was given this opportunity. So he stood for a moment, just listening and watching, literally comparing the two women, apples for apples. Who had the better looking features? Who showed mercy, kindness or vulnerability? And who was just plain nasty?

It was clear that he had made a huge mistake, so as Meagan finally at her wits end shouted, "Damn it! I just need to know why you did this Tony! We have had a wonderful relationship up to this point and I loved you the best I knew how. Please speak to me." She stood there looking him deeply in his eyes waiting for a response.

He looked her deeply in her eyes, shook his head and said, "I obviously made a huge mistake. The woman I thought I couldn't trust, the one I thought would sell me down the river and break my heart in a million pieces is the woman still standing here telling me she loves me. And the woman who I made the huge mistake to go back to, the one I thought would protect my heart, is the very same woman who is selling me out and betraying me?"

Tony looked at Gabrielle and reached his hand out and touched her gently on the back of her elbow and said, "You have to go now." He escorted her to the door.

Looking back towards Meagan, who was now wiping the tears off of her face, Gabrielle shouted back,

"I hope you don't believe a thing that comes out of this liars' mouth. If he hurt me, he will hurt you too. Don't trust what he says girlfriend."

What Gabrielle said would have ordinarily stung Tony but as it stood, her words rolled off of his back like water to a duck. He didn't get angry. He never raised his voice. He never said a cross word. In fact, he said nothing as he escorted her out then closed and locked the door behind her. As he went back into the house to talk with Meagan, she was looking hurt and angrier than when he walked Gabrielle to the door.

"I can't believe you would do this to me. I have never cheated on anyone I have ever been with. Why is it that men have to do this? What did I do Tony? What did I do to deserve this?" Meagan asked with tears streaming down her face.

"It had nothing to do with you or what you did more than it had to do with me and my own fears and how I handled it. I fucked up, plain and simple. Coming out of my last relationship, I think I was in a place that I couldn't believe words anymore and all you said, all I saw, all looked too good to be true. I let my fear chase me back into something familiar, something I thought was safer than pushing forward into the unknown. It was a coward's way to do things. I know that and there is no excuse for it. I fell prey to my weakness and can't begin to tell you how sorry I am."
Tony said this feeling like the ass end of a mule. How could he have been so blind; so weak to see something so good and not only didn't have the strength it required to see if it was indeed good, or no good, for him but the courage to tell the truth either way?

The truth is he was beat down - all the way down. For as much as he wanted to believe that what he suffered at the hands of DD, her family, her friends and each and every horrible thing that passed during that relationship, affected him in a major way, he was afraid and weak for having extended himself so far; but more than that, he had begun to believe that he was as small as DD made him feel. He didn't deserve someone like Meagan. He knew if that was his truth, he would never be happy and he would ultimately end up the same piece of shit that seemed to be floating around this toilet bowl of life, stinking from one corner of the world to the other. This couldn't be him? This couldn't be his truth. No, this was a lie! From the pit of hell!

And for a moment, the enemy almost had him throwing up his hands in self-loathing and pity, using the fiery darts of the truth to shoot him down. Then he remembered the blood. He remembered 2 Corinthians 5:17 *"Therefore if any man is in Christ, he is a new creature; the old things pass away, behold the new things come."* Suddenly he realized how he had been duped into believing that he would never be happy again without DD, and how he was only worthy of a love that hurt and tore him down. How the only good thing that had come into his life since her that was actually ready and willing to love him in the way he actually deserved to be loved, he was set on running from. Because he had stopped believing. Stopped believing in himself, and stopped BELIEVING in anything good that way. He had taken his eyes off of God and looked down and fallen into the ocean. At that very moment his eyes still fixed to the ground in shame.

"Look at me Tony. Tell me how you could do this to me? You don't deserve me! YOU don't deserve my love or what I have to offer as a woman! You ain't worth me at all! You are a liar and men like you deserve nothing but to suffer! You're right. You are weak and full of shit too! Gabrielle's right, you're just a damn liar!" Meagan shouted as she turned her back and headed up the stairs to get the things of hers she had left there in his house.

At first it was tough for Tony to speak. After all, she was right; he had been a liar in this circumstance. He could see clearly that Meagan was hurting but had far more to say by way of real content. She wasn't just speaking from a wounded place. She actually wanted answers and was sincerely concerned for the relationship they had built, despite the circumstances. When she came back downstairs, he was finally able to speak as she paused before heading to the door.

"Can we sit for a moment longer and talk about this thing?" He said softly and full of shame.

Without question, argument, or foul mouth, she simply sat down. This took him by surprise because he honestly didn't expect that she would want to hear anything that he had to say since she had already deemed him a liar among other things.

He took his time as he spoke, and she gave him the opportunity to speak without interruption or fight. She wanted to hear as much as he wanted to explain. He explained his history and the events that lead him to this dark place he had found himself in. Those to do with DD and others that pre-dated her. All the way back to some childhood events that shaped these very fears and his mountain of work against them. He explained how he viewed her, the way he felt about her, his fear of being in love with her and she leaving, and how he never wanted to be alone or feel those feelings again. It was primarily this fear that drove him back into the arms of a woman he KNEW was not right for him because she was an old familiar feeling. One he knew how to handle and sadly held less fear than she represented. By conversation's end they had both confessed their fears as well as their love for one another and vowed to work through those things together. She decided to stay and give him the benefit of the doubt and look beyond his behavior and not allow that one poor judgment to form who he was in her mind.

After all the grace he had given DD, it was nice to be given some back. After all, he had earned that much. But it was his transparency in this matter that brought this note due and he knew it. He knew it was going to take that and then some to get past this for the both of them. As it turned out, she appeared to be equally as amazing as he thought of himself in this area. That day, they dragged out all of their fears and insecurities into the light of day and shamed the devil for his trickery. They prayed and rededicated themselves to His service together and to one another. It was an emotional and amazing once in a LIFETIME afternoon that HE NEVER THOUGHT HE WOULD LIVE TO SEE. Up till that very moment, he frankly didn't think he was worth that from a woman of her caliber. It appeared it was indeed harvest season.

Harvest Season

It had been just about a year since Tony and DD split up and his life was DRASTICALLY different. It was a true testament to the Lord and Tony's ability to take up all of his life's lessons through this new found school of obedience. He could literally look around and see his harvest. It was his season. It was difficult at first. When he made the decision to allow DD to leave his life, he was crushed and couldn't see himself loving again. Now the Lord blessed him with a woman who truly understood, loved and supported him. She jumped right in from day one on Team Tony and whatever project was on the table. From the first bump in the road, she proved she was all in. He was amazed. She did all those little things that keep a person truly loving another. She worked out with him, lifted weights, ran, and even did P90X when he was in the mood. She helped him with his eating habits. She was just as concerned with his health and well being as he was and it showed each day as she prepared him healthy meals at home, instead of the crap he had grown accustomed to.

She held down two jobs just like he did and was truly a partner in parenting. She and Sharon even got along to the point that Sharon called her up to check on their little man. It was truly a different world, with no bitterness, no anger, no DEATH THREATS. Since they shared no children and Meagan didn't have any children of her own, they had plenty of time for romance. They moved in together into a wonderfully spacious four bedroom home on a corner lot with a huge front and back yard, a two-car garage that doubled as their gym. As a bonus, they both got their very own private office spaces to work on their own little projects. His move came sudden as he was determined not to run from the ghosts of his past or DD's memories.

When they split he decided he was not leaving that dwelling. He intended to stay right there, and deal with all the things that came up for him upon her and Kayden leaving. It was hella hard at first, looking at those walls the girls had painted for him on a weekend he was out of town. It was really Kayden's gift to him

502

and she was so very proud to do it for him. She was so excited about it she could barely wait for her mother to get it out of her mouth. He was equally as proud as she had become the daughter he had always wanted. That was one of the most difficult things he had to deal with, the absence of a love so innocent, and so pure. There was nothing larger in one's life than the love of a child. Once you take one into your heart it stays there forever. Turning her bedroom into his office space was equally as hard so things were difficult for some time.

But as time passed and the Lord cleaned his dark places fresh, those feelings began to pass. Eventually, with the exception of little memories that came back like waves gently breaking the shore, or his little man asking about Kayden, Tony had come to dwell in the very same home they had shared as if they had never been there. It must have been time to move on because one day as his brother came over, he handed him a notice that had been placed on the door. He was completely unaware that the home he was renting was coming up for foreclosure and someone had quietly taped an order for eviction on his door. He was in a panic and his mind raced as the notice was for two days. Once he got a stay on the order, he discussed it with Meagan and they decided that this would be the beginning stages of the eventual combination of their life. They found that wonderful home and immediately went in to purchase it. He would never again be surprised by another eviction.

Somewhere in the middle of this process of eviction he went from anxious and worried to sitting in the calm of what he first viewed as a storm but later realized was God's will moving his life to a NEW AND BETTER ONE. It was just absolutely miraculous how things had moved and changed in his life. Even the truck he and DD had shopped for together, which she had even given him some of his down payment for, had been moved from his life. He had helped DD shop for a new car as her old bucket had finally kicked and in the midst of that, found a Chevy Trailblazer for himself.

But one day, shortly after moving into his new home, he woke up to find that the car lot he had purchased his truck from had repossessed it. He and the company were disputing the contract as he found an error that would add a substantial amount to the cost of the vehicle. He skipped only ONE payment and they had taken the truck back. Two days later, he returned to the dealership and found that due to the error in his contract, he was not liable for the truck and it would not negatively affect his credit. This error allowed him to able to purchase a brand new INFINITY G35, fully loaded, black leather interior, a 3.8 liter engine with turbo, low profile body type, four doors and a Bose sound system. He had fallen right back into the lap of luxury for an additional $80 a month which the savings in gas would easily allow him to afford.

It was like he was living a fantasy but throughout these ordeals he could see God moving in each situation. The final thing was his job. When the state held up his teaching certificates his district was forced to let him go and for the first time in the months, he was human and went into worry mode. Unlike Meagan that entered his life slowly or the visions he got about the house or the car, the loss of income in his mind threatened to steal all of those things away, including possibly Meagan. He went to her afraid and concerned about how she might react. To his surprise, she buckled right in and took on a second job. He knew DD would have left. Hell, she left every time the wind blew so he held fear of the same outcome with Meagan but he couldn't have been more wrong. He lost his job and for a month Meagan went to two jobs while he searched for his future.

As it turned out, a job he had gotten but then lost two years ago was not only open again but offered to him. He went from teaching to assistant principal in the district closest to him. The district he worked in prior paid more. Even with the promotion it was only a small jump up in salary but it was a jump up never the less. It was motion picture like and if he hadn't experienced

God's greatness, the goodness of the Lord in the land of the living first hand he might have even doubted these things himself. However, having bore witness, he was just overwhelmed with not only the blessings but the love that filled his heart for the Lord and His promise.

Perhaps the greatest of all these things was his entrance into Omega Psi Phi. He met an Omega man named Ron who he befriended and helped find his way to his now chosen way of life. Tony was back to enjoying all his interests from years past. He was playing golf, pool and darts. He even got the chance to play on a flag football team, a softball team and more spades and dominoes than he had played in years. He truly had friends that called and checked on him almost daily. He went from being friendless and dwelling among people who he couldn't trust, to being around educated, fun, like-minded men. Tony was a HUGE believer in giving back to where he came from. This idea didn't extend to only the particular community he was from but the urban or communities of color in general and he had always given back, no matter where he lived. Now he and his friends, his "bruhs" got to do that together and he was more filled with the love of Christ and life than he had ever been at any other time in his life before.

He was blessed. His life was so FULL of joy and love like the Psalms he applied to his life and knew was God's promise to him.

"Psalms 128 Blessed is every one that feareth the Lord; that walketh in his ways. For thou shalt eat the labor of thine hands: happy shalt thou be, and IT shall be well with thee. Thy wife shall be as a fruitful vine by the sides of thine house: thy children like olive plants round about thy table. Behold, that thus shall the man be blessed that feareth the Lord. The Lord shall bless thee out of Zion: and thou shalt see the good of Jerusalem all the days of thy life. Yea thou shalt see thy children's children, and PEACE upon Israel."

PEACE, the one word he had sought for his entire life had finally arrived. He was certain there would be rougher days. After all, every season wouldn't be harvest season but his faith was strengthened and renewed in a way that was unspeakable in any real measurable way. All of his trust, strength and faith were based in his beliefs. Now he had seen, "the good of Jerusalem" with his very own eyes. And that mighty Sword he thought was meant to be wielded in battle along side DD, against the world, was sharpened each day as he and Meagan read God's word together as "iron sharpens iron" but remained sheaved. Most of the world's battles were left to the Lord and those he needed that sword for, those spiritual battles within himself or family were easily defeated, secured years prior in the gaining of his wisdom in that school of obedience.

She was the perfect wife, balanced between his rational mind, equally yoked in matters of the world. Of course in the spiritual world as well, she never strayed too far from Tony's leadership nor God's word; it was incredible. She was incredible, having been through her own life's trials that had already brought her to the feet of the father. She, having learned about the path to the home in the mountains long ago, was here before Tony, to live, love and GROW together. She arrived equipped to love him, having loved HIM and herself first, just as God had promised. She was the ideal metal to form their union, the perfect living sword, the perfect living, walking word of God. Just as the apostle Paul said that we are all living letters to the word of God, so shall they be a testament to his greatness in the land of the living. Through hell and high water, both of them finally arrived to meet their covenanted soul mate. And it did not always look good upon its approach by any means; it was not pretty as those fools might tell you. No, at times is was down-right ugly as the world could be but they had persevered through much, forgave much, forgotten much and forbore much too, to sit in the company of one another; but they were at last there.

He was finally solid as was their union. He, his wife and children was supremely built into and for the perfect union of all of the great things this world had to offer and those the Lord had shown him the pathway to in his strength, perseverance, obedience, faith, manhood and trust in God and His word. There are so many more love filled words I wish this narrator could find to express just how wonderfully bountiful, how immaculate this love that battered crucible had built under so much heat. But, alas, this place is best left to the silence of ones own imagination. But one thing is for certain, he, she, THEY could have never made it without THEE Almighty. Bless God. Yet it wasn't completely about Meagan. She was but the physical manifestation of God's love. Anyone who laid eyes on their family knew what love looked like. Tony and Meagan had worked hard at it so they knew. But if after all Tony and Meagan had been through, they had to describe it, what might they say?

*　　*　　*

Galatians 5:13 For you are called to freedom, brothers. Only do not use your freedom as an opportunity for flesh, but through love serve one another.

So what is LOVE? Does it exist? Or is this idea so many have chased down the romantic path of Harlequin novels and pretty movies just a cruel figment of one's imagination? Can something that wondrous truly be? For we have searched endlessly for it. Surely if this thing were real, I would have undoubtedly found it by now. It has been like some torturous joke. Most shake it off crying, "Who needs it?"

While these thoughts creep inside the minds of cynics within my chest. A heart tells of another tale. One of loving and losing many times. There deep down in the bottom of my soul, I concede I'm but a lost frightened child frantically weeping out of control just for a taste of this "love" But I be lost:

"1 John 3:18 Little children,
let us not love in word
or talk but in deed and in truth."
Until I have seen the face of his promise

DEFEATED, by this I know love is real. This I cannot deny.

Yet I question,

"Is this love supposed to give me profound insight on life and all else?

"Or does it simply serve to madden me, tear me down, one interval at a time?

"Maybe it is that feeling one gets when you are 'floating on air' or those butterflies I have heard talked about? Possibly it is the 'firework's or 'lack of appetite'?

Alas, it is for naught because even a fool knows that here is a poor place for reason and logic.

Out of the silence come a small voice, trembling at first, barely audible through the sobs of pain, and let us call this voice our conscience, our God voice, slowly it says:

I would like very much to tell you that this is a story of what we believe as traditional romance, that it is what dreams are made of, that it conquers all, sent straight from heaven on wings of an angel. For if this was true it could not hurt so badly. The reality, the lesson, is far worse.

John 14:23 Jesus answered him,
"If anyone loves me,
he will keep my word,
and my Father will love him,
and we will come to him
and make our home with him.

The lesson is he will love you when you learn to be obedient as all fathers do. When you can prove to him that you have kept his word in your heart, not in word but in deed.

1 Peter 1:22 Having purified your souls
by your obedience
to the truth
for a sincere love,

(Then shall you)
love one another earnestly from a pure heart.

No this is no LOVE STORY but a STORY ABOUT LOVE! A story each one of us must walk, through Him that gives all things. We must come to this eternal truth about love through him and only him.

Mathew 6:33 But seek ye first
HIS KINGDOM and
HIS RIGHTEOUSNESS,
and all these things will be added to you.

Loving Him will light the path to show you the essence of true love which already lies within you, FIRST FOR YOURSELF then all others.
Ephesians 4:2 with all humility
and gentleness, with patience,
bearing with one another in love

No this is a story about a mere man who stumbled most of his life through many things but mostly love; love of his family, parents, friends and sadly worst of all himself, which kept him blind to God's love. Through God's word he found his way back to the ultimate and true measure of love. Once he was able to align his thoughts and, most importantly, his actions with God's word.
Philippians 2:2 complete my joy
by being of the same mind,
having the same love,
being in full accord and of one mind.
It is the moment you realize your life weighted against THAT LOVE MEANS NOTHING. You may beg, saying, "Just to have that gentle touch or warm embrace" mistaking these things for the genuine article. However, within you KNOW such a thirst has never been nor can be quenched. As you run your hands across that smooth flesh for one brief moment, you may experience, as intended, all the answers to the universe.

509

Realizing nothing is impossible but it be fleeting if not done correctly.

If foolishly you remain, you will look deep within her eyes and know you have crossed a line that at last means do or die. You either love forever or sacrifice yet another portion of your soul to despair.

I heard him shout from this place still doubtful and lost, seeking still this romance of flesh and the world.

"Oh dear God it must exist, for I would give all that thee has made perfect and sacred to touch it just once more. To look love in the face again I would sell the world's fate for but a glimpse and bare no ill conscience."

What powerful devil is this?

Love?

I think not.

What is love?

Is it utter madness which drives men to their knees?

Or Ambrosia bestowed upon us mere mortals at the pleasure of the Almighty?

Or is it just YOU, GOD AND DESTINY?

1Kings 3:13 Moreover,
I will give you
what you have not asked for . . .
both riches and honor . . .
so that in your lifetime
you will have no equal among kings.

This ... IS MY STORY

Galatians 2:20 I have been crucified with Christ.
It is no longer I who live,
but Christ who lives in me.
And the life I now live in the flesh
I live by faith in the Son of God,
who loved me and gave himself for me.

BLESS GOD!
AMEN

www.ingramcontent.com/pod-product-compliance
Lightning Source LLC
Chambersburg PA
CBHW071629260626
47170CB00001B/18